Hadn't he been saying for months that trouble was a distinct possibility?

A familial alliance between Splotze and Borovnik signalled a major power shift in that thaumaturgic ally volatile region—and change always sent the cockroaches scuttling. Hadn't he put Bestwick on alert for precisely that reason? He'd have done a damned sight more, only Lord Attaby had over ruled him, citing delicate trade negotiations and the easily pricked sensibilities of Borovnik's capricious Dowager Queen.

And now it seemed he'd been proven right. Again. Danger to do with the wedding, that if not averted could easily lead to all-out war. A war with thaumaturgics this time, he could feel the danger in his bones, and the United Magical Nations' accords be damned.

But how to stop it? *How?*

Well, there was only one answer. He needed eyes and ears in the wedding party. And with Bestwick unaccounted for, quite possibly dead, he'd have to send someone else.

The question was, who?

And even if he could find the right man…how the hell was he going to get him invited to a bloody royal wedding?

Praise for the Rogue Agent series:

"Mills' whimsical prose keeps the plot jumping and the reader laughing."   —*Publishers Weekly*

"A fun mix of steampunkish fantasy, spy adventure, and screwball comedy."   —*Locus*

Books by Karen Miller

Kingmaker, Kingbreaker
The Innocent Mage
The Awakened Mage

The Godspeaker Trilogy
Empress
The Riven Kingdom
Hammer of God

The Fisherman's Children
The Prodigal Mage
The Reluctant Mage

Writing as K.E. Mills

The Rogue Agent series
The Accidental Sorcerer
Witches Incorporated
Wizard Squared
Wizard Undercover

undercover

⊰ rogue agent book four ⊱

K.E.MILLS

www.orbitbooks.net

Copyright © 2012 by Karen Miller
Excerpt from *The Legend of Eli Monpress* copyright © 2012 by Rachel Aaron

Orbit
Hachette Book Group
237 Park Avenue
New York, NY 10017
www.orbitbooks.net

Orbit is an imprint of Hachette Book Group. The Orbit name and logo are trademarks of Little, Brown Book Group Limited.

The Hachette Speakers Bureau provides a wide range of authors for speaking events. To find out more, go to www.hachette speakersbureau.com or call (866) 376-6591.

The publisher is not responsible for websites (or their content) that are not owned by the publisher.

Printed in the United States of America

First United States edition: May 2012

10 9 8 7 6 5 4 3 2 1
OPM

*Paul Haines, whose astonishing
courage is an ongoing inspiration.*

wizard undercover

PROLOGUE

Puffing and panting, dripping unladylike sweat down her cheeks and off the end of her freckled nose and with her stylish, brand new spectacles fogged, Melissande slipped and staggered her way along yet another narrow, barely lit, cobblestoned Grande Splotze alley.

I'm an idiot. What am I? A raving nutter. I should've known I'd be sorry if I wore high heels.

Well. High*ish*. A good two and a half inches, at any rate, which at this particularly fraught moment was two and a half inches too many.

I swear on Sultan Zazoor's best war camel, I don't care what the occasion is, the next time I get mixed up with one of Gerald's little missions I'm bloody well wearing ballet slippers!

Or better yet, football boots. The studded kind. With reinforced steel toes.

Assuming, of course, there is a next time. Assuming that this time doesn't end with us well and truly corpsified.

She risked a downwards glance at her pale green silk-swathed chest, where Gerald's lolling head was awkwardly pillowed. Oh, lord. He did look bad. *Don't die, Gerald. Please don't die.* Feeling him start to slip yet again, the fierce drag on her shoulders and back burning hotter with every unsteady step, she gave a little grunt, blinked fresh sweat out of her eyes, and tried to firm up her grip around his barely moving chest. If she dropped him he'd likely crack his skull on the cobbles, just like an egg.

Which would put the icing on our very lumpy cake, and no mistake.

Directly in front of her, arms clamped around Gerald's knees, Bibbie was having her own difficulties staying upright. Not long after the night's fireworks finished, a chilly rain had washed through festive Grande Splotze, chasing the crowds of revellers indoors even before the curfew. Now the capital's inconveniently empty streets were as treacherous as an ice rink.

So any minute now we'll be skating, I expect. Wonderful.

Without warning, the narrow, poorly lit alley took a precipitous right-hand turn. Cursing, Bibbie hopped and skipped and jiggled around it—and lost her footing. But then, praise Saint Snodgrass, with an alarmed squeak she found her balance and went on cursing, more inventively than ever.

Keeping up, but only just, Melissande clutched Gerald's chest so tightly she expected to hear the sharp snap-snap-snap of his ribs.

"Do be *careful*, Bibbie! And shut up!" she hissed, frantic, at the back of Bibbie's head. "We don't want those murderous pillocks to hear us! And whatever else you do, *don't drop Gerald!*"

"No, really?" Bibbie retorted over her shoulder. Her neatly coiffed hair was coming down in a tangle of plain pins. "Aren't you the spoilsport. I was hoping to roll him down the street like a hoop!"

Melissande scowled. If her arms hadn't been full of unconscious secret government agent she'd have happily slapped Monk's wretched sister.

They staggered on, still panting and sweating, but mercifully no longer cursing, until they reached the end of the alley. Now the air wasn't only coldly damp, it was smelly as well, ripe with discarded refuse and possibly a very dead cat. Melissande tried to hold her breath.

"Which way?" said Bibbie, between heaving gasps. "*Mel*, which—"

"I'm not sure. Give me a moment."

Bibbie groaned. "Must I?"

Ignoring her, Melissande filtered the disgusting air between her teeth as she racked her tired brain for inspiration. If only she and Bibbie had gone with Gerald the day he went to investigate Abel Bestwick's lodging. But he'd made them stay behind because they were only honorary janitors, and for all he knew Abel Bestwick had all kinds of secret janitorial information strewn about his rented home. Information they weren't cleared to see. So instead of knowing in practice where they were going, she and Bibbie only knew in theory: 45b Voblinz Lane, smack dab in the middle of fancy Grande Splotze's insalubrious slummy bits. She spared lolling Gerald's upside down face an unfriendly glance. If all three of them got out of this scrape in one piece she'd have a few pithy things to say about being treated like a second-class honorary agent.

"*Melissande!*"

"Yes, yes, all right. Go left," she said, haphazard.

"Left?" Bibbie echoed, doubtful. "Are you sure?"

"No, but at least there's half a chance we'll be going the right way!"

"Oh, Saint Snodgrass's elbow," Bibbie muttered. "Fine. Left it is." But instead of getting a move on she cocked her head, listening. "I can't hear anything, Mel. Are you quite certain those buggers are still chasing us? I threw down a pretty good confusion hex, y'know."

"Bibbie, you and me and Gerald are all that stand between them and utter ruin. That's what I call motive. Besides, with their thaumaturgics do you honestly think they're going to stay confused for long?"

"Yes, well, when you put it that way . . ."

"Exactly. Now let's go!"

They shuffled out of the stinking alley and headed left along a slightly wider and marginally less odiferous thoroughfare. Each side of the street was lined with slovenly buildings, leaning shoulder to shoulder like two lines of drunken sailors. A few crooked chimney pots belched half-hearted, noxious smoke. As with every other alley and lane in this dreadful part of Splotze's capital, only a few gaslights were properly working and none of them was draped with festive garlands. Dim lamps shone behind tatty curtains here and there, but nobody stirred beyond the safety of their four dilapidated walls. But probably it wouldn't matter if they did. Grande Splotze's townsfolk were no match for the villains they were dealing with.

And speaking of villains . . .

Having caught her breath a little, Melissande strained her hearing. But she couldn't hear any malevolent footsteps behind them. The only sounds were her bellows breathing, and Bibbie's, and Gerald's hoarsely squashed exhalations, and the uneven clipping of their reception-worthy heels on the city's slick, uneven cobbles.

So was I wrong? Have we lost them after all? Oh, please, please let it mean I was wrong!

"Bibbie, I think maybe—"

And then it didn't matter what she thought because Bibbie misstepped a second time, turned her ankle and with an anguished yelp let go of Gerald's knees.

"Bibbie!" she shrieked, and dropped rump-first to the wet cobbles, Gerald clutched in her arms.

Ignoring her, Bibbie hopped in a circle. "Ow! Ow! Ow!"

"Bibbie, be *quiet!*"

"Oh, be quiet yourself!" moaned Bibbie. "Can't you see I've broken my leg?"

No, because she was too busy making sure Gerald was still with them. Luckily, Monk's careless sister had chosen a fitful pool of gaslight in which to sprain her wretched ankle, so she could get a halfway proper look at him.

Oh, dear. Oh, lord. He's getting worse.

"Gerald," she whispered, patting his pale cheek. "Gerald, can you hear me? Gerald, are you there?"

He didn't answer. Not even his closed eyelids flickered. In the uncertain light his lips looked dangerously pale. Equally alarming was the fine sheen of sweat coating his skin. She pressed gloved fingertips to his neck and waited for the reassuring thub-thub of a pulse. It came at last, far too slowly.

"Well?" said Bibbie, bent in half and rubbing her kid-skin covered ankle. Her voice was steady enough but her eyes were frightened. "How is he?"

"Not dead yet."

"If only we knew what poison they used," Bibbie fretted. "Melissande, are you sure there'll be something at Abel Bestwick's lodgings that'll save him?"

No, of course she wasn't. Only she couldn't say that. For all her bravado, Bibbie's courage was hanging by a thread.

Not to mention mine.

"There should be," she said, chafing Gerald's cold hand. "Bestwick's a janitor, he must have some kind of emergency medicine kit."

"And if he doesn't?"

"Then he'll have a crystal ball hidden somewhere. One strong enough to reach Sir Alec. And Sir Alec will know exactly what to do."

"How?" Bibbie demanded, her voice catching. "When we can't tell him which poison that bastard gave Gerald?"

Yes, well, trust Emmerabiblia Markham to spot the flaw in her plan.

"Can you walk yet, Bibbie? We have to get on."

Gingerly, Bibbie put some weight onto her right foot. "I think so," she said, wincing. Then she frowned. "You know, I really should risk—"

"*No,*" Melissande snapped. "Are you out of your mind? With Splotze's etheretics as bad as they are, a levitation hex might explode Gerald to smithereens. Now help me up, then grab hold of his knees again. We can't stay here, Bibs. It's not safe."

Awkward and clumsy, they got Gerald slung between them once more like a lumpy sack of potatoes. If only he weren't such a dead weight. If only he could open his eyes.

If only he'd not drunk that damned cherry liqueur.

"Right," said Bibbie. "Which way now?"

Her own pulse racing, Melissande stared around them. A short stone's throw further along the street was the entrance to another laneway. Should they go that way? She had no idea. What they needed was a bird's-eye view of Grande Splotze.

"I'm not sure. Lord, I wish Reg was here."

Bibbie rolled her eyes. "Which one?"

"Emmerabiblia Markham! That's a *dreadful* thing to say!"

"Yes. Well." Sounding shamefaced, Bibbie settled her pale pink satin-clad shoulders under the heaviness of Gerald's sagging lower half. "Don't tell me you've never thought it. Honestly, trying to remember which bits of our lives this new Reg remembers, and which bits she doesn't, and constantly being reminded that she isn't *our* Reg, that's not much fun either."

No, it wasn't. But what could they do about it? Their Reg was gone and the new Reg was the only one they had left. The sooner they all got used to that fact, the better.

"Anyway," said Bibbie. "I'm ready. Are you ready?"

"Yes," she said curtly, blinking away the sting of inconvenient grief. "Let's go. And we'll keep going until we reach the end of this street."

Limping only a little bit, Bibbie started walking. Melissande fell into step behind her, pulse racing. Dangling between them in his elegant evening wear, looking less rumpled and more important than ever they'd seen him, Gerald wheezed the damp night air in and out of his lungs.

"Look!" said Bibbie, after a few moments. "There's a street sign, at last."

Still slipping and staggering, nearly bursting a blood vessel trying to catch any sound of pursuit, Melissande squinted through her foggy spectacles at the faded board hanging by one rusty nail from the house on the corner.

"Groontzeshilsitz Place," she said, stumbling over the surfeit of syllables and sibilants. "Sound familiar?"

Bibbie snorted. "Not the way you pronounce it."

She peered both ways. "Looks like a dead end to the right. We'll have to go left. Or turn around and take that little laneway after all. Or—"

"We can't," Melissande said, shaking her head. If we go back, we'll run straight into trouble."

"Y'know," said Bibbie, "I really do hate it when you're right."

"Ha," she said. "You should be used to it by now."

They shuffled around till they were pointed in the right direction, then kept going. Several unsteady steps later, Bibbie cocked her head again.

"Do you hear that?"

That was a sluggish sloshing sound, growing more definite the further along the street they walked.

"It's the Canal," said Melissande, and briefly closed her eyes. *Oh, Saint Snodgrass be praised.* "That means we're going the right way. Gerald said Abel Bestwick's haunt was directly across from it."

"Yes, he did," said Bibbie, suddenly doubtful. "Only *across from the Canal* sounds awfully vague."

"Now who's being the spoilsport? Come on, Bibbie, *hurry.*"

With an effort that sent her cross-eyed, Melissande picked up the pace, forcing Bibbie to shuffle along faster as well. Every muscle she owned was howling in protest. She had three blisters on each foot and was sweating so much that she thought she could easily drink the Canal dry, even if there were thirty dead cats floating in it.

Miraculously, they'd managed to reach the Canal's deserted public promenade. Stumbling to the watery thoroughfare's walled edge, Bibbie looked over her shoulder. "Wait—wait—I need a moment. I have to stop."

"All right," Melissande said, rasping. "But only a moment, Bibbie. We're running out of time."

They lowered Gerald to the cobbles and fell against the Canal wall, heaving for air. Melissande clutched at her side, where a white-hot pain was sawing her in two. Despite it, she stared across the city rooftops in the direction of the Royal Palace. Oh, dear. There was a definite *glow* in the night sky, shimmering crimson above the tiles and chimneys and gilding the crowns of the distant trees.

"Y'know, Bibbie," she said, wheezing only a little bit now. "On second thoughts, perhaps setting fire to the reception hall wasn't such a good idea after all."

With no gaslight close by it was too dark to see Bibbie's face, but she felt the searing touch of her friend's glare.

"Is that so?" Monk's sister demanded. "Well, correct me if

I'm wrong, Your Highness, but aren't you the one who shrieked *Quick, quick, we need a diversion!*"

"Yes, all right, I did," she said, caught, "but I meant for you to knock over a tray of drinks, not indulge in a spot of wholesale arson! Hartwig's going to be terribly upset."

"Right!" said Bibbie. "That's *it*. Next time *you* create the diversion!"

"Oh, come on, Bibbie, don't be like that! I'm only saying—"

Bibbie stamped her foot. "I don't care what you're saying! From here on in, Your Royal Snootiness, you can take care of your own bloody dirty work, because nothing I do is ever good enough for you!"

"What? *What?*" she spluttered. "Emmerabiblia Markham, that is the most—"

But before she could finish refuting such a rankly unfair accusation, the dank night air was unexpectedly full of feathers and beak and claws and a loud, angry indignation.

"Oy, you pair of hoydens!" Reg screeched. "Put a sock in it, right now! And then you can tell me what you've done to my Gerald!"

CHAPTER ONE

Three and a half weeks earlier . . .

"Right," said Mister Jennings, the Department of Thaumaturgy's leading technician. "That does it, I think, Mister Dunwoody. The monitoring crystals are all in place. How do you feel?"

So nervous I can't see straight, Gerald thought. But since obviously he couldn't say that, he shrugged. "Fine, Mister Jennings. I feel fine."

"Hmm," said Mister Jennings. A few years past middle age, he was corded with sinews and afflicted with adenoids, and a faintly fragrant pomade slicked his thinning grey hair close to his skull. Lips pursed, light brown eyes wearily cynical, he made another tiny adjustment to the clear crystals he'd fixed to his patient's forehead. "Good. That's good."

In other words, *I know you're a big fat liar, Mister Dunwoody, but for your sake I'm going to pretend I believe you.*

Satisfied at last, Mister Jennings glanced at the small, bare room's ceiling. "All set here, Sir Alec. Anything you wanted to say?"

"*No*," came Sir Alec's crystal-thinned voice. "*You may proceed, Mister Jennings.*"

Trying not to feel the trickle of sweat down his shirt-covered ribs, Gerald frowned.

What, Sir Alec? No last words of encouragement? Not even a feeble, half-hearted good luck? Miserable bastard.

Except that wasn't true. Not really. Soothing platitudes just weren't his chilly superior's style—something he should be used to by now.

"Now then, Mister Dunwoody," said Mister Jennings, and patted his shoulder. "Breathe slow and deep and keep as still as you can. Mapping your *potentia* for the grimoire hexes shouldn't be a problem, but once we start extracting them, well, there'll be a bit of discomfort. Can't be helped, I'm afraid. But I'll be right outside, keeping a nice close eye on you. Most important thing is, don't fight what's happening. You'll want to, but you'll only make things harder on yourself if you do."

"I see," he said, his mouth drier than the Kallarapi desert. "Ah—have you any idea how long this will take?"

Mister Jennings rubbed his chin. "Can't say as I do, I'm afraid. This isn't something as gets done on a regular basis, you know. And then every wizard's different, isn't he?"

The look in his eye added: *And some of us are more different than others.*

"Yes, of course," Gerald muttered. "Thank you, Mister Jennings."

As the small, bare room's door closed quietly behind the thaumic technician, he made an effort to relax. It might have been easier had he not been strapped down on the padded table. Or if there'd been something soothing overhead to look at. The empty expanse of white ceiling was oddly intimidating, even if he could only see it through his one good eye. Intimidating too were the broad strips of battered leather Mister Jennings had secured across his chest, hips, thighs and ankles. Honestly, he felt like he'd been abandoned in one of the less savoury establishments certain politicians had recently been caught frequenting, with abruptly career-ending results.

The crystals on his forehead weighed heavier than lead.

"*Right then, Mister Dunwoody,*" said Mister Jennings's disembodied voice. "*I'm activating the mapping hex now. You shouldn't feel anything more than a slight tingle. Be sure to say something if that's not the case.*"

He swallowed, wishing he'd thought to loosen his collar. "I certainly will, Mister Jennings. Thanks for the warning."

Some time passed. Was that a tingle? He couldn't tell. It was hard to feel anything beyond the heavy thudding of his heart against the wall of his chest. With his eyes closed he could almost hear the thick, red gushing of blood through his veins.

"*Right then, Mister Dunwoody,*" said Mister Jennings. Beneath the deliberate cheer there sounded a note of caution. "*All done.*"

"Really?" Surprised, Gerald blinked. "That was fast. And I hardly felt a thing. Are you sure all those grimoire hexes are properly mapped?"

"*He's quite sure, Mister Dunwoody. Kindly refrain from telling the expert how to do his job.*"

Oh. "Sorry, Sir Alec. No offence intended."

"*None taken,*" said Mister Jennings. "*Now, sir, we'll start the extraction. I'll have it over and done with soon as I can, I promise.*"

And whatever Mister Jennings intended, that wasn't the least bit reassuring at all.

"Thank you, Mister Jennings," he croaked.

But there was no point complaining. He was the one who'd pushed to have the grimoire hexes his appalling alternate self had given him sucked out of his *potentia*, where general wisdom declared all acquired incants resided. Sir Alec, not at all keen on the idea, had counselled patience. When that didn't work, Mister Jennings had been brought in to explain in stomach-turning detail the many and disgusting things that could go wrong with the extraction procedure. Not wanting to listen to either of them, he'd all but stuck his fingers in his ears.

"At least give the Department time to learn something of the effects of these hexes before you have them removed," Sir Alec had said at last. "After all, Mister Dunwoody, you can't overlook the fact that you're in a unique position to further the sum of our thaumaturgical knowledge."

Oh yes he bloody well could. He'd had more than enough of playing guinea pig for the Department. Besides, after enduring the grimoire hexes' sickening taint for eleven days, he was starting to feel desperate.

To his surprise, even Monk, who'd seen what the other, terrible Gerald Dunwoody had done, the damage those dreadful hexes could inflict, hadn't wanted him to do this.

"It's too risky, mate," he'd said, lanky dark hair flopped over his face. "Jennings's procedure is practically experimental. What if something goes wrong?"

Trouble was, things were already going wrong. The other Gerald's grimoire magic was giving him terrible dreams. Every night since his return from the other Ottosland he'd woken in a cold sweat, shaking, with those seductive grimoire hexes churning dread through his blood. In a terrible way they were alive . . . and they wanted to be used. But when he'd tried explaining that, all he got was blank stares. Monk shoved a bottle of brandy at him. Sir Alec told him it was his grief talking, and that as a janitor he could not afford to indulge in counterproductive and self-indulgent emotions.

The only person who took his fears seriously was the other Reg.

"You trust your instincts, sunshine," she said, head tipped to one side, eyes bright. "You're the one that bugger mucked up with the manky stuff, aren't you? If you think his grimoire magic's trouble, then it's trouble. So don't you go taking no for an answer from that beady-eyed Department stooge."

Gerald still couldn't decide if it helped or hurt, that her trenchant advice sounded so familiar. So right. As though it was really his Reg talking. Taking the advice, he'd dug in his heels and, for once recognising defeat, Sir Alec had relented.

So now here he was, strapped to a padded table in the bowels of the Department's rambling, obscure Nettleworth headquarters, waiting to be doused with the thaumaturgical equivalent of paint stripper.

Who says I don't know how to have a good time?

A hint of warmth in the crystals attached to his sweaty forehead stirred him out of thought. And then . . . no, it wasn't his imagination. That was a definite tingle. A few booming heartbeats later, the tingle intensified. He felt his muscles twitch in protest, and heat surge through him like a tide of boiling water.

"Bloody hell!"

"*Just relax there, Mister Dunwoody,*" said Mister Jennings, encouraging. "*We don't want you doing yourself a mischief, do we?*"

No, they certainly didn't. With an effort, Gerald uncramped his fingers. Willed his frantically beating heart to slow down. Took a deep breath and tried to relax his spasming body.

In vain.

The boiling water transmuted to thick, boiling molasses. He was being cooked alive from the inside out. Buried memories thrust themselves unwanted to the surface. This was his torment in Lional's cave all over again, it was—

Actually, it was much, *much* worse.

"Mister Dunwoody, do you understand what you're asking for?" Sir Alec had demanded, so severe. "The other Dunwoody's grimoire magic will resist extraction. Vigorously. Are you prepared for that?"

Of course he'd said yes, he understood completely and was perfectly prepared—even though he knew he wasn't. But he'd had no intention of letting that stop him.

Which, on reflection, might've been a mistake . . .

He could feel himself thrashing against the wide leather restraints. Everything hurt, but the worst of the pain was in his head, behind his eyes, where it threatened to shatter his skull. The small, bare room spun wildly around him. There was blood in his mouth, metallically tangy. He'd bitten his tongue.

"*Steady on, Mister Dunwoody. You're doing fine.*"

Fine? Jennings was mad. Let them swap places and the Department's best technician would soon realise this wasn't *fine*. He wanted to shout out the pain, but he couldn't. Sir Alec was watching and he had to prove his superior wrong. He had to bear this, no matter how bad it got, and deny Sir Alec the chance of saying *I told you so*.

"*Coming along nicely, Mister Dunwoody,*" said Mister Jennings's disembodied voice. "*But it'd help if you didn't jiggle about quite so much.*"

Only that was easier said than done, wasn't it? Ignoring

instructions, his tormented body thrashed itself from side to side, flailing against Mister Jennings's merciless extraction incant. And beneath the torment he could feel something else, an odd, hollow, *sucking* sensation. Not pain, yet somehow worse than pain. Just as Sir Alec had warned, the other Gerald's poisonous hexes were fighting their removal. Like ticks burrowed into tender flesh, they battled to stay put. Could a wizard's *potentia* bleed? His felt like it was bleeding.

Gerald heard his harsh, deep breathing turn into shallow pants. The pain was intensifying, squibs of bright light and heat bursting behind his tightly closed eyes. Fresh beads of sweat trickled, scorching his skin.

"*Really, Mister Dunwoody, you need to keep yourself still,*" said Mister Jennings. Now he sounded anxious. "*We're getting down to the nitty-gritty and we don't want any nasty accidents.*"

With an effort that rolled both eyes back in his pain-stormed skull, Gerald forced himself into immobility. He thought he heard his joints popping and cracking with the strain. Bits of his body were numb, where he struggled against the leather straps that kept him on the table.

"*Well done, Mister Dunwoody,*" said Mister Jennings. "*Nearly there. Just be a good chap and brace yourself. Things could get a mite uncomfortable now.*"

Only now? If he'd had the strength to spare, he'd have laughed.

But then even that brief spark of levity died as the heavy crystals on his forehead burst into flame. Or felt like it. He did shout aloud this time, he couldn't keep the pain decently, properly hidden. Not with the top of his skull ripped clean off. The air sobbed in and out of his labouring lungs and his fingers were clenched so hard he thought the bones would break. His belly twisted and heaved, threatening to empty. And then he felt a gush of something wet and warm, followed by a sharp slap of shame. His bladder had let go, as though he were a child.

"*Hold on, Mister Dunwoody!*" Mister Jennings urged. "*One last hurdle. Hold on!*"

But he couldn't. He was done. Even as a final blast of pain

surged through him, he felt himself drift upwards from the padded table and float away into welcome darkness.

A hand on his shoulder, not so gently shaking, brought him back with a thud. Dragging his eyes open, feeling an ache in every bone, tasting fresh blood in his mouth, Gerald frowned at the bleary, anxious face hovering above him.

"*There* you are," said Mister Jennings, his nasal voice unsteady with relief. "Gave me a proper nasty turn there, you did, Mister Dunwoody, going off like that. Not the kind of happy ending I was looking for. But never mind. You're upright and breathing, more or less. I've unhooked you from the extraction crystals and undone all your straps, so here. Have a drink."

With Mister Jennings's arm helping him sit up, Gerald took a large, grateful swallow of whiskey from the flask the technician held to his lips. Closed his eyes as it seared a path to his belly, took another, to be on the safe side, then politely declined any more.

"Is Sir Alec still here?" he said, feeling his bitten tongue tender against his teeth.

Stoppering the flask, Mister Jennings shook his head. "He's taken himself off to town. Told me to tell you to go straight home, and stay there recuperating until you're sent for."

"I see." Torn between relief and resentment, Gerald blotted his sweat-slicked cheeks on his sleeve. "And when will that be, Mister Jennings. Do you know?"

"I do not, sir," said Mister Jennings, mildly reproving. "That'd be between you and Sir Alec."

"Yes. Of course. Sorry. Ah—Mister Jennings—"

But Mister Jennings was avoiding his incomplete gaze. "I know what you're wanting to ask, Mister Dunwoody, but I've been told by Sir Alec to leave the particulars to him. I'm authorised to say the extraction went well enough, all things considered. No more than that."

All things considered? Gerald stared. What did *that* mean? Was he clean of filthy grimoire magic or wasn't he?

His light brown, cynical eyes surprisingly sympathetic,

Mister Jennings tucked the whiskey flask back into his lab coat's stained, capacious pocket.

"There's a change of clothes waiting for you in the showers, Mister Dunwoody. And Sir Alec's arranged a driver to take you home. I'd advise a hearty meal and an early turn in to bed. I'm sure you'll feel better after a good night's sleep." He nodded, a small, unexpected gesture of respect. "Good day to you, sir."

Acutely aware of every strained, insulted muscle, Gerald made his way through a honeycomb of drab grey corridors to Nettleworth's showers, which were blessedly deserted. As promised, there was a fresh change of clothes and a bag for his soiled suit waiting for him. Arranged by Sir Alec? Had to be, surely. How remarkably gentle of him. And also unexpected.

Slumped beneath the shower's steady sluicing of hot water, Gerald rested his head against the wet tiles and let his eyes close. With Sir Alec gone and Mister Jennings ordered to silence, he was alone with all his unanswered questions. So, was he brave enough to seek inside for those answers? A part of him desperately wanted to know the truth. Another part shrank from knowing it, so soon after the ordeal of extraction. For if the news was bad . . . if the procedure had failed . . .

A stab of self-contempt. He was a janitor. He had obligations. If the extraction had failed this time, then he'd just have to try it again. And again, and again, as many times as it took, until he was entirely rid of the other Gerald's malignant grimoire hexes.

He took a deep breath . . . and looked inside.

Whispering, seductive, dark magic called his name. Tempted him. Taunted him. Promised the unspeakable in a honey-sweet voice.

For a few unsteady heartbeats, despair threatened to overwhelm him. So what if he could feel the pitted gaps, the healing tears, where Mister Jennings had managed to suck out most of that other Gerald's unwanted, unasked for enhancements? Most wasn't all.

And I want them all gone.

Needed them gone, quickly, before he got used to being different. Gave in to that honeyed voice, because it was easier than fighting. Because he wanted to. Because—because—

It was a long time before he could risk leaving the solitary safety of the showers. And when he did . . .

"Errol," he said blankly, face to face with his nemesis three flights of stairs up from the showers. Damn. Listening to habitual, rebellious impulse he'd left his etheretic shield switched off—and the last thing he needed was this tosser feeling the changes in his *potentia*. "What the hell are you doing here?"

"None of your damned business," said Errol, his saturninely Haythwaite good looks as polished as ever. "Step aside. I'm busy."

And so self-involved, as usual, that he hadn't noticed anything different in the object of his contempt.

Relieved, Gerald shook his head. So much had changed since their days at the Wizards' Club, but it seemed Errol was determined to ignore that inconvenient fact. Which meant the arrogant tosser needed reminding. So he stood where he was, blocking the narrow, rabbit-warren Nettleworth corridor like a cork in a bottle.

"Sir Alec's not here."

"Did I ask if he was?" Errol's lips curled in a familiar sneer. "No. Because I'm not here to see Sir Alec. Now run along, Dunnywood. There must be a dustpan and brush with your name on them around here somewhere."

Lit match to dry paper, Gerald felt his uncertain temper ignite. Felt what remained of the grimoire magic bare its uncivilised fangs in a snarl. The narrow corridor misted in a rising storm of red.

Eyes widening with an unexpected and gratifying apprehension, Errol stepped back.

"You know what your problem is, Errol?" Gerald said, conversational. Every nerve in his body was threatening to catch fire. But there wasn't pain, precisely. Or, if there was, it was the kind of pain he could easily learn to bear. "Your problem, Errol, my old chum, is you were never taught any manners. Oh, you were taught polish. You were taught how to jibber-jabber with your plonking, over-bred peers. But you were never taught ordinary, every day *courtesy*. Bit of an oversight, that. So here's a suggestion. Why don't *I*—"

"Mister Haythwaite," said a bored voice behind him. "There you are."

"Mister Dalby," said Errol, sounding as close to meek as he could likely get. "Yes. I—ah—I just got here."

"Which means you're late," said Mister Dalby. "Mister Scrimplesham's waiting. Run along."

Errol swallowed. "Yes. Of course."

Heedless of Mister Dalby, watching, still inclined to make his point, Gerald didn't shift quite far enough out of Errol's path. Forced to brush against him, Errol hissed a sharp breath between his teeth. With a smile, Gerald pulled his spiky *potentia* back into himself. His burning nerves extinguished. The misted corridor faded from scarlet to clear. As he watched Errol out of sight, he felt a tickle of surprise.

Mister Scrimplesham? But he was Nettleworth's expert in matters of disguise. Best obfuscatory hexman in the entire Department, it was said. Better even than Monk, and that was saying something. Why the devil would Errol be needing to see old Scrimpy?

Behind him, Frank Dalby sniffed. "Think you're clever, do you, Dunwoody?"

A moment, then he turned to meet the senior janitor's unimpressed stare. "Sorry, Mister Dalby. I don't know what you mean."

"Yeah, you bloody do," said Dalby, and sighed. "Now just you listen up. Personally, I could watch you smear that little ponce into raspberry jam and not turn a hair. No great loss. World's full of rich tossers. But if you did you'd cause trouble for the guv'nor, and I won't be having that. So you mind your p's and q's with Errol Haythwaite, understand? Or you and me, Dunwoody, we'll have ourselves a problem."

Frank Dalby's fierce loyalty to Sir Alec, his former fellow janitor, was no secret around Nettleworth. Nor was it a secret that his mission success rate was second only to Sir Alec's, and that his kill count was higher by at least three. Not that such things were openly discussed. They were just . . . known. And taken into account.

The last thing Gerald Dunwoody needed was a problem with Frank Dalby. He stood on cracked ice with the senior janitor as it was. Prudently, he backed down.

"Sorry, Mister Dalby. I let my temper get the better of me."

Dalby's stare softened a trifle. "Like I said. Haythwaite's a tosser. Do yourself a favour and forget him."

With Frank Dalby so out of character chatty, Gerald decided to chance a question, even though the matter was none of his business. "What's he doing here? Errol's a domestic agent. I thought his lot and ours weren't meant to cross paths."

Metaphorical shutters slammed down behind Frank Dalby's weary eyes. "I'm a busy man, Dunwoody. I can drive you home now, or you can stand about chatting to yourself as long as you like and leg it home under your own steam later. Up to you."

He felt his jaw drop. "*You're* driving me home? But—"

"Fine," said Dalby, turning. "Suit yourself. Just don't you bloody go telling the guv'nor I didn't try."

"No—no—wait," said Gerald, leaping after him. "Wait, Mister Dalby. I'm coming."

And because he wasn't stupid, no matter what Errol said, he kept his mouth shut all the way back to Chatterly Crescent.

Afterwards, alone in the kitchen because Monk was busy inventing things in Research and Development and Reg had taken herself off for the day, exploring her new home, he sat with a cup of tea and tried very hard to ignore how the grimoire hexes still tangled in his *potentia*, promise and poison . . .

. . . and how sickeningly satisfying Errol Haythwaite's fear had felt.

"Oh good, Alec. You waited," Ralph Markham said, coming into his Department of Thaumaturgy office as burdened as a mule. With a groan of relief he dumped the over-stuffed files he was carrying onto his already cluttered desk. "I was afraid you'd give up."

Sir Alec raised his glass, half-full of best Blonkken brandy. "If not for this, I might have. Shall I pour you one?"

"Please," said Ralph, closing the door.

Obliging his sometime friend, sometime foe, Sir Alec rose from the comfortable leather armchair reserved for special guests and poured a second glass of brandy. There were those who'd say, disapprovingly, that it was far too early in the afternoon for alcohol. But given what he'd sat through at Nettleworth, and the frustrated exhaustion stamped into Ralph's heavy face, it wasn't an opinion he shared.

Not today, at least.

"Thanks," said Ralph, taking the glass. "Bloody domestic security meeting ran over. I tell you, if Gaylord was tipped out tomorrow he could earn a decent living blowing hot air into balloons."

Sir Alec smiled. "Anything I need to know about?"

"Officially?" Ralph swallowed deeply, then belched. "Of course not. Domestic matters are not your concern."

"And unofficially?"

Perching on the front edge of his heavy mahogany desk, Ralph glowered into his glass. "Unofficially, this black market wizard is kicking our arses. Four more cases of illicit hexes in the past two weeks. One's a fatality. Lady Barstow."

"Yes. I heard."

"I tell you, Alec, if we don't pinch this nasty piece of work soon . . ."

He shrugged. "Well, Ralph, you know what I think."

"Oh, don't start," said Ralph, impatient. "If I thought there was a snowball's hope in summertime of Gaylord and the rest agreeing to your people and his joining forces then we both know I'd leap at your offer. But those shortsighted fools won't have a bar of it and I can't afford to expend political capital on twisting their arms to make them agree."

"No, you'd rather wait until this criminal wizard brings Ottosland to its knees so they're forced to come crawling to you, cap in hand." Sir Alec smoothed his grey tie. "Which might be gratifying, I grant you. But Ralph, is it wise?"

"Alec, what would you have me do?" Ralph demanded.

"So far this—this *weasel* has confined his activities to home soil. As much as I'd like to, I *can't* over-ride Gaylord and involve your janitors." He raised a hand. "And don't, for pity's sake, try to use Errol Haythwaite against me. Loaning Scrimplesham's services to one of Gaylord's agents is *not* the same as ignoring the inflexible rules regarding agency territorial purviews."

Sir Alec topped up his glass then returned to the comfort of the guest chair. "Well, it's your decision, Ralph. And never fear, I'll be on hand to pull your chestnuts out of the fire when this blows up in your face."

"Thank you," said Ralph, gloomily, and downed the rest of his brandy. "Just don't gloat too loudly when the time comes, that's all I ask. You're not the one who has to put up with Gaylord day in and day out."

Which, for Ravelard Gaylord's sake, was fortunate. Repressing a shiver of distaste, Sir Alec sipped more brandy. Let his head rest against the armchair's high back and enjoyed the smothering glow of fine, fermented peach.

"You look a bit washed up yourself," said Ralph, shifting from the desk to the office's other armchair. "How did it go?"

Because he couldn't make use of Jennings without Ralph being told, and because telling the truth was out of the question, he'd concocted a story about a training mishap that had left Gerald Dunwoody tainted with the wrong kind of magic. Trusting him, Ralph hadn't questioned the tale.

Now, instead of answering, he dropped his gaze to the amber depths of his brandy. As a man of many and varied experiences, he prided himself on his carefully cultivated self-control. Unexpectedly, though, that discipline was shaken by what Gerald Dunwoody had stubbornly endured at Jennings's hands.

"Not much point lambasting yourself, Alec," Ralph said gruffly. "Accidents happen." He cleared his throat. "Are you going to tell him?"

Sir Alec looked up. "That the extraction wasn't entirely successful? Unnecessary. I've no doubt Mister Dunwoody's already worked it out for himself."

"I meant," Ralph said carefully, "are you going to tell him the extraction failed on purpose."

On purpose. That had an ugly ring to it. And why wouldn't it? What he'd done was ugly. But then that was what Sir Alec Oldman excelled at. The dark, dirty, ugly little tasks, performed in secret, shrouded in half-truths and outright lies. He did the things that needed to be done, for the people of Ottosland who wanted them done but didn't want to know the unpleasant details . . . and who'd bay for his blood if they ever found out.

"In time," he said at last. "When I can trust he'll not take my actions amiss."

"And you're sure that time will come, are you?"

"Dunwoody's not a fool, Ralph. Once the heat of the moment has passed, he'll understand."

Ralph shook his head. "You hope. Have to tell you, Alec, if it were me, I'm not sure I would."

"That's hardly surprising, Ralph," he said, indulging in a little malice. "You're not a janitor."

The sly dig earned him a look. Then Ralph drummed his fingers on the arm of his chair. "It's a big risk you've taken. Grimoire hexes are bad enough. I mean, they're restricted for a reason. But matched with Dunwoody's rogue *potentia?* Who knows what mischief that might brew?"

Sir Alec set aside his unfinished brandy. "Nobody. Which was always the point, wasn't it? To find out. And I seem to recall you thought it was the thing to do, when I raised the matter."

Which he'd done most reluctantly. But with Ralph's already deep involvement in Gerald's case, not to mention the need for his support, he'd had no choice. In this, as in so much else, he and Ralph were wary allies.

"Yes," said Ralph, frowning. "And despite my reservations I still do. An accident like this—you'd be mad not to take advantage. It's not like we can go around deliberately feeding that kind of grimoire muck to our people."

"But?" Sir Alec prompted, knowing there was more.

"But I wish it had been anyone other than Dunwoody. That unnatural young wizard is already too dangerous."

Sometimes it seemed he spent half his life defending Gerald Dunwoody. "We're all of us dangerous, Ralph, in our own little ways. Don't fret. I keep that young man on a suitably short leash."

"I know, Alec," said Ralph, levering himself out of his armchair. "But you'd do well to remember that leashes can snap. Now, I'm sorry, but you'll have to excuse me. I'm due for an early dinner with Wolfgang and the rest of the family. But look—before I go, is there anything I should know?"

"D'you mean has your nephew done anything appalling of late?" Standing, Sir Alec shook his head. "No. Not to my knowledge."

"*Wonderful*," Ralph groaned. "That can only mean we're overdue for a disaster." He collected his coat, hat and brief case. "I tell you, I do wonder what I did to deserve Monk. Him *and* his sister. There ought to be a law."

Sir Alec patted his shoulder in passing. "Well, Ralph, why don't you devise one? Since there's no plan in place to apprehend your black market wizard, it seems to me you must have plenty of time."

And on that satisfying note, he took his leave.

CHAPTER TWO

"*Oy!*" Aylesbury slapped his hand on the round dining table's antique lace tablecloth. "Monk! Stop acting deaf, you grubby little stoat! I said pass me the gravy before you and Emmerabiblia guzzle the bloody lot."

Seated opposite his irascible brother, Monk turned to their sister. "You know, Bibs, I think I need to visit the doctor."

"Why, Monk?" said Bibbie, her eyes alight with mischief. "What's wrong?"

"Something very peculiar. Whenever anyone forgets to say *please*, I'm stricken with an odd kind of paralysis."

"Really?" Bibbie fanned herself in mock distress. "Monk, that sounds awful. If I were you, I'd—"

"Now, now, you two, stop teasing Aylesbury," their mother said, calmly passing her eldest offspring the gravy boat. "This is the small dining room, not the nursery."

Slopping more horseradish onto his plate, Uncle Ralph snorted. "Could've fooled me, Sofilia."

Their mother smiled sweetly. "Speaking as a Thackeray, Ralph, I'm sure that's true. With one or two notable exceptions—" She patted her daydreaming husband's arm. "I'm afraid the Markhams are rather easily befuddled."

"Eh?" Uncle Ralph sat back in his chair. "Wolfgang! Are you going to let your wife insult the Markham name with impunity?"

As their father continued to dream thaumaturgics and eat his dinner, unheeding, and their mother and Uncle Ralph fell to familiar, good-natured bickering, Monk rolled his eyes at Bibbie, who giggled, then settled his gaze on Aylesbury. Feeling the scrutiny, Aylesbury paused in fastidiously cutting away the fat from his roast beef and looked up.

"What?"

Monk shrugged. "Nothing. Only I think you might've missed your true calling. I'd bet the Central Ott morgue is crying out for a man with your knife skills."

Eyeing him coldly, Aylesbury set down his cutlery and reached for the gravy boat. "If you volunteered yourself for me to practice on I'd consider offering my services."

Hmm. Was his brother joking? Most likely not. Where he was concerned, Aylesbury's sense of humour was conspicuously lacking.

"*Anyway*, Ralph," said their mother, waving an airy hand. "It's neither here nor there, is it, because though I was born a Thackeray I'm now a Markham by marriage. And everyone knows it's perfectly acceptable to insult your own. Emmerabiblia, stop eating. Who's going to marry you if you're the size of a cart horse?"

A pinched line appeared between Bibbie's perfectly arched eyebrows. "Another cart horse?" she suggested, and looked over her shoulder at the family's stoically silent senior footman. "Cheevers? The roast potatoes, please."

"Really, Emmerabiblia," their mother sighed, as Cheevers fetched the dish of potatoes from the serving board. "You are tiresome. Next you'll be saying you don't want to get married!"

Bibbie helped herself to a crisply golden potato, then dismissed Cheevers with a smile. "And so I don't. Not yet, anyway. I'm far too busy."

She sounded cheerful enough, but Monk felt his insides twist. Bibbie's trouble was that she *did* want to get married. To Gerald.

And that's the last thing I want for her.

Though it made him feel a traitor to their friendship, he couldn't settle with the notion of Gerald and his sister getting . . . involved. Not only because his best friend was one of Sir Alec's secretive, dangerous janitors, but because after their ghastly adventures in that other Ottosland, he was more convinced than ever that if Bibbie and Gerald did act on their feelings, she would only end up hurt.

Because the Gerald who came back isn't the same Gerald who went.

Aylesbury was favouring Bibbie with a scathing stare. "Come now, Mother. Emmerabiblia's never going to convince someone to marry her while she's footling about with that ridiculous hobby of hers."

Pink with indignation, Bibbie glared. "Witches Incorporated is not a *hobby!* We are a legitimate business enterprise, and—"

"Don't, Bibs," Monk said, treading lightly on her foot. "He's trying to get a rise out of you."

"It's true," Aylesbury retorted. "The rest of the family might be too soft-headed to protest her nonsense but I don't suffer from the same complaint! You must know, Emmerabiblia, that you and that misguided, ragtag bit of royalty you've teamed up with are turning the Markham name into a laughing stock."

Monk winced as Bibbie sucked in a furious breath. Oh, lord. She was going to lose her temper and reveal the truth about Witches Inc.'s interesting little arrangement with Sir Alec's secret government department. But before he could intervene, Uncle Ralph leaned a little sideways and clapped Aylesbury hard on his velvet-clad shoulder.

"Now, now, nephew, come along," he said, in a heartily patronising tone calculated to raise Aylesbury's hackles. "Don't be so stuffy. These are modern times we're living in, eh? Gels like to have a bit of fun, doncha know? And I think the Markham reputation can withstand a bit of girlish romping." He chuckled. "But speaking of weddings, what d'you all make of this fuss over Splotze and Borovnik's upcoming nuptials?"

Typically mercurial, Bibbie abandoned temper. "Melissande was invited to attend," she said sounding pleased and proud. "The wedding *and* the royal tour." She flicked a mordant glance at Aylesbury. "Which only goes to show that she isn't ragtag."

"Really, Emmerabiblia? How very prestigious," said their

mother, brightening. "Perhaps you could wangle your way into her retinue."

Rousing from his reverie, their father smoothed back his unruly salt-and-pepper hair. "What are you on about, Sofilia? You don't approve of royalty."

"Really, Wolfgang, do *try* not to be dense," said their mother, with an impatient *tsk*. "For all their faults, royalty can occasionally prove useful. There'll be scads of unspoken-for young men gadding about this wedding. Who knows what kind of eligible personage our unwed and rapidly aging daughter might meet?"

"*I* know, Mother," said Bibbie, with a glittering smile. "Not a one, because Melissande's declined the invitation. Something about the Crown Prince of Splotze and his wandering hands."

"Oh," said their mother, disappointed. "Well. That's terribly unobliging of her, I must say. As your friend she should be prepared for some trifling inconvenience if it means you could meet the right man. Monk, you're dallying with the young woman, aren't you? What are you doing to see that she changes her mind about attending this wedding?"

Monk trod on Bibbie's foot again, more emphatically, and favoured their mother with an apologetic smile. "Sorry, Mama, but when it comes to persuadability Melissande is quite a lot like you. Once she's made up her mind, there's no changing it."

"Well, I call that sadly lily-livered!" their mother retorted. "For your poor sister's sake, Monk, I demand that you try!"

There was no point arguing. "Yes, all right. But I'm not making any promises." And now it was time to change the subject. He looked at Uncle Ralph. "I must admit I haven't been paying a lot of attention to the Splotze-Borovnik fuss, sir. I'm still working on that big project for—" Just in time he remembered Aylesbury, who was employed by Ottosland's largest international trading company and didn't possess the right kind of government clearances. "That's to say, I've been busy. D'you honestly think something as simple as a wedding can patch up more than two hundred years of disputes and skirmishes and the occasional all-out war?"

"I can't say," said Uncle Ralph, after a considering moment. "But at least it'll give them something different to skirmish over. Weddings? From my experience they're little more than an excuse to settle old feuds and start new ones."

"Uncle Ralph, are you saying there's going to be trouble?" Bibbie said, pushing her emptied dinner plate away. "Because with Melissande not going to Splotze, and New Ottosland not wanting to risk various trading concessions, now it'll be King Rupert flying the flag at the wedding and it would be awful if something happened. He's the only brother Mel's got left and she's terribly fond of him."

"There!" said their mother, signalling Cheevers to start clearing the table for the dessert course. "That is *precisely* what I'm talking about. Your friend's brother. King Rupert. What is he if not a perfectly good unmarried monarch cluttering up the landscape? If this Princess Melissande was *really* your friend, Emmerabiblia, she'd introduce you to him. Monk, why haven't you arranged it?"

"Mama . . ." He sighed deeply, ruefully resigned. "Probably she would, if I asked, but even if I did, as a rule kings don't marry commoners."

"Commoners? With the blood of Thackerays and Markhams coursing through her veins, Monk, your sister is anything but *common!*"

"I know," he said patiently, because at times like this their mother required careful handling. "Only, Mama, you can't be serious. I mean, if Bibs married Rupert she'd have to go and live in New Ottosland."

"*And* get all excited about butterflies," Bibbie added, wrinkling her nose. "Because according to Mel, that habit's stuck. So I think I'll pass on Rupert, thanks all the same."

"And you know, Sofilia," Uncle Ralph added, "she's not likely to find the right sort of chap at this bloody Splotze-Borovnik affair. It'll be crawling with foreigners of dubious lineage. Last thing this family needs is Emmerabiblia making sheep's eyes at someone unsuitable from Graff or Harenstein or Blonkken."

Being careful to keep his expression safely amused at

indignant Bibbie's expense, Monk looked at their important, powerful uncle and wondered. For all his joviality, there was a shadow in his eyes. So either something was bothering him about the Splotze-Borovnik wedding . . . or else some other cloud was looming on the thaumaturgical horizon.

But what could it be? I've heard no rumblings. And if something was up, Gerald would've told me.

At least, he'd like to think so. Only things between him and Gerald hadn't been entirely comfortable since their return from the other Ottosland. They were keeping mismatched work hours, and when their paths did cross, in the kitchen or on the stairs of his inherited town house, it never seemed to be the right time for a fraught conversation. And anyway, he had no idea what to say.

I know you tried to kill me, mate, but no hard feelings. You weren't yourself. And incidentally, how's that grimoire magic working out for you? Had any more overwhelming homicidal urges lately?

No. No, he couldn't say that. Trouble was, it seemed he couldn't say anything that didn't run the risk of revealing a harsh truth: that every time he looked at his best friend, just for a split second he remembered that hideous killing hex, the cruelty in Gerald's face, the pain and the disbelief and the horror of impending death . . . and was afraid.

So, perhaps he shouldn't have spoken against Jennings's extraction procedure after all.

Pushing aside the sharply painful memories, Monk returned his attention to the family dinner. Cheevers and his underling were leaving the dining room, having served up the final course of raspberry fool, and Aylesbury was banging on about the importance of the wedding with regards to the stability of international trade.

"—exactly my point, Uncle Ralph. It might not be an ideal solution, but something has to be done. The Splotze-Borovnik Canal is a vital shipping thoroughfare. I hate to think how much money's been lost thanks to all those wasted years of bickering."

Stirred again from dreams of fantastic thaumaturgics, their

father slapped the table. "It's the greatest mistake in history, that bloody Canal," he declared, his deep-set eyes glittering. "All it's done is give Splotze and Borovnik even more excuses to fight. And how stupid were they, eh, to sign treaties that prevent the use of thaumaturgical measures to keep the peace? Superstition and ignorance instead of enlightenment, and for no better reason than their etheretics are unreliable. I tell you, it's been one misstep after another, ever since the day they opened their muddy ditch for business."

Aylesbury stared, aghast. "But, sir—you can't mean that!"

"I bloody well can," their father retorted. "And if you'd stop wearing those stupid neck ruffs that make you look like a lachrymose poet, you'd get a decent flow of blood to your brain and realise I'm right."

"But Father, you're *not* right," Aylesbury insisted, his colour dangerously high. Very fond of his neck ruffs, was Aylesbury. A stalwart aficionado of the romantical fashions. "Perhaps if you spent less time footling about with useless theoretical thaumaturgics, and more time out in the real world dealing with actual issues of economics and trade and politics, you'd—"

"Oh, blimey," Bibbie murmured. "Here we go. Do something, Monk."

"Why me?" he said, raspberry-and-cream laden spoon halfway to his mouth. But it was only a token protest. They'd never listen to Bibbie and there was no-one else. His mother and Uncle Ralph had long since given up when it came to keeping the peace between Wolfgang Markham and his eldest son.

But I'm the idiot who can't help throwing himself into the fray.

As Aylesbury and their father paused to take a heated breath, Monk cleared his throat. "I say. I've been thinking. It's pretty sad about Lady Barstow, isn't it?"

"Indeed it is," their mother agreed, with an approving flicker of one eyelid. "Not my favourite person, it's true, but she'll be missed. Very good on a committee, was Persephone Barstow. You could always rely on her to provide edible biscuits." She turned. "What has Gaylord to say about her death, Ralph?"

Uncle Ralph choked on a mouthful of dessert. "Sofilia,

please, this is hardly the time or place to discuss—besides, I can't—" Peevish, he dabbed pinkish cream off his chin with his damask napkin. "Dammit, I was hoping to leave work in the office for one evening, at least."

Monk had to smile. "A forlorn hope, sir. Y'know—" He sat back, comfortably full of roast beef and raspberries. "Looking at the matter purely academically, I can't help but be a *bit* impressed by the incant that did for Lady Barstow. Bloody ingenious, hexing her teapot like that. Your average punter won't think past natural causes. How d'you suppose—"

"Ingenious?" Aylesbury shoved his own raspberry fool to one side, untouched. "Monk, you make me sick. The wizard responsible for this has to be *stopped*, not *admired*. Lady Barstow might've been a vacuous blot but she didn't deserve to die like that." He leaned forward. "Infantile adoration from thoughtless idiots like you is one of the reasons this thaumaturgical madman hasn't been caught." His lips curled in a sneer. "Perhaps instead of witlessly fawning over the man and his growing list of misdeeds, you could spare a little of your vaunted genius for catching him."

Stunned to silence, the whole family gaped. One supercilious eyebrow raised, Aylesbury smiled, sardonic.

"Oh, come on, Uncle Ralph. Surely you didn't think you could keep this nefarious wizard's exploits under wraps forever? I might not be in the government's employ, but I am still a Markham. And while I don't pretend to be Monk, neither am I a *cabbage*."

"Now then, Aylesbury, I don't recall anyone ever calling you a cabbage," said Uncle Ralph, shockingly subdued. "Your aptitude scores are nothing to wink at."

Aylesbury sneered. "So I am right? When it comes to these odd deaths and thaumaturgical mishaps, the authorities know they're not random? Someone *is* standing behind the curtain, pulling the strings?"

"Hmmph." Uncle Ralph ran a finger round the inside around the edge of his collar. "Well. Since I know I can speak freely beneath a Markham roof . . . yes. But as for this damned black marketeer and his filthy hexes, while I can't go into details, for obvious reasons, I will assure you the Department is doing all in its power to bring the man down."

"We know you'll catch him," said Monk, as his parents exchanged looks and held hands under the table. Funny how they always thought nobody would notice. "Word around the Department is that Gaylord's got his best agents on the hunt."

"What?" Uncle Ralph's eyes bulged alarmingly. "D'you mean to tell me, Monk, that you and the rest of Research and Development's ramshackle collection of reprobates spend the day gossiping about highly sensitive government matters that are none of your bloody business?"

"No—no, of course we don't," he said, leaning away from his irate uncle. "Sorry. Didn't mean to—that's to say, I wasn't—look, forget I mentioned it. My lips are sealed. I don't know a thing."

"*Actually*, Uncle Ralph," said Bibbie, heroically rushing to the rescue, "I think it's a bit insulting, the way you keep on referring to Ottosland's mystery criminal as *he*. For all you know, your evil mastermind is a witch. I mean, when it comes to committing heinous thaumaturgical acts, you must agree that a witch is perfectly capable of being every bit as dreadful as a wizard."

Their mother turned. "Wolfgang, darling, I don't understand. Where did we go wrong?"

"Steady on, Mama," said Monk, as Bibbie's eyes widened with hurt outrage. "That's not fair, y'know. Bibs—"

Ignoring him, their mother added, "I'll tell you one thing, Wolfgang. Emmerabiblia's zaniness does not come from *my* side of the family! She's a Markham throwback, which means you'll have to deal with her!"

"Thanks ever so, Mother, but I don't feel like being dealt with," Bibbie snapped. "I feel like going home. Monk, I'm off to warm up the jalopy. If you're not sitting in the passenger seat by the time it's toasty, you can walk back to Chatterly Crescent."

And in the highest of dudgeon, she flounced out of the small dining room.

"Lord," said Aylesbury, laughing. "I do love our family

dinners. They save me from buying a ticket to the theatre."
He stood. "But even the best of entertainments must come
to an end. I've a conference in Aframbigi tomorrow and a
mountain of papers to read through before I leave. Good
night, Mama." He kissed their mother's powdered cheek.
"Good night, Father." A perfunctory hand-shake. "Good night,
Uncle Ralph." A reserved nod of his head.

Their mother sighed. "Aylesbury dear . . ."

Aylesbury dear grimaced. "Monk."

Monk waggled his fingers. "Aylesbury."

"Really, Monk, you should try harder to get along with
him," his mother scolded, once his brother was gone. "Poor
Aylesbury. He might not be a cabbage, but I'm afraid there's
no escaping the fact that next to you he is a trifle *leafy*."

He shot his mother a sly look. "Perhaps he's a throwback
on the Thackeray side."

"Really!" his mother said, then glanced at the dining room
door and sighed again. "Oh dear. I suppose I should go and
mend fences with your impossible sister. You know, Monk, it's
very poor of you to encourage her. I'm not at all sure it was
the right thing to do, letting her live with you in Uncle
Throgmorton's house. Not after saying she could start that
little witching business with that princess of yours. A great
many eyebrows were raised both times, and I'm still waiting
for most of them to come down."

"Now, now, Sofilia," said his father, taking her elbow before
she could launch into a proper tirade. "You're going to need
some help, mending that fence. Give us a few minutes, Monk.
And if you've some time in the next few days, you should
drop back round. I've developed a new etheretic combinant
meter, and I'd like your assessment."

Monk grinned. Wolfgang Markham, world-renowned thaumaturgist, was an easy man for a son to admire . . . but
sometimes hard to live up to.

But not now. Now being his son is the easiest thing in the world.

"Of course, sir. I'm free the night after next, if that suits."

"Good," said his father, and stood. "Come along, Sofilia."

As his parents withdrew, Monk looked at Uncle Ralph.

"Honestly, sir, you've got the wrong end of the stick. The other lads and I don't—"

"I know," his uncle said heavily. "You've faults aplenty, but idle tongue-flapping's not one of 'em. Don't mind me, my boy. It's been a long day."

It was strange, really, being related to one of the most important government men in Ottosland. There was such a sharp line they had to draw, between their encounters at the Department, and then at family gatherings like this. Even stranger was being privy to things that by rights Ralph Markham should know, but didn't, because him finding out would lead to terrible repercussions. Not an idle tongue-flapper?

Bloody hell, sir. You don't know the half of it.

Uncle Ralph drummed his fingers on the tablecloth. "That friend of yours. Dunwoody. Seen him today, have you?"

Monk felt a frisson of unease stir the hairs on the back of his neck. "No, actually. Ah . . . why?"

Instead of answering, Uncle Ralph seemed to debate with himself. Then he pulled a face. "He's undergone a classified and slightly dangerous procedure, Monk. It means he might not be feeling quite himself, so be sure to look in on him when you get home."

His mouth sucked cinders-dry. Bloody hell. The grimoire extraction. That was today? *Why the hell didn't Gerald tell me?*

"Yes, sir."

"I can see from the look on your face you know what I'm talking about," Uncle Ralph added, resigned. "So you know what it means. If you're not satisfied with Dunwoody's appearance, raise the alarm. But discreetly. Understand?"

"Of course, sir."

"Good lad," said Uncle Ralph.

It was one of the most startling things he'd ever uttered.

Driving home with Bibbie, too preoccupied to pay much attention to her fuming complaints about overbearing, old-fashioned mothers, too numb to feel his usual terror at her recklessly extravagant driving, Monk gnawed at his bottom lip and wished he'd not eaten that third helping of roast beef.

Why hadn't Gerald told him about the procedure? Was his silence another symptom of their ailing friendship? Doused in misery, as Bibbie rambled on he nodded in what he hoped were all the right places, offered an encouraging grunt every now and then, and felt his belly churn more and more nervously the closer they got to home.

Leaving his sister to garage the jalopy, he had her let him out by the gate. As he reached the bottom of the steps at the end of the path, he heard a familiar rustle of feathers.

"Evening, sunshine."

Reg. She was perched on the big flowerpot by the front door, light from the window limning her long, sharp beak and making her eyes gleam.

"Evening," he said, stopping. "What are you doing out here?"

Her tail feathers rattled. "Enjoying a little peace and quiet."

There was something in her voice. "Oh. So . . . you know?"

"That our daft Mister Dunwoody spent the day having himself spring cleaned?" She sniffed. "Yes. I know."

Monk folded his knees until he was sitting on the nearest step. "You think getting rid of those foul grimoire incants was daft?"

"No. That was smart. Going it alone was daft."

He couldn't argue with that. "Have you seen him?"

"I spoke to him. From the other side of his closed bedroom door. He's not interested in company." Reg chattered her beak. "I'll try again in the morning."

Yes. Reg had often been the only one who could talk sense into Gerald. He just had to trust that at least that much hadn't changed.

"I'm worried, Reg. He's not the same."

In the darkness, a cynical snort. "Neither am I, sunshine. And neither are you. We're all of us different now, aren't we, Mister Markham? One way or another."

He realised then that he wasn't ready to answer that question, or to talk in any meaningful way about what had happened in the other Ottosland. About the Reg who'd died there, or the Monk who'd died here and the Gerald who'd killed them both. Those things were too enormous. Still too close. He needed more time.

"Is Gerald all right, d'you think?"

"No," said Reg, looking down her beak at him. "But you don't need me to tell you that."

Groaning, Monk dropped his head in his hands. "Oh, Reg. What are we going to do?"

Another rattle of tail feathers, and then a flap and a thud as she landed on his shoulder. "Right now? You're going to pour me a brandy. Then we're both going to take our beauty sleeps. And come tomorrow? Well. We'll see."

He stood, his knees creaking. "Don't mention this to Bibbie. Or Mel, for that matter."

"Ha!" said Reg, and whacked him with her wing. "Do I look like I came down in the last shower of turnips?"

"No, Reg," he said humbly.

"No," she echoed. "Now gee up. My brandy glass isn't about to fill itself, is it?"

CHAPTER THREE

"Ooooh, *Ferdie*," said Mitzie, breathless. "Should we? I don't think we should. What do you think?"

Grinning, Abel Bestwick slid his arm around the buxom kitchen maid's willowy waist, then accidentally-on-purpose let his eager hand slip south to caress her delightfully plump behind. What did he think? He thought that if Sir Alec knew he was dipping his wick on Department time he'd find himself in very hot water. But seeing as how Sir Alec was several countries eastward, chances were his superior would never find out. And anyway, after living nearly four years as Ferdie Goosen, pantry-man in the Royal Palace of Splotze, he was owed whatever chances of wick-dipping wandered his way.

Sometimes it was a real bugger he'd been born half-Splotzin. And an even bigger bugger he looked all Splotzin through-and-through and thanks to his mother spoke Splotzin like a native.

"What do I think, Mitzie?" he murmured, nibbling at her ear. They were tucked out of sight in the palace kitchens' vast drygoods pantry, surrounded by beans and sugar and flour and herbs and suchlike. "I think even lackeys like us deserve a noon break from our toils. And it just so happens I overheard the head groom mentioning he and the lads would be gone most of the day, taking the horses with them. So you and me, we can duck into an empty stable or up to the hay loft and—" He closed his fingers on her ample flesh. "Bounce."

Mitzie squealed, her lavish eyelashes fluttering. "Ooooh,

Ferdie. In broad daylight? Idn't that playing dice blindfolded?"

"Bit of danger adds spice," he said, and dared a kiss. "You feeling spicy, Mitz? My itsy bitsy mittens?"

She kissed him back. For all her protestations she was no innocent, Mitzie. She'd only been in the kitchens a few months, but he'd sized her up on her first day as a lass who wasn't a stranger to bouncing. His luck, for once, that her come-hither eye had alighted on him.

"I'll meet you round back of the stables, by the manure pile," she said, giggling. "Don't be late, Ferdie."

And then she slipped away, not a moment too soon, for he'd barely tipped a fresh sack of flour into the drygoods pantry's big stone crock when the cook-in-charge barged in shouting for more salt. He did a lot of shouting, did Cook. In that respect he was the opposite of Sir Alec, who never raised his voice . . . and was about a hundred times more frightening because of it.

As soon as Cook stopped shouting and waving his fat arms, Abel pointed. "Salt's there, Cook. Came in fresh just yesterday."

"No, no, no, that is the wrong salt!" Cook bellowed. His cheeks were scarlet, his jowls wobbling like badly-set calf's-foot jelly. "You are stupid. You think I create the finest medallions of veal poached in malmsey for the Crown Prince and Princess and His Highness and the foreigners using plain marsh salt from *Ottosland?*" He spat on the stone floor. "*Pah* for your Ottosland! Where is my beautiful sea salt from Beleen?"

Abel blinked at him. "I don't know?"

"*Pah!*" No respecter of lackeys, Cook brandished his ham-hock fists. "But you are the senior pantry-man! Why don't you know?"

The answer to that was simple—because Cook insisted on jealously guarding his collection of recipes and his weekly menus, so that the underlings who cooked in his wake and the kitchen's general lackeys never knew from one day to the next what ingredients would be needed.

But if he said that, Cook might well toss him out on his

arse, which wouldn't please Sir Alec at all. So he bit his tongue, looking suitably chastened. On the inside, though, he was seething. Enough was enough. As soon as the royal wedding was done with he was going to ask Sir Alec for a different assignment. It wasn't just the scarcity of wick-dipping, though that didn't help. No, it was the daily bollocking from Cook, and the mind-numbing, bone-breaking physical labour that went with being a pantry-man and the relentless, grinding reminders of his despised lackey status and the ever-present background tension over that bloody Canal. The whole bloody set-up was giving him the gripes. He was homesick. Fed up to the back teeth with all things Splotze. Desperate for a pint or several of good Ottish brown ale.

Cook was slamming his way around the drygoods pantry's shelves, searching like a madman for his precious Beleen salt. As if it could make that much of a bloody difference! Salt was salt, wasn't it? If it was white and salty, what else could any sane man possibly want? Clearly, Cook needed to get out more. He needed to do a little wick-dipping of his own, instead of spending his days making love to pots of bubbling stew.

Panting, Cook slewed around. "You, there, you stupid, blind pantry-man!"

"My name's Goosen," Abel said, feeling truculent and unfairly put-upon. "Ferdie Goosen."

"A good name, then, for you are a goose!" Cook snapped. "You will run down to the township and you will find me Beleen salt! Go now, goose-man. Run your feet off. *Run!*"

In this world, in his current disguise, he had no choice but to obey Cook as he'd obey Sir Alec. Cursing under his breath in gutter Splotzin, denied even the comfort of some good, plain Ottish oathing, Abel took to his heels. If he was lucky, he'd find Cook's bloody salt and still make it to the stables in time to meet Mitzie.

"Ferdie!" Pouting, Mitzie stamped her foot into the soft ground beside the odiferously steaming manure pile. "You are late! I am leaving. I only stayed until now so I could do *this!*"

And she smacked his face.

Slapping one hand to his smarting cheek, Abel grabbed her wrist with the other and tugged her, protesting, into the deserted opulence of the royal stables.

"Don't blame me, Mitzie love, it was Cook's fault," he wheedled. "I had to run an errand for him, and I promise I ran it as fast as I could."

Still pouting, she folded her arms. Her generous charms swelled provocatively above the demure neckline of her blouse. Abel felt his breath catch.

"Please, Mitzie. We've still got time. And I won't sleep tonight, I swear it, if I can't dream happy dreams of a little bouncing with you!"

"I don't know, Ferdie," she said, looking past him to the square of sky framed by the stables' wide, open doorway. "Look where the sun is. We don't have much time."

He grinned, knowing he had her. "Then we'll be quick."

"Not too quick!"

"No, my little mittens," he promised, and pulled her with him towards the ladder up to the hay loft, where the horses' loose fodder and straw were stored. "Just quick enough."

Bouncing with Mitzie to their happy destination wiped away the aggravation of his scurrying salt search for Cook. Later, moist with the aftermath of sweet exertion and stuck with stray bits of straw, they sprawled side by side, happily smiling.

"Just quick enough," said Mitzie, and kissed the tip of his nose. Then, to his great regret, she started lacing her delightfully loosened blouse. "Only we'd best be back to the kitchens, Ferdie. We'll be noticed, else, and trouble idn't what I'm after. I'll go first."

"Wait!" he said, as she scrambled up to put the rest of her rumpled self aright. "I want to do this again. Don't you?"

Knowing, nimble fingers fiddling with her reddish-blonde hair, she dimpled. "I might. You've got some bounce in you, for an old man."

Old man? He wasn't thirty till next year! But then to a lass not far past seventeen, perhaps that was old. Saint Snodgrass knew working for Sir Alec had aged him.

"And will you dance with me at the Servants' Ball, Mitzie?"

Another saucy smile. "I might. Now, Ferdie, mind you stay behind so there'll be no spying us together," Mitzie said, pausing as she descended the hay loft ladder. "And no bragging on this when my back's turned. If I do hear there's bragging, Ferdie, it's a mischief I'll be doing you."

He pushed onto his elbows. "And if you don't hear it?"

"You keep mum?" She tossed her head, eyes bright with promise, her sweetly kissable lips pouting. "Then could be we'll bounce again, by and by."

Smothering a laugh, Abel settled himself to wait until she was safely away. After he'd counted nearly five minutes, with all the straw picked out of his hair and clothing, decently laced and buttoned like a well-behaved palace lackey, he laid a hand on the hay loft ladder—then pulled it back as though the old, splintered wood had burned him.

Curse it! Someone was returning to the royal stables.

Heart leaping in his chest, he flung himself face-down into the loose, dusty straw and listened to the clip-clop of horses' hooves on the herringbone brickwork. After a few more moments they stopped.

"Groom! *Groom!*"

And that was a Harenstein accent, roughly wrapping itself around the guttural Splotze tongue. Official go-betweens and negotiators of the unlikely upcoming nuptials, the Harenstein wedding party had been in Grande Splotze for several weeks. He'd managed a good look at them, since being a lackey meant he was able to scurry about the place with none of the hoity-toits paying him any more attention than if he were an umbrella. No alarm bells had rung. But then, why would they? Harenstein wasn't a danger. Without its efforts there'd be no wedding.

"Damned vermin," said another voice, speaking in Steinish this time. "Lazy shrulls."

And that speaker sounded no more familiar than the first. Abel winced. From the sound of them they weren't of the lackey class, so that meant there were at least two Steinish dignitaries he'd overlooked. Damn. Might be best not to mention that in his next report. Not unless he had to. Sir Alec would be far from amused.

"We'll have to see to the nags, Dermit," the disgruntled voice added. "The marquis isn't to be kept waiting."

More clip-clopping. Leather creaking. The squealing groan of a stable door that wanted oiling. Abel risked a look over the edge of the hay loft and saw the two men and their horses disappearing into their respective stables, only three boxes along from the hay loft ladder. Dare he risk leaving while they were still here, and so close by? He had to. He was already late. And since he'd taken Cook's salt to him straight away, he couldn't plead a delay in the town. Linger here any longer and by the time he did get back to the kitchens there'd be screaming and ranting and probable dismissal in disgrace.

Curse it.

Holding his breath against an inconvenient sneeze, Abel bellied his way backwards over the edge of the hay loft and made his stealthy way, rung by rung, down to the ground. The two Harenstein officials were still complaining about having to care for their own horses. Typical arrogant upper-class snobbery . . . which in fairness he shouldn't criticise, since their whining was keeping them too preoccupied to notice him.

And then, as his feet touched the brickwork, he realised the men had stopped their complaints and instead—instead—

Oh, Saint Snodgrass save us!

"Yes, Volker, all is ready," the first man said in answer to the second's question. "Bribes paid, hexes in place. And we have the extra hexes, just in case. This abomination of a wedding will founder. How often must I reassure you?"

"Do not blame me for wanting reassurance, Dermit," said Volker. "You know well the saying—there is many a slip 'twixt cup and lip. I am not yet convinced we have done enough."

"We have done all that we dare," said Dermit, sounding scornfully dismissive. "Would you risk our lives? Do not worry. Remember, we are not alone in this."

The other man snorted. "Perhaps we should be. To trust there, Dermit, is dangerous. What if someone should suspect that we and—"

"Who would suspect such an alliance? It is unthinkable, which is why it will stay secret and we will remain safe."

"I do not share your confidence. We are risking our lives. I think we should reconsider—"

"We reconsider nothing, Volker!" Dermit snapped. "What will happen on the way to Lake Yablitz has been meticulously planned. I tell you there is *no* danger to us. Or are you now thinking to question my judgement?"

Chilled to his marrow, Abel scarcely heard Volker's grudging reply. What the devil? This plotting made no sense. With Harenstein instrumental in brokering the match, why would they—

"Hey! You there! You're not a stable lad. What d'you think you're doing, loitering here?"

Abel spun round, nearly leaping out of his shoes in his fright. Damn. It was Mister Ibblie, a senior palace minion, the brass buttons on his dark blue tunic proclaiming his superiority. Of all the wretched bloody timing!

"Sorry, sir," he said, sidling away from the hidden men of Harenstein. Pretending utter ignorance, because Ferdie Goosen had no business knowing the difference between important Ibblie and a tree stump. "I was sent with a message for the head groom, sir. But seems he's not about, so—"

Frowning, Ibblie approached. "Sent by whom? You're a kitchen lackey, from the look of you. What—"

An ominous iron groan, as a stable door was pushed open. Almost frozen with horror, Abel slid his gaze over his shoulder. One of the Steinish plotters was staring at him, blue eyes cold and calculating, one broad, blunt hand resting on the worn knife-sheath belted at his hip. Beyond him the neighbouring stable door opened, and the second plotter stepped out. Thinner in the face than his friend, a violently suggestive pale scar slashing the width of his right cheekbone.

Abel turned back to Ibblie, his skin crawling as though he wore a shirt made of ants. "Sorry, sir. I think I've muddled myself. You're right, I shouldn't be here at all. The message is for the gatekeep." He bobbed his head. "Excuse me. I'll get on."

"Yes, you do that!" snapped Ibblie. "And be sure I'll mention your incompetence to the head cook!"

Prickling with alarm, Abel managed, barely, to hold himself

back to a swift walk. They wouldn't follow him, surely, those murderous plotters from Harenstein. Not with the palace secretary standing there, an inconvenient witness.

As he reached the hedge with the gate in it, which opened into the palace's extensive kitchen gardens, he dared a look behind him . . . and choked. Those bastards. They were following.

Throwing caution to the proverbial winds, Abel ran.

Mid-afternoon in sunny Central Ott.

Pretending leisurely indifference, Sir Alec sauntered along pedestrian-thronged Haliwell Street, which bustled with brisk trade. There was no better place in Ottosland's capital for the training of junior agents in the art of clandestine operations without benefit of thaumaturgics. Today, having won a short and bracingly sharp argument with Frank Dalby, whose purview this fell under, he was training two hopeful would-be janitors.

On the other side of the wide, busy street, in between passing carriages and automobiles, he caught sight of Mister Pennyweather, who was oblivious to the fact that doggedly persistent Frank Dalby had been following him for the last quarter hour. Were this real life, and not a training exercise, and were they not in Central Ott but instead some far-flung thaumaturgical hotspot, Bocius Pennyweather would by now be an unfortunate statistic.

The blithering fool.

On the other hand, he still held out cautious hope for Chester Baldrin, currently five shops to the rear on his side of the street. Mister Baldrin had neatly evaded Grady Thomquist, the Department's other regular field trainer, and continued to remain almost inconspicuous. Sir Alec was vaguely aware of relief. Provided he could keep finding more Chester Baldrins, the Department's future would remain secure.

In the short term, at least.

Because the two young men were supposed to believe that this chance to follow their superior was entirely haphazard, he ducked into a haberdashery and purchased a half dozen unnecessary handkerchiefs. Then, to test his trainees more rigorously, he took a seat next to the railing in the outdoor area of a popular tea room and waited.

But not for long.

Just as his unsweetened lemon tea was placed before him by a waiter, disastrous Mister Pennyweather caused a commotion by darting across the street under the nose of a startled carriage horse. Making a bad situation worse, he then walked right past the tea room's outdoor seating area and made eye contact.

Lips thinned, Sir Alec raised an eyebrow.

The young fool's stride faltered and his face turned beet red. As he dithered, blocking the sidewalk, inviting irritated glances and a flurry of complaints from inconvenienced pedestrians, Frank Dalby slid up to him like a shadow, pressed a finger into the small of his back, and snarled.

"*Mister Pennyweather, you blockhead, you are dead.*"

Across the street, Chester Baldrin kept walking without so much as a glance in their direction. When Grady Thomquist appeared on the edge of the pedestrian-knot in front of the tea room, Sir Alec idly snapped his fingers. *Training exercise over.* Thomquist nodded, and took himself off after Mister Baldrin.

Bocius Pennyweather was staring at his feet. "Sorry, Sir Alec. Sorry, Mister Dalby."

"Idiot." Frank grabbed him by the coat sleeve and hauled him close. "No names. Get back to the office. We'll have words on this later."

"Yes, sir. Sorry, sir," Mister Baldrin whispered, and fled.

Sir Alec signalled to the waiter. "Another tea, please. Plain, with milk and five sugars. And some cream cakes."

"I knew Pennyweather was a crock the moment I clapped eyes on him," said Frank, sliding into the second chair as the waiter obediently retreated. "Do us all a favour, would you, and send him packing back to Customs."

"I'll agree Mister Pennyweather's not fit for field work," he said mildly, once he was sure no-one was paying them attention. "But his analytical skills are impressive."

Frank grunted. "If you say so."

"I do," he said, and decided to indulge himself further, with a cigarette.

A short, round matron wearing a shockingly green-and-purple checked day dress and far too many ostrich plumes in her puce turban stopped in front of them to peruse the tea room. She was accompanied by a parcel-laden maid, wilting in black and white, who tried not to look longingly at the shade and food. Noticing, the beplumed matron swatted her on the shoulder then launched into a tirade about slatternly servants who didn't know when they were best off.

Sir Alec listened to the harangue for a few moments, then inhaled deeply on his cigarette and exhaled, strategically.

"*Well!*" said the turbaned matron, wheezing, and moved off. Shooting him a grateful glance, the maid scuttled in her wake.

As Frank rolled his eyes, the waiter returned. Marvelling, Sir Alec watched as his former partner fell on the horribly sweet tea and cream-filled cakes like a man starved for weeks in the wilds of Apineena. How he remained skinny as a rake, eating like that, was a mystery.

He set the cigarette aside and sipped from his own cup. "So. Mister Pennyweather is out. And Mister Baldrin?"

Frank smacked his lips. "He's got a bit of promise, but I'll want to see him handle some tricky thaumaturgics before I start turning cartwheels."

Sir Alec hid a smile. There were times when Frank made him look like a giddy enthusiast.

"Right, then," said Frank, and let out a gentle belch. "That's them sorted. Now, about our other problem child."

It was funny, really. Inside the building at Nettleworth, Frank was taciturn and self-contained. Never anything less than dutifully deferential. But get him back into the field, away from Department hierarchies and protocols, and the years fell away until they were simply janitors again, standing shoulder to shoulder and back to back against the swiftly multiplying evils of the world.

He hated to admit it, but there were times when he missed that uncomplicated camaraderie, quite keenly.

"You're referring to Mister Dunwoody, I take it? Well, what about him?"

The glint in Frank's eyes was derisive. "You bloody know what."

As much as he trusted Frank, he'd not told him the entire truth of Gerald Dunwoody's most recent escapade. No need to burden him. No need to run the risk. How much Frank had guessed for himself, he didn't ask. Quite a lot of it, he suspected. Especially since Frank had been the one to dispose of that other, deceased Monk Markham. But his former partner wouldn't push to know more and he'd not bear a grudge over a prudently-held silence, either.

"Mister Dunwoody will be fine," he said, and sipped again from his cup. "He just needs a little more time to adjust."

Frank wiped his fingers clean of cake cream. "You really think he can hold the line against grimoire magic?"

Sir Alec blinked. *Oh. I didn't think he'd guess quite that much.* "Frank—"

"Ha." Frank downed the rest of his ghastly tea, then rattled the cup back onto its saucer. "That business in East Uphantica left me with a quirk in my *potentia*, remember?"

Lord. East Uphantica. Twelve—no, thirteen—years ago, that was. Not his finest hour. Sometimes it still astonished him, that Frank could forgive those scars.

But then he was always much kinder than me.

"I caught a whiff of the muck Jennings left behind," said Frank, leaning across the table and lowering his voice. "Dunwoody's always *forgetting* to turn on his shield. Past time you hauled him back over the coals for it. Especially now."

"Apparently," he said, knowing Frank could tell he was shaken. Not minding too much, because it was Frank. "Mister Dalby—"

Lip curling, Frank sat back. "Yeah, yeah, I know. I'm just saying."

The popular tea room was doing a lively trade, voices raised in conversation and laughter, glasses and cups rattling, cutlery chinking against porcelain, chairs scraping. In the street, carriage horses clopped, automobiles chugged, and on the sidewalk pedestrians raised dust beneath their hurrying feet. They were safe talking here, but even so . . .

"Yes. But you'll not say any more."

"I'll say this," said Frank, frowning. "You watch your bloody step, Ace. That Dunwoody, he's a can of worms. You keep on poking it, and one day you might find there's a snake buried in there."

Aggravated, Sir Alec signalled the waiter for the bill. "Thank you Mister Dalby. I do know what I'm doing."

"Yeah?" Frank got up, dug around in his pocket, pulled out a crumpled bank note and tossed it onto the table. "Let's hope so, for all our sakes. I'll see you back at Nettleworth." He touched two sardonic fingers to his forehead. "Sir."

Returning to his office some thirty minutes later, intending only to jot down a few notes for an upcoming inter-Department meeting before joining Frank in his education of Bocius Pennyweather, Sir Alec saw the small, flashing crystal ball on his desk and halted.

Only a handful of people were entrusted with its vibration. And every one of them knew they should only call him on it as a last resort. He had a telephone, a general crystal and the Department's communications room for anyone desirous of a regular conversation.

He closed the office door, crossed to his desk and coded in the password that would release the ball's recorded message.

A familiar and totally unexpected face swam into focus.

"*Sir Alec! Sorry not to come through regular channels. Had no choice. Don't think I know who to trust!*"

Abel Bestwick, one of his long-term sleeper janitors. Sweaty, panicked, his voice ratcheted too high, the words spitting out too fast.

"*Dammit, why aren't you there? Sir Alec, there's something funny afoot. I've just—*"

A spasm of pain crossed Bestwick's pale face. He lifted his hand, staring. Blood dripped between his fingers.

"*Oh. That blade must've been longer than I—*"

Another spasm of pain, more severe. Groaning, Bestwick

seemed to collapse into himself. And then a sharp sound from beyond the scope of his crystal ball's recording field snapped his head round. He breathed in, sharply.

"*Sir, it's the wedding! They're trying to—*"

A loud crack. A flash of light. Abel Bestwick's face vanished.

Stunned, Sir Alec picked up the small crystal ball. Had to fight not to shake it, as though shaking it would bring Bestwick back. He replayed the short message. Replayed it again. And again. And then, frustrated, threw the damned ball hard at the far wall. It struck, leaving a dent in the paper-covered plaster, and thumped to the carpet.

"*They?* Who's *they?* You bloody *idiot*, Bestwick!" he fumed. "Living in Splotze has rotted your brain, has it? Four years of indolence has turned you into a *pudding?*"

The most basic emergency protocols, unheeded. Every janitor on assignment had them hammered into memory.

If you must make an emergency report, stick to the salient facts. No blathering.

And what was that bloody recording, if not a prime example of *blather*. So what if he'd been hurt? It was a risk every janitor took. Bestwick *knew* that. And he knew better than to blather. Or he had done, four years ago.

I left him over there too long.

But this wasn't the time for self-recriminations and post mortems. He'd assess his own culpability once he'd sorted out the mess.

The wedding.

Obviously Bestwick meant the Splotze-Borovnik affair. And hadn't he been saying for months that trouble was a distinct possibility? A familial alliance between Splotze and Borovnik signalled a major power shift in that thaumaturgically volatile region—and change always sent the cockroaches scuttling. Hadn't he put Bestwick on alert for precisely that reason? He'd have done a damned sight more, only Lord Attaby had over-ruled him, citing delicate trade negotiations and the easily-pricked sensibilities of Borovnik's capricious Dowager Queen.

Now it seemed he'd been proven right. Again. Danger to

do with the wedding, that if not averted could easily lead to all-out war. A war with thaumaturgics this time, he could feel the danger in his bones, and the United Magical Nations' accords be damned.

But how to stop it? *How?*

Well, there was only one answer. He needed eyes and ears in the wedding party. And with Bestwick unaccounted for, quite possibly dead, he'd have to send someone else.

The question was, who?

And even if he could find the right man . . . how the hell was he going to get him invited to a bloody royal wedding?

CHAPTER FOUR

Still wrapped in her pink flannel dressing gown, because it was early and she was alone—well, except for Boris and he didn't count—Melissande sat at her desk in the office and worked her way through Witches Incorporated's neatly kept account book.

"Y'know," she remarked to the sleepily attentive cat, "I'm starting to think we might not sink like the proverbial lead balloon after all."

Curled up on Bibbie's desk, green eyes slitted, Boris twitched his tail.

"Yes, really. I mean, all right, we'd have probably sunk already without Sir Alec's totally self-serving assistance, but leaving that aside . . ."—which she was more than happy to do—". . . there's no getting away from the facts. Nearly three-quarters of our clients last month came from legitimate, *non*-Sir Alec sources. Word of mouth, mostly. And that's the kind of advertising money can't buy."

Saint Snodgrass be praised. Because they didn't have the money to buy any kind of advertising, beyond a tiny entry each month in the *Wizarding Times*. And they could only afford that by going without their sticky buns every other week.

Bibbie was getting very scathing about that.

"Which is a problem, Boris," Melissande added, "because without Bibbie we *would* be sunk. She might be scattier than a flock of deranged hens, but it's her thaumaturgical genius that keeps people coming back."

Boris flicked his whiskers, agreeing.

"If only Gerald didn't have to go on pretending he's nothing more than a Third Grade wizard," she said crossly, double-checking her addition of the figures in column three of the ledger. "I tell you, Boris, we'd be using gold bars for paper-weights if that wretched Sir Alec would just let him off his leash once in a while. I mean, honestly, how much could it hurt?"

But that was never going to happen. Not so long as Gerald remained a janitor. And despite the awfulness of what had transpired in that mysterious other Ottosland, she couldn't imagine Gerald ever abandoning the Department. Or the Department letting itself be abandoned, for that matter.

"So I suppose we'll just have to keep muddling along, relying on Bibbie's formidable talents," she sighed. "But if Bibbie decides she's bored with Witches Inc., or if her Uncle Ralph gets it into his head she'd be an asset to the government even though she's not a man, or if she gives up the notion of living happily ever after in wedded bliss with Gerald—which, let's face it, might not be a bad idea—and decides to go adventuring abroad to mend her broken heart, then honestly, Boris . . . I don't know *what* I'll do!"

You could always marry Monk and live happily ever after in wedded bliss yourself, her treacherous inner Melissande slyly suggested.

The thought made her blush, then slap the office ledger closed.

"He has to ask me first," she pointed out to the cat, putting the cap back on her fountain pen. "And Monk's been a bit preoccupied lately."

"Not to mention slow off the mark," said an almost familiar voice from the open office window. "Ducky, you do know what they say about women who sit about in empty rooms talking to themselves, don't you?"

Reg. Sort of. Melissande snatched up the pen cloth and wiped a smudge of ink from her fingers. "I wasn't talking to myself, thank you. I was talking to Boris."

With a hoot, Reg flapped from the windowsill to the ram skull on the battered filing cabinet. "If you think that makes it better, madam, you'd best think again."

Drat the bird. Some things really were exactly the same.

"Where have you been, anyway?" she demanded. "Why didn't you come home last night?"

Reg's sharp brown gaze shifted, evasive. "I was busy."

"Doing what?"

"None of your beeswax," said Reg, and rattled her tail feathers. "Do I ask how you pass your evenings? No, I don't. Though I might, if you ever did anything but sit in here fretting over the agency and talking to that moth-eaten excuse for a feline."

"Fretting over the agency is part of the job description," she retorted. "And anyway, I do plenty of other things with my evenings, which you'd know if you'd been here for longer than five minutes!"

Ghastly silence.

Melissande watched her fingers clench. *Damn.* "Oh, Reg. I'm sorry. I wasn't thinking. I didn't mean—"

But before she could stumble her way through the rest of her difficult, apologetic explanation, somebody rapped sharply on the office's outer door.

"Oh, yes," said Reg, feathers fluffing, sounding distant. "That's what I came in to tell you. Your manky Sir Alec's here. And he's brought a friend."

She leapt up. "Sir Alec? Here? Now? *Why?* It's practically the crack of dawn!"

Another rap on the door.

"Reg, there's something going on, isn't there? Something to do with Gerald."

"No," said Reg, after a moment.

A rush of cold apprehension. In more ways than not, this was still Reg. "That's a fib. Reg, tell me the truth *right now* or I'll—"

"Miss Cadwallader? Miss Cadwallader! Kindly open the door. It's important that we speak."

Sir Alec, sounding briskly impatient. Nothing new there.

On principle, she ignored him. Give the Sir Alecs of the world an inch and the next thing you knew, they were merrily galloping over the horizon.

"Reg, *please*. I *know* something's going on. Gerald's been so awfully secretive ever since . . . well, you know. And there's a look in his eye that—frankly, it frightens me. Please, you *have* to—"

Rattle rattle went Reg's long tail. "I don't have to anything, ducky. Now just you give that boy some breathing room. I know you mean well, but he doesn't need you or anyone else poking—"

"I say, Melly, do stop faffing about," another voice called through the locked office door. "Because if you really must know, I need to use the conveniences."

Melissande turned so fast she nearly fell over. "*Rupert?*"

But before she could open the door to her only living brother and the agency's dubious, double-edged government benefactor, it swung wide of its own accord.

"Excuse me!" she snapped at Sir Alec, who led the way inside. "That was incredibly rude!"

Sir Alec considered her as he put in his pocket the key he wasn't meant to possess. "Whereas leaving visitors to bellow on the doorstep is the height of good manners?"

"Not when they're invited, no," she retorted, tugging her shabby flannel dressing gown a little tighter to her ribs. "But since I *didn't* invite you—" She held out a hand. "—*or give you that key, don't expect me to repine over my dearth of social polish."

"I say, Melly, steady on," said Rupert. "No need to bite off poor Sir Alec's nose."

"Trust me, sunshine, it's better than biting off other bits," said Reg, from her ram skull. "Which I'm more than happy to do." She jerked her beak sideways. "Lavatory's through there, incidentally."

"Ah," said Rupert, with a pained smile. "Yes. Actually, I only said that so Melly would open the door."

Though she was worried and cross, Melissande laughed. Then she threw her arms around him. "Oh, Rupes. It's lovely to see you. But why are you smothered in that ridiculous cloak and hat?"

"I'm in disguise," said Rupert, hugging back. "We don't want anyone to know I'm here, which is why we're bothering you so early."

Leaning away from her brother, she stared into his lean, much-missed face. "Yes, and why *are* you here? Zazoor hasn't decided to invade, has he?"

"No, of course not," said Rupert, removing the hat. "You'd go a long way to find a more reasonable man than Kallarap's mighty sultan. Besides, I paid the final installment of our in-arrears tariffs last month."

"Oh," she said, and looked past Rupert to Gerald's aggravating superior. "So that means this is your doing, Sir Alec. I might've known. What's gone wrong now?"

Probably no other subordinate, or dependent, or whatever she was, dared speak to Sir Alec Oldman in that particular tone of voice—which was why she made a point of doing it. Men like Sir Alec grew so used to ordering people about, risking their lives and their sanity, that they very quickly became unbearable if they weren't put firmly in their place every so often.

He might even come to thank me for it, one of these days.

But not today, apparently. "Do sit down, Miss Cadwallader," he said, with a sharp, dangerous courtesy. "And allow me to explain."

"No, why don't you sit down, Sir Alec? I'm going to get dressed. And by all means feel free to leave that key on my desk while you're waiting."

Sir Alec, in his habitually sober grey three-piece suit, neatly shaved with every short mousey brown hair in place, favoured her with one of his most acidic smiles.

"I'm afraid I can't oblige you there, Miss Cadwallader. The key is mine, you see. Just as the building is mine. In a manner of speaking. Though perhaps it's more accurate to call me its custodian."

She blinked. "Are you telling me the government has bought this entire building?"

"Yes," said Sir Alec, irritatingly calm.

Good lord. Her heart was thumping, not calm at all. "When?"

"Recently."

"How recently?"

"Very," said Sir Alec, with a careless little shrug. "I believe the ink has just dried on the deeds of transfer."

"Does Gerald know? What does he think?"

Sir Alec raised an eyebrow in that aggravatingly supercilious way of his. "Are you suggesting I base my decisions upon the opinion of a junior subordinate?"

"I'm suggesting it might've been nice if you'd warned us!" she said, fuming. "A change of landlord has an impact on a business, you know."

Another acidic smile. "Don't worry, Miss Cadwallader. I wasn't intending to raise the rent. Yet."

She narrowed her eyes. Was he joking or serious? As usual, it was impossible to tell. "How generous."

"Not at all," he said smoothly. "Now, please, Miss Cadwallader, do go and get dressed. My business is somewhat urgent."

Yes, well, wasn't it always? Biting her tongue, Melissande flicked Rupert a warning look then withdrew to her tiny bedsit in the office's second room, where she hauled on the first clean and ironed day dress that came to hand, found stockings with no holes, or at least none that would show in the respectable gap between hem and ankle, buttoned on her shoes then hastily brushed, plaited and pinned up her hair. Sometimes she flirted with the idea of getting the rusty red mass of it chopped off in a daring crop. Except her long, thick hair was almost her only genuinely glorious attribute. It seemed silly to discard it.

Besides. Monk said he liked her hair the way it was.

When she returned to the office, she found Sir Alec pensive by the window, Rupert seated in the client armchair, Reg eyeing the pair of them suspiciously from her vantage point on the ram skull, and her desk alarmingly empty of cat.

"Where's Boris?"

"Threw himself headfirst out of the window," said Reg. "But he landed on his feet, worse luck."

She rolled her eyes. "If I thought for a moment you actually *meant* that . . ."

"Ha," said Reg, and fluffed out her feathers. "How would you know what I do or don't mean, ducky? Seeing as I've only been here five minutes."

Uncomfortably aware of Sir Alec's sudden, pinpoint scrutiny, Melissande feigned an attack of deafness. "Does anyone want tea?"

"No," said Sir Alec. "Miss Cadwallader, word has reached me that there is a credible threat to the Splotze-Borovnik wedding. Without going into details, let me just say that the Ottosland government has good reason to fear the consequences, should anything go wrong during the upcoming nuptials. Therefore it falls to me and my Department to nip this threat in the bud."

"And to me, it seems."

Reluctantly, Sir Alec nodded. "Yes. And to you. Indeed, without your assistance I fail to see a solution to the problem."

Oh. Feeling cornered, Melissande looked at her brother. "And Rupert? What has any of this to do with him?"

"His Majesty is here because—"

"Thank you, Sir Alec," said Rupert, with the merest hint of a bite. "Best you let me handle this." He smiled, but his washy blue eyes were serious. "Melly, darling, do sit down and I'll explain."

Heart sinking, she perched on the edge of her desk. "Please, Rupes, don't tell me he's got you tangled up in his dreadful janitoring business too."

"Only very slightly around the edges, I promise." Leaning forward, Rupert braced his elbows on his knees and steepled his fingers. "Insofar as he needs me to ask you to attend the Splotze-Borovnik wedding as New Ottosland's representative."

"Rupes . . ." Melissande shook her head. "You've already

asked me, remember? It was thanks but no thanks then, and it's thanks but no thanks now."

"Yes, well, the thing is, you see, Melly, *now* Sir Alec needs you to say yes, please."

"But why?" she said, resisting the urge to glare at Sir Alec. "I mean, what possible use is it for me to attend the wedding? It's not as though I can go romping about Splotze pretending to be a janitor."

Rupert shifted in his chair, uncomfortable. "No, indeed, Melly, you certainly can't."

"Under *any* circumstances," said Sir Alec. "Let me make that perfectly clear. No. One of my agents will accompany you."

"I see," she said, willing herself not to snap at his high-handed attitude. "And I take it you expect me to slide him into the wedding party without any awkward questions being asked?"

"Precisely."

So, she was to be a stalking horse. How glamorous. "And when you say *one of my agents*, d'you mean the agent already stationed in Splotze? I take it there is one."

Sir Alec's grey gaze was cool and watchful. "Yes. But he is currently . . . unavailable."

The hint of tension in his voice had her skin crawling. *Oh, damn. There's trouble. And now I know where this is going.* "You're sending Gerald."

"I assume you have no objection."

Reg broke her silence to rattle her tail feathers, ominously. "Well if she doesn't, I do. If I were you, Mister Smarty Pants, I'd be thinking twice about sending my Gerald anywhere. Given the givens of recent events."

"I agree," Melissande said, nodding. "It's too soon to send him off janitoring again."

Sir Alec stared at her, his gaze abruptly glacial. "In your opinion."

"Melly," said Rupert, sounding uneasy, "perhaps it's not your place to question how Sir Alec conducts the affairs of his Department."

"It's all right, Your Majesty," said Sir Alec. "Your sister is simply expressing her concern for a friend."

"A concern I'd have thought you'd share, Sir Alec," she pointed out. "Gerald might be a rogue wizard, but that doesn't make him indestructible."

"No. It makes him unique," Sir Alec said, very clipped. "And under the circumstances, Miss Cadwallader, unique is what I require. Like it or not, and largely thanks to your connection to both him and the Crown Prince of Splotze, Mister Dunwoody is the most suitable agent for this assignment." His cool grey gaze flicked to Reg. "Various *givens* notwithstanding."

Melissande felt a fresh warning prickle on the back of her neck. Something was going on here between Reg and Sir Alec and Gerald was in the middle of it, of that she had no doubt. It was why the bird had stayed out all night, and why she was now giving Sir Alec a look fit to turn a lesser man to wilted compost.

"Besides, Reg," Sir Alec added, undaunted, "I can't think of anyone who appreciates more completely than you do, the need for good men and women to stand against evil. And considering present company, that's saying something. Don't you agree?"

Reg looked down her beak at him. "I don't recall saying you shouldn't make a stand, sunshine. But you can't ask me to believe Gerald's the only man you know with legs."

"Mister Dunwoody is not a child," Sir Alec said sharply. "And I very much doubt he'd want you treating him like one." He turned. "Or you, Miss Cadwallader."

Well, he was right about that much at least. Drat the man. Melissande shifted her accusing stare to Rupert. "And you're prepared to go along with this, are you?"

Rupert shrugged. "I'm here."

Ha. And to think she'd been happy to see him. Resentful, she glowered at Sir Alec. "So . . . assuming I do this, how would it work? I attend the wedding in my official capacity as Princess Melissande of New Ottosland, representing His Majesty King Rupert, and Gerald tags along as—what, exactly?"

"Some kind of minion, I'd have thought," said Sir Alec, eyebrow lifted again. "Royalty is always breaking out in minions, isn't it?"

She bit her lip, thinking. "Well, I suppose at a pinch I could call him my secretary. Although why I'd need to take a secretary to a wedding, I'm sure I don't know."

"You're forgetting, Mel," said Rupert. "It's not just the wedding. There's the wedding tour beforehand."

Oh, lord. Of course. "But—but the tour is slated to last for days!" she protested. "I can't possibly leave the agency to fend for itself. Not for days. Not with just Bibbie to sail the ship. She'd capsize it before lunch."

Reg snorted. "Not to mention no princess worth her tiara is going to travel anywhere with nothing but an unattached young man as her escort. You try pulling a stunt like that, ducky, and they'll turf you out of the international princess club faster than you can say *Oy, you there, how about a curtsey, then?*"

"Actually, Sir Alec, that's perfectly true," said Rupert, disconcerted. "What Melissande gets up to here in the Old Country as plain Miss Cadwallader is rather winked at back home. Out of sight, out of mind, y'know. But if she's going to Splotze as Her Royal Highness, well, she simply cannot flout tradition. There would be . . . repercussions."

"Lord Billingsley and his decrepit cronies?" Melissande pulled a face. "Honestly, Rupert, it really is past time you pensioned them off."

Sir Alec cleared his throat, lightly. "Perhaps Miss Markham might care to play the role of royal lady's maid in this particular production?"

"*What?*" She slid off the edge of her desk. "Sir Alec, are you stark raving bonkers? Bibbie as a lady's maid? Bibbie to walk three steps behind me, curtseying every time I hiccup? *Emmerabiblia Markham?* Tell me, have you *met* her?"

"Miss Cadwallader, I—"

"And anyway, if you rope me *and* Bibbie into this nonsense, along with Gerald, that means there is no more Witches Inc.

I'd have to close the doors. And I won't do that, I've worked—
we've worked—too hard for too long and—"

"*Miss Cadwallader!*"

She couldn't help it. She flinched. Even Rupert, who'd been
king for quite a while now and was finally used to putting his
foot down without scaring himself silly that he was turning
into Lional, looked alarmed.

Perched on her ram skull, Reg tipped her head to one side
and waited.

"You need not fear for Witches Incorporated," Sir Alec
continued, in a far more conciliatory tone. "I shall see that
its doors remain open while you are in Splotze."

Melissande stared at the faded carpet. If he said he would,
then he would. She knew that much about him. But on principle, she didn't like to capitulate too easily. She looked up.

"And what about Boris?"

"Your cat will also be cared for."

Slowly, she lowered herself back to the edge of her desk.
"You don't even know if Bibbie will do it."

"Ha!" said Reg, with another rattle of tail feathers. "That
scatterbrained flibbertigibbet turn down the chance to romp
around on foreign soil being a secret government agent? Don't
be daft, madam. You try keeping her out of this and she'll do
you a bloody mischief, mark my words."

Drat. The bird was right. Sighing, Melissande looked at Sir
Alec. "I suppose it has to be Bibbie?"

"I'm afraid so," said Sir Alec, markedly unenthusiastic.
"Since there are no female janitors. It's a case of making the
best of a bad situation."

Oooh, he could be a sarky bugger when he felt like it.
"Well, fine, only Monk's not going to like this idea. And what
about their parents? Bibbie's still under age. Not by much,
but still. You can't send her off janitoring without first asking
them."

"Mister Markham's preferences do not largely figure in my
decision-making, Miss Cadwallader," Sir Alec said, very chilly.
"As for his parents' position, I'm sure you're aware that the

Markhams have a long and illustrious history of serving their country in whatever capacity their country requires. I don't anticipate any difficulty."

And if he was wrong it was more than likely that Sir Ralph, so important and influential and as dedicated as Sir Alec, would allay his brother and sister-in-law's concerns for their daughter with whatever flummery he could think of. As a career politician, he could probably do it in his sleep.

Melissande felt her insides jump with nerves. "You've got an answer for everything, haven't you?"

"No, Miss Cadwallader," Sir Alec said quietly. "If I did, this conversation would not be necessary."

Bugger the man for a boat-load of monkeys. She was *not* going to feel sorry for the horrible position he was in.

"And now that the situation has been thoroughly explained," Sir Alec continued, "I must have your answer. Will you attend the Splotze-Borovnik wedding in your capacity as New Ottosland's princess, thus providing Mister Dunwoody with the cover he needs to undertake a mission that might well prevent the outbreak of war?"

Oh, well, yes, fine, if he was going to put it like *that*.

"Sir Alec," said Rupert, before she could reply, "I feel bound to point out that when you asked me to assist you in this matter, you did not phrase your request in quite those terms. In fact you entirely failed to mention that if she attended this wedding my sister might well be in danger."

The look Sir Alec gave him was daunting. "Your Majesty, given the nature of my work, to which you were long ago made privy, I rather thought the question of danger was a given."

Rupert stood, slowly. The sunshine pouring through the open office window woke his silvering blond hair to golden fire, caught a glitter in his eyes, and traced the edge of his sharply tightened jaw. Melissande, watching him, was suddenly very much reminded of Lional.

She leapt between the two men. "Right. Be quiet, both of you. In case it's slipped your notice, I'm no more a child than

Gerald is." She rested her hand on Rupert's iron-tense arm. "Yes, Rupes. It'll be dangerous. But what Sir Alec's asking of me is no less than he's spent his whole life asking of himself. So it's not like he's being a hypocrite." She tightened her fingers. "The thing is, if this weren't desperately important Sir Alec would *never* ask for my help. He loathes the fact that civilians are mixed up in his precious Department business. And because it's important, I have to say yes. Even if it means braving Crown Prince Hartwig of Splotze."

"I'm sorry?" said Rupert. "What are you—"

"Oh, you know," she said, and shook his arm a little. "Hartwig at New Ottosland's last centennial celebrations. He couldn't keep his hands to himself, remember? And Hartwig being Hartwig, I very much doubt if anything's changed. It doesn't matter that he's married, either. He was married when I was sixteen. But you don't need to worry. I'm pretty sure I can keep him at bay and still avoid an unfortunate international incident."

Rupert was neither amused nor appeased. "I'm not talking about a trifling matter of wandering hands, Melissande! What Sir Alec is asking—"

"Trifling?" She smacked him. "Honestly, Rupert, if you'd ever had Hartwig's hands slipping below *your* equator you wouldn't be using words like *trifling*."

And that made her brother smile, as she'd intended. She smiled back, then turned.

"As for you, Sir Alec? I'll thank you to remember that Rupert isn't one of your subordinates, he's the crowned sovereign of a nation. I don't ever want to see you raise an eyebrow at him, or hear you speak to him in that snooty tone of voice, ever again. Understood?"

After a moment of silent consideration, Sir Alec offered her a slight bow. "Understood . . . Your Highness."

"Good."

"I take it this means you're agreeing to my proposal?"

"Under protest," she muttered. "I still think you're wrong sending Gerald. But since it's clear I can't talk you out of it . . ."

"No, I'm afraid you can't."

She sighed. "Well, that still leaves Bibbie. Will you allow me to tell her she's needed? If she is coming, I'm going to have to educate her in the protocols of royal lady's maidship anyway, so you might as well." She sniffed. "After all, it's not like I can tell her any dire government secrets, is it, since you've been very careful not to reveal any."

Another slight bow. "By all means."

On the ram skull, Reg chattered her beak. "Oy. If you don't mind. What about me?"

"Yes?" said Sir Alec. "What about you?"

"Well, you're not leaving me behind!"

"D'you know, Reg," said Sir Alec, dangerously bland, "I rather think I am. I'll ask you to bear in mind your—" A glance at Rupert, who didn't know everything about what his sister and her friends got up to. "Unusual circumstances."

Reg's feathers trembled from beak to tail. "What? You're going to use *that* as an excuse to keep me here while you send my Gerald gallivanting off to an international war-in-waiting? In *his* condition?"

"Reg . . ." Sir Alec's steady gaze was more unforgiving than honed steel. "You're forgetting that Mister Dunwoody isn't your Gerald. He might well be, one day, in the fullness of time. And I'm sure I hope that will be the case. But today, you and he are very little better than strangers. Moreover, you would be a distraction that he can ill afford. He is burdened enough at the moment, don't you agree? Surely, if you do care for him, you'll not add to the weight."

Tears pricking, Melissande held her breath. Sir Alec, in his cool, detached, totally unsentimental way, was right. Drat him again. And oddly, because he was so coolly detached, she thought she'd never seen him so deeply moved.

As for Rupert, he was looking confused. She shook her head, just a bit, and let her eyes plead for his silence.

With a sad little sigh, Reg deflated her feathers. She'd gained some much-needed weight over the past week or so, but she was still too thin. Forlorn on the ram skull, she hunched her head to her chest.

"Fine," she snapped. "You win. But I'm warning you, sunshine. If anything happens to Gerald I'll—I'll—I'll poke you in your bloody unmentionables. Just you see if I don't!"

CHAPTER FIVE

Bibbie's delighted squeal was so loud it was a wonder she didn't shatter the office window.

"*Really?* Sir Alec *really* wants me to be one of his janitors? Oh, Melissande!"

Heart rapidly descending towards her neatly buttoned shoes, Melissande held up her hands.

"No, Bibbie, that is *not* what he wants. In fact, I think I can safely say that is the *last* thing he wants."

Delight instantly transformed into dudgeon. "But he wants *you?*"

Oh, lord. "No, Bibbie, he doesn't," she said carefully. "All he wants is this problem with the Splotze-Borovnik wedding, whatever it is, to go far, far away. And if that means he has to involve us then he will. But only with great reluctance. In a very bad mood."

Bibbie flounced round her desk and dropped into her chair. "How d'you know he was in a bad mood?"

"Ha!" said Reg, who'd shifted from her ram skull to the windowsill. "Your precious Sir Alec was *born* in a bad mood."

Bibbie's beautifully manicured fingernails tapped a tattoo of displeasure on her old, scuffed desk. Then she sighed.

"Fine. So tell me about the problem with the Splotze-Borovnik wedding."

Melissande retreated to the client armchair and sprawled, heedless of wrinkling her day dress. When Reg didn't make a cutting remark about princesses who carried on like ruffian football players—*and why not? Is it because she doesn't know she's supposed to, or because I really am in disgrace?*—she fixed Monk's beautiful, temperamental sister with an earnest gaze.

"I'd tell you if I could, Bibbie, only Sir Alec refused to tell me. Not the particulars, anyway. According to him, all we need to know is that Gerald will be on assignment, I'm to provide him with a reason for being there and you're coming along to protect my reputation. Absolutely *no* janitoring from us, at all, under any possible circumstances *what*soever. Or else."

"What?" Bibbie sat up, fresh colour rushing to her peaches-and-cream cheeks. "D'you mean to say we're going as—as—*gels?*"

She nodded, gloomily. "I'm afraid so."

"*Oh!* That *manky* Sir Alec!" Incensed, Bibbie zapped her bowl of paperclips with such a strong levitating hex that instead of floating, they melted.

"Do be careful, Bibbie!" Melissande protested. "Paperclips don't grow on trees. Melt any more and I'll have to dock your wages."

"Really?" Bibbie folded her arms. "D'you know, Mel, you've never been the same since you did that stint in the Wycliffe Airship Company office." Her hot stare shifted. "Don't you think so, Reg? Don't you think she's just like that dreadful, miserly Petterly woman? I swear, next thing we know she'll be pilfering the bloody biscuits!"

"Petterly woman?" said Reg. "Sorry. Never heard of her."

And lo, the second ghastly silence of the day.

Clearly mortified by the mistake, her sapphire-blue eyes wide with dismay, Bibbie reached a hand towards Reg, then let it fall. As though she hadn't seen the gesture, Reg ruffled her feathers then sleeked them to her too-slender body.

"Think I fancy a lazy turn or two about the city. I'll see you young hoydens at supper. Mind my mince is fresh, or we'll be having words."

And with a soft flapping of wings, she hopped around on the windowsill, launched herself into the mid-morning air and swiftly vanished.

"Blimey," said Bibbie at last. "How *awful*. Mel, you have

to believe me, it was an accident. I just didn't think, I keep forgetting she's not—that she wasn't here for the Wycliffe case or—really, they look practically the *same*, and—"

"It's all right, Bibs," Melissande said gently. "We're still getting used to her. Reg understands it's going to take time for things to settle down."

Bibbie shivered. "If they ever do."

"They will," she said, sounding far more confident than she felt. "Now, about this wedding business . . ."

"Yes?" Bibbie said, brightening a little. "What?"

"Even though Sir Alec clutched his cards so close to his chest I'm astonished he could breathe, I'm positive that trouble really is brewing. I think something's happened to his janitor in Splotze. And that can only mean there's a certain amount of—well—"

"Danger?" Bibbie's eyes sparkled. "Excellent. I'm so tired of Gerald and Monk having all the fun. It's about time you and I were allowed into the thick of things! *Gels*." She made a rude sound. "By Saint Snodgrass's elbow, I'll give them *gels*."

Helplessly, Melissande stared at her. At moments like this, Bibbie seemed like a child. But then, was it fair to expect she'd understand? She hadn't seen Lional and his dragon and what they'd done to New Ottosland. To Gerald. Evil had never left its filthy fingerprints on careless, mercurial Emmerabiblia Markham.

"Excuse me?" said Bibbie. "Melissande Cadwallader, don't you *dare* think at me in that tone of voice! I know *exactly* what I'm letting myself in for, thank you. Wasn't I in Permelia Wycliffe's firing line when she was brandishing the poisoned hairpins? Didn't I shadbolt myself on purpose to help Monk?" Her lips trembled. "And wasn't I standing mere inches away from that other Monk when he died?"

"Yes," Melissande admitted. "But this is different, Bibbie. We'll be in a foreign country, a long way from home and help. If someone really is trying to disrupt the Splotze-Borovnik wedding, well, chances are they're not wearing kid gloves."

Bibbie shrugged. "So? I don't always wear kid gloves myself, you know. Trust me, Melissande, if anyone tries to get clever with me, or with you, or with Gerald for that matter, I'll—"

"Yes, but Bibs, don't you see?" Bubbling with agitation, she shoved herself out of the client armchair and picked her way between the office's clutter of furniture. "That would be *precisely* what Sir Alec's trying to avoid."

The potted Weeping Fireblossom was looking parched. Needing a moment to think, she fetched the watering can from her room and splooshed the poor thing.

"We simply *can't* rush about Splotze drawing attention to ourselves, Bibbie," she added, setting the emptied watering can by the office door. "That might put Gerald in even worse danger than he'll already be in. Besides, I'm going to this wedding in my official Royal Highness capacity, remember? Which means whatever I and my staff do will reflect upon Rupert. I won't have him embarrassed or backed into an awkward corner or embroiled in some ghastly international incident because of you, is that clear?"

"Yes, Your Highness," said Bibbie, sickly sweet.

Glowering, Melissande returned to the client armchair and sat, trying not to notice the unoccupied ram skull on top of the filing cabinet. "You can joke all you like now, Bibbie, but once we're in Splotze you will have to call me Your Highness. You won't be able to speak in public until you're spoken to. And you'll have to wear very plain, very *un*Bibbie dresses. Trust me, you aren't going to enjoy being my lady's maid at all."

Bibbie waved an airy hand. "Nonsense. It's going to be a rollicking adventure. But I give you fair warning, Mel . . . I'll do my best not to embarrass you, but I won't stand idly by twiddling my thumbs if I see Gerald's in trouble. Besides, we both know that if I didn't save him you'd never speak to me again."

Unfortunately, that was true. Filled with foreboding, Melissande nibbled the edge of her thumb. Then a thought occurred. "Of course, Bibbie, if your parents object to the idea of you coming with us, and Sir Alec can't convince them to let you risk yourself on his say-so, then—"

"Stop sounding so hopeful," said Bibbie. "The Markham hasn't been born yet who'd think twice about throwing his or her offspring onto the sacred altar of duty."

"Oh." So Sir Alec had been right about that? Damn. She nibbled her thumb again. "Yes, but your mother is a Thackeray, and—"

"And when it comes to duty," Bibbie said, grinning, "the Thackerays think the Markhams are amateurs."

Really? No wonder Monk was so driven to be the best Research and Development thaumaturgist in government history.

But even so . . .

"I think perhaps you're underestimating the strength of parental feeling," she said. "After all, Bibbie, you are their only daughter."

"What's that got to do with the price of eggs?"

"Well, it's a bit late now for them to think of hatching a replacement, isn't it?" she pointed out. "You know. If anything happened to you."

Bibbie's grin faded. "Oh yes, I see what you mean."

"So maybe you shouldn't set your heart on coming with us, just in case your mother and father—what?"

Staring into mid air, Bibbie was holding up one intimidating finger. "Melissande," she said, dreamily thoughtful. She wound a curl of blonde hair around the finger. "Your brother. Rupert. By any chance is he still about?"

A little pang. "No. He had to portal home again before anyone realised he'd popped out."

Bibbie pouted. "That's a pity. I suppose, since you're going to Splotze on his behalf—well, his and Sir Alec's—he'll be greeting you—us—upon our return? Congratulations on a job well done, and so on, and so forth?"

"I don't know," she said, trying to blink away the memory of Rupert's worried, washy blue eyes as Sir Alec hustled him out of the office before they'd had the chance to talk properly, in private. "Probably. Why?"

Instead of answering, Bibbie yanked open her desk's middle drawer and pulled out her small but exquisitely calibrated, very expensive personal crystal ball. Fingers dancing over its surface, she hummed a vibration address under her breath, then waited. A moment later, from her vantage point in the armchair, Melissande saw the back of someone's head swim into focus out of the crystal ball's clouded depths.

"Oh," said Bibbie, staring at the someone's face. "It's you, Aylesbury. I don't want you. I want Mother. What are you still doing there, anyway? I thought you were meant to be in Aframbigi on business."

"*I've been delayed,*" said the deep, not unattractive voice of Monk's older brother. "*I'm going tomorrow, or the next day. Not that it's any business of yours. Why do you want Mama?*"

Although Bibbie smiled, her eyes remained scornful. "I've something to tell her. Not that it's any business of yours. Now do stop being difficult and fetch her, would you?"

The back of Aylesbury's head vanished, to be replaced a moment later by the back of a head covered in tight blonde curls. Sofilia Markham. Melissande felt herself shrink a little. She'd met Monk and Bibbie's mother a number of times since she'd taken up residence in Ott, at this social event and that one. Their encounters had been perfectly polite. But even though Sofilia Markham knew that her younger son was paying attention to the king of New Ottosland's only sister, there'd been no invitation issued to a dinner at the Markham mansion. No, not even to a piddling afternoon tea.

And even more telling, as far as she knew Monk had not once pushed for it.

Is it any wonder I lurch from one day to the next without any idea if he's serious or not? I mean, if he can't make up his mind, how am I supposed to make up mine?

A question it was best she didn't dwell on. At least not at the moment. But sooner or later, she'd have to.

Sofilia Markham was going on about some important university dinner she and her genius husband were due to host. Bibbie sat stiff and straight in her chair, mouth opening and closing as she tried to get a word in edgeways.

In the end she gave up and shouted. "Mother! Please! There's something I need to tell—I mean, ask you!"

Interrupted mid spate, Monk and Bibbie's mother caught her breath. "*What?*"

Bibbie smiled, winningly. "Well, Mother, the thing is, Melissande—my friend the princess, remember?—well, her brother King Rupert has asked her to do a favour for him, but she can't unless I do a favour for her. So I need you to say that I can. Do this favour for Melissande, I mean. Which, you know, is like me doing a favour for King Rupert."

The back of Sofilia Markham's head looked suddenly very interested. "*Really, Emmerabiblia? How terribly fortunate. Wonderful timing! What kind of favour?*"

"Well, she's had a change of heart, and now she is attending the Splotze-Borovnik wedding for her brother, King Rupert, and she wants me to go too. As a companion. You know, royal protocol and so forth. Because she's a princess. So can I go with her, Mother? Please?"

Melissande stared. How many times did Bibbie need to mention Rupert's name? Or his title? Or her own, for that matter? Did Bibbie think her mother's wits were wandering? And what did Sofilia Markham mean, this was terribly fortunate and wonderful timing? That was a very odd thing to—

Bibbie's fresh squeal of delight shattered the thought.

"Oh, Mother, thank you! I knew you'd think it was an excellent idea. And you'll smooth Father's feathers if they get ruffled, won't you? I mean, it's funny how things turn out, isn't it? Gosh. Only, y'know, I think this should be our little secret. Not a word to anyone but Father. Because you just *know* that nasty cat Honoria Diddlecombe and her crowd will turn grass green with envy when they hear, and then try and spoil things for me. And now I must dash, I've got so much to do. If I can't come to dinner before we leave, I promise I'll come as soon as we get back. Thank you, again. I'll see you soon, I hope. Goodbye!"

As Bibbie disconnected the crystal ball vibration, Melissande pushed out of the client armchair. "Bibbie—"

Holding up that imperative finger, Bibbie tugged the office telephone towards her—in the interests of fair play, this month it took pride of place on her desk—and dialled.

"Yes, hello, this is Emmerabiblia Markham. I wish to speak to Sir Alec."

With a roll of her eyes, Bibbie listened to the voice on the other end of the telephone.

"No—no—now, look, I'm sorry, I think you mustn't be paying attention," she said, interrupting. "This is *Emmerabiblia Markham*. Now stop being tiresome and fetch Sir Alec to the telephone, or transfer this call, or whatever it is that you do out there at Nettleworth."

"Really, Bibbie," Melissande murmured, not sure whether to be appalled or impressed. "Have you never heard the one about catching more flies with honey than vinegar?"

Bibbie huffed, impatient. "Yes, well, if I was there I'd just bat my eyelashes at him, wouldn't I? But I'm not, so I have to be firm. If you knew—oh! Sir Alec! This is—oh. Good. Well, then, I'm just calling to let you know that my parents are perfectly fine with me going to Splotze with Gerald and Melissande, *and* they've said they'll keep it secret, so there's no need for you to speak to them, or send Uncle Ralph to do it, if that's what you were thinking. In fact, it would be a good idea if you didn't mention this to Uncle Ralph at all. Not until I've gone, anyway.—Why?" Bibbie rolled her eyes again. "Fancy you having to ask me that, seeing as he's your friend.—Well, because Uncle Ralph is tediously old-fashioned about some things and—" More eye-rolling. A sigh. "Yes, Sir Alec. *Yes*, Sir Alec. Yes, I *promise*, Sir Alec.—Didn't I just say I would? *Yes*. Goodbye."

"What did you promise?" said Melissande, as Bibbie slapped the telephone receiver back in its cradle.

Bibbie groaned. "What d'you think? That I'd remember I'm not a janitor, that I'm going as a lady's maid and nothing more, and that I won't go looking for trouble or distract Gerald or give him away. *Honestly*." She returned her crystal ball to its place and pushed the drawer sharply shut. "You'd think Sir Alec thinks I'm a *nincompoop*."

"I wouldn't say that," Melissande said, cautious. "A bit over-enthusiastic sometimes, perhaps."

"Ha," said Bibbie, scowling. "I'll give *him* overenthusiastic."

Then her expression lightened. "But never mind boring, stuffy Sir Alec. What matters is that Mother's agreed I can go, and she'll make sure Father doesn't get all twitty and mulish and difficult about it."

"Yes," she said, and folded her arms. "Let's talk about that, Bibbie. Not that I'm not pleased you're coming, but you did rather belabour the point about doing King Rupert a favour."

"Did I?" said Bibbie, the picture of innocence.

Melissande gave her a look. "You know bloody well you did. What's going on?"

"Nothing."

"No, it's something," she retorted. "Bibbie, by any chance is there a ridiculous notion floating about the Markham mansion that perhaps you and my brother might possibly—I mean to say, that you and he could—"

She couldn't finish the preposterous sentence.

Bibbie heaved her deepest sigh yet. "Well . . . yes."

"*Emmerabiblia Markham!*"

"Now, now, Mel, there's no need to panic," Bibbie protested. "*I'm* not the one dreaming of tiaras. It's a silly idea Mother's got into her head, that's all. I mean, as you say, the notion's ridiculous, isn't it? Me marrying your brother and you—"

Surely three ghastly silences in one morning was setting some kind of record.

"Look," said Bibbie, very sober now. "Mel. If it'll help, I'll have a word with Monk. I'll do more than have a word. I'll hex him to the eyebrows until he—"

"*No!*" she said, and banged her fist against the filing cabinet. "Emmerabiblia Markham, you'll keep your nose out of whatever it is that's between me and Monk. I know you mean well, and I appreciate it, truly, but you really must mind your own business."

"All right," said Bibbie, after a moment. "Only whatever you're going to do about it, I wish you'd hurry up. The fun is fast going out of watching you two treading all over each other's toes in this dance."

"Really?" Melissande said crossly. "Then I suggest you close your eyes, and tell me where you've got to with Doctor Jellicoe's bunion plasters."

Chilled, Gerald watched the desperate message from Abel Bestwick for a third time. He could feel Sir Alec's tightly controlled impatience like a blast of hot air from a furnace. And of course, his enigmatic superior was right. Even if he watched the recording a hundred more times he'd glean no further information from it. The blood wouldn't suddenly become any less red and Abel Bestwick's pain and fear wouldn't magically diminish.

"The wedding tour leaves Grande Splotze in three days," said Sir Alec, very cool, as though the sight of his janitor bleeding like a stuck pig was neither here nor there. And who knew? Perhaps it wasn't, to him. He'd been in the business a long time. "And it will wend its way around the capital's home districts before returning to the capital to celebrate the nuptials. King Rupert has agreed to suffer an incapacitating stomach complaint, thus opening the door for Miss Cadwallader to represent New Ottosland at the festivities."

Impressive. Sir Alec's reach had no limit, apparently. "And I'll be going with her?"

"As Her Royal Highness's personal secretary," said Sir Alec, his chilly grey eyes ever so faintly amused. "And general dogsbody." The amusement faded. "Miss Cadwallader will also be accompanied by Miss Markham, who will act as her lady's maid."

Gerald blinked. *Blimey. When Monk hears about this he's going to go spare.* He could easily go a bit spare himself. Bibbie, playing at janitor? His Bibbie? Well, all right, so she wasn't precisely his. Most likely would never actually be his. But he cared about her. More than cared about her, if he could bear to let himself admit the truth.

His heart sat in his chest like a lump of ice. "Ah . . . sir . . . is that wise?"

"Wise?" Lips tightening, Sir Alec snapped his fingers over the small crystal ball, relegating Abel Bestwick's fear and pain to memory. "Of course it's not wise, Mister Dunwoody. It's the most reckless thing I've done all year. And given what I've done recently . . ."

Shackled together by secrets, they stared at each other across the severely neat desk.

"I understand why you'd want to handle it this way, sir," Gerald said at last, still unhappy. "What with Melissande's convenient connections. It's not like we have a lot of time up our sleeve. And doing it this way keeps things all in the family, so to speak. Less complicated. Fewer explanations and cover ups if I have to . . . get clever."

Sir Alec gave him a look. "Indeed."

But he still didn't like it. "I don't suppose . . ." He shifted in his chair. "Look, is there any chance Bestwick's . . . I don't know. Misread the situation?"

"And then what?" Sir Alec said tartly. "In a fit of embarrassed remorse stabbed himself to make his story more plausible?"

No, probably not. "Sir, you must admit his claim is nebulous. Has there been any independent confirmation of trouble?"

"None," said Sir Alec. "I've had Mister Dalby running down every last source he can think of, but so far no new information has come to light. As best as we can ascertain, both Splotze and Borovnik are in transports of delight at the prospect of this wedding."

He thought about that. "Maybe," he said eventually. "But Splotze and Borovnik have neighbours. Graff, for example. Not a month goes by that they aren't kicking up some kind of dust with Borovnik. Up till now, Splotze has never bothered itself over those problems. The wedding might change that. New family loyalties, and so forth. Borovnik might assume that from now on Splotze will weigh in on their side of any future disputes. Graff won't like that. And then there's Blonkken, and its special relationship with Splotze. Whenever Splotze gets control of the Canal, Blonkken's shipping tariffs go down. What if Borovnik sweet-talks Splotze into keeping the tariffs high? That's hardly going to put a smile on Blonkken's face. And while they might all be signatories to the UMN accords, that's not to say they can't, or won't, get creative with their thaumaturgics if tempers really start to fray. Or worse, go all sly and secretive with them. Midnight assassinations, that kind of thing. And what about *us?* Ottosland can't afford—"

Halting him with a raised hand, Sir Alec favoured him with a look that might almost be called approving. "At least you're familiar with the current geopolitical landscape. That will save a certain amount of time. Now, touching upon the details of this assignment. There's nothing you can tell Miss Cadwallader about the protocols and particulars of travelling as a royal. I expect you to be guided by her in that regard. Obviously you'll conduct yourself with all due restraint. Under no circumstances can you betray the fact that you are acquainted with Miss Cadwallader and Miss Markham in any personal sense."

"No, sir, of course not." And then a thought occurred. "Sir, it's highly unlikely anyone in the wedding party will know me. They probably won't even look at me. That sort never notice dogsbodies. But Bibbie? Miss Markham, I mean? Leaving aside her—ah—" He cleared his throat. "Well, to be blunt, sir, her beauty . . . with the number of international personages who've been entertained at the Markham mansion over the years—"

"Miss Markham will need to be suitably obfuscated," said Sir Alec, betraying irritation. "Although not by Mister Scrimplesham. The fewer people who know of this, the better. I'm sure that you and Miss Markham can arrange matters so that even her parents wouldn't recognise her."

Yes, that should work provided Bibbie went along with it. And he rather thought she would. Remarkably, there wasn't a vain bone in her body. And he had the sinking feeling she'd do a lot worse than give herself a few warts if it meant the chance of playing at janitors.

Oh, lord. This is such a bad idea.

"Ah—speaking of her parents, sir. They're content that you're involving her in this?"

The question came out far more accusing than he'd intended. But really, what Sir Alec proposed was madness.

For all her precocious brilliance, Bibbie was an innocent. She hadn't been forged in the kinds of fires he'd faced, and Monk had faced, and Melissande too. The thought of Bibbie being scorched by such flames hurt him.

An odd look crept into Sir Alec's eyes. "Miss Markham has already obtained her parents' permission for the trip to Splotze. And I have no doubt she'll play her part satisfactorily."

He might not, but I do. He's never seen Bibbie when she gets carried away.

"Does that mean they know Bibbie's mixing herself up in Department business?"

Sir Alec's lips thinned. "What Miss Markham's parents are aware of is not your concern."

In other words, probably not. And probably they weren't going to find out, either, because Sir Alec would do or say whatever he had to in order to ensure that Bibbie played her useful part in the quest to find Abel Bestwick and unmask the villains wanting to destroy the marital union between Splotze and Borovnik.

He really is the most appallingly ruthless bastard.

"Mister Dunwoody," said Sir Alec, very sharply. "Were you in Abel Bestwick's shoes right now, hurt, possibly hunted, would you not wish me to do everything in my power to see you brought safely home, and the assignment for which you spilled precious blood followed through to a successful conclusion?"

Yes. He would.

So does that make me an appallingly ruthless bastard, too?

Discomfited, Gerald cleared his throat. "Then you think Bestwick's still alive, sir?"

Sir Alec slid out from behind his desk and crossed to the window. The drab, inconsequential little suburb of Nettleworth spread its bleak streets beyond the dirty glass. It was barely past midday, but the sun looked tired already.

"Until I am provided with evidence to the contrary, Mister Dunwoody, I always assume that my agents are still alive."

He was touched by unexpected shame. "Of course."

"Tell me," said Sir Alec, with his back almost turned. "How are you, after Mister Jennings's procedure?"

Coming out of the blue, the question surprised him. Immediately wary, he resisted the urge to fold his arms.

"It didn't kill me."

Sir Alec flicked him a look. "Obviously. Mister Dunwoody—"

"Well, what d'you want me to say, sir? I mean, you're sending me on this assignment. You must think I'm fit for duty. Surely that's all that matters."

Gerald waited for a reprimand. Taking that kind of tone with Sir Alec was more dangerous than juggling sharp knives with his one good eye closed. But instead of snapping out a reprimand, Sir Alec breathed a soft sigh.

"I gave Mister Jennings instructions not to discuss with you the results of the hex extraction."

He frowned. "I know. He said."

"Mister Dunwoody, you astound me," Sir Alec said, turning. "Will you sit there and tell me you don't have any questions about what was done to you?"

"No, sir. But since I don't expect you'll give me honest, straightforward answers, what's the point in asking them?"

"You won't know if I'll answer you honestly and straight-forwardly if you don't ask, Mister Dunwoody."

"Fine," he said, no longer caring about his tone, or sharp knives. "All right. The procedure failed. Mister Jennings didn't manage to extract all the grimoire hexes. But is that because he couldn't? Or because you wouldn't let him?"

CHAPTER SIX

"Bloody hell, Gerald!" Monk breathed, awestruck. "You actually said that? And what did Sir Alec say?"

Up to his elbows in sudsy dishwater, Gerald took a moment to scrub the bottom of a pot. For all her besetting sins as a cook, at least Bibbie was keen. And for once her sausages, mashed potatoes and onion gravy had been edible. Only it did mean spending rather a long time in the kitchen afterwards, cleaning up.

"Gerald!" Monk prompted, snapping his tea towel in a vaguely threatening manner. "What did the cagey bugger say?"

He put the scrubbed pot on the sink's drainer, then glanced at the ceiling. "I wonder how much longer the girls are going to be? I mean, I know your sister's a raving beauty but it shouldn't be taking her this long to brew up the right obfuscation hex. I never should've let Melissande shut the door in my face. Or throw smelly socks at you until you ran away. I tell you, those two are up to something."

"And in other startling news," Monk growled, "water is wet. Gerald, what is going on? Why won't you answer a simple question?"

Why? Because the question wasn't simple, and neither is the answer.

I was mad to start this conversation.

"Sir Alec didn't say anything," he said, scrabbling around the bottom of the sink to make sure he'd not missed a teaspoon. "Mister Dalby burst in, all hot and bothered about some hiccup in Fandawandi, which meant I became superfluous to requirements. So I toddled home to read up on the history of Splotze and Borovnik, and practice bowing like a minion."

Monk lifted the drained pot and started towelling it dry. "Oh."

He'd left no teaspoons behind. Playing for time, trying to avoid possible unpleasantness, he emptied the sink of sudsy water, then started wiping down the table.

With nothing else to dry, Monk put the pot in its cupboard then hung the damp tea towel on its hook. Glancing at him, Gerald saw that his friend's usually open-as-a-book face was firmly closed. Damn.

"Look . . . Monk. I really am sorry I didn't tell you I was going through with the extraction procedure. Only—"

"I know," said Monk. "You said. Let's not beat the dead horse, Gerald."

"No, let me finish," he insisted. "You were right. Jennings's procedure is bloody risky. I was afraid that if you had another go at talking me out of it, well . . . I might listen."

"Oh." Monk hooked his ankle around the nearest kitchen chair, pulled it away from the table and sat down, back to front. Then he rested his chin on his folded arms. "D'you wish I had, now? Talked you out of it?"

Remembering the startled fear in Errol's face, the treacherous pleasure of it, the whispering seduction of power in his blood, Gerald began wiping down the nearest bench. "No."

Silence, while he pretended to care about spotless benches and his friend brooded. At last, Monk sat up.

"So what d'you think? Did Sir Alec hobble Jennings?"

Gerald shrugged. "I don't know. And I don't suppose it matters, does it? What matters is that Mister Jennings didn't manage to extract all the hexes, which means I have to find a way to live with what's left until you find a way to get rid of it."

"And I will, mate," Monk said darkly. "My word as a Markham. Only first I have to clear my desk of a few things I can't afford to shove onto a back burner." He dragged the fingers of one hand through his unruly hair. "Is that all right?"

It'd have to be, wouldn't it? "Sure."

"Good," said Monk, not quite hiding his guilty relief. "Ah—don't suppose you can tell which hexes got left behind, can you?"

Finished wiping benches, Gerald fussed over rinsing the cloth. It was hard to meet Monk's eyes, talking about this. He wasn't to blame for trying to kill his friend, he knew that, but even so . . .

"It's tricky," he said at last, "I can tell which hexes Jennings managed to extract. Like—the power to control a First Grade wizard? That one's definitely been knocked on the head."

Monk hooted, not very amused. "Yeah, I'll bet. Catch the Department letting you hang onto that one. What else?"

"There were a lot of shadbolt hexes. They haven't gone, exactly, but they're kind of . . . smudged. I can't read them any more."

"Shadbolts." Monk shuddered. "You're well rid of that muck, mate. Trust me."

Yes, he certainly was. "I've lost the compulsion hexes, too. Before my encounter with Mister Jennings, if the fancy had struck me I could've made you cut out your own tongue with a pair of rusty garden shears." His turn to shudder. "Or Melissande's. Bibbie's. Anyone's."

Monk was staring, wide-eyed. "Bloody hell!"

Finished rinsing, Gerald turned to the kitchen hob. Should he mention bumping into Errol? Confide in his friend how the urge to smash the arrogant bastard had risen in him like a scarlet tide and threatened to sweep away both conscience and humanity?

No. No, I don't think so. Things are complicated enough as it is.

Monk grimaced. "So you've no idea what got left behind?"

"Not no idea," he said, still wiping. "Those hexes the other me used to punish witches and wizards who crossed him?" He tapped his temple. "They're still stuck in here, like burrs. Mister Jennings couldn't budge them for love or money. And I think—" He swallowed. "I think it might be easier to kill, now."

"Oh," said Monk.

They stared at each other, both remembering the other Ottosland and the killing hex that neither of them could escape, even though it had failed. Monk was the first to look away.

Damn. "And there's other stuff," Gerald said quietly. "Only I can't put my finger on it. It's a feeling, more than anything. I know more than I did. I just don't know what I know. Y'know?"

"But you're still *you*, mate," said Monk. He almost sounded uncertain. "Right? You're still our world's Gerald Dunwoody."

And this was why he'd not wanted to talk about it. How could he possibly explain to Monk what it felt like to have his *potentia* so horribly tampered with? To no longer be sure that he was himself, that he could trust himself, from one breath to the next, when sleeping deep inside, too lightly sleeping, was the urge to obliterate whatever irritated him?

Monk's such a decent bloke, he'd never understand.

"I mean, Sir Alec's not a fool," said Monk, sounding close to anxious. "If you weren't all right he'd never let you out of his sight. He wouldn't be sending you to Splotze if you weren't all right. And *you* wouldn't risk the girls, mate, would you? You'd stay home if you weren't all right. Right?"

And that was a far trickier question. The bald fact was, he had a great deal to prove. To Sir Alec. Sir Ralph. The Department. Most of all to himself. And he needed to prove it, soon, before doubt crippled faith.

"Look, Monk," he said, tossing the kitchen cloth into the sink. "I'm not going to lie to you. I do feel different. It's as though there's more of me inside my skin. And I feel *darker*, too. Like there's a shadow in between me and the world. It's not as thick as it was, but . . . it's still there."

"I see," said Monk, after a moment. He looked sick.

"But I promise you, I *swear*, I'll *never* endanger the girls," he added swiftly. "If I thought for a moment I couldn't be trusted to keep them safe I wouldn't let Sir Alec mix them up in this wedding business."

"So . . ." Monk dragged a hand down his face. "There is

something going on over there. This isn't just Sir Alec with the wind up."

Gerald hid a wince. Careful, now. Careful. He mustn't mention Abel Bestwick's graphic message. If Monk got a bee in his bonnet he was perfectly capable of futzing the entire mission. As expected, he'd already gone spare over the notion of Bibbie playing janitor. It wouldn't take much of a nudge to send him over the edge again.

"All I can tell you is that our man in Splotze has landed himself in hot water. But we don't know how hot, and we don't know who's boiling the kettle. It could all turn out to be a big misunderstanding. That's why I'm going, to figure the lay of the land. But trust me, Monk, I won't let the girls get within sniffing distance of trouble."

"Oh, yeah?" Monk snorted. "Think you can hobble those two if they get the bit between their teeth, do you?"

He was saved from answering by Melissande's return. "Are you two still in here?" she said, hands on hips in the kitchen doorway. "Honestly, how long does it take to wash a few dishes?"

"Where's Bibs?" said Monk, neatly side-stepping the domestic bear-trap. "Don't tell me you've made her hex herself so hideous she can't bear to show her face!"

"On the contrary," said Melissande loftily. "I've managed to kill two birds with one stone. Gentlemen, I give you Gladys Slack, lady's maid to Her Royal Highness Princess Melissande of New Ottosland."

She moved out of the way, and into the kitchen walked a modestly downward-looking young lady with glossy dark brown hair pulled into a bun and melting brown eyes framed by thick horn-rimmed spectacles, whose plain black skirt and prim cream blouse and sensibly low-heeled button shoes and knitted stockings did nothing to disguise the tempting figure beneath.

"Well, *that's* no good," said Gerald, feeling his heart crash and bang against his ribs. "Where's the hooked nose? The beady eyes? Where are the warts with hairs in them? Blimey, Melissande. She might not look like Bibbie but she's still beautiful!"

"Exactly," said Melissande, as Bibbie stood like a mouse with her hands demurely clasped before her and her gaze still downcast. "She doesn't look like Emmerabiblia Markham, which means if there's anyone in the wedding party who's ever dined at the Markham mansion they won't think twice when they see her. But she's still guaranteed to attract Crown Prince Hartwig's wandering hands, which means they won't be wandering over *me* this time, so I can avoid creating an international incident, which I'm sure Sir Alec will appreciate."

Gerald swallowed. What about him creating an international incident? He didn't want Crown Prince Hartwig's philandering hands all over Bibbie! Except he couldn't say that, could he? He didn't have the right.

"And Bibbie? You seem very comfortable speaking for her about this, Mel," he snapped. "What's her opinion?"

"She doesn't have one," said Melissande, lofty again. "She's a maid. But if she did, it would be identical to mine. Yours would be, too."

His jaw dropped. "I beg your pardon?"

"Begging's good. Very miniony. Keep it up," Melissande said, encouraging. Then she sighed. "Honestly, Gerald. Don't be so thick. Minions ministering to royalty possess no thoughts that haven't been inspected and approved first. You do *remember* Lional, don't you?"

Of course he did. But he'd hoped Melissande had forgotten him. Instead here she was doing the most *appalling* impersonation of her imperious dead brother. Ignoring her, he turned to Bibbie.

"Look, Bibs—"

"I'm sorry, sir," said Bibbie, in a mousey little voice. "I'm afraid I don't know who you mean. My name is Gladys, and I'm sure I shouldn't be speaking to any young man without Her Highness's permission."

There wasn't even the hint of a mischievous twinkle in Bibbie's changed eyes. Giving up, Gerald rounded on Monk.

"So you're just going to sit there, are you, like a drunk flea on a dog? You've nothing to say about Melissande tossing your sister into the clutches of this grabby Crown Prince Hartwig?"

Monk grinned. "No. If Hartwig's stupid enough to put his hands where they don't belong, Bibs'll take care of him. She's had a lot of practice."

"Wonderful," he groaned, reluctantly accepting defeat. "Where's Reg? I know she'll be on my side."

Melissande and Bibbie—Gladys—whoever the devil she was being—exchanged cautious looks.

"Reg?" said Melissande. "She's—ah—taking a post-prandial flap about the neighbourhood."

Oh, no. "You had a fight?"

"Of course not," Melissande said quickly. "Just . . . a difference of opinion. Don't worry. She'll be back soon."

Uncomfortable, they stared at each other.

"It is going to work out, isn't it?" said Bibbie, alarmingly uncertain. "With Reg, I mean. The day will come when we don't look at her and think *You're the wrong one*. Won't it?"

Nobody answered her.

Soon afterwards, Bibbie unhexed herself then went back upstairs to change out of her Gladys Slack attire. Melissande and Monk withdrew to the parlour for a bit of privacy, and possibly to argue some more about Bibbie, and Gerald shut himself in the library with paper, pen and ink and his mission briefing notes so he could order his thoughts. He read them twice, once quickly, once slowly, and then, ideas and random observations simmering, started scribbling.

Two scrawled pages later, a gentle rustling of feathers turned his attention to the open window.

"And that's you, is it?" Reg enquired politely, from the sill. "Thinking *You're the wrong one* every time you look at me? Sorry now you didn't leave me behind to die too, are you?"

So she'd heard that? Damn. A sharp pain was brewing in his temples. Sighing, Gerald let his head fall against the back of the chair.

"Don't be daft, Reg. Of course I'm not sorry."

A feathery whoosh and flap as she glided from the

windowsill to the arm of the chair opposite. "And don't you try to kid a kidder."

He cracked open his good eye. "I'm not."

"No?" Her dark eyes were gleaming in the lamplight. "And I s'pose you're not peeing-your-underdrawers terrified that you're going to wake up one morning and find you've turned into *him*, either."

"Not peeing-my-underdrawers, no," he said, after a brief hesitation. "But I'll admit to an occasional looseness in my bowels."

"Ha!" Her tail rattled. "And so they should be loose, sunshine. He was a nasty piece of work and no mistake, your opposite number."

"Which means *I'm* a nasty piece of work, surely," he countered. "Doesn't it?"

"That's up to you," Reg said, shrugging. "Every man's captain of his own ship, Gerald Dunwoody. You made the right choice the first time. All you have to do is make it again."

"And again, and again, and again," he murmured. "Every hour of every day, for the rest of my life. And how much harder is that going to be, with his magic inside me like he's perched on my shoulder?"

"But it's not all inside you, is it? Not any more."

"Trust me, Reg. Enough of it is. And if Monk can't pull a rabbit out of his trousers, it always will be. D'you know, I nearly flattened bloody Errol Haythwaite?"

Reg chuckled. "Bloody Errol Haythwaite could do with a bit of flattening."

"It's not funny!"

"Gerald, Gerald," she sighed. "Lose your sense of humour, my boy, and you really will be in a pickle."

And that was when she sounded like his Reg. He felt the memory jolt through him, bright flames in the sunlight as she crumbled to ash. Smothered a groan. A familiar, feathered weight came to rest on his shoulder and a long beak rubbed gently against his cheek.

"I know it's hard," she whispered. "I know you miss her. It's easier for me. I got my Gerald back. That other manky bastard, he's just a bad memory. But I know it's not the same for you, Gerald. I won, and you lost, and how that's going to end up I honestly can't say."

"No," he croaked. "Me, neither."

"I'll go, if you want me to," the other Reg said, with only the slightest tremor in her voice. "I managed before I met you and I'll manage if I leave. No need for you to worry about that. If having me around makes it harder for you to do your job, then I should go. Just say the word, Gerald, and you'll not lay an eye on me again."

"*No!*" he said, sitting up. "Reg, are you mad? Of course I don't want you to go. *No-one* wants you to go. Things might be a bit difficult at the moment, but they won't always be. And I absolutely want you to stay. We all do."

Instead of replying, Reg hopped from his shoulder to the library's writing desk and cast her eye over his various scribblings.

"Not bad, not bad," she said, when she'd finished reading. "In another ten years or so you might make a halfway decent secret government agent. Only you're mad if you only take one crystal ball with you. You'll need at least three. More if you can manage it. Because if your luggage doesn't get left behind, dropped over the side of a riverboat, down a mountain or into a bog, or end up confused with someone else's so it's shipped to Jandria by slow hot air balloon, then I'm not the dispossessed Queen of Lalapinda." She looked at him over her wing. "And no matter where I happen to be, I am."

"Yes, Your Majesty," he said, grinning despite the evening's heartache. "At least three crystal balls. I'll make a note."

She sniffed. "Yes. Well. See that you do. Because if you've only got one and you lose it at a delicate moment, meaning you've got to nick someone else's in order to save the day, all you need is some other snooty guest's busybody minion poking his nose where it's not wanted and you'll be answering awkward questions and drawing attention to yourself. And *that* won't please your Sir Alec, will it?"

"No," he said. "Reg . . ."

With a rustling of feathers she hopped around to face him. "Gerald?"

Heart thumping, he stared at her. This was as good a time as ever to say it. And he had to say it. *Had* to.

"Reg, if ever you see me turning into him, you must speak up. And if I won't listen, if I try to brush you aside, you must go to Sir Alec. He'll know what to do and he'll do it, no hesitation. He's very good at his job."

Reg chattered her beak. "Now, Gerald—"

"No, Reg. I mean it," he said, leaning forward. "You promise me. Right now. I need this. I need to know I can trust you. Just in case the day comes when I can't trust myself." He swallowed. "And it might come. We both know that. So please, don't insult me by telling me I'm talking nonsense."

"Oh, Gerald," said Reg, and gave her tail feathers an aggravated rattle. Then she sighed. "*Fine*, you wretched boy. Yes. I promise."

Was it his imagination, or did the shrouding shadow lighten then, just a little? He touched his fingertip to her wing.

"Dammit, Reg. I wish you were coming to Splotze. But since you're not, do me a favour, would you? Keep an eye on Monk? Because he adores Bibbie, and Mel, and he's going to worry himself sick over them. Besides, you know what he's like. He can no more stop himself from inventing things than Melissande can help giving everyone orders."

"Ha!" said Reg, eyes gleaming again. "And won't madam be in her element, with *two* of you to boss around from sun up to sun down and half way into the night!"

Half laughing, half groaning, Gerald sprawled backwards in his chair. "Saint Snodgrass's teeth, Reg. Don't bloody remind me!"

Standing with Frank Dalby in Nettleworth's dingy Ops room, staring at the enormous relief map of the Central Northern Continent where Fandawandi spread like a threadbare carpet across nearly half of the humpy landmass, Sir Alec pinched the bridge of his nose, hard.

"I must be going blind," he muttered, glaring at the glowing, unbroken line that traced the thaumaturgically protected edges of Fandawandi's territory. "Or senile. For the life of me I cannot fathom how these bandits are getting the *dirit* weed past Fandawandi's checkpoints and across the border into Dibaloo."

"Neither can I," said Frank, his expression dour. "And since we don't have an agent in Dibaloo, or any kind of political influence there, that means it's only a matter of time before the bloody stuff's smuggled from there onto boats crossing the Damooj Strait, then starts showing up on the back streets of Ott and every-bloody-where else you'll find young fools cursed with more money than sense."

"Yes, while the Fandawandi authorities mop and mow and wring their lily-white hands," Sir Alec said. He thumped his fist to the edge of the relief map. "Why the devil they've not taken steps to eradicate *dirit* is beyond my comprehension!"

"You know bloody well why," Frank said roughly. "Because when they're not busy wringing their hands, those same Fandawandi authorities are putting them out for bribes to turn a blind eye. What do they care if a muck-load of Ottish youngbloods fry their brains smoking poisonous herbery?"

"Well, I'm going to damned well make them care. Mister Dalby—"

The Ops room's door burst open. "Sir Alec. A moment of your time, if you'd be so obliging."

Frank's scowl deepened. Sir Alec frowned him into blandness, then turned. "Sir Ralph," he said, with every appearance of cordiality. "Good morning. Did we have an appointment?"

Ralph's colour was high, a sure sign of danger. "We have one now. Your office, if you please."

If it had been anyone other than Ralph, and if the witness to such blatant bad manners had been anyone other than Frank Dalby, there would have been hell and more to pay.

Fortunately for Ralph, that was not the case.

"Right, Mister Dalby," he said, his tone as cool and conversational as ever. "We'll continue this discussion later."

Frank nodded. "Yes, sir."

"After you, Sir Ralph," he said, extending his hand. "I'm sure you remember the way to my office."

Ralph remembered. The door hadn't even closed behind them before he spun about, fists clenched and chest heaving.

"What the devil, Alec! What the damned bloody *devil!* You're involving my niece in your janitor shenanigans? Where the hell do you find the nerve, involving *my niece?* Without so much as a *word* to me first? I think I deserve a damned sight better than *that!*"

Sir Alec hesitated, then chose to stand by his office's cold fireplace. "How did you find out?"

"What does that signify?" Ralph demanded, his eyes bloodshot with outrage. "The point is, I *did*. And now you'll kindly put a stop to it."

"It signifies," he said, priding himself on the fact that not even Ralph would know how tightly he was controlling his temper, "because the Splotze-Borovnik mission is already on shaky ground, and if—"

"It was my bloody nephew, all right?" said Ralph, close to spitting. "Monk told me. He's supposed to be working on a new thingamajig for Bailey's crew but instead I found him farting about with an obfuscation hex! Naturally I asked him what the hell he thought he was doing, wasting his time with frippery when he knows he's on a deadline, and he spilled the beans."

Swallowing a sigh, Sir Alec rested an elbow on the fireplace's mantel. *I'd haul him and Dunwoody over the coals, if I thought there was any point*. "Of course he did."

"I'm serious about this, Alec," Ralph said, taking a thunderous step toward him. "I won't have you dragging little Emmerabiblia down your dirty, dangerous alleyways! It's bad enough Monk's caught in your orbit. You can't have his sister too."

"I'm afraid I must, Ralph," he said, gently. "This business in Splotze might be nothing, or it might be a powder keg getting ready to blow. Which means I don't have the luxury of playing favourites with who can and can't help me keep a lid on things before they go up. Like it or not, your niece is in the right place, at the right time, with the right friends, to be of use. So I am going to use her, Ralph. Because that's what I do."

Stricken silent, Ralph stared at him. Then, with a stifled curse, he collapsed into the visitor's chair, pulled a handkerchief from his vest pocket and pressed it to his sweaty forehead.

"I always knew you were a ruthless bastard, Alec, but you've surpassed yourself today."

He was a fool to let the words wound him, but Ralph had always been more friend than foe. Mask perfectly in place, Sir Alec moved from the fireplace to his desk and sat behind it.

"Your niece is a Markham through and through, Ralph. What's more, if she'd been born a boy we both know she'd likely be giving your reprobate nephew orders by now. But just because she's a girl is no reason to waste her . . . or underestimate her. Besides, she's not going to Splotze as a janitor."

"She's going as a lady's maid, I know," Ralph said gruffly. "But she's still going, isn't she? And so's Dunwoody. *Dunwoody?* Alec, how can you ask me to trust my only niece to his care? Dammit, man, he's tainted with grimoire magic. What if he runs amok?"

"If I thought that were a possibility then he'd be under lock and key," Sir Alec retorted. "Ralph, because I asked for his assistance, the King of New Ottosland is sending his sister to the damned wedding. Would I ask such a thing, would I risk a diplomatic disaster, if I thought Princess Melissande's life would be at risk?"

Ralph glowered. "Of course you bloody would. New Ottosland could drown in quicksand tomorrow and it'd be a year before anyone noticed it was gone."

"Ralph . . ." He shook his head. "Not a week passes when you and I don't ask someone's son or nephew to put country before self. How can we do that, how can we ask them to ask their families to bear that burden, if you and I are unwilling to bear it ourselves?"

"The devil with that, Alec!" said Ralph, his voice catching. "I'm the one with the burden, not you. You're an only child with no family. Emmerabiblia's my flesh and blood!"

"I know," he said. "And I'm sorry. But I can't let that count."

A long silence. Then Ralph tucked his handkerchief back into his vest, and stood. "No. You can't. And though it pains me to say it, neither can I. But if anything happens to her, Alec . . . if anything happens . . ."

Leaving the threat unfinished, he walked out.

CHAPTER SEVEN

To avoid even the remotest possibility of a raised suspicion, Sir Alec decreed that his agent and his agent's camouflage should enter Splotze by way of New Ottosland. That entailed a midnight portal trip from the bowels of Nettleworth to King Rupert's palace, where they would wait until it was a polite time to turn up on Crown Prince Hartwig's doorstep.

"There you are!" Rupert greeted them, grinning with unroyal enthusiasm as, leaving their luggage behind, they stepped out of the portal and into the opulent reception chamber that Lional had built. "All in one piece, I take it?"

Clutching her expensive beaded reticule, feeling smothered in her suitably royal pale pink silk ensemble, complete with whalebone corset and far too much of her late mother's jewellery, and with residual etheretic spots dancing before her eyes, Melissande shuffled to make room for Gerald and Bibbie.

"More like three pieces," she said. "Rupert, what are you doing here?"

"What does it look like, Melly? I'm your Official Portal Conductor for the evening. Sir Alec wants this kept hush hush, remember?"

She looked her brother up and down, noting the patched hole in the elbow of his cream shirt sleeve and the distressing bagginess about the knees of his faded moss-green velvet trousers. "So you thought you'd turn up in disguise? Honestly, Rupert, if Lord Billingsley could see you now, he'd faint. You look like a—a gardener!"

"Like Father, you mean?" Rupert said lightly. "If that's the case, Lord Billingsley should feel right at home. Except, you know, I'm very careful *not* to dress like a gardener when that old fogey's about. I suppose I could've greeted you in my dressing gown, but I thought that might not be quite the thing."

"Yes, well, you playing Portal Conductor isn't quite the thing, either," she said. "I mean, honestly, Rupes. Do you even know what you're doing?"

"Actually, you dreadful scold, I do. And as far as tonight's little jaunt is concerned, Sir Alec assures me his boffins say we'll have a clear window. But I double-checked their long-range etheretic readings, just to be sure." He chuckled. "Turns out I'm rather a dab hand at portal conducting. So if this whole being king business ends up not working out, at least I can be sure of some gainful employment! Hello, Gerald. Good to see you again."

Sighing, because clearly Rupes was in one of his butterfly moods, Melissande stepped aside so her brother and Gerald could clasp cordial hands. Feeling Bibbie staring at New Ottosland's casual king, all a-bubble with repressed excitement, she was very careful not to look at the wretched girl.

"Your Majesty," said Gerald, offering a slight bow. Wizard to king. Equal to equal. "It's been too long."

"Hasn't it, though?" Rupert agreed warmly. "But no doubt that Sir Alec of yours is keeping you on the hop. Doesn't strike me as a lazy layabout kind of chap."

Gerald almost smiled. "Ah . . . no. When it comes to Sir Alec, those aren't the first words that spring to mind."

"And how have you been? Mel doesn't tell me much. Well. Really, she doesn't tell me anything. Very good at keeping secrets, my sister. Though I do understand you've joined her at the agency?"

"That's right, sir," said Gerald. "When I'm not acting under orders from Sir Alec, I'm giving the girls a hand with their clients."

"Excellent," said Rupert, approving. "It's good to know they've a sound chap like you to lean on." With a pat on

Gerald's shoulder, he turned. "And speaking of the girls . . . Melissande, I don't believe your charming friend and I have been introduced."

Oh, lord. That wasn't a roguish twinkle in Rupert's washy blue eyes, was it? She could feel Gerald, beside her, retracting like a snail.

"Sorry," she said. "I forgot you two haven't actually met. Your Majesty, this is Emmerabiblia Markham. Bibbie, my brother, His Majesty King Rupert the First."

"But please, you must call me Rupert," said Rupert, taking Bibbie's outstretched hand in his. Smiling, he touched his lips to her knuckles. "Melly's told me so much about you, I do feel as though I know you quite well already."

Bibbie was dimpling. "It's a great pleasure to meet you at last, Rupert. Melly adores you so completely, and I'm sure that now I know why."

Melissande felt her stomach turn over. Oh, lord. Monk's incorrigible sister was *flirting* with him. So much for her protestations of disinterest in tiaras.

Bibbie, how could you?

And then, belatedly noticing the laden gold-and-silver tea trolley pushed against the wall, and the small table and chairs placed strategically nearby, she breathed a sigh of relief.

"Rupes, you thought of refreshments? How hospitable of you. I'm impressed. So now you can toddle back to bed and we can amuse ourselves quite happily until it's time to go. No need to worry about the portal, Gerald can operate that for us, can't you, Gerald?"

"Oh, yes, of course," said Gerald. "I'm—"

But Rupert was wagging a finger at her. "No, no, *no*, Melissande. I won't hear of it. We hardly had a chance to speak the other day, Sir Alec hustled me out of your office so fast. You can't deprive me of this chance to enjoy your company. The busy life you lead these days, Saint Snodgrass alone knows when we'll catch up again."

Bibbie batted her eyelashes. "Quite right, Rupert. Make hay while the moon shines, that's my motto."

"And a charming motto it is, too," said Rupert, terrifyingly gallant. "Shall we, Miss Markham? Or might I be so bold, given these extraordinary circumstances, as to call you Bibbie?"

Another devastatingly dimpled smile. "Rupert, I'll be cross beyond measure if you don't."

Breathless with horror, Melissande watched her brother escort Monk's appalling sister across the opulent portal chamber to the table, seat her, then trundle over the gold-and-silver tea tray.

She glanced sideways. "Gerald . . ."

"What?" he said, his voice tight with self-control.

They'd never properly discussed his feelings for Bibbie. What she knew of them, she knew mostly from watching him watch the girl he'd convinced himself he could never have. But while there might well be some solace in the notion that the sacrifice was noble, it could only be shattering to see the object of that sacrifice batting her eyelashes at another man. Worse, a *king*. Not that Rupert was looking particularly kingly, in his patched shirt and baggy trousers. And even when he was done up in his royal best, not even the kindest sister would mistake him for shockingly handsome Lional. But the absence of dashing good looks aside, Rupert *was* a king and Gerald . . . wasn't.

"Well, you two, don't just stand there," Rupert called, expansively genial. "Come and drink this tea while it's hot. And you must try the scones. Zazoor sent me three crates of best Kallarapi dates and the palace cook's been going mad trying to use them up."

So they sat at the table for nearly an hour, drinking tea and eating date scones and cream cakes and discussing the world at large. There was much rueful merriment from Rupert about the ongoing difficulties of modernising his tiny kingdom without entirely abandoning Tradition with a capital T. Bibbie overflowed with sympathy. She could completely understand, she said. Didn't she battle the forces of hidebound tradition every day at home? She was so deeply impressed that Rupert never dreamed of treating his sister like a *gel*.

Melissande pushed her empty plate away, decisively hinting. "No, indeed, as brothers go Rupert's very nearly a paragon.

And now, while this little interlude has been delightful, I'm afraid we really must be pushing along. By my reckoning it's past ten o'clock tomorrow morning in Grande Splotze, and we'll be expected."

"Oh," Bibbie groaned. "Really? Does that mean it's time to put on Gladys Slack?"

Rupert looked bewildered. "I'm sorry? Who is Gladys Slack?"

"Gladys Slack is my lady's maid," said Melissande. "And yes, Bibbie, it's time she made an appearance. Same goes for Algernon Rowbotham, Gerald."

"Ah," said Rupert. There was a smidgin of disapproval in his voice. "And Algernon Rowbotham's to be your secretary, I suppose?"

"He is," said Gerald, who'd hardly said a word since they sat down. "Thanks to some hex disguises we've worked out, we'll be unrecognisable."

Bibbie giggled. "We just have to cross our fingers that we don't break out in a rash. That can happen, you know, Rupert, with these kinds of thaumaturgics." Another giggle. "Once, my other brother Aylesbury lost a bet with Monk and he had to wear a hex for a whole month. Brought him out in green spots. The young lady he was seeing at the time laughed at him so hard he had to rusticate in the country for ages. I don't believe he's forgiven Monk to this day."

"Yes, well," said Gerald. "With all the tweaking I've done to our hexes, Bibbie, I doubt we have to worry about spots of any colour."

"Oh, I'm sure," said Bibbie, waving a careless hand. "Gerald's always fiddling with incants and things, Rupert. He's almost as bad as Monk when it comes to having no time for anything else."

Rupert shook his head. "Extraordinary, the things you witches and wizards can achieve these days. You know, Gerald, when this little matter of the wedding's taken care of, I really must have a chat with your Sir Alec. I'm sure there's a great deal to be done in New Ottosland, thaumaturgically speaking, and I can't imagine anyone better to give me the benefit of his experience."

Melissande tried to picture Sir Alec as a thaumaturgical consultant, and failed.

"Or," Rupert added, "perhaps, Bibbie, *you* might care to share some insights with me. I'm sure you'd offer a most unique perspective."

Oh, lord. "That's a very interesting suggestion, Rupert," Melissande said, standing. "Only we really don't have time to talk about it now. Gerald and Bibbie might be dressed for their parts, but I'm afraid their faces are all wrong."

"Of course," said Rupert, disappointed. "Duty before pleasure, always. Melissande, perhaps we could have a word while Bibbie and Gerald are assuming their disguises, yes?"

"What is it?" she said, as Rupert drew her aside. "Is everything all right?"

The rackety nonsensicality she remembered in him from his butterfly days faded. "That's a silly question, Mel, don't you think?"

"Oh, *Rupes*." She stroked her hand down his arm. "Honestly, there's no need to worry. I'm not the one who'll be in danger. That's Gerald. He's the janitor. I'm just the other half of his disguise."

Her brother frowned. "You thought there'd be no danger when you agreed to help Permelia Wycliffe, and look how that turned out."

"Careful, Rupes," she said, giving him a little poke. "You're starting to sound like the very opposite of a paragon."

"And you, Princess Melissande," he retorted, "are becoming uncomfortably reckless. I wish you'd remember your position. And mine. D'you know what'll be said about me if anything happens to you?"

Closing her fingers on his shirt front, she shook him. "As if you ever gave a fig for what other people say!"

"They'll say I held you too lightly," he continued, ignoring her. "And they'll be right. Melissande, it's not too late to change your mind. You don't work for Sir Alec or his dubious Department. There's no reason for you to risk yourself like this."

She smoothed the wrinkles she'd left in his shirt. "Would

you still say that if I wore trousers all the time, instead of the occasional dress when I have to? I don't think so. Please don't tell me you're going to break my heart now by treating me like a *gel*."

"Melissande . . ." Sighing, Rupert touched his knuckles to her cheek. "I've already lost my brother. I couldn't bear it if I lost my sister too. I'm not cut out to be an only child."

She stepped back. "And *I'm* not cut out to be a dress-up doll princess. Of course I have to do this. Quite apart from any considerations of international tranquillity, there's Gerald. He needs my help, Rupert, and I owe him. *We* owe him. This kingdom. The chance to make a better future for our people. Oh, everything. And I know you're a man who's scrupulous about repaying his debts."

Rupert's face clouded until he looked so sad and serious she almost wished for the gormless butterfly prince to return. Then, without speaking, he crushed her in a desperate embrace that threatened to turn her ribs into matchsticks. She hugged him too, just as hard, heedless of her corsets, until she was in danger of flooding with tears. Then she released him, and stepped back.

"Right, then," she said briskly. "I think that's quite enough unseemly emotion for one visit. Gerald? Bibbie? Are you—"

"Gosh," said Rupert, staring. "How utterly bizarre."

Before them stood meek Gladys Slack, with her dark bun and her brown eyes and plain spectacles, her black skirt and white blouse, and Algernon Rowbotham, wearing inconspicuous brown tweeds. His straw-coloured hair was slicked close to his skull and his green eyes peered short-sighted through his own wire-framed spectacles. Ink splotched his fingers.

Used to the startling transformations by now, Melissande grinned. "Clever, isn't it? Not so much as a hint of Bibbie or Gerald. I tell you, Rupes, between them those two possess more thaumaturgics than Sir Alec's entire Department."

"So I see," said Rupert. "Extraordinary." He didn't sound altogether approving.

"And now we really do have to go," said Gerald, in a voice hexed half an octave higher than normal, with a slight nasal whine added to it for good measure. "Thanks for your assistance, Rupert. I know the Department is deeply grateful."

"So long as the Department takes good care of my sister," said Rupert, "it will have my assistance whenever there's need."

Gerald nodded. "I'm sure Sir Alec understands that, Your Majesty." Walking forward, he held out his hand. "I promise you I do. I'll keep her safe, sir."

Rupert took Gerald's offered hand and shook it, firmly. Then he turned to Bibbie and bowed. "Bibbie. Or should I say Miss Slack? It was delightful to meet you. I look forward to seeing you again soon."

Bibbie, who was taking her role as Gladys more seriously than any actress, sank into an impeccable curtsey. "You're too kind, Your Majesty."

"Right, then, Rupes," said Melissande, and stood on tiptoe to kiss his cheek. "We'll be off. Now, mind you don't portal us to Babishkia by mistake and please, don't let that dreadful old goat Billingsley bully you while I'm gone."

With a nod at Bibbie and Gerald she led the way back into the portal, then smiled at Rupert until the doors closed in her face and the whirling thaumaturgics whisked them away.

"Princess Melissande! You've come! How *utterly* delightful!"

From his subservient position in the rear, with Bibbie demurely reticent beside him, Gerald watched Melissande stand formidably straight.

"Crown Prince Hartwig," she said, her austere reserve pitch-perfect and quintessentially, royally *Melissande*. "How kind of you to meet me. I wasn't expecting such an honour."

"My dear Melissande, so formal!" Splotze's ruler protested, his Ottish correct but strongly accented, approaching with both heavily beringed hands outstretched. "When you and I have known each other for so many *delightful* years. You must call me Twiggy when we are spared the rigours of public observances. And I shall call you Melly, just as that good chap Rupert does."

Anyone less twig-like, Gerald couldn't imagine. Splotze's Crown Prince was nearly as wide as he was tall, an impression not helped by the miles of gold braiding on his crimson tunic and trousers.

"Well, Twiggy," said Melissande, accepting his hands so she could hold them at bay, and suffering him to kiss her noisily on both cheeks. "That sounds lovely. And tell me, how is Brunelda?"

The Crown Prince sighed, lugubrious. "Sadly afflicted with the gout. Today is not a good day, or she'd have come with me to greet you." Another sigh. "Don't tell her I told you, eh? There's something quite lowering about a Crown Princess with the gout. I'm afraid Brunelda feels it keenly."

"I imagine she does," said Melissande. "I understand it's a most uncomfortable complaint."

"Yes, yes, it's devilish discommoding," said the Crown Prince, vigorously nodding. "I've had to turf her into a spare bedchamber, Melissande. She was quite cutting up my sleep!"

Wincing, Gerald dropped his gaze to the gold-chased tiles beneath his feet. Sir Alec would go spare if his mission ended five minutes after it began because Melissande lost her temper with their stuffy, middle-aged host.

Bite your tongue, Mel. For pity's sake, for all our sakes, please bite your tongue.

"Oh, dear, poor Hartwig," she sympathised. "That's too utterly bad. And you with so much to contemplate, now that Ludwig's getting married at last."

He breathed out relief. Shame on him for doubting the redoubtable Miss Cadwallader. After a lifetime of dissembling in the face of Lional's tempestuous instabilities, of course she wouldn't stumble over such a small hurdle. Stupid of him to think that she might.

"Oh, lord, *Ludwig!*" said the Crown Prince, rolling his bloodshot brown eyes. His florid complexion burned brighter as he tugged his luxuriant fox-red moustache. "If you have the smallest care for me, Melly, do not utter my brother's name. Not after last night. He went out carousing with some men from Harenstein and didn't stumble home until dawn." Reluctantly releasing her, he waved a hand about the palace room into which they'd arrived. "Now, here's a sweeter topic for conversation. How d'you care for my privy portal chamber, eh? A bit of extravagance, really. With our dodgy etheretics it only works one day out of five, if we're lucky! But even so—it's pretty delightful, don't you think?"

No, pretty hideous, Gerald thought, but kept his face blank. *Hartwig and Lional must've attended the same art classes.*

Melissande, escorted by the Crown Prince, was taking a slow turn around the portal reception chamber, exclaiming in apparently sincere admiration at the plump, naked cherubs and the taxidermied foxes and stoats and the enormous glass domes under which were trapped colourful, taxidermied birds, caught forever in mid-flight.

Domes . . .

Shuddered by memory—*that other Ott's parade ground, full of the other Gerald's hideously tortured victims*—Gerald thought he felt the gold-touched tiles beneath his feet tilt.

Bibbie sidled closer. "Ger—I mean, Algernon. Mister Rowbotham. Are you all right?"

He nodded, a curt dip of his head. Bloody Bibbie. *Flirting* like that with Melissande's brother. Did she think he was made of cold stone?

But how stupid am I, to feel betrayed by a little flirting? I haven't declared myself, have I? I don't even know if she cares. If she's ever thought of me as anything more than her brother's best friend.

With a wrenching effort, clenching his fingers so his neatly trimmed nails bit his palm, he drove the treacherous thought deep inside. Dammit. Let Bibbie distract him on this mission and Sir Alec would rightly skin him alive—assuming that said distraction didn't get him killed first. Which it might well do, if he wasn't careful.

On second thoughts, maybe bringing her as camouflage wasn't such a good idea.

Rebuffed, Bibbie inched away again. A glance at her profile showed him her feelings were hurt.

Yes, well, my girl. That's what those of us born and bred in Nether Wallop call tit for bloody tat.

Melissande, adroitly managing to evade Crown Prince Hartwig's suggestive hand hovering near her waist, paid the eye-searingly over-decorated chamber one last fulsome compliment, then halted.

"Now you know, dear Twiggy," she said, fingertips brushing his braided forearm, in a voice amazingly close to a simper, "that while it's a lovely morning here, back in New Ottosland it's still practically midnight and I'm afraid any moment now I'm simply going to *wilt*. Would you be a dear and excuse me until afternoon tea? I'm sure I'm keeping you from any number of important matters and I feel quite overcome with guilt."

Clearly not one to be easily dissuaded, the Crown Prince snatched Melissande's hand and pressed a damp kiss to it.

"Of course, Melly. What a brute I am, keeping you on your delicate feet so I can boast of my lovely new portal chamber, when you should be reclining in the palace's most sumptuous guest suite."

Another kiss, this time accompanied by an ardent look from beneath his wildly untrimmed greying eyebrows. Gerald had to bite his cheek at the way Melissande's face fixed itself in an expression of coy delight.

"Not at all, Hartwig," she said, her voice shifted from simpering to strangled. "But if you could send for someone to show me upstairs, and see that my luggage goes up too, I'd be very grateful."

The Crown Prince's eyes gleamed. "*How* grateful?"

Melissande slid her hand free and turned. "Oh, yes, and Hartwig, dear, I should make my staff known to you. I hope you don't mind that I brought a staff with me. It's Rupert, you know. Such a stickler for the proprieties. And d'you know, I did rather promise the *New Ottosland Times* that I'd record a few memories of this momentous occasion, for their readers to peruse and enjoy. So to keep Rupert happy there's Slack— step forward, Slack, and curtsey to the Crown Prince—and to fulfill my obligations to the *Times*, there's my secretary, Rowbotham. Yes, my good man, bow. So that's who they are, should you see them flitting about the place."

The Crown Prince of Splotze barely spared them a glance. Not even Gladys Slack's lithe curtsey and trim figure seemed to disturb him.

"Yes, yes, of course it's all right you've brought a staff, Melissande," Hartwig said, still fatuously smiling. "Good God, only two? You should see how many hangers-on have accompanied the Marquis of Harenstein! I've bloody near had to build a whole new wing to the palace, excuse my Babishkian. And as for Dowager Queen Erminium—" He swallowed, hard. "But there you have it, it's her daughter who's marrying Ludwig so I expect that can't be helped. A piddling two servants? You, my dear, are the very model of restraint. And as for sending you upstairs with a lackey, shame on you for asking. I'll take you up myself. So, shall we?"

Capturing Melissande's arm, Crown Prince Hartwig led the way out of the portal chamber. Gerald tipped his head at Bibbie, who tilted her chin, and they fell into step behind.

"So, Twiggy, aside from the bride-to-be and her party, and the Marquis of Harenstein, who else is here?" said Melissande, as they climbed the palace's spectacularly swooping central staircase. The walls were hugely frescoed with scenes from classical myth: Devonia and the Bull, the Blind Twins of Teresco, the Ascension of the Lark. Very little had been left to the imagination, but instead of modestly averting her gaze Bibbie was avidly staring. Well. Avidly staring in the manner of a demure lady's maid. Gerald, watching sideways, had to grudgingly admit she was doing a good job with her disguise.

"Who else?" said the Crown Prince, supremely indifferent to the bows and curtseys coming at him from all directions, as dozens of harried-looking servants rushed about in a pre-wedding frenzy. "Let's see. So far we've got the guests from Harenstein, Blonkken, Graff and Aframbigi cluttering up the place. Can't take a step without falling over one of them. Still waiting for Ottosland's foreign minister. He's cutting it fine, since we're leaving on the grand wedding tour day after tomorrow, but that's Ottosland for you. Always expecting the world to wait on its pleasure." He cleared his throat. "No offense meant, of course. I mean, you've only arrived just now but that's different. Old friends, you and I, Melly. Not about to stand upon ceremony with you."

"Oh, there's no offense taken, Twiggy," said Melissande airily. "Feel free to insult Ottosland all you like. *New* Ottosland is quite definitely its own country. And what's more, I know *exactly* what you mean about the government types of Ott. Quite unbearably autocratic, most of them."

"Yes, *aren't* they," said the Crown Prince, with feeling. "But how do you know?"

Melissande shrugged. "Oh, I spend rather a lot of my time in Ott, these days, on Rupert's behalf, and what with one thing and another I've come to know its government denizens quite well."

"My dear," said the Crown Prince, pressing Melissande's hand. "You have *all* my sympathy."

As the staircase continued to unwind above them, they left the frescoes behind and entered a world of old, cracked paintings and more moth-eaten stuffed animal heads. Keeping a blank face with some difficulty, Gerald couldn't help remembering his arrival at Lional's palace, and a similarly endless tramp to his apartments with Melissande as his guide.

Bloody hell. This mission better not turn out to be New Ottosland all over again.

If for no other reason than this time he didn't have Reg around to save his hide.

Wheezing as they tackled the next flight of stairs, Splotze's Crown Prince spared Melissande a curious look. "So you're swanning about Ott at old Rupert's behest, eh? Funny. I could've sworn Brunelda showed me a newspaper photo a while ago, of you with some young jackanapes, talking about you starting up a witching agency or something. Not even calling yourself by your proper title. Extraordinary. Brunelda read that and needed her smelling salts brought."

"Oh," said Melissande, after the merest hesitation. "Really? Well, can you ever believe what you read in the newspaper? I mean, really?"

"So it's poppycock? Oh, good. Brunelda will be pleased."

"Not exactly *poppycock*," Melissande said, cautious. "It is true I'm dabbling in a little thaumaturgic venture, but that's for Rupert too. He has plans for New Ottosland, you see, and it's easier for me to look into certain opportunities than it is for him, being the king. You know what *that's* like."

The Crown Prince laughed, wheezily, then guided them off the staircase and onto a landing which led to a long narrow corridor. "I certainly do. If only the common man knew what we suffered, bearing the burden of a crown."

As Bibbie gurgled a little in her throat, Gerald managed, but only just, not to swallow his tongue.

"So, Twiggy," said Melissande, apparently unmoved by the Crown Prince's ludicrous lament. "Is anyone else joining us on the wedding tour?"

"Oh, did I forget to mention them?" said the Crown Prince, sounding gloomy. "There is one more guest, yes. Lanruvia."

"Really?" said Melissande, surprised. "Lanruvia?"

She wasn't the only one who'd not expected that. Gerald felt his pulse race. Lanruvia? Sir Alec was going to go spare.

"But why Lanruvia?" Melissande persisted. "Splotze doesn't have much to do with them, does it?"

The Crown Prince shuddered. "No. Of course not. But someone—don't recall who—insisted on an invitation for them. A last minute thing. Can't say I'm thrilled about it, but no one's interested in my opinion. I'm here to foot the bill and keep out of the way."

"Oh, Twiggy," said Melissande, and sounded genuinely sorry. "It can't be *that* bad."

Crown Prince Hartwig halted in front of a wide set of double doors. "You wait. You'll see. Now, here we are, my dear. Your secretary's at the end of the corridor, the green door, and you're in here. Don't fret about your things, they'll be brought up in a trice." He cleared his throat. "These were my mother's rooms, y'know. Wouldn't give them to anyone else."

"Oh, *Twiggy*," said Melissande. "Don't you dare make me cry. Just be about your important business and leave me to settle in."

"Well!" said Bibbie, as soon as the Crown Prince was safely on his way back down the staircase. "What a ghastly old man. I hate to admit it, but Mother's right. Aside from your brother,

Melissande, I can't think what the rest of the world sees in royalty!"

Melissande sighed. "No, well, I expect you need to have been brought up with it. Now d'you mind if we don't stand in the corridor gossiping? There'll be a maid along any moment and it's bound to look odd."

Gerald cleared his throat. "Actually, you two can settle in without me. I need to get cracking. Sir Alec's anxious that I nose about Bestwick's lodgings, just in case he's still there, or left something behind if he's not."

"Still there?" said Bibbie. "But if he's still there after all this time, won't that mean—" She wrinkled her nose. "Oh. That's disgusting."

"No, Miss Slack, it's my job," he said, repressive. "So if you'll excuse me? And don't worry if I'm gone a while. These things tend to take time."

"Wait," said Melissande, as he turned away. "You can't go alone. If there is a plot afoot, you could be in danger. Bibbie and I should—"

"No, you shouldn't!" he snapped. "Are you mad? There might well be all kinds of classified material where I'm going and if there is and I let you see it, Sir Alec will *pillage* me. You two are here as Rupert's royal sister and a meek little lady's maid. You're going to stay here and *be* them. Understood?"

Not waiting for an answer, he left the girls standing in the corridor and headed down the stairs.

CHAPTER EIGHT

On the Gerald Dunwoody list of Things To Do, *visit Splotze* had always ranked high. It was a country of great natural beauty, with deep lakes and richly forested mountains, rippling green meadows and picture-perfect milch cows and goats. The headily potent cherry liqueur his parents had brought back from their trip-of-a-lifetime, Splotze's most famous and lucrative export, was a pretty decent incentive too. If he had time, he'd have to buy himself a bottle or several while he was here.

And who knows? he considered, tromping down yet another flight of opulent stairs. *It could be that with this marriage between Splotze and Borovnik, always assuming I can prevent it falling apart at the last minute, there'll be lots of trade benefits and liqueur prices might actually come down.*

In which case somebody, somewhere, would surely owe him a medal. Or possibly a lifetime's supply of Splotze cherry liqueur. After all, a man could dream . . .

Nobody in Crown Prince Hartwig's anthill-busy palace paid attention to him as he descended to its imposing ground floor Grand Entrance hall. In keeping with the country's martial past—indeed, its martial present, thanks to all those tedious bloody Canal skirmishes—the hall was crowded with an amazing array of armour for man, horse and dog. Though fashioned for violence, the pieces were also works of art. Chased with intricate etching, loops and whirls and filigrees of infinite variety, inlaid with gold and copper and semi-precious stones, they stood testament to the irrepressible human urge to create beauty even out of barbarity.

Carefully, Gerald lowered his etheretic shield a little and examined the impressive collection through the lens of his *potentia*. To his surprise, he felt nothing. Not so much as one visor, greave, gauntlet or spiked dog collar had been fashioned with the use of thaumaturgics. Only good old fashioned love, blood and sweat had gone into their creation. That the pieces had been crafted long before ratification of the United Magical Nations' accords prohibiting the manufacture of thaumaturgical weapons made it even more astonishing.

Just as impressive was the fact that he couldn't detect any trace of thaumaturgical residue on the exterior of the armour, either. Which meant that the battles fought by the armour's inhabitants had also been fought the old-fashioned way.

He wasn't sure whether he should feel admiring, or appalled.

Sliding his shield back into place, he headed for the palace's grand and guarded entrance. Still no-one challenged him. Interesting. Once someone was inside the palace it seemed nobody cared who they were or what they were doing. The assumption was, apparently, that anyone who was inside the palace belonged *because* they were inside. A definite lapse in security, there.

On the other hand, unless visitors were portalling directly to Hartwig's little personal indulgence, the only public way into the palace was through its grand front doors. And that meant enduring the stern scrutiny of six tall guardsmen ranged across the foyer, a few paces from the doors. They wore suggestively militant uniforms of dark blue and gold, unsheathed daggers belted at their trim, muscular waists, and carried very tall, very sharp double-pronged pikes. It was a safe bet neither weapon was for decoration.

So that's something done right, at least, Gerald thought, relieved. *Because being a rogue wizard doesn't make me a one-man army.*

For a moment he was tempted to hex the guards with a no-see-'em, to make sure that Algernon Rowbotham was able to move about the place freely. But would that be wise? What if there was a changing of the guard while he was out breaking into Abel Bestwick's lodgings? Well, yes, he could simply hex the new guards too, on his return, but either way he'd be bumping into the same problem. The no-see-'em incant was slippery and powerful. He'd have to switch off his etheretic shield entirely to use it, which would leave him vulnerable to detection by the thaumic gauges and monitors and tripwires and so forth riddling the place. And since most of them had been developed by Monk and his friends in Research and Development, he'd be detected.

Or would he?

Heart sinking, he looked the answer to that square in its face. No. He'd not be detected. Not if he took advantage of his unique personal thaumaturgics. With a nip here and a tuck there and a bit of squirrelling with the various devices' matrixes, he'd be able to hex the palace guards without a soul—or one of Monk's monitors—being any the wiser.

But if I flout the rules for no better reason than just because I can, well, it makes me someone who thinks the rules are for little people. Lesser wizards. It makes me that other Gerald Dunwoody.

The thought churned him sick.

Somebody brushed past him, needing to get outside. So much frantic activity. Surely palace security was on highest alert. And yes indeed, it was, because one of the eagle-eyed, tautly attentive guards was watching him without appearing to be watching him. Not a good sign. The last thing he needed to do was raise official suspicions.

Recalling Rupert's remarkably effective gormless butterfly prince routine, Gerald offered the interested guard a foolish, slack-lipped smile and crabbed his way close enough for conversation.

"Ah . . . excuse me? I say there, so sorry to bother you when you're busy, only there's something I feel you ought to know. Oh dear." He rubbed at his nose, feeling its real shape beneath the obfuscation hex's snubby illusion. "I say, d'you speak Ottish?"

The guard, a tall, bronze-skinned young fellow with

typically Splotzeish ginger-red hair and a truly amazing breadth of muscled shoulders, looked down his long, narrow nose.

"Yes," he said, his voice heavily accented. The merest hint of a sneer curling his lip suggested the question was an insult. Or perhaps being forced to sully his tongue with Ottish was the insult. According to the Department's briefing notes, Splotze was at once dazzlingly cosmopolitan and fiercely nationalistic. It was an interesting, and sometimes combustible, combination.

Gerald risked another foolish smile. "Wonderful! Well, the thing is, y'see, I'm on Her Royal Highness Princess Melissande of New Ottosland's staff. We've just arrived, through the Crown Prince's private portal. Princess Melissande is invited to the wedding, y'know."

The guard didn't quite manage to swallow his sigh. *Tourists.* "We know the approved guests for Prince Ludwig's wedding. Her Royal Highness is welcome to Splotze."

"Excellent!" Gerald said, beaming. "Well, it happens I need to toddle off for a bit. And I just wanted to make sure you know who I am, so you'll let me back into the palace when I return."

The guard thought for a moment. "Name?"

"Rowbotham. Algernon Rowbotham."

More thought on the part of the guard. Risking a glance at the young man's five brothers-in-arms, Gerald saw that although their gazes remained strictly front-and-center they were closely listening, ready to take action should they perceive any threat.

Thinking concluded, the guard held out his hand. It was heavily callused, as though he spent many hours training with his dagger and his sharp, double-pronged pike.

"Papers."

"Oh, yes. Of course," said Gerald, and slid his own uncalloused, yet still lethal, hand inside his boring tweed coat and extracted from its concealed pocket the identity paperwork so meticulously prepared for him by Beevish Trotter, the Department's document specialist. "Here you are. All in order, I hope!"

The guard scanned Algernon Rowbotham's particulars then scanned them again, for good measure. Waiting for his false identification to be approved, Gerald noted from the corner of his eye three remarkably vivid individuals mounting the marble steps leading up from the palace forecourt and into the Entrance hall.

Well, well. So the Lanruvians really are here. I wonder what for? And why Sir Alec didn't know they'd been invited . . .

The Lanruvians were impossible to miss or ignore, with their scalp-locks dyed bright emerald and lips tattooed cobalt blue. Tall and disturbingly thin, the three men were swathed head to toe in sand-white woollen robes. Their shimmering skin was very nearly the same shade. One of them had beads of jet and ivory dangling from his pierced nose, marking him as his wedding party's Spirit Speaker. The Lanruvians were thaumaturgists, after a fashion, but their etheretics were wrapped so tightly in the chains of religious mysticism that as far as the Lanruvian people were concerned they might as well not exist. On that score Lanruvians weren't terribly unlike the Kallarapi. Only compared to them, the Kallarapi were the life of any party.

Watching the guards draw themselves that little bit taller as the Lanruvians approached, Gerald hid his consternation. With his etheretic shield engaged it was much harder to feel their inner power, but it was there, elusive as a name on the tip of his tongue. *Smarmy*, Crown Prince Hartwig had called them, and he wasn't entirely wrong. There was a slickness to the Lanruvians that couldn't sit easily with anyone who possessed an aptitude for thaumaturgics.

Blimey. I hope they're not the ones causing trouble. Because if they were, his job was going to be nigh impossible. *And then Sir Alec really will go spare.*

As the Lanruvians passed unchallenged into the palace, just a rap of five pikes to the marble-covered floor in honour of the Crown Prince's guests, the guard held out the false paperwork. "You are free to go, Mister Rowbotham, and free to return." A sardonic smile. "Enjoy your little visit to Grande Splotze."

Gerald shoved the papers back inside his tweed coat. "Thank you! D'you know, I think I will!"

He'd memorised a suitably havey-cavey route from the palace to Abel Bestwick's lodgings, one that made sure he took in some of the more popular attractions a visitor might wish to see in Grande Splotze. As the crow flew it was no more than a brisk three-quarter hour's walk to his destination, cutting through various side-streets and alleyways, but it was the kind of route that only someone familiar with Grand Splotze would use. If Algernon Rowbotham was seen nipping along it smartish, like a man who knew precisely where he was off to, eyebrows would rise. And if they weren't friendly eyebrows, well, the next thing being lifted might well be a knife. Not that there was any reason to think that Algernon Rowbotham, secretary to Princess Melissande, would be the object of scrutiny.

But under the circumstances, he couldn't afford to take the chance.

On a deep breath, Gerald marched off to give his best impression of a gormless tourist-about-town.

Splotze's royal capital was abuzz with a feverish anticipation of the upcoming wedding. Being very late in autumn, with a definite nip in the air but no picture-postcard snow to delight visitors from warmer climes, this was the time of year that tended to fall between two seasonal sightseeing stools. At least, ordinarily. But the pending nuptials between Hartwig's young brother, Prince Ludwig, and Borovnik's only daughter, the Princess Ratafia, had turned *ordinarily* on its head.

The people of Splotze were easy to spot, with their abundant hair in varying shades of chestnut red and the men sporting moustaches most walruses would gladly claim. But for every proud local, Gerald saw a face that didn't belong. His own folk from Ottosland, with their indefinable yet distinctive cast of features. A great many dark-haired, dark-eyed Borovniks, which was only to be expected. They were very well behaved, for once. In startling contrast to their trim swarthiness were the floridly well-fleshed visitors from Blonkken, with their blond hair thick as straw. They were almost as well-fleshed as the tourists from Graff, with whom they shared a common ancestry and a great many squabbles. And if that weren't enough to turn Grande Splotze into a human zoo, there were also ebony-skinned Aframbigins, wiry-haired Steinish folk and even a few silk-wrapped Fandawandins shimmering in the cool sunshine like Rupert's late, lamented butterflies.

Indeed, Grande Splotze was so crushed and crowded with visitors that Gerald was slowed to a maddening hop-step-and-shuffle as he made his way from the palace to the township's heart. Not wanting to draw attention to himself, just in case someone was watching, instead of causing a fuss when confronted by yet another pedestrian of the voluminously-attired female persuasion, he simply stepped into the gutter. Sadly, the city's gutters weren't empty. By the time he'd navigated the length of Palace Way and reached the junction with Bessleslitz Circus he was mired well over the instep with a variety of evil-smelling substances he didn't dare investigate too closely.

Bugger, he thought, casting another look behind him at the cheerful crowd. *If I am being followed, how will I know?*

The thronged centre of Grande Splotze was gaily festive. Garlands swooped from lamp post to curlicued, wrought-iron lamp post, intricately entwined in royal blue, gold and crimson. In the middle of each swoop was a portrait of the prince and princess, and if a certain amount of artistic licence had been taken with Ludwig's likeness, well, it was a wedding, after all, starring the prince as The Dashing Bridegroom.

And it wasn't just the lamp post garlands that created the air of celebration. Every shop front was festooned with bunting, every window graced with a larger version of the happy couple's official portrait. In the pastry shops' displays he saw cakes baked in the royal likenesses, some of them terrifyingly life-like. One ambitious baker had produced a figured cake to actual size and standing upright, with Ludwig and Ratafia's iced hands coyly clasped—which seemed on the whole to be a sad waste of flour, eggs and sugar. He couldn't imagine anyone *eating* the thing. Surely they'd be tried for treason if they did.

With one last horrified look at the life-sized cake, acutely mindful of Sir Alec back in Nettleworth doubtless impatient for a report, Gerald hurried on, making sure that Algernon Rowbotham took a moment to stare admiringly at the famously mosaicked Town Hall, then ogle the surprisingly unclothed statues in the Groblemintz Gardens. Both times he risked lowering his shield again, but couldn't detect any trace of untoward thaumaturgics.

Probably I'm not being followed. Probably I'm letting Bestwick's message give me unnecessary collywobbles. But my motto from here on in is Better Safe Than Sorry . . .

The major landmark of interest in Grande Splotze was, of course, the Canal: source of so much prosperity and misery, and the ultimate cause of the upcoming nuptials. Thanks to a coin toss between the respective rulers of Splotze and Borovnik, back in the days when the Canal was still only a dream, it began in Grande Splotze.

Also thanks to his Department briefing notes, he knew that the actual nuts-and-bolts business of the Canal, the cargo barges, lived in a shipyard some safe fifteen miles down-water from the royal capital. It meant that this end was used mostly for sightseeing and celebratory business. Indeed, according to Melissande, there would be two spectacular fireworks displays launched from barges tethered in the Canal itself, one to see them off on the wedding tour *and* one to welcome them back. At least that was something to look forward to.

Assuming, of course, that he foiled the pending plot.

Reaching the Canal promenade, Gerald spied the lofty observation tower that, for a modest fee, visitors were invited to climb in order to enjoy a spectacular view of the city. Shading his eyes against the cheerful sunlight, he tipped his head back. Blimey, it was high. That meant a lot of stairs. But he had to climb it. Sir Alec had warned him that Abel Bestwick's choice of lodgings had everything to do with strategy, and nothing at all with comfort. It might be a bit of harmless gawking for Algernon Rowbotham, but for Gerald Dunwoody, bereft of Reg and her useful bird's eye view, Grande Splotze's famous tower presented the perfect opportunity for him to get a look at his fellow agent's neck of the woods before wandering off the well-trodden tourist path.

He paid his fee and started up the stairs. Four hundred and twenty-three treads later, jelly-legged and gasping, he staggered onto the viewing platform.

The first thing he felt was the wind whipping through the blond hair that startled him every time he looked in a mirror. Close on its heels came a punch of strong thaumaturgics from the safety barrier erected around the platform's edge. Recovered enough to properly observe his surroundings, he shuffled out of the way of those folk who'd survived the climb in better shape than he had, then waited for a gap to appear in the three-deep crowd of tourists already ooohing and aaahing over the sights.

After waiting several minutes, he created a gap of his own. And while, yes, absolutely, it was the kind of thaumaturgical behaviour that often got frowned upon, he didn't care. He wasn't a sightseer, he was a janitor on a mission, and he didn't have all day.

The most remarkable thing about standing so high above Grande Splotze was the chance to see, in person, just how close it was to Borovnik. He'd seen its proximity on a Department map of the region, of course. Had seen how the Canal, which long ago had been a treacherous, inconsistent and unreliable river, now neatly and predictably divided the two countries. But maps were maps and never felt quite real. Even at ground level, it wasn't much better. Trees got in the way, and buildings, and in the sprawling city a man could easily feel like an ant.

But up here, he was an eagle. At least, all right, maybe not an *eagle*. But some kind of bird. Probably Reg would call him a moth-eaten sparrow, but the principle remained the same. Up here, wind-whipped and still panting a little from that leg-breaking climb, he could see for miles . . . and note, a little nervously, that Borovnik's well-trained military didn't have far to march at *all* before they'd reach the Canal and soon after that, Splotze.

On the whole, he thought it was a good thing that not only had Splotze and Borovnik signed treaties preventing the use of any thaumaturgics in their tedious Canal disputes, but that they'd actually *honoured* them. Because if they hadn't . . .

Right now I'd most likely be standing in a smoking thaumaturgical crater, instead of on top of this tower admiring the not-quite-distant-enough spires of Borovnik's capital, Gajnik.

And if he didn't succeed in averting a crisis over the Splotze-Borovnik wedding, that could still happen.

But never mind, Dunnywood. No need to feel pressed.

With a last appreciative look at the surrounding countryside—blindingly green fields, home to sheep and cows, and dots of woodland and cherry orchards and higgledy-piggledy hedgerows, all very picturesque—he turned his attention to the tidy sprawl of Grande Splotze. And yes, there was the palace, golden and glittering. The main street, with its shops, the town hall and the Gardens. Crossing to the western side of the platform, he saw there was a smaller canal running at a sharp angle off the main Canal. Interesting. It hadn't been on the city map he'd studied. With a small, cynical smile he saw that it bifurcated the city's western residential district into the haves and the have-nots. On the tower side of the small canal, the houses were large and manicured. But on its far side . . . they weren't. There, the houses were slovenly and mean-sized, fit only for servants and the poor. Somewhere down there, in that huddle of shoddy dwellings and tightly tangled, narrow alleys and laneways, was Abel Bestwick's modest lodging.

And if I don't get a look at it soon, and report home, Sir Alec is going to have my guts for garters.

Climbing down the tower's stairs was only a little less trying than climbing up, what with all the squishing and holding his breath so upward-bound sightseers could squeeze past. At last, safely back on the ground, Gerald looked around the busy promenade and plaza. Bloody hell, so many people. Before he went any further he needed to make sure he was still alone.

So he lingered on the haves' side of the small canal, ensuring his anonymity and feeling briefly sorry that Melissande and

Bibbie were stuck back in the palace. Because really, this was delightful. Not far from the tower was a brightly painted gazebo on a large square of lush green grass, from which an enthusiastic band of musicians serenaded the crowd. Keeping the music company were tame Jandrian monkeys turning tricks, dancing dogs in silly skirts, gaudily dressed clowns on stilts handing out fresh flowers to the ladies, a trio of daring fire-eaters, a sword swallower, a snake-charmer, several jugglers and a giant walking to and fro with a dwarf on his head—both of them inviting Grande Splotze's visitors to call down blessings on the upcoming royal wedding. So innocent. It was worlds away from plots and danger and terrified janitors staring at their own blood.

But I can't afford to think about that.

As sure as he could be that he remained unnoticed, he slowly edged away from the eddying crowds until he reached the fantastically constructed and painted iron bridge hooping over the small canal that would lead him into the heart of have-nots territory . . . and from there to missing Abel Bestwick's lodging.

Nearly an hour later, muffled by the shadow of a steeply overhanging eave across the way, Gerald frowned at the shuttered front window and dilapidated front door of 45b Voblinz Lane, where Abel Bestwick had crawled into bed every night for the past four years. Like all the dwellings in this have-not part of the city, 45b was in desperate need of some tender loving care.

It was actually half a house. Some enterprising landlord in the past had taken 45 Voblinz Lane and sliced it in two with a single dividing wall. From the look of things 45a was unoccupied, and had been for some time, which doubtless suited both Abel Bestwick and Sir Alec. Neighbours could be nosy, and a great deal depended upon Bestwick remaining largely unremarked.

Still. No neighbours, and not much life in this ramshackle lane beyond a skinny stray cat and a few anaemic-looking pigeons? Lord, what a depressing place to live.

Doing his best not to breathe too deep of the damp, narrow lane's malodorous air, Gerald tried to imagine being Abel Bestwick, a wizard undercover on long term assignment. Ghastly. Unthinkable. At least, not when the task demanded living this kind of life. Kitchen lackey in the palace, slaving and scurrying and hiding, snatching up whatever crumbs of useful information fell in his path and feeding them back to Sir Alec. Knowing that one day, *one day*, he might snatch up a crumb that could mean the difference between life and death for someone. Hoping for it, surely, so that his many sacrifices wouldn't have been for nothing.

He shivered. Fingers crossed Sir Alec never asked that of him. Because he was pretty sure he couldn't bear it . . . and in saying no, he'd likely cause a lot of strife.

But that was borrowing trouble, and he had more than enough already. He'd been standing here for over half an hour, and not a soul had walked by. Time to break into Abel Bestwick's sad little home and see what useful information the man had left lying about.

Only please, please, don't let him be lying about. I've seen enough dead bodies to last me three lifetimes.

Doing his best not to look furtive, Gerald crossed the narrow lane to number 45b. To be on the safe side, Sir Alec had given him a master de-warder that would get him past any thaumaturgical security safeguards Bestwick had left in place. He started to fish it out of his pocket, then hesitated.

I wonder.

Pretending he was a regular kind of visitor, he knocked on Abel Bestwick's badly painted, ill-fitting, rust-hinged front door. And as he knocked, he let slip his etheretic shield—only to realise, with a sickened twist of his guts, that he had no need of his peculiar talents. The abrupt ending of Bestwick's message to Sir Alec wasn't, as they'd hoped, due to Splotze's frustratingly erratic etheretic field. No. Someone—he couldn't tell who—had already smashed through Bestwick's security, with enough bludgeoning thaumaturgic force to shred the warding hex and leave it in fading tatters.

Bugger.

Cautiously, Gerald let himself into Bestwick's unlit lodging, closed the door behind him and sealed it with a hex he knew for a fact not even Monk could disable. And then, screwing his eyes shut, he dropped his shield entirely and took a deep breath.

Don't be here, don't be here . . .

He coughed in the darkness, tasting the stale air, feeling a tickle of dust, smelling mould from something fruity. But that was fine. That was wonderful. He *couldn't* smell the stench of death. And he had no sense of company, either. He was alone. Opening his eyes, he groped by the front door for the gas lamp igniter, found it, and flicked it on. After a moment, and the slightest whiff of gas, the lamps caught alight and lifted Bestwick's lodging out of shadow.

The shoebox of a front room was a wrecked mess.

"Damn," he said softly, looking at the smashed and splintered remains of an old, battered table, two equally old and battered dining chairs, a faded armchair and a tall, possibly fifth-hand bookcase. The books it had contained were gutted, their ripped pages tossed about like early wedding confetti.

Dried blood stained the old blue carpet a darker, rusty brown.

Skirting the sickening evidence of violence, he picked his way through the debris of Abel Bestwick's life to the even smaller shoebox of a bedroom. There he found a splintered wooden truckle bed, its straw mattress slashed and spilling its dry, grey guts. The sheets were ripped, the blanket reduced to fraying ribbons, the single, ungenerous pillow disembowelled like the mattress. Ruined, too, Abel Bestwick's meagre wardrobe of clothes. Not even his smalls had been spared, knifed to ribbons and dust cloths and strewn across the floor.

The shutter on the bedroom window was loose. Pushing it open, just a little, Gerald saw a smear of blood down the outer wall. Did that mean Bestwick had made his escape this way? It seemed a fair assumption, since he wasn't here.

Well done, Abel.

Every drawer in the cramped coldwater kitchen had been upended, knives and forks and spoons and a spatula tossed onto the miserly bench. Shards of mismatched crockery and a drinking glass cracked and splintered underfoot. That meant he almost missed Abel Bestwick's wrecked crystal ball. It was the damaged thaumics that caught at him as he was turning away. Turning back, carefully crouching, he poked at the burned, crushed crystal. So who'd done this, then? Bestwick or his attacker?

But before he could even begin to work it out, he felt a rotten twist in the erratic ether, felt his darkly enhanced *potentia* burn hot and hurting in sudden alarm. And then, before he could react, before he could save himself, *run*, the wickedly hidden entrapment hex he'd unwittingly triggered unfurled its poisonous tendrils with whipcrack speed to wrap him in a tight and lethal embrace.

"Bloody hell," he whispered, stunned. "Oh, bloody, *bloody* hell."

Holding his breath, he pushed as hard as he dared against the constricting hex. Indifferent to his rogue *potentia*, the hex pushed back. Pain seared every nerve.

"*Bugger!*" he swore, blinking away a scarlet mist. The pain eased, but not enough. Heat surged. Sweat prickled. His heart battered its cage of ribs. With a groaning effort he tried to see the hex's matrix, tried to unravel the tangle of strands. The hex resisted, tightening its hold, smearing his vision. Somehow it could blind whomever it held prisoner.

Damn. Damn, damn, damn . . .

He groaned again. "Hell's bells, Monk. Why aren't you ever around when I need you?"

CHAPTER NINE

"Monk! Hey Monk! Come to the phone, it's for you!"

Up to his aching eyeballs in randomly oscillating counter-intuitive tetrathaumicles, Monk cursed.

"Damn. It's not Bailey, is it?"

"I don't know who it is."

"Then can't you take a message?"

"Do I look like your secretary?" Walthorpe demanded, indignant. There was a heavy thumping of heels as he marched back to his cubicle. "Take it yourself."

"D'you mind?" Dalrymple demanded from the other side of Research and Development's cramped particle experiments lab. "I can't hear myself think with you two bellowing back and forth like bloody fishmongers."

"Don't blame me," Walthorpe protested. "Markham's the one who won't answer the telephone."

As Monk opened his mouth to refute that calumny, his carefully constructed containment field overloaded and the oscillating counter-intuitive tetrathaumicles sparked and spat and died in a nasty shrivelling cloud of expended thaumic energy.

"Bollocks!" He kicked the nearest bit of bench. "That's *nineteen* hours of work gone up in smoke!"

"Never mind," said Walthorpe. "At least it gives you time to answer the telephone."

Monk cursed again, then stamped out of his smelly cubicle to the lab telephone on its rickety desk beside the triple-sealed door. With a glare back at Walthorpe's cubicle, he snatched up the receiver.

"*What?*"

"And a very good afternoon to you, too, Mister Markham," a cool, self-contained voice said in his ear.

Bugger. "Oh. Sir Alec. Sorry."

"I need to see you, Mister Markham," said Sir Alec, indifferent to apology. "Now would be a good time."

Monk bit his tongue. A good time for who? Not him. He was so far behind on his current project he'd need a miracle of temporal thaumaturgics to finish it on deadline.

"Right now? Are you sure?"

A pause, and then a faint sigh. "Quite."

Oh. "Yes. All right. Only—"

Sir Alec disconnected the call.

Staring at the humming receiver, Monk fought down a surge of unease. What the hell? Why was he being yanked away from R&D in broad daylight with a call to a telephone number Sir Alec had no business using?

Lord, please don't let anything have happened to Bibbie. Or Melissande. Or Gerald.

This was the first time he'd been stranded alone with all three of them to worry about. He didn't like it. And when this mission was done with he was going to say so, very loudly, until somebody promised it wouldn't happen again. Because if it did, hell, if it turned into a regular occurrence, then being friends and relations with those three was going to take years off his life.

"Well?" said Walthorpe, coming out to lean on the open side of his cubicle. His thin blond hair was waving wildly about his face, charged with ambient, random tetrathaumicles. He looked like a startled dandelion. "Who was that, then? A secret admirer?"

He pulled a face. "Idiot. No, it—ah—it was my tailor. I've some altered shirts to collect. I won't be long."

I hope.

"You're going out?" said Walthorpe, comically crestfallen. "Oh. But I wanted you to—"

"Did I hear you aright?" said eavesdropping Dalrymple, popping up from his cubicle like an outraged jack-in-the-box. "You're dashing off to fetch some bloody *mending?*"

Blimey, Norris Dalrymple could be hard work. From the day he'd set foot in R&D, nearly a year ago, in his perfectly pressed three-piece suit that always stayed pristine, with or without a lab coat, and his perfectly polished spectacles and his corrugated brown hair plastered with pomade and never imperfectly parted, he was the kind of bloke you wanted to trip up in passing, just for the pleasure of seeing him go splat.

"Actually, Dalrymple, no," Monk snapped. "But since you don't like it when I'm called away without explanation . . ."

Dalrymple's face darkened. "I see. Well, then, Markham. Best you run along. God forbid the lowly likes of us keep you from your oh-so-important clandestine business."

Torn between his own irritation and an inconvenient sympathy, he shrugged. "Sorry, old chap. It's not like I can help who I was born related to."

Dalrymple subsided, muttering. "Treats the place like a bloody *cafeteria*. There are proper procedures. Rules. Not to mention deadlines. Arrogant, insufferable . . ."

"Never mind him," said Walthorpe. "He's brewing an ulcer. Go, if you have to. Is everything all right?"

Lord, it better be. "Of course."

But Walthorpe was no fool. "Yeah. Look, Markham, leave your cubicle. I'll desaturate it for you while you're gone. And if Bailey does call I'll fob him off."

"Thanks, Wally," Monk said, touched. "I'll try not to be all day. And when I get back I'll take a gander at that third-level splice you're working on. I'm not sure, but to artificially induce etheretic subsoms I suspect you'll need to go deeper. Maybe a fifth-level splice. Have a think about it, anyway, while I'm gone."

Mildly cheered by the memory of Walthorpe's almost boyish excitement, he drove his jalopy white-knuckled to Nettleworth. There he let himself into the dismally nondescript Department building through its dingy back entrance, jumping at the tingling buzz of the thaumic detector as it read his *potentia* and let him pass.

When he tapped on Sir Alec's open office door, Gerald's superior didn't look up, just waved him in and continued to read the report spread across the desk. Knowing better than to sit uninvited, Monk did his best to read the report for himself, upside down, while standing in front of the desk with his hands in his baggy pockets looking like he'd never *dream* of doing anything so impolite.

What he read threatened to send him shrieking from the room.

After a few moments, Sir Alec cleared his throat. "Mister Markham."

He was too shaken to even attempt a denial. "But sir, I thought we'd smashed the *dirit* weed trade."

"Did you?" Sir Alec shuffled the report's pages together, slid them into a folder and set it to one side. "That was rather naïve, wasn't it?"

Monk fought the urge to wince. "I'm guessing you didn't ask me here to talk about *dirit* weed."

"Naïve and yet, at the same time, peculiarly perspicacious," said Sir Alec, his smile acidic enough to etch glass. "Sit."

"Sir," said Monk, and sat with a bump in the old wooden visitor's chair.

"Regarding the mission to Splotze," said Sir Alec, his grey gaze cool and watchful, as ever. "Miss Cadwallader informs me they are safely ensconced in the palace, with Mister Dunwoody and your sister's false identities duly established. As we speak, Mister Dunwoody is attempting to ascertain the status of the agent whose whereabouts are currently unknown. I hope to hear from him shortly."

Giddy with relief, he nodded. "That's good to know, sir. Thank you. Ah—was that all, sir? Only I'm right in the middle of this bloody awful project and—"

Sir Alec folded his hands on the desk. "No, Mister Markham, that is not all. I have spoken with Sir Ralph, and he has agreed that, given your undesirable yet inevitable famil-iarity with the Splotze-Borovnik situation, and taking into account the fact that my Department finds itself temporarily over-stretched—" That watchful grey gaze flicked with cold contempt to the *dirit* weed report. "—I am within my purview to request your assistance."

Despite his deadline agitation, Monk felt a warm glow of pleasure. *Ha. So Bibbie's not the only honorary janitor in the family.* "Yes, sir. Of course, sir. Anything I can do. Just name it. Anything."

Sir Alec raised an eyebrow. "Thank you. Mister Markham, I need you to do a little discreet digging. I have asked Miss Cadwallader to provide me with the most recent wedding guest list, as well as the names and nationalities of all those guests' retinues. As soon as I have it, I will pass it to you and you will educate yourself about these people so that you might, in turn, educate me. No detail about them should be considered too obscure—and it should be noted that I don't much care how you go about discovering the information, provided you don't get caught." Another acidic smile. "If you do get caught, then you can expect to discover me afflicted with amnesia."

Of course he bloody could. "But . . ." Monk shifted on the uncomfortable chair. "What you're asking. That's spying, or something very like it. I thought you were talking thaumaturgics. I can do thaumaturgics. But I'm not trained to—"

"Training has nothing to do with it," said Sir Alec. "You're a Markham. Intrigue is in your blood."

"Yes, well, that's very flattering, Sir Alec, only—"

"Mister Markham," Sir Alec said, severe, "if you think the notion of once more dragging you into this Department's business affords me any pleasure you're entirely mistaken, but I don't have a janitor to spare and you, as it happens, are uniquely qualified for this task."

He blinked. "I am?"

"Yes. Thanks to your family, you know people who know people who will not talk to me but *will* talk to you, and who can very likely tell you what *I* need to know. So *talk* to them, Mister Markham. Help me to help your friend Mister Dunwoody. Again."

Blimey. Was he imagining things, or did Sir Alec sound rattled? "Yes, sir. Of course, sir."

And then, belatedly, an unwelcome thought occurred. His current project, hurtling towards deadline and nowhere near completion. Had Uncle Ralph bothered to consult with Bailey on lending him to Sir Alec? Bailey, who called three times a day demanding an update. Bailey, who'd taken to accosting him in the men's room, wild-eyed and practically foaming at the mouth. Bailey, who—

Sir Alec sat back. "Do not concern yourself with Bailey, Mister Markham. He will not interfere."

Dammit, how did the man *do* that? How did he always know? "Really, sir?" Monk said, not managing to hide his doubt. "Because Bailey, well, he's—"

"Taken care of," said Sir Alec.

"Oh. Right. Good. Only—" Monk cleared his throat. "The monitoring system I'm building for him? Actually, Sir Alec, it's pretty crucial, really, and—"

"Trust me, not as crucial as this."

His mouth dried. "Oh."

"Yes. *Oh.*" Sir Alec's eyes were like chips of ice. "Mister Markham, should the Splotze-Borovnik wedding be disturbed by any violent activity then no new thaumaturgic monitor that you could devise will prevent a conflagration the likes of which has never been seen. Believe me, it will make the Jandrian conflict look like a nursery school spat."

Because of that piddling Canal? But the Jandrian conflict had killed tens of thousands. Since when had the Splotze-Borovnik Canal been worth so many lost lives?

Feeling sick, Monk stared at Gerald's difficult superior. "Sir, Gerald said that you said my sister wouldn't be in danger. She's just window dressing. That's what he said you said. Sir."

"And I did say it," Sir Alec replied, his voice thin and distant. Then, steepling his fingers, he turned his head, just a little, to frown out of the office window. "But that was before I learned Lanruvia is attending the wedding."

"*Lanruvia?*" Monk swallowed, his heart knocking hard enough to crack a rib, surely. Because he was a Markham, and because his parents had always trusted him, he knew a lot more about a lot of things that most people had never heard of. Probably not even Gerald or Melissande knew what he knew about the deeply treacherous currents running through the waters of international thaumaturgical politics. "But why?"

"I don't know, Mister Markham," said Sir Alec, sounding grim. "But between us I am rather hoping we can find out. Because as doubtless you know . . . wherever Lanruvia treads, trouble is bound to follow."

With Sir Alec's alarming words of warning ringing in his ears, instead of returning directly to his cramped cubicle in Research and Development, Monk went home to the Markham mansion.

"Hello, Dodsworth," he said, as the butler stepped back from the front door to let him in. "Don't suppose my brother's about, is he?"

"He is, Mister Monk," said the butler warmly. "I believe you'll find him in the Octagonal Library."

"Then that's where I'll be, if you need me. Thanks."

"You're welcome, sir," said Dodsworth, pushing the heavy front door closed. "Have you eaten, sir, or can I bring you some luncheon?"

He nearly said *No, don't bother, I won't be here that long*, then changed his mind. He was ravenous, and lunch served from the Markham mansion's kitchen was infinitely preferable to what he could scrounge for himself back at R&D. Especially since he suspected that Dalrymple would've done his best by now to make sure there'd be nothing left worth eating in the cafeteria.

"Thanks," he said, and patted Dodsworth's stooped shoulder. "You're a scholar and a gentleman."

Dodsworth's smile was deprecating. "Neither, sir. But I'm sure it's kind of you to say so. I'll see you upstairs shortly."

Because he'd been expecting it, Aylesbury's lack of enthusiasm at his appearance didn't sting. Well, not much. Truth was, he was so used to it now that if his brother had evinced pleasure at seeing him he'd likely faint from the shock.

"You're still here, then," he said, closing the library door behind him.

Seated at the large reading table, Aylesbury shook his head without looking up. "My brother, ladies and gentlemen. Master of the obvious."

"Sorry. All I meant was that Bibbie mentioned your Aframbigi trip's been delayed. I hope that's not too awkward."

"Do you?" Aylesbury rested one finger on his place in the report he was reading and lifted his unenthusiastic gaze. "I can't imagine why."

As always, that undertone of mocking cynicism. But he couldn't let it distract him. Bibs and Melissande and Gerald were counting on Monk Markham to save the day.

"Anyway," he said, closing a little of the physical distance between himself and his brother. "Have you got a moment? I wanted to ask you something."

Aylesbury scowled. Because this was a business day he wasn't wearing his neck ruff and velvets, and his earlobe was empty of his favourite dropped pearl. Instead he looked like any ordinary wizard, in a plain charcoal grey suit and restrained dark red tie.

"Look, Monk," he said, not even attempting a cursory courtesy. "I might not be in the office, but that doesn't mean I've got time to lark about. With the Aframbigi trip on hold it means I'm back to juggling three other clients, all of whom are convinced the other two don't matter a toss."

Monk dropped into the nearest overstuffed leather reading chair. "It's important."

"So's this! Find someone else to pester."

It was hard, but he kept his temper in check. "Trust me, Aylesbury, if there was someone else I would. But it's you, or no-one. And this can't wait."

Intrigued despite himself, Aylesbury sat back and considered him with tightly narrowed eyes. "Fine. I'm listening. But not for long."

"Thank you," he said, managing to keep the sarcasm at bay. "So, what can you tell me about whispers from Lanruvia?"

"Lanruvia?" Aylesbury's eyes widened. Then he shrugged.

"Nothing. There haven't been any whispers. Not for years."

It wasn't the answer he wanted to hear. "Are you sure? I mean, your people have a lot of interests on the Andabedin Continent. And there's not much that escapes the notice of local businessmen and traders."

Aylesbury's lips pinched in annoyance. "Yes, Monk, I'm sure. What, d'you think I'm being untruthful?"

No. Not exactly. But ever since childhood, whenever Aylesbury found something his little brother wanted he did his best to make sure he never got it.

So maybe I do think he's lying. But really, is that fair? I mean, he's got no earthly reason to.

"Why d'you want to know, anyway?" said Aylesbury. "Nobody in their right mind crosses paths with a Lanruvian."

Ah. "It's a work thing. Someone mentioned something in passing and it tweaked my interest."

"Yes, well, I'll bloody well tweak you if you're not careful," Aylesbury retorted. "I've got better things to be doing than—"

"Please, Aylesbury," he said. "Indulge me, just this once."

Aylesbury laughed, his expression scornfully impatient. "No, Monk, I won't. There needs to be one person in the world who refuses to indulge the great Monk Markham."

This wasn't the time for one of their childish argy-bargies, so he throttled resentment. "*Please.*"

Clearly baffled, Aylesbury threw up a hand. "Fine. Ever since that near miss in '91, everybody within spitting distance of Lanruvia sleeps with one eye open. I promise you, little brother, those slippery buggers are minding their manners. You hardly see them around any more." He sneered. "But if you don't believe me, why not ask Uncle Ralph? In fact, why not ask him in the first place, instead of bothering me?"

"Because sometimes the last person to know what's happening in a place like Lanruvia is a man like Uncle Ralph."

Aylesbury drummed his fingers on the arm of his chair. "This isn't you pulling my leg, is it?" he said, after a moment. "You really are windy. Monk, what's going on? And don't give me that tripe about *something in passing*. It's more than that."

Yes, indeed, his brother was far from being a cabbage. "Ah . . ." Monk rubbed his chin. "Honestly, Aylesbury, I'd tell you if I could. I *will* tell you, once I'm cleared to. But in the meantime, could you keep an ear out for whispers about Lanruvia? Please? Because—"

He turned as the library door opened and Dodsworth entered carrying a large silver tray, on which were two covered plates and two glasses of red wine.

"Luncheon, gentlemen," the butler announced. "Might I place it on the large reading table?"

"Do what you like it with it," Aylesbury snapped, standing, and began shoving his reports into his briefcase. "I've a long-distance conference. I'll be in my private study. Don't disturb me unless one of Father's experiments blows the roof off. And as for Lanruvia—" He flipped the briefcase catches shut. "You should think about cultivating a few more contacts, Monk. Last time I looked I wasn't your dogsbody."

Monk watched his brother march out of the library, then sighed. Bloody typical. With Aylesbury, in the end everything was reduced to the personal. Trying not to mind, he turned to the butler.

"The large table's fine, Dodsworth. And since we now seem to have a spare serving, why don't you join me? There's no point letting good food go to waste."

Dodsworth hesitated. "Really, Mister Monk, that's most kind of you but—"

He slid off the arm of the chair. "Dodsworth, I insist. In fact, I'll not take *no* for an answer."

So Dodsworth set out the two plates, uncovered them, placed the covers and the silver tray out of the way, and joined him at the large reading table for a fragrant slice of Cook's best venison pie.

Grinning, Monk lifted his glass of wine in a toast. "Here's mud in your eye, Dodsworth."

"Indeed, sir," said the butler. "You are too kind."

Savouring his first gravy-rich mouthful of flaky pastry and meat, Monk was struck by a thought. *Can I? Should I? Sir Alec did make it clear it was results he cared about, not methods.*

And he doesn't strike me as being a snob . . . Besides, from the outside, life as the Markham family's butler looked awfully dull. He'd be doing their old family retainer a favour if he enlisted his help. Surely, after a lifetime of good care, he owed Dodsworth a little adventure in his old age.

And with Aylesbury so bloody unhelpful, I'm not sure I can do what Sir Alec wants without him.

"I say, Dodsworth," he said slowly. "You're a butler."

Dodsworth considered him gravely. "Indeed, sir. I am."

"And you know a lot of other butlers, don't you?"

"That I do, sir. Yes. Were you perhaps thinking of engaging a man for Chatterly Crescent, sir? If so I would be pleased to—"

"What? No!" he said, recoiling. His own butler? How ghastly. Bad enough he had to answer to Bibbie for his scattered socks. "No, this is something else. Look. All these butlers you know. I don't suppose any of them buttle at Ott's foreign embassies, do they, by any chance?"

Dodsworth gave him an old-fashioned look. "Ah—Mister Monk . . ."

"I'll take that as a yes," he said, grinning. "Right. Good. So, listen carefully Doddsy, my old chum. There's something important I need you to do."

Trying not to breathe too deeply, Gerald blinked the ceaseless sweat out of his stinging eyes. How much time had passed since he'd tripped this stinking entrapment hex? It felt like years . . . but he guessed it wasn't more than a couple of hours.

Oh, lord. The girls will be going spare.

He was going a bit spare himself, to be honest. The hex holding him was the most powerful of its kind he'd ever encountered. Every time he caught hold of one strand, started teasing it undone, the other strands tightened to strangling point. All this time fighting it, and he was exhausted. Defeated. Covered in wire-thin bruises. He could feel them, and see some of them, snaking round his wrists and between his fingers.

So much for being a rogue wizard. I'm an idiot, that's what I am. If only I'd listened to Sir Alec and left that grimoire magic where it was . . .

Because with his luck, the other Gerald had given him the perfect key to unlock this thaumaturgical door. But he'd never know now, would he? All he knew for certain was that no key lurked in the grimoire magic's remaining dregs. He'd looked. So he was trapped here, with every chance that the men responsible for his capture, for Abel Bestwick, were on their way back right now, eager to see what insect wriggled in their clever web. And when they found him, they'd kill him. Or worse.

Come on, Dunnywood, come on. Think what Errol Haythwaite would say if he could see you now. Think what Reg would say, or Monk, or Sir Alec. Think!

A tickle in the back of his empty, aching mind. Words, a memory, drifting dreamlike to the surface.

I know more than I did. I just don't know what I know. Y'know?

He'd said that to Monk, in the kitchen at Chatterly Crescent. A lifetime ago, or so it seemed.

I know more than I did. I just don't know what I know. Y'know?

Yes, all right, he'd said it. But what did it mean?

He knew what he was afraid it meant. He was afraid it meant that he *did* have the power to break free from this hex . . . but only if he crossed a terrible line. Because there was *using* the grimoire magic and there was *becoming* the grimoire magic. And lacking a specific hex, to escape his entrapment he'd have no choice but to embrace it so completely that he became it.

The thought terrified him.

But did he have a right to that fear? With so much at stake—a brave man missing, hurt, possibly murdered, two nations in peril, the threat of bloodshed spreading further as treaties and alliances dragged more nations into war—wasn't his fear a bloated self-indulgence that would cost more innocent lives?

He could hear Sir Alec, curt and impatient.

Yes, Mister Dunwoody. So what are you waiting for?

Help. Rescue. A last-minute miracle. Only this time they

weren't coming. No Reg. No Monk. No Melissande. No miracle. He was on his own. This time he'd have to rescue himself . . . or not.

And if it's not, if I choose to give in to fear . . .

Then chances were he'd destroy the world anyway. Or at least, this corner of it. Not directly, perhaps, but his inaction would make him responsible. And didn't he already have enough innocent blood on his hands? Hadn't he sworn an oath to himself?

Never again.

Fear to the left of him, terror to the right.

Pick your poison, Dunwoody. Pick your poison and drink.

With a stifled groan, Gerald sank into his rogue *potentia*. Glittering. Powerful. Welcoming. *Changed.* Still healing in so many places where Mister Jennings's extraction procedure had torn it apart. He brushed lightly against those tender scars and moved on, moved deeper, towards those new, dark places he'd tried so hard to deny. He could feel them. Taste them. Hear them singing in his blood.

There.

Eyes closed, his throat coated with fear, he fought the urge to turn tail and run. Fought it sweating. Fought it panting. The entrapment hex howled, constricting him so tightly he thought he'd be sliced to bloody pieces. A long way distant he heard someone whimpering. Swiftly realised it was himself. Ignored the pathetic sound.

The lingering grimoire magic was a black pool in his soul. With a silent, despairing cry he half-leapt, half-fell. Cried out again, in pain and wonder, as it closed over his head. Flooded him, burned him, and turned him to ice. He felt his rogue *potentia* flare. Felt every wounded place in it mend. Felt its melding and remaking as the remaining grimoire magics changed his *potentia* again, changing him into something new. Something more than a mere rogue wizard.

Oh, lord. What have I done?

Gerald opened his eyes . . . and was shocked to find that Abel Bestwick's small, wrecked coldwater kitchen looked exactly the same. The only thing different in it was him.

"Right," he said, and was surprised to hear he still sounded like Algernon Rowbotham. "To hell with this."

He took a deep breath and tensed every muscle in his body. Saw with his mind's eye the entrapment hex's binding filaments fly apart. A ripple, like a shadow crossing the sun. A sting of heat. A shiver of protest. The hex resisted, then gave way.

He was free.

Breathing slowly, though his heart raced, he waited for his roiled *potentia* to calm. When he was himself again—his new self—he lifted his hands. They were unblemished, the wire-thin bruises healed. The pain was gone, too. He felt stupendously alive. And he could see—he could see—

Bloody hell. I can see.

With *both* eyes, he could see. His blinded eye had been made whole again. The permanent reminder of that deadly battle with Lional and his dragon, of the little lizard life he'd taken, was vanished. Undone. As though it had never been.

But even as he started to laugh, an echo of dark thaumic energy struck him like an angry hand.

Elation vanished. He looked down at the floor, at the pieces of smashed crystal ball on the scarred timber before him. Not Abel Bestwick's doing, this destruction. The fingerprints here belonged to the wizard who'd crafted the entrapment hex. So. For whatever reason, Bestwick had left his crystal behind and his attacker—or maybe attackers, in his desperate message he'd said *they*—had smashed it out of spite.

But what if they'd managed to extract information from it first? What if they now knew that Bestwick had called someone. What if they knew *who?* What if—

He leapt to his feet. Knowing it was reckless, and not caring, he unleashed his full *potentia* and sought for enemies unseen.

Nothing. No-one. He was still safely alone.

Then he caught a hint of something else. Something new, yet somehow darkly familiar. Following instinct, he returned to the ruined living room and stood adrift in the mess. It was in here, he was certain. Whatever he'd missed the first time, it was here. He could feel it through the powerful deflection incant that had defeated him before—before—

Before I leapt without looking.

And yes. There it was. Embedded in the blood stains that had soaked and dried the old carpet. Kneeling again, Gerald hovered his fingertips above Abel Bestwick's blood. Let out a long, slow breath and opened himself to evil.

The grimoire magic inside him leapt to life, like to like.

"Dammit," he said softly, as his remade *potentia* rippled and writhed and his belly started to heave. "Oh, Bestwick. You poor bastard. How am I meant to help you now?"

CHAPTER TEN

S prawled face up on the guest chamber's ridiculously large, high bed, Bibbie flopped her arms wide, dangled her legs over the end of the counterpaned mattress and sighed, gustily.

"Honestly, Melissande. It's not much fun being cooped up in here. I thought this janitoring business was going to be *fun.*"

Melissande, peering into the room's ornate dressing mirror, held up one of her late mother's gold-and-emerald earrings and let it dangle beside her cheek.

"And *I* thought Hartwig would take one look at Gladys Slack and start drooling," she said, admiring the effect. "But he didn't. I wonder if there's something wrong with his eyes?"

"Since there's no way I can answer that without getting into trouble, I'm going to pretend I didn't hear you," said Bibbie. "Now can we please get back to—"

"No," she said, frowning at Bibbie's disgruntled reflection. "Because trust me, Miss Slack, nobody's having fun around here tonight, most especially me, since a whip and chair won't go with my gown and short of a whip and chair there'll be no way of keeping Hartwig at a decent distance at the reception. Not with gouty Brunelda still confined to her couch."

Bibbie hooted. "Oh, Mel. I'm sure you're exaggerating."

"Really?" Offended, Melissande slewed round on the padded crimson velvet dressing stool. "So you're saying you can't imagine Hartwig, or anyone else for that matter, getting— *carried away*—in my presence?"

Bibbie flopped her legs like a mermaid wondering where her tail had got to. "Don't be silly. But it's an official State Dinner, Melissande. The Crown Prince of Splotze isn't going to make a cake of himself in front of all those important guests." She sniffed. "Of which *I* am not one."

At moments like this it was hard to remember precisely *why* she was fond of Monk's sister. Just like Monk, Bibbie could be thoroughly obtuse, self-involved and *clueless*. It had to have something to do with being a genius. So much of the Markham siblings' intellect was occupied with being brilliant, it seemed there wasn't much room left for anything else.

"Of course you aren't invited to Hartwig's State Dinner," she said. "You're my lady's maid, remember?"

"Who's being relegated to the *Servants' Hall!*" Bibbie wailed.

"The Servants' *Ball* in the Servants' Hall," she corrected. "Personally, I think it sounds like fun. You'll get to eat food that's actually food, and kick up your heels in a jig afterwards, while *I'm* stuck sucking tadpoles' eyes off toothpicks then spending the rest of the night keeping Hartwig at a desperate arm's length while getting my toes trodden on in one dreary quadrille after another."

"Oh, Mel, *not* tadpoles' eyes! *Nobody* eats—"

She shuddered. "Trust me."

Unfortunately, Bibbie was feeling too hard done by to be properly sympathetic. "Yes, well, even with the tadpoles it's still a State Dinner, isn't it? And I've never been to one. Monk and Aylesbury have, but I'm always left out of things. That's the thanks I get for being born a *gel*. It's all right for you. You might be a gel too, but at least you're royal."

Melissande shook her head. Obviously Monk's sister hadn't been paying the least bit of attention to all those tales of life in New Ottosland.

"Believe me, Bibbie, you're better off as you are. Being royal is like living in a cage."

Bibbie made a rude sound. "Maybe, except from what I've seen it's a pretty swanky cage."

"Yes, perhaps, sometimes," she admitted, "but at the end of the day a prison's still a prison even if the bars are gilded."

"Well, if you hate the idea of this State Dinner so much, Your Highness, we could always swap places," said Bibbie, suddenly hopeful. "Monk and I once cooked up a wonderfully effective doppleganger hex. I'm pretty sure I remember it. We could—"

"No, Bibbie, we *couldn't!*" Exasperated, Melissande resisted an urge to throw the earring at her. "You don't know the first thing about behaving like a princess. You don't know anything about Hartwig. And you certainly don't know enough about me and Rupert and New Ottosland to fool him when he starts romping down memory lane, which I promise you he will."

"And whose fault is that?" Bibbie muttered. "I'd never even *met* your brother before—"

"Yes, and while we're on the subject of Rupert . . ." She fixed Monk's incorrigible sister with her best gimlet stare. "*What* was all that *flirting* about, back in New Ottosland? Honestly, Bibbie, I didn't know where to look! And as for poor Gerald . . ."

One of Bibbie's swift, impish grins lit up her altered face. "I know. Good, wasn't it? He got really *tetchy*. I thought for a moment he might actually turn grass green!"

"So you did all that flirting to make Gerald jealous? Using my brother?" she said, tossing the earring back in its velvet-lined box. "Emmerabiblia Markham! How *could* you?"

At least Bibbie had the grace to squirm. "But I had to do something, Mel. I mean, it was either make Gerald notice me by flirting with your brother or ask Reg to poke him in the unmentionables on my behalf. And while I know *our* Reg would poke him, I'm not nearly so sure how co-operative this new one is."

Melissande sprang off the dressing stool and relieved her feelings with some stamping about. "Right now I don't give two fat ferrets about the romantic adventures of Emmerabiblia Markham. If you *ever* put Rupert in that position again I'll—I'll—" Whipping round, she fisted her hands on her hips. "You do realise, I suppose, that he was halfway to taking you seriously?"

"Oh," said Bibbie, blinking. "Really? Well. That's awkward."

"It certainly is! Rupert might be a king, but he's not *sophisticated*, Bibbie." She thumped herself back on the dressing stool. "After growing up in Lional's shadow, and all those years of pretending to be a gormless dimwit, well, he's got some cosmopolitan catching up to do. Right now he's no match for feminine wiles. He's no match for *you*. And even if he were, that isn't the point! *Gerald* doesn't deserve to be treated like that, either. Really, Bibbie, it's too bad."

Bibbie's bottom lip trembled. "I thought you'd understand. I mean, Monk's just as hopeless. They're peas in a pod, those two, when it comes to admitting their feelings. And I *love* Gerald, Melissande. I can't imagine loving anyone else. So if I don't give him a gentle nudge, then what? I spend the rest of my life pining? Well, bollocks to that!"

Though she was still cross on Rupert's behalf, and Gerald's—and a little pricked by the uncomfortable reference to pining—she had to laugh. "Miss Slack! Such vulgarity from a royal lady's maid!"

But it wasn't really a laughing matter. The last thing this mission needed was romantic misunderstandings and bruised hearts getting in the way.

"Look . . . Bibs . . ." She sighed. "This isn't the time or the place for demanding declarations from Gerald. Sorting him out will have to wait till we get home. And even then, please, you must leave Rupert out of it. He has quite enough grief to be going on with, thanks to that old goat Lord Billingsley wheezing down his neck."

Disconsolate, Bibbie flopped again. "Fine. I'll wait. But if I die a spinster, Your Highness, I shall come back from the afterlife and make *your* life a bloody misery!"

Oh dear. Bibbie really was glum. Biting her lip, trying to think of something cheerful, Melissande was struck by a fortunate thought. "Actually, Bibs, I think you're missing something."

"Am I really?"

"Yes."

"About what, exactly?"

"Tonight, of course."

Propping herself up on her elbows, Bibbie squinted. "Well, don't keep me in suspense."

"Oh, Bibs, don't you see?" Melissande said, exasperated. "While I'm upstairs, dodging Hartwig and putting faces to names on the wedding guest list, you'll be downstairs, won't you? With Gerald. It's the perfect opportunity for you to show him first-hand that you're not a gel in need of his manly protection. In short, this evening gives you the best chance you've ever had to dazzle Gerald on his own turf."

"Oh, yes?" said Bibbie, still squinting. "And how am I s'posed to investigate an international-crime-in-the-making surrounded by bootboys and scullery maids?"

Melissande heaved another sigh. "Honestly, Bibs, don't be so obtuse. The Servants' Ball will be crawling with wedding guest minions, and minions always know who's doing what with whom and how often. But Gerald can't talk to so many people by himself, can he?"

"True," said Bibbie. Puffing, she wriggled herself upright and cross-legged on the billowy bed. "Go on."

Encouraged, Melissande waved her hands enthusiastically. "Well, then, Abel Bestwick's been here for years. He might be a janitor, but he'd hardly be human if he hasn't made at least one friend. You can make it your mission to find out who that is and what he or she knows. Gerald's success here could depend upon it. Imagine how impressed he'll be if you end up saving the day!"

Bibbie nibbled a fingernail, pondering the possibilities. "Yes," she said at last. "Except this mysterious friend— assuming he or she exists—might not know anything. I don't think it's likely Abel Bestwick would've blabbed janitor business, even to a friend. Can you see Sir Alec leaving an agent here alone for so long if he didn't know how to hold his tongue?"

No. Not at all. Stymied, Melissande slumped—then snapped up straight as fresh inspiration struck. "But he or she might not know that they know something important! And even if they don't, or even if there isn't a friend, *someone* has to have been the last person to see Bestwick in the palace before he bolted home to warn Sir Alec about the wedding. And that's your other job, Bibbie. Finding out who that is and getting him or her to confide in you."

"Confide in me?" said Bibbie, nonplussed. "Why the devil would some complete stranger want to pour out their secrets into my ear? I mean, yes, I s'pose I could encourage them a bit, I do know a rather effective little tittle-tattle hex, only Sir Alec did say—"

"And Sir Alec was right!" Melissande raised a warning finger. "Don't you dare try hexing people. You'll get us sent home in disgrace. Or worse, you could ruin things for Gerald."

"Which wouldn't endear me to him at all," Bibbie agreed. "Fine. No hexing. Only how am I meant to—"

She grinned. "Easily. The only thing royal servants enjoy more than a good gossip is having a good whinge about all the dreadful things we do to make their lives impossible."

"Ah," said Bibbie, impish again. "So all I have to do is start whinging about *you* and I'll have more confiding friends than I know what to do with?"

"Something like that," she said, beginning to wonder if this was a good idea after all. "But don't get carried away. Just start the ball rolling with some good, vigorous complaints and then throw in a few leading questions. Gently steer the conversation round to Abel Bestwick, and see what happens."

"Yes," said Bibbie, of a sudden looking uncertain. "But Mel, this is only going to work to my advantage if Gerald's there to see my brilliance in action. What if he insists on being upstairs with you? What if he invokes the wrath of Sir Alec if he's banished to the Servant's Ball with me and the other miniony riff-raff?"

"He won't," she said. "He can't. Algernon Rowbotham's no more invited to the State Dinner than Gladys Slack is. Gerald might want to go, but in the end he has to do what I say."

Bibbie's lingering frown scrunched into a scowl. "In that case, you can tell him to stop trying to protect me for my own good!"

Oh, lord. Best to squash such a dangerous thought here and

now. "I'm sorry, Bibbie, I can't," she said firmly. "Whatever's going to happen between you and Gerald will happen without me." She held up a hand, forestalling Bibbie's protest. "It's not that I don't want you to be happy. I do. But no good ever comes from friends meddling with friends in affairs of the heart."

"Really?" said Bibbie, plaintive again. "Are you sure?"

She folded her arms. "Positive."

"Yes . . . well . . ." said Bibbie. "I s'pose so."

Praise Saint Snodgrass. Another crisis averted. "Good. Now, come along, Miss Slack. The day is fast running away from us. Time for you to shake out my gown then run me a bath. Be sure you put lots of rose oil into it. If memory serves, Hartwig's allergic to roses. That might be my only hope."

"Blimey," said Bibbie, groaning, and flailed her way off the vast bed.

"That's Blimey, *Your Highness*, if you don't mind," said Melissande, very prim, and laughed as Bibbie made another rude noise.

Though she loved them dearly, the emerald earrings weren't going to suit. So while Bibbie excavated the wardrobe, Melissande fished around a bit more in her jewellery box. In the end she chose her great-grandmother's chandelier rubies. They were a nightmare to wear, all heavy gold and large-cut blood red stones, but they were the best fit with the gown she'd brought for the State Dinner. And what was a little pain, in the service of one's adopted country?

She put the earrings aside, ready for polishing, and turned to see Bibbie brandishing a dress at her. "It's this one, Mel, isn't it?"

This one was the blue-and-gold dinner gown that a lifetime ago she'd worn to Lional's coronation banquet. It was the only flattering gown she'd dared let herself possess, then, and she hadn't worn it since. Nearly threw it away, after—after everything changed—only it had cost a small fortune and since New Ottosland taxes paid for it, she couldn't bring herself to commit such waste.

"Yes, that's right, only please don't wave it about like a damp tea towel!"

"Sorry," said Bibbie, rolling her eyes. She shook out the folds of heavy silk, then laid the elaborately bead-and-crystal sewn dress over a plushly padded chair. "It's rather gorgeous, this. What a shame Monk's not here to see you in it."

Yes, wasn't it? The dress really was very becoming . . . but instead of a chance to bask in Monk's admiration, she was facing an evening of being boggled at by Hartwig. Bibbie was right. This janitoring business was turning out to be no fun at all.

"There," Bibbie said, and gave the expensive dress one last smoothing pat. "And now I'll go and stink up the place with oil of roses."

But instead of retreating to the guest suite's private bathroom, she wandered to the nearest window and peered down into the palace gardens far below.

"I wonder where Gerald's got to? He's been gone for ages. Don't you think he should be back by now?"

Yes, she did. "Perhaps he got lost," she said, trying to ignore a treacherous sizzle of nerves. "Grande Splotze is a bit of a sprawl, you know."

"Lost? Gerald?" Bibbie drummed her fingers on the windowsill. "You don't think he could've run into trouble, do you?"

Precisely because she *did* think it, because when it came to trouble Gerald was more attractive than honey to flies, she made a scornful tutting sound.

"No, of course I don't, Bibbie. After all, he's a rogue wizard. Wherever he is, I'm sure he's fine."

Dizzy with nausea, Gerald bent double over the nearest bit of refuse-clogged gutter and heaved up another burning mouthful of bile. It seemed that not even his newly enhanced *potentia* could protect him from the persistently lingering savagery of blood magic.

Head pounding, guts aching, he pressed his fists to his knees and slowly straightened. Where the devil was he? A long way from Abel Bestwick's wrecked half-house, that much he knew for sure. Otherwise . . .

Am I lost? Hell, don't let me be lost. I'll never hear the end of it if I am.

Splashed on the cracked cobblestones at his feet, more of Abel Bestwick's blood. The splotchy crimson trail had enticed him out of his fellow janitor's living room and into the alley behind the run-down lodging. Bludgeoned by the stench of blood magic he'd blindly followed the dried smears as they led him streets and streets away from the Canal and the centre of Grande Splotze, out to the ragged edge of the city's slummy district. The dwellings here were even more depressing and dilapidated than those in Voblinz Lane. If not for the occasional suspicious twitching of a curtain as he passed, he'd have thought them deserted.

"Dammit, Bestwick," he said, rubbing his belly. "Where *are* you?"

Balled in his pocket was one of the agent's dirty socks. Monk said you couldn't improve on a good, smelly sock when it came to a seeking. But even with that, and with the strongest locator hex he knew, Abel Bestwick remained stubbornly elusive. Sir Alec had warned him that field agents dosed themselves regularly with an *obscurata* incant but he'd not lost any sleep over that. He was Gerald Dunwoody, rogue wizard. Abel Bestwick had no hope of hiding from him! But it turned out his rogue status hadn't made any difference. Bestwick was gone, vanished like mist in sunlight.

Bloody hell. If I don't find him, Sir Alec really will go more than spare.

Throat tight with frustration, Gerald dropped to one knee in the filthy lane and touched his fingertips to Bestwick's dried blood. Then he held out his hand and waited for the answering tingle from the next splash, somewhere ahead.

Nothing.

"What?" he muttered, and tried again. *Come on, come on, come on.* But though he strained his senses to the point of fresh nausea, still he felt nothing. The trail had gone cold.

"*Dammit!*" he said, shoving to his feet. "Bloody, bloody, bloody—"

The sound of a front door opening behind him made him

turn. A skinny woman wrapped in an old, faded apron stood on the front step of her shambling, paint-peeling cottage, scrawny arms folded, thin face pinched with suspicion.

"You there," she said, accusing in rough Splotzin. "What's that you're up to? This idn't no place for strangers. Be off."

Praise the pigs. A sign of life. Wiping his hands down the front of his tweed coat, Gerald hastily rearranged his face into its gormless butterfly prince expression.

"Oh! Good day, madam! I'm sorry to bother you!" he said, switching languages, and crossed the lane towards her. "Only I'm looking for a friend of mine, and—"

The woman stepped back inside her cottage and slammed the door in his face.

"And I guess that means you can't help me," he finished. "*Damn*."

Uncertain, frustrated, he stared along the lane, willing Bestwick to magically appear. He didn't, the miserable bugger.

Just you wait, Bestwick. When I finally catch up with you, we're going to have words.

He blew out a harsh breath and looked at the sky, where the sun was slipping swiftly towards the unseen horizon. Damn. If he didn't get back to the palace soon the girls would likely send out a search party. But he couldn't go back empty handed. How was he meant to explain that to Sir Alec?

The grimoire magic that had healed his bruises, healed his ruined eye, seethed with quiet power under his skin. Waited for him to call on it, like a dragon tamed to his fist. Heart thudding, he pulled Bestwick's manky old sock from his pocket, closed his fingers around it, and let his eyelids drift shut.

Come on, Abel. We've got work to do. Come out, come out, wherever you are . . .

The grimoire magic lashed through him, dropping him to his knees. He scarcely felt the pain of skin and bone striking cobbles. Astonished, appalled, he wrestled it into submission. Channelled it into one last effort to find Sir Alec's missing man.

Fireworks exploded behind his eyes—and then, like Abel Bestwick, the world disappeared.

"All right," said Bibbie, pacing the guest bedchamber's plush carpet. "That's it. I'm going to look for him."

Freshly bathed, smelling of roses and wrapped in a quilted silk dressing gown, Melissande leapt to bar her way. "No, Bibbie. You can't."

"Melissande, I *have* to!" Eyes bright with tears, Bibbie fought back a sob. "I can't just sit here, not knowing what's happened! He could be bleeding in a gutter, or lying in a hospital, or—"

"Or on his way back right now without so much as a scratch," she said, and put a restraining hand on Bibbie's arm. "Bibs, if you kick up a fuss you could put him at risk. Is that what you want?"

"Don't be a *gudgeon!*" said Bibbie, wrenching free. "What I want is—"

They both startled at the loud knocking on the guest suite's front door.

"Gerald, for pity's sake, where have you *been?*" Bibbie demanded, as he pushed past her into the antechamber. "Mel and I are—"

"Shut the door, shut the *door*," said Gerald, glaring. "D'you want some passing housemaid to hear us?"

As Bibbie pushed the door closed, biting her lip, Melissande shook her head at him. "Gerald, I'm glad you're all right, but really, you can't be in here. What if—"

"I need your small green dressing case, Mel," he said, riding roughshod. His Algernon hair was all over the place, and there was dirt on his sleeves and hands and the knees of his tweed trousers. "Where is it?"

She stared. "My small green—Gerald Dunwoody, *what* is going on?"

"Dammit, Melissande!" he said, turning on her. "Just give me the bloody case!"

"It's in the bedchamber," Bibbie said, eyeing him warily. "I'll fetch it."

"Hurry," said Gerald.

Melissande folded her arms. "Whatever's happened, Gerald, snapping and snarling at us isn't going to help."

A fraught moment, and then his shoulders slumped. "You're right. I'm sorry."

"So, what have you hidden in my dressing case? I hope it's not that scaled-down First Grade staff Monk arranged for you. I haven't forgotten what it did to your ties."

He started to pace. "No. I was going to bring it but I changed my mind. *Bibbie!* Come on, I have to—"

"All right, all *right*," said Bibbie, hurrying back. "Honestly, Gerald, you're starting to sound like—"

Ignoring her, he snatched the dressing case from her grasp, undid its clasps and upended its contents onto the floor. A small, unfamiliar crystal ball rolled out of the embarrassing tumble of sensible camisoles.

Gerald snatched it up then turned. "Sorry, Mel, but I couldn't risk carrying it with me. There's always a chance of someone searching my things."

"It's all right," she said, completely unnerved by the look in Gerald's hexed eyes. "It's a direct link to Sir Alec, I suppose?"

"Yes," he said curtly, putting the ball on the antechamber's occasional table. "Now, if I thought there was any point trying to keep you two out of this I would, but since there's not, just stay still and quiet. What Sir Alec doesn't know won't hurt him or us."

A shared look with Bibbie, then Melissande nodded. "Fine."

"We'll be church mice, Gerald," Bibbie added, coming to stand with her. "Cross our hearts."

"You'd better," said Gerald, then activated the crystal ball. It fogged, then swirled a muddy, unpromising brown. He cursed. "Bloody Splotzeish etheretics. Come on, come on . . ."

Melissande chewed her thumb. "What's the matter?"

"The vibration won't settle."

"Can't you fix it?" said Bibbie.

"No," Gerald snapped. "Not even I'm strong enough to realign the etheretics of half a bloody continent. And what part of *be quiet* didn't you two understand?"

Oh, dear.

A few more moments and the etheretics settled enough, barely, for the crystal ball to establish a tenuous connection with Sir Alec.

"*Mister Dunwoody. Report.*"

"Sir Alec," said Gerald, his voice tight and oddly formal. "Bestwick's not in his lodging, and he didn't leave anything helpful behind. But I'm afraid that whoever attacked him did. When they left 45b, they were tracking him. With blood magic."

Bibbie stiffened, swallowing a gasp.

In the small crystal ball, Sir Alec's face blurred and wavered.

"*Blood magic? Mister Dunwoody, are you sure?*"

"I threw up four times following the blood trail Bestwick left behind him," said Gerald. "And I've still got a splitting headache. So, yes. I'm pretty sure."

"*I take it you've no idea of Bestwick's current location?*"

"No, sir. The trail went cold a mile or so from Voblinz Lane. Either he managed to stop the bleeding or he found transport out of the area."

"*Or his attackers caught up with him. Or—*"

"Yes," Gerald said heavily. "Or he died, and his body's either not been discovered or it's lying unclaimed in the Grande Splotze morgue. But if he is still alive, sir, then he could be anywhere by now. I'm sorry."

"*Not your fault,*" said Sir Alec. "*By the time I—*"

The rest of his reply was lost in a sparkly etheretic snowstorm. When it cleared a few moments later, Sir Alec's voice was uncharacteristically alarmed.

"*—hear me, Mister Dunwoody?*"

"Yes, sir, you're back," said Gerald. "But I don't know for how long."

"*When do you leave on the wedding tour?*"

"The day after tomorrow. I'll keep looking for Bestwick between now and then."

"*Without raising suspicions?*" said Sir Alec, skeptical. "*Algernon Rowbotham has no good reason to be poking about the Grande Splotze morgue.*"

"I have to do something. I can't just—"

"*Yes, you can, Mister Dunwoody. Right now we're playing a waiting game. Overplay your hand and this will end in tears.*"

Pinching the bridge of his nose, Gerald came to terms with harsh reality. "Yes, sir. Sir, blood magic hexery isn't what you'd call common—or legal. Have you got someone who can start nosing out any wizards capable of supplying it?"

In the crystal ball, Sir Alec's face broke apart, then reformed. "*I'll task Mister Dalby. It's not like he has anything better to do.*"

His weary scorn was hurtful to hear.

"Ask Monk," Gerald suggested. "He's a dab hand at solving thaumaturgical puzzles."

"*I'll see,*" said Sir Alec, unenthusiastic. "*At the moment Mister Markham is—*"

Another burst of etheretic static. It took longer to clear this time.

"Sir, this connection's about to clap out for good," Gerald said quickly, then tugged a small square of bloodstained carpet from his inside coat pocket. "I've got a sample of the hex. I'll send it to Uncle Frederick tomorrow."

"*Good,*" said Sir Alec. "*And in the meantime, keep me informed of—*"

"Uncle Frederick?" said Bibbie, once they'd given up hoping the connection to Sir Alec would re-establish. "That's a secret Department address, I suppose?"

Nodding, Gerald shoved his ghastly souvenir back inside his patchily stained tweed coat. "Yes. I don't want a portal record of anything going directly to Nettleworth."

"No," said Bibbie. Then she shivered. "Blood magic. Gerald, whoever's behind this . . . they really mean trouble, don't they?"

He gave her a look. "Did you think the threat would turn out to be a prank?"

"I hoped it might. Because now it means other people really could get hurt."

"People like you and Melissande," he said, frowning. "Hell. I wish you hadn't come."

As Bibbie took a breath, ready to argue, Melissande put a warning hand on her arm. "But we did, Gerald, so that's that.

Look—" She cleared her throat. "Are you all right? I don't mean to fuss, but you've gone rather green about the gills."

Gerald dragged a hand over his disordered hair. "I'm fine. Tracking Bestwick took it out of me, that's all. That blood magic, it's filthy. Five minutes to catch my breath and I'll be right as rain."

Frowning at him, she wasn't so sure of that, but this wasn't the time to argue. "Yes, well, I'm afraid five minutes is all you've got. So you'd best hurry back to your own room. It's almost time to go downstairs, and you can't escort Bibbie to the Servant's Ball looking like a goat-herder."

With a tired smile, Gerald clicked his heels. "Yes, Your Highness. Your wish is my command."

"I don't like this, Mel," said Bibbie, as the door closed behind him. "He's not telling us everything. I can feel it."

"Probably he isn't," she agreed, "but whatever you do, Bibbie, you mustn't nag. Right now Gerald's not our friend, he's Sir Alec's secret agent, and he can't afford to be distracted."

Distressed, Bibbie was shaking her head. "But—"

"*No*, Bibbie. No buts," she said, in her best royal highness voice. "Now come along. It's time to get dressed."

CHAPTER ELEVEN

The house on Chatterly Crescent felt horribly empty without Bibbie, Melissande and Gerald for company. To Monk, it didn't matter that Melissande didn't actually live there. The point was, she'd long since fallen into the pleasant habit of dropping by three or four times a week, so it felt like she lived there, and now there was a great big Melissande-shaped hole beneath the old mansion's roof.

"Blimey," said Reg, perched on the back of a kitchen chair. "It's a bit bloody quiet around here, isn't it?"

Half-heartedly smiling, he looked up from the range, where he was trying not to fry eggs and bacon into lumps of greasy charcoal.

"You're reading my mind, Reg."

The bird rattled her tail feathers, then balanced on one foot so she could scratch the side of her head. "And there was me thinking I could do without all the domestic drama." She sniffed. "Fancy being wrong at my time of life. It's enough to bring on a case of the dropsicals."

"I didn't think birds could contract the dropsicals."

"Ha! Rumours of my aviosity have been greatly exaggerated." A moment's brooding silence, then Reg shuffled a bit. "That manky Sir Alec of yours. He'll tell us if Splotze goes pear-shaped, will he?"

Wonderful. Trust Reg to stick her beak right into his imagination's sore spot. Moodily, Monk poked at his crisping bacon. "Of course."

"Because I wouldn't put it past that bugger to keep his trap shut. His kind swallow secrets the way toddlers guzzle gumdrops."

"You're wrong, Reg," he insisted, then prodded his frying eggs so hard he breached their wobbling yellow yolks. Damn. "But he won't have to. Splotze won't go pear-shaped. Not with Gerald on the job. And the girls."

"'Course not," said Reg, being valiant. "I don't doubt it for a moment."

Except she did, and so did he. Feeling cross and put upon, he fetched a plate and tipped his messy bacon and eggs onto it. Then he fetched Reg's minced beef from the larder ice box and placed both suppers on the comfortably scarred kitchen table, which was supposed to have three more places set at it—and didn't.

"Brandy?" said Reg hopefully, hopping down from the chair.

Monk thought about it, tempted, then shook his head. "Not with bacon and eggs. Or raw mince, for that matter. Besides . . ." He slid into his own chair and picked up his knife and fork. "Between you and me and the wine cellar, I think we've all of us been imbibing a bit too freely of late."

"Ha!" said Reg, with an indignant ruffling of feathers. "Speak for yourself!"

"Look, Reg," he said, sighing. "I know you're feeling frazzled. I am, too. But brandy won't help. We just need to be patient."

"If I'm frazzled," Reg said, glaring at her minced beef, "you can blame that manky Sir Alec. He should've let me go with them."

With an effort Melissande would've admired, Monk restrained himself from throwing the salt cellar at the damned bird.

"As I've already agreed, more than once, probably he should've, yes. But he didn't, Reg, which is typical and let's face it, not surprising. So let's leave the poor dead horse alone, shall we?"

Reg's feathers fluffed again "I bet he'd have let the other Reg go with them."

Oh. Well. *Really* damn. He'd been hoping she wouldn't reach that conclusion. Because while he couldn't say for certain, what with Sir Alec being a right unchancy bastard and not inclined to share his inner thoughts, he also knew first-hand that the man was unpredictable. Sending Bibbie to Splotze? He hadn't seen *that* one coming. So yes . . . it was entirely possible he'd have sent the other Reg along as part of Gerald's unlikely team. But it wouldn't help to tell this Reg as much.

All of a sudden it was very important that he concentrate on cutting his bacon strips into handy bite-sized pieces.

"Well?" Reg said, belligerent. "Don't just sit there massacring those charred bits of dead pig. Answer me! He would've, wouldn't he?"

Lord, if only Melissande was here. She knew exactly what to say when the bird started one of her rants.

And to think I was going to work late and changed my mind. Why didn't I work late? I'd rather face Dalrymple than the bird's inquisition, any day.

He sighed. "Reg . . ."

"*Yes*, he bloody well would've," said Reg, determined not only to beat the dead horse but to bounce up and down on its corpse for good measure. "And what's more, even if he'd *tried* to keep her out of it, I'll bet that other Reg wouldn't have let him, would she? She'd never have taken no for an answer. Come on, Mister Markham. It's an easy question. In fact, I've already answered it. Doing all the work here, I am. That other Reg—"

"Is dead," he said quietly, and tried to ignore the ache in his throat. "So it doesn't matter what she would or wouldn't have done, or what Sir Alec might or might not have allowed, does it? She's dead and you're not. Now if you don't mind, Reg, I'd like to finish my supper. Cold fried egg gives me wind."

"Sorry," said Reg, after a short, subdued silence. "I don't mean to upset you. I know I'm not—I know I can't—well. Sorry."

And that was the most alarming thing of all, hearing her small and pained and uncertain. Saying sorry in that tiny voice, and meaning it. *Reg.* It brought back the dreadful memory of her dead twin, stuffed in that horrible cage, the other Gerald's helpless prisoner.

"No, Reg, *I'm* sorry," he said, letting his knife and fork drop. "There's no point pretending this situation isn't bloody awkward, because it is, but I don't want you feeling like you have to apologise because you're alive. I never want to hear you apologise for that." He let out a sharp breath, feeling a tremble in his gut. "It's not your fault she's dead."

Head tipped to one side, Reg regarded him with a disconcertingly knowing gaze. "No. And it's not yours that *he's* dead. That other Monk."

The tremble in his gut tightened into a pain. "Yeah, okay, look—"

"No, Mister Markham, you look," said Reg, with a sharp rattle of her tail. "I might not be her, but that doesn't make me blind or stupid. You need to stop breaking your heart over what happened, sunshine, because there was no saving him. That other Monk. Believe you me, his Gerald was always going to kill him sooner or later. It's just your bad luck he ended up dying here."

The memory of the other Monk's cruel death, still raw, still too near, closed his aching throat.

"So what say we start over," said Reg, her careful gaze not shifting from his face. "No more wallowing in yesterday. No more flogging corpsed horses. They're dead, we're not, and life carries on."

It sounded horribly heartless, put baldly like that. But she was right. Short of creating a thaumaturgically transduced temporal slipshift, recent events could not be undone.

And while that might be doable, maybe, not even I'm mad enough to give it a go.

"Agreed," he sighed. "We'll start over, starting now. Only . . ." He impaled a piece of crispy bacon on the end of his fork. "I'm not so sure about Gerald. If he can put it all behind him, I mean. That leftover grimoire magic? I'm telling you, Reg, he's so scared of the filthy stuff he can hardly see straight. He's scared of himself. And I'm worried he'll—"

She chattered her beak. "Just you leave that boy to me. Because here's what I know, if I don't know anything else: whichever Reg I am, sunshine, first and foremost he's my Gerald. And I'll bloody well set myself on fire before I let him go the way of that other one."

Whatever she'd been once, human, a witch queen, with possibly dubious powers, she was a frail, vulnerable bird now. More vulnerable than ever, given her ordeals in that other world. Even so, Monk felt bolstered by her stark declaration. More and more he was coming to believe that in her heart, where it counted, despite all the differences, she was still *Reg*.

He nodded. "Good. But when he gets back from Splotze, I think you and I need to—"

They both turned their heads at the sound of the front door bell, deeply chiming.

"Bugger," said Reg. "Expecting visitors, are you?"

As he pushed back his chair, the door bell chimed again. "No. You?"

"Ha," she snorted. "Very funny. Now go see who that is before they break the bloody bell."

He opened the front door to find his brother scowling on the welcome mat. "It's about time. What are you, Monk? Deaf?"

"Aylesbury," he said stupidly. "Was I expecting you?"

With a roll of his eyes, Aylesbury shoved past him into the shabby foyer. "How should I know what you're expecting? You can't even answer your own front door in a timely manner."

Bugger. It was turning into one of those kind of nights. Resigned to aggravation, Monk closed the door and trailed after his brother, who was acquainted enough with Great-uncle Throgmorton's old house that he didn't need to ask directions to the parlour.

"Do help yourself to a drink, Aylesbury," he said, entering the large, comfortably untidy room.

His brother was already pouring a generous measure of brandy into a glass. A swift quirk of one eyebrow was his only response to the sarcasm. Without asking if he could pour his host a drink, too, he downed the brandy, sploshed another generous measure into the glass, then turned.

"So. Lanruvia. Seems I was a trifle . . . behind the times. Apparently they're dipping their toes into murky waters again."

Oh, lord. Monk crossed to the drinks trolley, poured himself three fat fingers of fermented peach and swallowed all of them in one go.

"What kind of murky waters?" he said hoarsely, as the brandy ignited a trail of fire down his throat and into his almost empty belly.

Aylesbury began an aimless wandering of the parlour. "I was pretty bloody peeved, you know, when Throgmorton handed you this place," he said, his gaze roaming the faded wallpaper and the tatty carpet and the wide, curtain-covered windows. "He knew I wanted it. That's why you got it, of course."

Monk said the only thing he could think of. "Sorry."

"Of course you are." Aylesbury sipped more brandy, then smiled one of his small, sardonic smiles. "Bet the old codger's spinning in the family sepulchre as we speak, knowing our dear little sister's taken up residence. Assuming he does know." Another smile. "We can but hope."

Monk considered his brother. Aylesbury in his day-to-day work clothes was always more approachable than the brother who aped a lost age in velvets and neck ruff. And he had driven all the way out here with news of Lanruvia. That counted for something, surely. Meant there was maybe some hope for them to be more than impolite strangers. So perhaps, just this once, they might find common ground.

"Aylesbury . . . why aren't we friends?"

Aylesbury choked on his brandy, then laughed. "Because you're a pillock."

Or possibly not. "I don't mean to be."

"And snakes don't mean to be poisonous, but they'll still kill you."

"You think I'm a *snake?*"

"I think you're a spoiled brat, Monk," Aylesbury said, shrugging. "I think you're so used to being fawned over as a genius you can't imagine being wrong or not entitled to adoration. Everything you want, you get. You always have. You always will. You break the rules, you're winked at. You ignore the rules, you're winked at. You make up your own rules, you're winked at. Your path's strewn with roses and the rest of us walk in shit." Another shrug. "That's what I think."

Monk blinked. His brother's indifferent dislike hurt, far more than he expected. Or wanted. "And yet you came to tell me about Lanruvia."

"Yes, I did."

"Why?"

Hitching his hip against the back of the old sofa, Aylesbury gestured vaguely. "You asked. Besides, I like those Lanruvian bastards even less than I like you."

He put down his empty brandy glass. "You still haven't told me what kind of murky waters they're splashing about in."

"That's because I don't know," said Aylesbury. "Not exactly. Nobody likes to talk about Lanruvia, Monk. The folk who have regular dealings with them know what happens to gossips."

"But you've heard something, you must have," he insisted. "Or you wouldn't be here."

"I've heard two things," Aylesbury admitted, after a teasing pause. "The first is that we had an enquiry about locating and shipping a thaumicle extractor to Maneez."

"Well . . ." Monk frowned. "Extractors are restricted, sure, but Maneez is on the approved list of purchasers."

"Maneez is, but Lanruvia isn't. And at the Trade Fair in Budolph week before last, I saw with my own eyes the Maneezi and Lanruvian delegates being very friendly."

"And that's unusual, is it?"

Aylesbury snorted. "No, Monk, I'm mentioning it because them hobnobbing in corners happens every bloody day of the week."

"Right. Sorry." He chewed at his lip. "And what was the other thing?"

"They got an invite to the Splotze-Borovnik wedding."

Distracted by the unsettling notion of the Lanruvians

mucking about with thaumicle extractions, he nodded. "Yeah, I know."

"You *know?*" Lips tightening, Aylesbury stared into his unfinished brandy. Then he finished it and slapped the emptied glass onto the nearest table. "I see. Doubtless Uncle Ralph, or one of his government cronies, mentioned it to you in passing. As they do. All the time. Must be nice, not to mention warm, hugging all those terribly important secrets to your skinny chest."

Damn. Monk took a step towards him. "Aylesbury, I'm sorry. I'd tell you what's going on if I could, but—"

Up came his brother's hands, in mock-entreaty. "No, no, that's quite all right. Wouldn't want Ottosland compromised, would we? Wouldn't want *you* compromised. Not *you*, the great and mysterious Monk Markham. No—don't bother. I can see myself out."

Stranded in the parlour, Monk flinched as the front door slammed shut. Then a flapping of wings, and Reg was gliding into the room. She landed on the back of the sofa and looked pointedly at the two empty brandy glasses.

"He's a bit of a plonker, your brother, isn't he?"

"You were eavesdropping?"

Reg's dark eyes gleamed. "I was holding myself in readiness in case fisticuffs broke out."

"Thank you. I think."

"You're welcome. Well? Was him dropping by worth letting your dinner get cold?"

Groaning, Monk collapsed into the nearest armchair. "I've no idea. But I'll pass on what he said. Perhaps Sir Alec can make sense of it."

"And speaking of that Department stooge," said Reg, her feathers fluffing with disdain, "he's left a message for you in your crystal ball. The one in the kitchen. Didn't sound particularly urgent but then you never can tell with that cagey bugger, can you?"

To hell with dignity. He ran out of the room, Reg flapping behind him.

The message was short and sweet. "*Contact me via this*

vibration." Because dealing with Sir Alec required razor sharp reflexes, and there was too much brandy sloshing about in his belly, he ate what remained of his cold bacon—it looked like Reg had helped herself while his back was turned, drat her—then activated his crystal ball.

"*Ah. Mister Markham,*" Sir Alec greeted him, looking washed out and weary but no more worried than usual, which was a relief. "*Good. You're free to talk?*"

"Yes, sir. Sir, is everything all right?"

"*Not really,*" said Sir Alec, very dry. "*Mister Dunwoody reports that Abel Bestwick appears to have met with some thaumaturgical foul play. Which means, Mister Markham, I need you to brush up on blood magic hexes. I should shortly have a sample for you to unravel.*"

Blood magic? Monk swallowed bile. Hell, what was Gerald mixed up in this time? And Bibbie . . . and Melissande . . .

And if Sir Alec can give me a heads up about blood hexes and not be looking more worried than usual, what does that say about a typical day in his Department?

Nothing he wanted to think about too closely.

"Yes, sir. I can do that. Only—" Deep breath, take the plunge. "Sir, blood magic hexes are pretty dicey. I'm not sure I like the idea of my sister—"

"*Your sister is in no danger, Mister Markham.*"

"Not yet."

"*You have my word she'll be extracted should circumstances merit.*"

Which was nice of him, but no guarantee. "Sir Alec—"

Sir Alec's etheretically transmitted face tightened with temper. "*Mister Markham, I refuse to argue this with you every time we have occasion to speak. Miss Markham is a gifted thaumaturgist who accompanied Mister Dunwoody of her own free will. I strongly suggest you stop thinking of her as a helpless gel made victim of my nefarious machinations.*"

Perched on the back of a handy chair, Reg rattled her tail feathers. "He might be a Department stooge, sunshine, but he's right. That giddy sister of yours is no fainting Fanny. So get a bloody grip."

Sir Alec's lips twitched. "*Indeed.*"

Feeling unfairly ambushed, Monk threw Reg a hurt look. "Yeah, well, gifted or not, Bibbie's safety is still my responsibility!"

"*No, Mister Markham,*" said Sir Alec, very quiet. "*Until the Splotze mission is concluded, the responsibility is mine.*"

Oh. Monk closed his mouth. Even through the etheretics of crystal ball communication, he could see something daunting in Sir Alec's grey eyes . . . and was surprised to feel his fears for Bibbie easing.

He nodded. "Yes, sir. Sir, there's something else. I have news about Lanruvia."

Gerald's unsettling superior listened without interruption, then frowned. "*You consider your brother's sources reliable?*"

"I don't know who his sources are, Sir Alec. But I do know Aylesbury. He wouldn't have told me if he didn't think the whisper was true."

"Even if he is a plonker," Reg added. "And he bloody well is."

Again, Sir Alec's lips twitched. "*Mister Markham, what progress have you made with the wedding guest list?*"

Should he mention Dodsworth, and the butler's efforts on his behalf? Probably not. What Sir Alec didn't know wouldn't hurt Monk Markham.

"None yet, sir. Soon, I hope."

"*As do I, Mister Markham.*"

"Sir Alec, what does it mean if the Lanruvians really are trying to get their hands on a thaumicle extractor?"

"*It means, Mister Markham, that we will be obliged to thwart their efforts.*"

Yeah. Right. Just like that. "I see."

"*Do you? How encouraging. Good night, Mister Markham.*"

Reg chattered her beak. "Blimey, but he's a sarky bugger! No wonder my Gerald ended up—"

"Ended up what?" said Monk, eyeing the remains of his cold fried egg with distaste.

"Never mind," said Reg, and fluffed all her feathers. "Now come along, sunshine. Either finish your dinner or bin it, because we've got work to do. I've forgotten more about blood magic than anyone else you know, so you can pin back your ears and get an education. All right?"

"All right," he said slowly. "But I think I ought to ask *how* it is you—"

"No," said Reg. "You really oughtn't. Not if you want to sleep tonight."

And on that trenchant note she flapped out of the kitchen. Monk binned his cold fried egg, and followed.

The Servants' Hall in Grande Splotze's palace was enormous. Buttoned into his precisely selected dinner suit—not too care-worn, not too sleek, designed to reflect well upon his royal employer without hinting at undue largesse—Gerald waited in a slowly shuffling line with Bibbie to be formally admitted, and looked ahead into what he could see of the crowded room. How mad was it, anyway, such a sprawling space? So many servants? Splotze's royal family was of middling size, as far as royal families went. Surely they couldn't need so many people catering to their every whim? Two hundred and twelve, according to the briefing notes.

Two hundred and twelve people whose lives and livelihoods hang on Hartwig's slightest whim. I don't know how they bear it.

Standing beside him, masked by Gladys Slack, Bibbie remained her beautiful, brilliant self. He felt a cold chill run down his spine. If only there was a way to send her home. After Abel Bestwick's lodgings . . . the entrapment hex . . . the blood magic . . . this mission could spin out of control at any moment.

Leaning close, Bibbie brushed her cheek against his shoulder. "What's wrong?"

His heart thumped. "Nothing."

"Really?" Bibbie murmured. "You're going to keep on trying to fool me? That is a waste of time, Mister Rowbotham. You're still upset. And you're walking differently. Did something else happen while you were out? Are you hurt?"

Her soft questions set his pulse racing. "Hurt? No."

"I don't believe you."

The line shuffled forward, and they shuffled with it.

"I'm fine," he insisted, even though it was a lie. His dragon magic slept lightly, a shallow breath beneath his skin. But she couldn't be feeling its presence. His shield was up. He was hidden, even from her. "Miss Slack, this isn't the time or place."

"Then make the time and choose a place," she said, her fingers tightening on his arm. "Because I am not—the princess. You can't fob me off with vague assurances and half-truths."

So many fellow-guests, crowded in front of them and behind. He couldn't shout at her, couldn't wave his arms and splutter. The most he could do was snap, "*Miss Slack*."

Bibbie dropped her hand and eased herself away from him. "I'm just saying."

Yes, she was . . . in her inimitable Bibbie style. Damn, how did she know always what he was thinking and feeling? And how was it she could make his heart leap even when she didn't look like Emmerabiblia Markham? But she could. She did. She was doing it now. It wasn't her face, it was her. The sheer *Bibbieness* of her, that shone through no matter what face she was wearing.

I saw what she could be, in that other Ottosland. What she might become, the worst flaws in her magnified . . . just as I saw all the worst parts of me. So how is it I'm not afraid of her the way I'm afraid of myself?

And he was afraid, now more than ever. After today, there was no going back. Not even Monk would be able to suck the grimoire magic out of him after what he'd done. It was his blood, his bones, the air he breathed. His life.

Bugger. Monk's going to go spare.

The line shuffled forward a few more paces. And yes, he was walking differently. He could feel it. With two good eyes again, his depth perception had returned to normal. Perhaps that explained the nagging ache in his head.

Or perhaps it doesn't. Perhaps I'm on the brink of thaumaturgical chaos . . .

No. No. He couldn't afford to think like that. He had a job

to do. A wedding to save. A few more minutes and he'd be up to his armpits in suspects. Well, possible suspects. Or possible sources of information that would lead to the thwarting of the plot against Splotze and Borovnik.

His heart thudded again, but not because of Bibbie. Lord, could he do this? Could he prevent yet another international disaster? He'd averted calamity three times already, that was true, but only by accident. He'd stumbled into those other crises unwittingly. What if he wasn't up to this task? Had Sir Alec lost his marbles, sending grimoire-tainted Gerald Dunwoody to Splotze? The whole bloody set up was so *nebulous*. And now with the discovery of that filthy blood magic, far more lethal than surely even Sir Alec had guessed, so much hung in the balance. There were so many dangerous knives to juggle, and he had the girls to worry about . . .

Hell's bells, I wish Reg was here.

Probably he should be flattered that Sir Alec had such trust in him. He should take it as a compliment and use his superior's confidence as a shield. Instead he felt crushed by the responsibility. The possibility of failure.

Besides, will he still trust me when he finds out what I've done? When he learns I'm no longer a simple rogue wizard?

A hand on his arm. He looked down, seeing not Gladys Slack but Bibbie Markham. His Bibbie. The girl he loved, and could never fear. She was staring at him with such an intent look in her changed eyes.

"Wherever you are, Algernon, it's time to come back," she whispered fiercely. "Whatever's wrong, we can fix it. But we'll have to fix it later."

She was right, Saint Snodgrass bless her. So he found a small, proper smile for her, royal secretary to lady's maid, then stepped up to the very stiff, very formal Splotze official barring their way into the Servants' Hall.

"Names?" the official said, looking down his large, Splotzeish nose.

Gerald cleared his throat. "Mister Algernon Rowbotham and Miss Gladys Slack, attached to Her Royal Highness Princess Melissande of New Ottosland."

The Splotze official looked for their names on his clipboard. "Ah. Yes." A reserved, thin-lipped smile. "Of course. On behalf of the Crown Prince and Princess, welcome to Splotze. Enjoy your evening."

Shrinking into herself, Bibbie bobbed the official a shy curtsey. "Oh, that's ever so kind of you, sir. Thank you. I'm sure we'll have a wonderful time."

"Yes," Gerald added, wishing he could kick Bibbie's ankle. "It was good of you to ask us. Come along, Miss Slack. Let's not hold up the line."

As soon as they'd entered the crowded Servants' Hall, Bibbie tugged at his sleeve.

"*Right*," she said, abandoning demure Gladys Slack. "So you take *this* side of the room, I'll take *that* side, and between us we should be able to talk to everyone here before the end of the night. And don't forget to keep an eye on me, because if I find someone you need to talk to, I'll give you a sign. All clear? Good. Then off we go!"

And before he could stop her, or sharply remind her that hello, he was the only janitor here, and she wasn't meant to be drawing attention to herself, or him, she'd plunged into the jostling crowd of staff and servants, leaving him with no choice but to do as he was told.

Wonderful. Thanks ever so, Sir Alec.

He took a moment to make sure of his etheretic shield, rearranged his altered features into an expression of non-threatening, slightly bucolic pleasantness, turned to the nearest Splotze-liveried minion and beamed.

"I say there. Good evening. I'm Algernon Rowbotham, from New Ottosland. What a perfectly splendid shindig. And if might I ask, sir, who are you?"

CHAPTER TWELVE

"Yes, yes, I couldn't agree more." Eyes brightening, the Marquis of Harenstein snatched a crab puff from a passing servant's silver tray and engineered it into his walrus-moustachioed mouth. "This is indeed an auspicious occasion," he added indistinctly, spraying a fine shower of pastry crumbs. "In fact, my dear—" A frown. "I'm sorry. *Who* are you again?"

Melissande smiled. *Tosser.* "Princess Melissande, Your Grace. King Rupert of New Ottosland's sister."

The Marquis of Harenstein's frown deepened. "New Ottosland . . . New Ottosland . . . oh, yes! Little patch of green in the middle of a desert, where Ottosland dumped its unwanted aristocracy and other assorted riff-raff. And you're sister to its king, are you? Don't think I've met him. Is he here?"

"No," she said, still smiling. Or perhaps her face had frozen into a rictus of horror. "I have the honour of representing New Ottosland on His Majesty's behalf."

Another tray of pastries squeezed by. With a grunt of pleasure, the marquis snatched again. "You simply *must* try one of these, y'know, my dear. Deep fried Harenstein goose paté topped with our finest Hidden Sea caviar. Delicacies, I promise you. A gift from Harenstein to the happy couple. One of many. No expense spared to celebrate the glorious event."

Melissande took the smallest appetiser on the tray then nibbled as little as possible from around its edges. The marquis inhaled his with gusto, and swiped a second one just as the tray was about to be swallowed by the press of chattering, drinking, eating guests.

I wonder if Hartwig's invited any doctors? she thought, torn between dismay and fascination at the marquis's inexhaustible appetite. *Because at this rate we're going to need one.*

The next servant to appear carried a drinks tray. The marquis pursed his lips, disappointed, then soothed his pique with a slender flute of something pale yellow and bubbly. Melissande followed his example, needing the fortification, and managed to surreptitiously toss her paté and caviar onto the tray before it moved on.

Oh, lord. This is going to be the longest night of my life.

And to think she'd not even attempted to chat with the Lanruvians yet, which she would do as soon as they arrived. Not that Gerald wanted her to. He'd turned practically beet red at the suggestion. But given the looming shadow of Abel Bestwick's disappearance, with everything horrible *that* implied, she couldn't afford to worry about threats of retribution by Sir Alec. Besides, she had the sneaking suspicion that while he claimed to want her safely sidelined, in truth Sir Alec was relying on her to do whatever she could to assist Gerald and, to her complete surprise, she realised she didn't want to disappoint him. Sir Alec might be chilly, self-contained and ruthlessly pragmatic, but he was also a good man. A man who, despite his flaws and under different circumstances she might have called a friend.

Which was more than she could say for the Marquis of Harenstein. He was complaining about the slow service, now.

"Yes, yes, it is terribly poor," she said, with all the sympathy she could muster. "I wonder, Your Grace, could you tell me the story behind this fairytale wedding between Prince Ludwig and Princess Ratafia? It's been very clever of you, a stroke of genius, really, to bring them together in wedded bliss. However did you manage it?"

The Marquis of Harenstein's broad chest swelled alarmingly with pride. "Why yes, my dear, it was a remarkable feat." His muttonchop whiskers wobbled as he let out a bark of self-satisfied laughter. "But the thing is, Princess Murgatroyd, can

I *trust* you, eh? Got to know if I can *trust* you if I'm to tell tales out of school!"

"It's Melissande, actually," she said, her voice freezing, before she could stop herself. The marquis's pebbly eyes bulged, as though he couldn't believe his ears. Damn. Smile, smile, and toss in a high-pitched, girlish trill of coy amusement. *What* a good thing Reg had been left behind. "But Murgatroyd's a lovely name, too. And *of course* you can trust me, Your Grace. We're all aristocrats here."

"Ha!" said the marquis, disbelieving, then flapped his hand across the crowded chamber towards its curtained doorway, where the unfashionably late Lanruvians were making their entrance. "Not them!"

Hartwig had arranged for a collection of string musicians to serenade the gathering before the State Dinner. What with the talking and laughing and chinking of glasses, their music had been pretty much drowned out . . . until the Lanruvians entered the reception chamber. Their arrival stilled tongues into a ripple of silence that left the musicians raucous.

"Bloody Lanruvians," said the marquis, disastrously, into the void.

Someone in the press of invited guests laughed, a nervous honking. Someone else tittered. And then the waters of renewed conversation closed over their heads, spiced with a giddy relief, and Melissande let out a breath.

Lord. I hope Gerald and Bibbie are getting on better than this.

The marquis intercepted yet another passing servant, took two more crab puffs to soothe his offended sensibilities, and to her surprise handed her one. Trapped, she ate it.

"So, Your Grace, you were saying?" she prompted, wickedly tempted to wipe her fingers down the front of his over-braided velvet coat. "About how you played matchmaker to the happy couple?"

Another self-satisfied bark. "Yes! Well, Princess Mona, when you get right down to it, all of us here on the Small Western Continent, we're just one big family. And families, y'know, they squabble, they disagree, but when push comes to get the devil out of my way, we have a care for each other. And all this biff and bash between Splotze and Borovnik, over one little canal? Not helpful, is it?"

"So you thought the time had come to say Enough is Enough?"

The marquis chortled. "Indeed I did! And I *did*. And now there's to be a wedding!"

"Yes, but how did you manage it?" Melissande persisted. "I mean, after so much intransigence on both sides, how did you—"

The marquis tapped the side of his prominently veined nose. "Ah, indeed, wouldn't *you* like to know?"

Yes, she really would, because it was almost impossible to believe that this overdressed blowhard was capable of tying his own shoelaces, let alone finagling such an unlikely marriage.

The man's a complete plonker. And a greedy old windbag, to boot. I'll bet someone else is behind this wedding.

Humming with speculation, she slid her gaze over to the Lanruvians. They were standing in an aloof knot on the far side of the chamber, watching the reception's goings-on like visitors at a particularly rowdy zoo.

"Actually, Your Grace," she said brightly, "I must ask you to excuse me. But I'm sure we'll chat lots more, during the wedding tour. And, oh, look!" She snapped her fingers, summoning another of Hartwig's tray-bearing servants. "I don't believe you've tried one of these yet, have you?"

Leaving Harenstein's deplorable ruler to salivate over the prune-stuffed crispy bacon, she fled as fast as the press of her fellow-guests allowed. Her heart boomed as she pushed her circumspect way through the crowd. Was it madness, to march right up to the Lanruvians and introduce herself? Probably, but how else was she going to engage them in conversation? She didn't want to wait until the tour. What if they weren't invited? Or had refused to attend? Tonight might be her only chance.

But she'd not managed to squeeze more than halfway across the chamber when the serenading musicians fell silent, and a pompous horn blast rent the air. The wedding party had arrived.

Bugger.

Bibbie was flirting again.

Because this time it was in a good cause, Gerald gritted his teeth and tried not to care—but that was easier said than done. The wretched girl was depressingly accomplished at it. Probably she'd been practising since she was three.

I wonder what it means that she's never flirted with me?

No. No. He was not going to think about it. This wasn't a social event. Bibbie wasn't flirting, she was working, and it was time he followed her example.

The Servants' Hall was warmly crowded. Because they were mere lackeys, and ought to count themselves fortunate they were getting any kind of jollity, the palace and wedding guests' minions weren't being treated to a reception ahead of a sump-tuous nine course banquet, or enjoying the talents of an exquisitely-trained string ensemble. No. *Their* food was laid out on long tables around the edges of what would become the dance floor, and they were expected to eat all of it standing up, entertained by a lone violin, a xylophone and someone haphazardly banging on a drum.

Appetite largely curtailed by the day's alarming events, Gerald helped himself to a roasted chicken drumstick, then retreated to a bit of empty wall to seek out any hidden foes while he was eating. But even that was proving a challenge. Lowering his etheretic shield was too risky, and not only because there might be someone present sensitive to the inex-plicable presence of a wizard. Bibbie was here, already alarmed about him . . . and it was practically certain she'd notice the new changes in his *potentia*, which he was nowhere near ready to discuss.

Leaving his shield up meant the Servants' Hall buzzed at him indistinctly through muffling layers of etheretic cotton. So frustrating. What if the mission went pear-shaped because he was too busy hiding to notice a vital clue?

There has to be better way. When I'm home again, I'll find it.

That bloody grimoire magic must be good for something more than demolishing entrapments and giving me nightmares.

On the other side of the noisy room, Bibbie was giggling at something a handsome minion from Borovnik was saying. Gerald scowled. Feeling his regard, she turned a little and carelessly caught his eye. Her lashes fluttered in a swift, almost imperceptible wink, and then she was turning away again. His stomach swooped.

I can't stand this. She's the love of my life. How can I risk her? My life's too unpredictable. Too dangerous. I'm too dangerous. Especially now. We can't possibly have a future.

Perhaps he should ask Sir Alec if he could do an Abel Bestwick. There had to be a thaumaturgical hotspot somewhere that could use the attention of a grimoire-enhanced rogue wizard. Because although the thought of exile was bad, the thought of watching Bibbie meet someone else, fall in love with someone else, make a life with someone else, was infinitely worse.

But he *really* couldn't afford to think about that here.

Get a grip, Dunnywood! If Reg was around she'd boot you up the arse so hard . . .

A trio of Splotze servants bearing trays of food and wine approached the clustered gaggle of Borovnik retainers. They accepted the personal service without any sign of embarrassment. So, what? They thought it was their due to be waited on by Crown Prince Hartwig's people? Why? Because their princess was marrying Splotze's junior prince? And did this bowing and scraping mean *Splotze* thought Borovnik was doing them a favour, handing over Princess Ratafia to Hartwig's brother?

If so, what did that say about the Canal Treaty? Would Borovnik end up with the lion's share of any concessions and tariffs? And if that were the case, how would the people of Splotze react when they found out? How would Splotze's various trading partners and regional allies react? Appalled, chicken drumstick forgotten, Gerald considered the geopolitical ramifications.

Blimey. This could get a bit bloody messy.

With a last teasing finger-wag, Bibbie abandoned the superior Borovniks and joined a little knot of Splotze girls, various flavours of maid from the way they were dressed, aprons and caps and skirt hems modestly brushing their ankles. The maids welcomed her with shy smiles and eager questions. Relieved, Gerald shifted his attention to Harenstein's people. There were seven of them, clotted in the hall's far corner. A lone Splotze servant plied them with food and drink. But why only the one? Why wouldn't they be treated with the same deference as the Borovniks, when it was Harenstein who'd brokered the wedding? Was there a conflict brewing between them and Splotze? Or was Harenstein more safely offended than Borovnik? Or could it be that Borovnik wished to see Harenstein taken down a peg, and had the leverage now to make sure it was done?

Gerald frowned, uncertain. So many eddies and undercurrents. If only he knew what they meant.

With any luck, Melissande's getting some answers upstairs. I hope she is. And I hope the waters settle on the wedding tour so I can see the rocks ahead before we crash into them.

Raised voices at the nearby food-laden tables distracted him from dire forebodings and doubts. The senior palace official in charge was leaning backwards, straining to keep his nose out of the reach of a large, sauce-splattered man waving both fists in his face.

"—insult you? *Me*, insult *you?* Mister Secretary Ibblie, *I* am the man insulted here. *You* are the insult! You are the man who seeks to ruin my life with your stupid accusations!"

"Cook, this is most irregular," Ibblie retorted in a furious undertone. "Get back to the kitchen. If you stayed there, where you belong, perhaps your underlings wouldn't be indulging in undesirable secret trysts in stables then irresponsibly wandering off, leaving you short-handed! And *then* perhaps you'd not be serving raw potatoes!"

Those close enough to have noticed the argument were openly staring at the two angry men. Staring himself, Gerald wondered how many—aside from the other palace staff—understood them, since they were shouting in their native tongue. Thanks to a few clever Department hexes, it wasn't just Splotzin he could now speak like a local. He was fluent in every major language and a few obscure ones, too. But since it might come in useful if other people thought he knew nothing but Ottish, he made sure to keep his expression uncomprehending. Beneath the blank mask, his thoughts tumbled.

Disappearing underlings. Does Ibblie mean Abel Bestwick? Bestwick worked here as a pantry-man, so it's a safe bet he does. I need to know what he knows. And the cook. The cook must know something too.

Goaded beyond endurance, Ibblie snatched up a fork, stabbed it into a serving bowl full of potatoes and brandished his proof in the fat cook's sweating face.

"Instead of complaining about how much work you have,you incompetent spoonsucker, bite this and *then* tell me it's not raw!"

The pair looked so comical, people started to laugh whether they understood the shouting or not. Startled, Ibblie stared at their amused, eavesdropping audience. His eyes widened and his cheeks darkened with angry embarrassment.

"Here," he said, shoving the impaled potato at the cook. Then he handed the man the serving dish. "Get back to the kitchens. We'll finish this later."

The cook retreated, burdened with tubers and muttering imprecations under his breath. Disgusted, Ibblie gestured the small band of musicians to louder, busier playing.

"I say," Gerald said, neatly stepping in front of the man as he made to leave. "Fabulous spread, sir. Very generous of the Crown Prince. I'll be sure to tell Princess Melissande so, when I see her."

"Thank you," said Ibblie in his impeccable Ottish, and plastered a hasty smile over his irritation. "Mister Rowbotham, isn't it?"

Gerald beamed. "Oh, call me Algernon."

"Wonderful," said Ibblie, and slid a little off to the side, suggestively. "So very pleased you're enjoying the evening. Algernon. But if you'll excuse me, I need to—"

"Though I must say," he added, blocking Ibblie again, "I don't envy you the organisation of this little shindig. Always something going wrong at the last minute, isn't there?"

"Wrong?" said Ibblie. To his credit, his voice didn't change. "I'm afraid you're mistaken. Nothing's wrong. Now I really should—"

"Nothing?" Prompted by some unfamiliar instinct stirring inside him, a sudden certainty that he could get this man to talk, Gerald clapped a friendly hand to Ibblie's arm. "Then what was all that business with the cook about, eh?"

Eyes glazing, Ibblie stilled. Into his face crept a blank softness. "The cook? The cook is an imbecile," he said, his voice sounding oddly distant. Mechanical. "He will not keep his place. He cannot control his underlings. He served raw potatoes. He is a disgrace."

What the devil? Letting his hand drop, Gerald glanced around the hall, but no-one appeared to be paying them any attention. The crowd of servants and minions was too busy laughing and eating to care about Ibblie. Where was Bibbie? He couldn't see her. Never mind. Best she be kept well out of the way, for now.

Woken instinct stirred again. No. Not instinct. Grimoire magic. He could feel it, a dragon's sigh. *I was right. I can compel a man to speak against his will.* Quashing a surge of astonished excitement—*bloody hell, this could be useful*—he looked back at Ibblie.

"Tell me more about the missing underling, Secretary Ibblie."

Ibblie blinked. "I—that is a matter for—palace business should not—"

He frowned as the man sputtered into silence. Clearly Hartwig's secretary needed a sharper prod to spill all the cook's beans. *I shouldn't, not here, it's taking too much of a chance. Besides, it's not right.* But this opportunity might not come again, so before he could second-guess himself, or let misgivings stay his hand, he let his etheretic shield drop and stared into Ibblie's unfocused eyes.

"*Tell me about the missing underling.*"

"Ferdie Goosen!" gasped Ibblie. "I caught him dallying in the stables. Roasted him for it, and Goosen deserted his position."

In other words, Abel Bestwick. At last he was getting somewhere. "Who was this Goosen dallying with? Who else did you see there?"

"Mister Rowbotham! *Mister Rowbotham!*"

Biting back a curse, Gerald snapped up his etheretic shield and turned, scowling. "Can't this wait, Miss Slack? I'm rather—"

"Wait?" Behind her window-dressing glasses, Bibbie's changed eyes were wide with concern. "No, Mister Rowbotham, it can't wait! I need to speak with you, *urgently.*"

Muttering like a man waking from dreams, Ibblie stepped back. Gerald opened his mouth to recapture him but it was too late. Ibblie's face was full of purpose again, and with Bibbie agog at his elbow he didn't dare risk a fresh compulsion.

"Very nice to chat with you, ah, Algernon," Ibblie said, with a slight bow. "Do enjoy the rest of your evening." With a nod to Bibbie, he withdrew.

Gerald watched the happy crowd swallow him, then turned. "*Miss Slack*—"

But Bibbie ignored his frustration. "What's the *matter* with you? Are you ill? You must be, or surely you'd have felt it!"

Oh. Damn. His altered *potentia*. Of course she'd noticed its stirring. "Felt what?" he said vaguely. "Sorry, I'm not sure—"

"That *awful* ripple in the ether!" said Bibbie, lowering her voice. "A few moments ago. I tell you, it made my head swim. I can't believe you didn't feel it."

He couldn't meet her eyes. "No, no, sorry. Can't say I did," he said, wandering his gaze around the room. "Are you sure you're not imagining things? It's awfully crowded in here, lots of different etheretic auras, all clashing, so perhaps—"

"Don't you *dare*," she growled, digging a finger into his ribs. "I did *not* imagine it. Something—or someone—dangerous is in this hall right now!"

Well, *damn*. "All right, all right. No need to drill a hole in me," he said, shifting. "Can you still feel it?"

He held his breath as Bibbie half-closed her eyes and sent her own formidable *potentia* seeking.

"No," she said at last, disappointed. "No, it's gone."

Saint Snodgrass be praised. Light-headed, he took her elbow. "Oh. Well, never mind."

"Trust me," she said grimly. "I'm not minding. Now that I know what to look for, I'll be on the highest of high alerts. You should be, too. Truly, one whiff of that disturbance and your hair will stand on end."

Gerald cleared his throat. "It certainly sounds alarming. Ah—you're sure it's not familiar, in any way?"

"No," said Bibbie, after some thought. "But then it did come and go very quickly. If I had more time I might recognise something."

More time? Ha! Over my dead body. "Then we'll have to keep our fingers crossed, won't we, that you feel it again."

"Honestly, I'd rather not," said Bibbie, shivering. "But since it's for the mission . . ." She glanced across the hall. "And speaking of which, what were you and our doorkeeper discussing?"

No point pretending. He'd never manage to fob her off. "His name's Ibblie. He's a palace secretary. And I think he might've been one of the last people to see our mutual friend. In the stables, of all places. He—"

But Bibbie wasn't listening. "Our mutual friend! *Drat*, I was so spooked by that etheretic surge—" She grabbed his wrist. "Come on Algernon. With me, quickly. There's someone you must meet. That's if she's still there. Oh, *lord*."

Gerald let himself be hauled through the crowd of revellers to the far side of the hall, where a buxom young maid moped beside a potted tree fern. When she saw Bibbie she blotted her tear-streaked cheeks with her sleeve.

"Oh, miss, there you be," she said, in strongly accented Ottish. "I thought you'd forgotten about me."

"No, no, Mitzie, I wouldn't do that," said Bibbie, taking hold of the girl's hands. "Mitzie, this is the man I was telling you about. Mister Rowbotham, the princess's private secretary. Mister Rowbotham, this is Mitzie. She's very worried about her friend Ferdie Goosen, who works in the palace kitchens, and I told her she should talk to you, sir, seeing as how you know so many important people."

"Of course," he said, and offered Mitzie a bow. "Anything I can do to help. Tell me, Mitzie, why are you so worried about this friend of yours?"

Mitzie bobbed an unsteady curtsey. "Well, sir, because he's not here, and he's meant to be." Her cheeks flushed a becoming pink. "He's my young man, y'see."

"Really?" Gerald arranged his face into an expression of kindly concern, but inside he was boggling. Abel Bestwick was dabbling with a local girl? *If Bestwick's not dead, Sir Alec will skin him alive.* "And you're quite sure this Ferdie knows he should—"

"*Yes*, sir!" she wailed. "Ferdie's gone, sir. And I don't care what Cook says, or Mister Ibblie, or *anyone*. He *idn't* a wastrel and a good-for-naught. Something's happened to him. I know it."

"Oh dear," said Gerald, heart sinking. "That does sound upsetting. Why don't you tell me all about it?"

Shortly after the wedding party's arrival at the reception, Hartwig extricated himself from the Lanruvians and made a beeline for the unattainable woman of his dreams.

"There you are, Melissande," he said fondly, seizing her hand in his. "And don't you look lovely."

Acutely aware of the many surprised gazes shifting their way, she smiled instead of pulling herself free. "Thank you, Your Highness. It's kind of you to say so."

"Not at all, not at all," Hartwig gushed. He was having trouble keeping his eyes off her cleavage. "And let me just say, my dear, how sorry I am about tonight's seating arrangements. Only the thing is, y'see, what with Brunelda ordered to stay off her gout, protocol demands that Erminium take precedent. You know. Little Ratafia's mother. Borovnik's Dowager Queen. Met her yet?"

"No, not yet, I'm afraid," she replied. "I don't believe she travels, and I've never been to Borovnik."

Hartwig snorted. "Don't repine. You haven't missed anything."

"Hartwig!" she muttered. "Do be careful what you say!"

"Why?" said Hartwig, tiresomely mulish. "I'm the Crown Prince of Splotze, this is my palace, this is my reception, I'm paying for everything, so I think I'll say what I like!"

There was a lively buzz of renewed conversation and the string ensemble was playing again, as the wedding party mingled with the reception's guests, but even so . . .

Sir Alec won't like it if I preside over an international incident five minutes after I got here.

"I quite understand, Hartwig," she said in a soothing murmur. "Only perhaps you shouldn't say it quite so loudly. I wonder, d'you think you could be a dear and introduce me to the Dowager Queen? Because she's looking at me rather oddly and I don't want any misunderstandings while we're on the wedding tour."

"Very well, Melissande," Hartwig sighed. "Only don't blame me afterwards. This is your idea, not mine."

Dowager Queen Erminium of Borovnik was very tall, very thin, and had never been beautiful. Which made it all the more extraordinary that she should be Princess Ratafia's mother, because Ratafia was lovely.

"So," said Erminium, whose wide mouth was pleated with many lines of habitual disapproval. "You're that scoundrel Lional's sister, are you? I hope you know you're lucky he met an untimely end? Rupert might be an idiot but at least he's not *encroaching*."

Melissande waited until the dull roaring in her head subsided. "I wasn't aware Your Majesty was acquainted with my family."

"When I was young and on the market, there was a suggestion that your father, Lional that was, might be a suitable husband for me," said Erminium. "I said no, of course."

With a pleased chuckle, his duty done, Hartwig rubbed his hands together. "Right then! Seems you two lovely ladies have potloads to talk about, so I'll just wander off and say a few words here and there before we go in for dinner, eh?"

Erminium spared him a dry glance. "By all means, Hartwig. Go away. You are quite unnecessary."

A servant walked past with a final tray of crab puffs. Melissande grabbed two and ate them, quickly, to give her face something to do.

"Now, Melissande. Why aren't you married yet?" Erminium demanded, skewering the servant with a glare that sent him hurriedly backwards. "You're three years older than Ratafia. Have you no sense of your obligations?"

Melissande blinked. "Ah . . ."

"You're not getting any younger," Erminium added, relentless. "Neither's Rupert, what's more. Is he going to start breeding soon? He'll want to. A king's first duty is to sire the next king. Well, Melissande? Say something!"

Mind your own business, you ghastly old hag? No, no, she couldn't say that. Such a pity. Bloody diplomacy, always getting in the way.

"Ah—well, my brother's been rather busy," she said. "But I do know the question of marriage is very much on his mind." Because that old goat Billingsley wouldn't shut up about it, but still. "I'm sure he's eager to find a bride, Your Majesty."

Erminium sniffed. "Well, if he can't hunt down a suitable gel tell him to apply to me. I've a spare niece that wants taking off my hands."

Oh, Saint Snodgrass protect me. "That's very kind of you, Your Majesty," Melissande said faintly. "I'm sure Rupert will be touched."

But Erminium had turned away, her stick-thin, silk-draped arm lifted a little, crooked forefinger beckoning.

"Here, Ratafia," she said, as her radiant daughter joined them. "This is Melissande of New Ottosland. She's that scoundrel Lional's sister. By all means be convivial while I have a word with Leopold Gertz, but don't go getting any ideas. This chit thinks she's fooling the world by calling herself *Miss Cadwallader* and prancing about Ott in trousers, currying favour with social misfits who refuse to accept they need a king."

As her mother went in search of Hartwig's Secretary of State, Princess Ratafia sighed. "Please forgive Her Majesty," she said, her soft voice lightly accented. "She does not mean to be abrupt. It's just that my wedding has her melancholy. She misses my father, King Barlion. It has been eleven years and she still has not forgiven him for dying."

"Oh," said Melissande. "I'm sorry."

"And I am sorry, too," said Ratafia, whose beauty up close was as overpowering as Bibbie's, in its distinctly Borovnik fashion. "About the loss of your brother, King Lional. It must have been a great shock."

Melissande, who until that moment had thought she looked quite fabulous in her crystal-beaded dinner gown and jewels, resisted the urge to give up once and for all and go find a spare pair of Gerald's trousers.

"Yes, it was a shock," she said, managing to keep her voice even. "Thank you."

Ratafia looked across the crowded room at Hartwig's very plain brother, Ludwig, who'd been waylaid by the Count of Blonkken. Her flawless face softened into a smile of haunting beauty.

"I fancied myself in love with Lional, you know."

"Oh," she said again. "I didn't know you knew him."

"Only from afar," said Ratafia. "We met once, in Graff, when he was still a prince. He danced with me five times in one night. I wept for days after we heard the sad news of his accident. I couldn't imagine there was another man who could make my heart beat so fast." Her perfectly sculpted lips parted in another smile. "And then I met Ludwig."

And what did that mean? Was it possible that mixed up somewhere in all the politics, there was also true love? Given the pressures of international relations, it seemed unlikely. On the other hand, stranger things had happened. But before Melissande could ask, the trumpets blared again.

Dinner time.

CHAPTER THIRTEEN

"I'm sorry?" Gerald said, staring at Mitzie. Thank Saint Snodgrass they were ensconced more-or-less behind the potted tree fern, and that the Servants' Ball was in full, uproarious swing. "You went looking for—ah—Ferdie in the Grande Splotze *morgue?*"

Mitzie nodded vigorously. "Yes, sir. After I couldn't find him in the hospitals. But he wadn't with the dead people, neither. I looked at all of them." She shuddered. "Even when they were old and horrible, or all runny, I looked. But Ferdie wadn't there. Oh, Mister Rowbotham! Something dreadful must've happened to him!"

"You looked at runny dead bodies," said Gerald, not risking a glance at Bibbie. "Gracious. That was very brave of you, Mitzie."

Fresh tears welled in her eyes. "Thank you, Mister Rowbotham."

"Although I'm a bit surprised Cook didn't offer to do it for you."

"Cook? Pah!" Mitzie blinked away the tears. "All he does is call my Ferdie nasty names and throw bowls at the wall because he don't have his senior pantry-man and he says his back's too bad for lifting."

"And what about Mister Ibblie? You can't ask for his help?"

Mitzie shrank. "Oh, no, Mister Rowbotham, sir. Mister Ibblie, he don't speak to kitchen maids. And even if he did, sir, Ferdie idn't meant to be any of my business. Besides, there'd be no help dere. Mister Ibblie told Cook he caught Ferdie out of bounds and Ferdie must've bolted on account of fearing he'd be punished and if he shows his face again he'll only be turned off so dere's no point in trying to find him." She hiccupped. "And Cook said Mister Ibblie had no right to chase away his pantry-man, kitchen staff are his say-so, and then Mister Ibblie told Cook it was his own fault for not keeping a stricter eye on us and after that neither of them had a care for Ferdie no more. It was just about them."

Well, damn. If only that didn't sound entirely bloody plausible. "There, there," said Gerald, and fished a handkerchief out of his pocket.

Mitzie took it with a watery smile and mopped her wet cheeks. "Dere weren't no-one I could speak to. Only I feel like I'm letting Ferdie down, sir, holding my tongue when I *know* something's wrong."

"Oh, Mitzie, you've not let him down," Bibbie said quickly, and slid her arm around the despondent kitchen maid's shoulders. "You braved the Grande Splotze morgue! If that's not friendship, I don't know what is."

Mitzie's cheeks pinked, and her eyelashes fluttered low to shield her eyes. "Oh, miss. You'd do the same, for Ferdie. He's got such a way with him, he has."

Gerald stifled a groan. It seemed more than likely that Bestwick's little ways were set to end his career.

Provided, of course, he's not lying dead in a ditch.

Trying to ignore the dread that thought woke, and the guilt of his own failure, he gave the kitchen maid an encouraging smile. "Yes, I'm sure you're right, Mitzie. Now, I wonder, d'you think we could go back over a few things? Just to make sure I have the story straight? You said the last time you saw Ferdie was in the stables. You're quite certain of that?"

"Yes, sir."

"And it was two days ago?"

"Two days afore yesterday, sir. Late lunchish time."

So, definitely the same day Bestwick sent Sir Alec his desperate message. The same day, it seemed, that Ibblie had seen him. "And what exactly were you doing with Ferdie in the stables? I don't think you said."

"Doing, sir?" said Mitzie, her voice strangled. Her blush this time was rosy red.

Belatedly, he realised. *Oh. Right.* Opposite him, Bibbie was working hard to keep her expression serious. Wretched girl. She was s'posed to be gently-bred. She was s'posed to be *mortified.* Instead she looked like she wanted to break into whoops.

"Yes, well, never mind, Mitzie," he muttered. "I'm sure what you do with your friends is none of my affair. I mean business. Just, if you could think back and tell me who else was in the stables with you?"

Mitzie looked puzzled. "Oh, sir, there wadn't nobody else. All alone, we were. We had to be." Another blush. "You know."

"Yes, yes, quite," he said hurriedly. "I see. Ah—does that mean you didn't see Mister Ibblie?"

She shook her head. "No, I never saw him, sir. I left first, y'see. So's we'd not set tongues wagging."

"And you're quite sure nobody's laid eyes on Ferdie since then?"

"*Yes*, sir," said Mitzie. "Everybody's been asked, sir. And there'd be no call to fib on it."

Not if there was nothing to hide, no. But clearly somebody was concealing the truth, because in the short space of time between Mitzie leaving the stables and Ibblie discovering Bestwick there, something had happened to alarm the agent about the wedding.

Unless Ibblie's the culprit, Gerald realised. *In which case he and I need to have another pointed conversation. In private, this time.*

Damp handkerchief strangled in her fingers, Mitzie turned to Bibbie. "Oh, miss, please, you have to believe me. Ferdie didn't run away. He told me how much he loves working in the kitchen and how one day he'd like to be a 'prentice cook, and I *believed* him. He was pantry-man here four years, y'know, and there's not a man alive stays slaving in the pantry with the likes of Cook if it's not work he's born to do! And—and he asked me to dance with him tonight, afore everyone to see us, he did. That idn't a thing a man asks if he don't have a true care for a girl."

Gerald met Bibbie's concerned gaze over the maid's bowed head. "I'm sure you're right, Mitzie," he said, carefully gentle. "So here's what I'm going to do. I'm going to tell Her Royal Highness, Princess Melissande, all about Ferdie. And then she'll ask Crown Prince Hartwig to look into his disappearance."

Mitzie looked up. "Really, sir?" she said, doubtful.

"Really. Princess Melissande has strong views about the way people should be treated. She doesn't give a fig if you're a servant or a prince. Isn't that right, Miss Slack?"

"Quite right, Mister Rowbotham," Bibbie said promptly.

"But, sir . . . the Crown Prince?"

"Oh, yes," said Gerald, firmly squashing his scruples. "Princess Melissande and the Crown Prince are excellent friends."

"Oh, sir!" Mitzie blinked, awestruck. "Thank you!"

Skewered with fresh guilt, Gerald patted her hand. "You're welcome."

"So now you can enjoy the evening, can't you?" said Bibbie. "Instead of sitting all by yourself in a corner, feeling weepy."

"Yes, miss, thank you, miss," said Mitzie. "Only I can't really, miss, because I'm only allowed an hour upstairs before I have to get back in the kitchens so's Effie can take her turn kicking up her heels. So I'd best go." She held out the damp handkerchief. "But *thank you*."

Reluctant, Gerald accepted the tearstained square of cotton then watched the kitchen maid out of sight.

"Poor little blot," said Bibbie.

He frowned at her. "Well? What d'you think?"

"I think," she said, sighing, "that it's going to be nearly impossible to find out what Ibblie knows, *especially* if he's mixed up in this. Which is starting to look likely. If he was in the stables plotting, and you-know-who overhead him then got discovered, well, of course you-know-who would run away, wouldn't he? And of course Ibblie wouldn't lift a finger to find him. The question is would he lift a finger to stab him? Because *somebody* pushed a knife into you-know-who. But I don't suppose we'll be able to find out who did it."

It was on the tip of his tongue to confess. Confide. Tell Bibbie everything about the entrapment hex, the grimoire magic, why she'd felt what she'd felt when he'd questioned Ibblie earlier. He'd not feel so terribly alone if she knew.

But I can't tell her. Not yet. Not until I know what it means.

Not until he could be sure she wouldn't turn away from him in horror.

She was looking at him, one eyebrow quizzically raised. "Mister Rowbotham?"

He forced a smile. "That was good work, Miss Slack, noticing Mitzie was upset about something."

"Yes, well." Bibbie rolled her eyes. "The waterfall of tears down her face was what you might call a hint."

"Don't dismiss it so lightly," he said. "My point is, thanks to you we've found our first suspect."

"And much good he does us," Bibbie muttered. "When he's untouchable, at least by a lady's maid and secretary."

"We can still try," he said. "And if it doesn't work, we can get Melissande to question him. But let's not forget, he's only a suspect. Ibblie could be completely innocent."

She snorted. "Nobody's completely innocent."

"So young and yet so cynical," he marvelled.

"You would be too if you'd grown up in my family. And besides, I'm not that young." Bibbie smiled, her eyes wicked. "I'll be my own woman soon."

"At which time the world will tremble," he said. And then, because her smile was doing dangerous things to his blood, he looked around in search of Mister Ibblie.

Most of the food had been consumed, and the Splotze servants who weren't condemned to tidying up, and the guest minions from Graff and Blonkken and Aframbigi and Fandawandi and Borovnik and Harenstein and elsewhere, were nibbling the leftovers or dancing or gossiping. But where the devil was Ibblie? Had he left the Servants' Hall? Because if he'd slipped away, then—

But no. There he was, deep in conversation with the lackeys from Harenstein. Gerald stared.

Is it him? Is he the one?

Ibblie was certainly senior enough, and trusted enough, to be involved in a plot without suspicion. Was he to be included on the wedding tour? That was something to find out. If he wasn't, then any move he made would need to be either before the wedding party departed Grande Splotze, or after it returned.

And we're leaving Grande Splotze the day after tomorrow. So that doesn't leave him much time, does it, if he wants to get his sabotage over and done with?

His nerves, which had been sleeping, leapt to fizzing life. Tonight? If the culprit was Ibblie, would he try something tonight? Surely the timing was perfect. Why would anyone suspect him when he was stuck downstairs presiding over the Servants' Ball?

Bibbie plucked at his coat sleeve. "What's the matter?"

"We should circulate," he said. "We're not going to learn anything more keeping this tree fern company."

"That's true," she agreed. "I know. Why don't I tackle Mister Ibblie?"

What? Let Bibbie confront a potential murderer? *I don't think so.* "No. If Sir Alec finds out you're—"

"Oh, pishwash to Sir Alec," she said, with an airy wave of her hand. "How's he going to find out? We're not going to tell him, are we? Besides, Gerald, what's your plan for tackling Ibblie? Are you going to march up to him and say *Excuse me, Mister Ibblie, I was wondering if you had any plans to scupper the royal wedding? Oh, yes, and how are you with a knife?* If he's guilty he'll lie, and if he isn't he'll think you're a madman and have you thrown out."

She was right, curse her. Especially since he couldn't use

his newfound compulsion power on the bloody man, not with her watching.

"And I suppose you think you can *flirt* the answer out of him?"

Bibbie batted her eyelashes. "Why, Mister Rowbotham. If I didn't know better, I might think you were *jealous*."

She was saved from a shaking by the motley musicians, who launched into a sprightly jig.

"I know!" said Bibbie, with the brightness he'd long ago learned to distrust. "I'll ask Mister Ibblie to dance! He won't say no, it'd be rude to refuse Princess Melissande's lady's maid, and while we're prancing about I'll tell him I found Mitzie crying, and that she told me about you-know-who, and then we'll see what he says about the last time he saw Ferdie Goosen."

Gerald swallowed. He wished he could forbid it, but since he couldn't risk lowering his shield she was their best chance of getting some answers. One melting look and Ibblie would surely be butter in her hands.

"All right," he said, resigned. "You do that, and I'll have a chat with some of the chaps from Borovnik. Only please, Miss Slack, be careful. This isn't a game. If Ibblie's our man that means he's dangerous."

"Double pishwash," said Bibbie, loftily. "How many times do I have to tell you? Stop treating me like a *gel!*"

If he said what he wanted to say they'd get into a shouting match, so he restrained himself. The effort nearly gave him a hernia.

"Fine," he said, teeth gritted. "Off you go, then. And make sure you dance him past me a few times. I got a good whiff of those dark thaumaturgics in you-know-who's lodging, and if I go looking I might smell them on him."

Bibbie flashed him a Gladys Slack smile that was almost as dazzling as her own. "Yes, Mister Rowbotham. Whatever you say, Mister Rowbotham."

Hell's bells, he groaned silently, as she headed for Ibblie. *That girl will be the death of me yet.*

*   *   *

Leopold Gertz was a damp little squib of a man. Which was odd, really, considering he was Splotze's Secretary of State. Surely Hartwig could've found someone with more personality for the job?

Honestly, Melissande thought, trying not to listen as he slurped his cream of artichoke heart soup. *I can't believe Hartwig couldn't have found me someone less dreadful to sit with!*

She'd been placed at the far end of the Great Table, with Leopold Gertz ensconced damply at her right hand, and because they were all seated side by side in one long row, there wasn't anyone to talk to across the table . . . even if she'd been prepared to commit such a breach of good manners.

Seated with them on the overly decorated dais, displayed like shop window dummies to the whole sumptuous State Dining Room, were Hartwig, Dowager Queen Erminium, Ratafia and Ludwig, of course, the Marquis of Harenstein and his child-bride Marquise, who looked any minute as though she were about to start sucking her thumb—or possibly fall asleep face-first in her soup—and all three Lanruvians. In typical Lanruvian fashion they managed somehow to sit apart, even when neatly sandwiched between Erminium and the marquis.

Curse it. If only Hartwig had sat me next to them. At the rate I'm going I won't get to say so much as boo to the buggers.

Interestingly, the various dignitaries from Graff, Blonkken, Aframbigi, Ottosland, Fandawandi and Jandria had been relegated to the dining room's second-best tables. From the look on the Ottish Foreign Minister's face—what was his name, again? Boggis? Beaver? Something starting with B. Battleaxe, it should be, the glares he was giving Hartwig—it was clearly counted an insult to Ottosland that he wasn't up there with them on display. And why wasn't he? she wondered. Was Hartwig punishing the great nation for messing him about?

It wouldn't surprise me. Hartwig can be a bit prickly, and Ottosland never seems to notice when it's giving offence.

Remembering the Wycliffe affair, Melissande pretended to enjoy her own soup—lord, she loathed artichokes, she'd almost prefer the tadpole eyes on toothpicks—while surreptitiously observing the Jandrian Minister of Foreign Affairs and his wife. Were they behind the attack on Abel Bestwick and the planned disruption of the wedding? Oh, surely not. *Surely* they weren't stupid enough to try more shenanigans after their still-recent close shave with international industrial espionage.

I mean, not even the Jandrians are that arrogant . . . are they?

She didn't know. Bibbie, being a Markham, might have an idea. One of the Markhams must. Sir Ralph. Possibly Monk. It was something to remind Gerald about, anyway, so he could discuss it with Sir Alec. Though doubtless Sir Alec was already taking a closer look at their old foe.

The rest of the noise in the dining room belonged to the bevy of other invited guests, captains of Western Continent industry, social and cultural luminaries and the like, who laughed and gossiped and clattered cutlery, gold and silver and jewels glittering in the luminous chandelier light. And of course the musicians, who were soaking the rarefied air with a selection of classical Borovnik music.

Melissande looked down at her soup bowl. Not even half emptied, which could easily be taken as an ill-mannered insult to her hosts. Her stomach growled a warning complaint. She really did *not* like heart of artichoke. As her stomach complained again she gave up, and pushed the bowl to one side.

Beside her, his own bowl scraped clean, Leopold Gertz dabbed napkin to lips. "Very nice, I'm sure." He glanced sideways. "You disagree, Your Highness?"

Oh, damn. "No, no, Mister Secretary. Unfortunately I—ah—I got a bit carried away at the reception. Too many crab puffs. Did you try one? They were delightful."

Leopold Gertz sniffed, damply. "I don't believe in crustaceans."

"Ah! Then that must give you something in common with our friends from Lanruvia," she said, seizing the chance before it slithered away. "I don't think they ate any crab puffs, either. I must say . . ." The rest of the table wasn't paying attention to either of them, so she shifted a little in her seat and tried her best to capture the man's attention. "It's lovely to see the Lanruvians getting about, taking part in things, isn't it? They're so reclusive as a rule. But I have to ask, why now? Why Splotze? Why do they care about this wedding?"

Leopold Gertz's eyes were a nondescript brown, their irises floating despondent in a bloodshot corneal sea.

"Who knows why the Lanruvians do anything, Your Highness?" he said, with a dispirited shrug of his skinny shoulders. "I did hear they were interested in using our Canal to transport goods from Harenstein to the Gardeppe Isthmus. Since the upcoming joyous event will usher in a new era of stability for the region, perhaps that's why."

Servants had magically appeared to remove their soup bowls. Leaning out of the way, Melissande frowned. "But you're not sure?"

"As I say, Your Highness." Gertz attempted a smile, and mostly failed. "Who can fathom the Lanruvian mind?"

"Well, I'd certainly like to try," she said, with a sickeningly coy little laugh. "They're so terribly intriguing. Whose idea was it to ask them to the wedding, d'you know? Hartwig couldn't recall."

"I'm afraid I can't either, Your Highness," said Gertz, disapprovingly repressive. "And even if I could, it wouldn't be proper for me to tell you."

"No, no, of course not," she said quickly. Her stomach growled again, this time so loudly that Leopold Gertz heard it. Startled, he blinked at her. She pretended it hadn't happened. "Mister Secretary—"

But then she forgot what she meant to say, because her stomach growled yet again then turned itself over on a surging wave of sickness. Her skin rushed hot, then cold and clammy. Dark spots danced before her eyes.

"Your Highness?" Leopold Gertz said, damply concerned. "Are you all right?"

Further down the table, Hartwig's brother Ludwig groaned. A moment later Princess Ratafia let out a pained little gasp.

"Mama—Mama—I don't feel very well!"

Stomach writhing, the dancing black dots duelling with scarlet blotches now, Melissande squinted around the dining room. Quite a few of the guests seemed to be in intestinal distress. Without warning, Ottosland's Foreign Minister bent double, half-slid from his chair, and began to heave up his artichoke soup . . . along with everything else he'd eaten so far.

Horrified cries. The scraping of chair legs on the polished marble floor. And then the ghastly, ominous sounds of more people succumbing.

But succumbing to what? Poison? Was this the dreadful plan? Wipe out the entire wedding party and a great many other important people for good measure? Hand pressed to her spasming middle, Melissande looked past Leopold Gertz to Hartwig. He was sweating profusely, and hiccupping, his eyes stretched wide in disbelief. Beside him, Ludwig was heaving like a drunken sailor. So were Princess Ratafia and her mother, the Dowager Queen. The Marquise of Harenstein was flapping her hands and squealing, revolted and hiccupping, as the marquis tried to pull her away from the mess. The musicians had stopped playing, appalled, and the servants were staring, abandoning the idea of serving the next course. And the Lanruvians . . . the Lanruvians . . .

Had extricated themselves from the carnage and were watching from a safe distance, unmoved.

Teeth clenched tight, Melissande battled the inevitable for as long as she could. But her offended insides were adamant. What had gone down just had to come up.

"*Bugger* it," she said, helpless . . . and started to retch.

Not surprisingly, Ibblie had succumbed to Gladys Slack's charms and was now partnering her in an energetic Splotze folk dance that involved a great deal of hand-clapping, heel-clicking, head-tossing and sultry meeting of eyes. The empty square within the border of tables was crammed full of palace lackeys and quite a few of the visiting minions who'd been unable to resist the lure of harmless entertainment.

Standing on the sidelines, Gerald fought to keep the scowl from his face. Bloody Ibblie was enjoying himself entirely too much. He was taking advantage. Taking liberties. He was clutching Bibbie's waist!

And for all I know, the man's a bloody villain!

He still couldn't say one way or the other. If he could think of a reason to send Bibbie out of the hall, he'd be able to corner Hartwig's secretary and learn the truth. But until then he was stuck with trying to read the man from behind his damned etheretic shield. As arranged, Bibbie had danced Ibblie past him five times, and each time he'd risked bursting a blood vessel trying to examine the man for thaumaturgical taint. He'd not felt any, but that didn't mean anything. He'd not felt that entrapment hex, either, until it was too late, and that was with his shield down.

Bibbie danced past yet again, and this time he managed to catch her eye in a warning. As the folk dance ended, and the couples broke apart, he nipped in smartish and gave Ibblie an almost friendly nod.

"Mind if I steal Miss Slack away from you, sir? Thank you!"

The band launched into a stately Ottish parade. Giggling, Bibbie set her hand primly on his shoulder and slow-marched beside him the length of the dance floor.

"Well?" she said in an undertone, mindful of the other dancers. "Anything?"

"No. You?"

"For what it's worth, I don't think he's been meddling with things Uncle Frederick wouldn't like," she said, neatly dipping at the corner without losing her balance. "And I didn't catch a whiff of what I felt earlier."

He'd never danced with her before. She was as graceful as a swan. "Good."

"No, it's bad," she said, as they dipped and turned again. "I'll just have to keep trying."

Oh, wonderful. "Did you ask him about Ferdie Goosen?"

"He didn't bat an eyelash. And when I wondered if everyone was pleased about the wedding, he said yes."

He gave her a look. "That was taking a risk."

"No, it wasn't," she retorted. "Don't be tedious, Algernon."

Tedious? He was terrified. Bibbie might be a powerful witch but she was no match for whoever had set that entrapment hex, or let loose the blood magic.

What if I can't protect her? What if she stumbles across this evil bastard by accident and I'm not there to save her? What if—

The sedate Ottish dance ended, and the musicians started up a new jig.

"I'm thirsty," said Bibbie. "Let's sit this one out."

So they retreated to the drinks table, accepted a glass each of fruit punch with bits of melon floating in it, and retreated to a safely empty stretch of wall.

Bibbie twizzled her wooden stirrer idly round her glass. "Nobody's watching. You should see if you can feel that nasty ripple in the ether."

Gerald sipped more punch. It was far too sweet. "I can't. I'd have to lower my shield."

"Then lower it," said Bibbie, shrugging. "I'll obfuscate for you. If there is a wizard here, he'll never know he's not alone."

"Miss Slack—"

She slid him a sharp, sideways look. "Why are we arguing, Algernon? You have to. You might not get another chance."

Damn. "Look, stop bossing me," he snapped. "He's my Uncle Frederick, not yours, which means I'll be the judge of what I do and when I—"

"Oh, Algernon," said Bibbie and, turning towards him, rested her hand on his arm. Her changed eyes were warm now, with sympathy. "Don't be a tosser. Are you afraid I'll be upset by the changes in your *potentia*? I won't. D'you think I care about . . . you know. *Grimoire magic*." She said the words silently, trusting he'd read her lips. "I swear, I couldn't care less. You're a good man, Mister Rowbotham. Nothing in the world has the power to change that."

She was wrong. He'd already changed it. In Abel Bestwick's

dismal little home he'd rewritten the rules. And without meaning to, she'd already told him it might have been his worst mistake.

Something—or someone—dangerous is in this hall right now.

He took a half-step back from her. "Bibbie—"

A commotion at the entrance to the Servants' Hall turned them both, and then one of the upstairs lackeys, splendidly silver-trimmed, flailed his way onto the dance floor shouting for Mister Ibblic.

Everyone stopped jigging as the music abruptly died.

"Lishboi?" Ibblie demanded, pushing forward. "What's the meaning of this?"

Lishboi was sheet white. "It's the Crown Prince, sir! And Prince Ludwig, and the princess! It's all of them, just about. Somebody's poisoned the State Dinner!"

Ibblie spat out a Splotzeish curse and plunged for the door. Ice-cold, Gerald plunged after him, knowing Bibbie was close behind. Following after them came the foreign dignitaries' servants. In a herd, they thundered up the stairs to the State Dining Room, hard on Ibblie's heels.

The magnificent chamber looked like a battlefield. It stank like one, too. Bodies were strewn everywhere, some of the wealthiest and most important people in the civilised world draped over tables and chairs or sprawled on the marble floor, heaving and groaning and spasmodically emptying their bellies.

"Oh, Saint Snodgrass!" Bibbie gasped, hand slapping over her mouth as they staggered to a halt not far into the stinking room. "Oh, *Algernon!*"

Ibblie was barrelling towards Crown Prince Hartwig and Prince Ludwig, who were seated on a dais at the far end of the chamber, wracked with pain. The servants from Borovnik and Harenstein barrelled after him, shouting at the sight of the Dowager Queen and Princess Ratafia and Harenstein's Marquise in similar distress.

"Where's Melissande?" Bibbie demanded. "I can't see— no, wait, there she is!"

Gerald watched as she shoved and slid and leapt her way

through the press of stricken dinner guests and their various appalled lackeys to where Melissande was slumped almost under the long table at the far end of the dining room's dais. He felt his breath catch, and throttled the terror.

Melissande's tough. She'll be all right. I have a job to do. She'd want me to do it.

To hell with the risk. He was one of the most powerful thaumaturgists in the world. So what if he'd been tainted with grimoire magic?

I control my potentia. It doesn't control me.

He let his shield drop. Wrapped his mind around his changed power, willing its new darkness to sleep, and with his safely rogue thaumaturgics went in search of villainy . . . and possible murder.

CHAPTER FOURTEEN

"*F*ood poisoning?" Sir Alec stared into the slight fogginess of his private crystal ball. Splotze's etheretics were acting up yet again, making the connection jittery. "Mister Dunwoody, are you sure?"

"*As sure as I can be,*" said his most promising and problematical janitor. "*The thinking is that the crab puffs are the culprits. The head cook's been off his game ever since Bestwick disappeared.*"

Bestwick. A possible connection, then? "This cook. You don't think—"

"*No, sir, he's not involved. At least, not on purpose. He just about collapsed when he was brought up from the kitchens and saw what had happened. Burst into floods of tears at the thought of his precious crab puffs ruined.*" A short. "*Not to mention his reputation.*"

"Tears, Mister Dunwoody, are not a foolproof indicator of innocence."

"*No, sir. But I made sure to read him, and I couldn't sense anything to suggest he'd mucked about with dubious magics.*"

"And you're confident you've not been misled?"

Even with the unreliable etheretic connection, he could see something shift behind Dunwoody's eyes. Honed instincts stirred, and he leaned forward.

"Mister Dunwoody?"

"*Yes, sir, I'm confident. The cook's not involved.*"

A flat statement, lacking room for doubt. Still . . .

Disquiet not eased, he decided to let the moment pass. For now. "And you have no other suspects?"

"*There was one,*" said Dunwoody. "*The palace secretary. But I've ruled him out too.*"

"So where does that leave us, Mister Dunwoody? Was the food poisoning accidental, or a deliberate attempt to sabotage the wedding?"

"*Sorry, sir,*" Dunwoody said, shrugging. "*I can't say yet. The investigative waters are a bit muddy. Turns out the cook's been helping himself to the good stuff in the palace wine cellar. He's hazy about the last couple of days.*"

Just what he needed. "In other words, he could have allowed tainted crab meat into his kitchens, or tainted it himself through drunken carelessness."

"*Exactly, sir. And if it was tainted when it got here the next question is, did someone deliberately taint it beforehand? But if it was fine when it arrived, and the cook's habits aren't to blame, then that points to someone in the palace taking advantage of his drinking to tamper with the crab.*"

Sir Alec pinched the bridge of his nose. Another thundering headache was brewing. "And how likely is that, d'you think?"

"*Well, sir, I suppose anything's possible,*" Dunwoody said. "*But honestly? It all seems too complicated to me. That kind of plot's got so many moving parts. An awful lot can go wrong with it.*"

Very true. "A more immediate interference, then?

"*Possibly,*" Dunwoody said, sounding doubtful. "*Only I couldn't detect any leftover thaumaturgics in the State Dining room. And when Bib—I mean, Miss Markham—inspected the kitchen, she couldn't sense anything out of place either.*"

That sat him upright, a muscle spasming beside his left eye. "I'm sorry? Mister Dunwoody, are you telling me you've made Miss Markham an active part of this investigation?"

Dunwoody stared out of the fogged crystal ball, his slightly distorted expression defensive. "*No, sir. At least, not exactly. It just made sense to let her look. I mean, she has had experience with thaumaturgical food tampering, remember?*"

As if he could forget the cooking competition debacle. "That isn't the point. The point, Mister Dunwoody, is that—"

Gerald Dunwoody held up his hands. "*Sir, sir, I know what you're going to say. But I can explain. Y'see, the thing is, Bibbie—Miss Markham, I mean—at the Servants' Ball, she made friends with a kitchen maid who knows Bestwick. A very useful connection, sir. I'd have missed it. Anyway, it gave her an excuse to go down to the kitchens, sir, to see if this Mitzie was all right. And while she was down there, well, she had a little poke around, thaumaturgically speaking.*"

"And was this her idea, Dunwoody, or yours?"

Dunwoody swallowed. "*Hers. But Mel—I mean, Miss Cadwallader—she thought it was a good idea too. So. You know. I was outnumbered.*"

"Outnumbered?" Astonished, Sir Alec stared at his man in Splotze. "Mister Dunwoody, you are an agent of the Ottosland government. You *outrank* them. Act like it!"

"*All due respect, sir, but that's easy for you to say,*" Gerald Dunwoody retorted. "*You're in Nettleworth. Besides, it would've looked very odd, me wandering about the palace kitchens. But nobody questioned one maid comforting another.*"

Unfortunately, Dunwoody had a point there. "Granted," he said grudgingly. "However, do let me make myself perfectly clear. This is the first and last time Miss Markham insinuates herself into this investigation. She and Miss Cadwallader are useful bystanders. They are *not* participants."

"*Yes, well, I'm sorry, Sir, Alex but I'd like to see you keep a lid on Miss Markham,*" Dunwoody muttered. "*Or Miss Cadwallader, for that matter. She's taking this personally, sir, and I can't say I blame her. She was dreadfully sick, y'know.*"

High-handed princesses taking things personally. Catastrophically talented witches poking about in kitchens. Pinching his nose again, he had to wonder if at last, in sending those two unconventional young women into the field, he'd not managed to outsmart himself.

He frowned at his agent. "You said this kitchen maid was friendly with Bestwick? How friendly, exactly?"

Dunwoody cleared his throat. "*Friendlier than you'd like. Sir.*"

Damn. He could already hear Frank Dalby's cursing. "I see."

"*It's hard to blame him*," Dunwoody added. "*Four years is a long time to spend in a pantry.*"

"Bestwick wasn't sent to Splotze to cavort with kitchen maids!" he snapped. "And if you can so easily forgive his lapse of good judgement, Mister Dunwoody, perhaps you're not the right man for the job either!"

Silence, as Dunwoody blinked at him. "*Sorry, sir.*"

"Miss Cadwallader," he said abruptly, angrily aware that weariness and frustration were betraying him into an unproductive shortness of temper. "How is she faring now?"

"*She's recovering, sir. Everyone is, who's been sick.*"

"Which begs the obvious question: who hasn't been sick?"

Gerald Dunwoody's misted, wavering expression darkened. "*The Lanruvians. They didn't touch the crab puffs.*"

Of course the Lanruvians. Everywhere he turned, the elusive bloody Lanruvians. "Who else?"

"*Leopold Gertz, Splotze's Secretary of State. The Marquis of Harenstein, but it seems that's because he has a cast iron constitution. According to Miss Cadwallader he was eating everything he could lay his hands on. A few political nobodies. Nearly everyone was afflicted, sir.*" He grimaced. "*It was a real mess.*"

Sir Alec drummed his fingers on the desk. "So then, to sum up: we're no closer to uncovering the source of the plot against the wedding than we were when you left."

"*No, sir.*"

"And the Lanruvians have done nothing at all to make you suspicious?"

"*They're bloody unsettling, sir, but that's hardly a crime.*"

"Granted. But keep a close eye on them, Mister Dunwoody. They are not to be trusted."

"*Yes, sir.*"

"And the wedding tour. Does it continue as planned?"

Dunwoody almost smiled. "*It does, thanks to Dowager Queen Erminium's bullying. I don't think there's much that old battleaxe wouldn't do to make sure the nuptials go ahead.*"

"Then, Mister Dunwoody, I advise you to remain vigilant. Next time there's an incident—and we must assume there will be a next time—we can't expect to get off so lightly. You're to use any and all means at your disposal to ensure the success of the Splotze-Borovnik wedding."

In the foggy crystal ball, Gerald Dunwoody frowned. "*Including what's left of the grimoire magic?*"

Careful, now. Careful. "If you must."

Even the etheretic uncertainty couldn't hide Dunwoody's displeasure. "*Really? So let me see if I understand you, sir. It's too dangerous for Bibbie and Melissande to help me, but using the most lethal thaumaturgics we've ever met is fine and dandy?*"

And now it was time to tread very lightly indeed. Gerald Dunwoody might well be the best weapon in his arsenal, but carelessly handled weapons had a tendency to go off at the most inopportune moments.

"I'd have thought the distinction would be obvious, Mister Dunwoody. While Miss Cadwallader and Miss Markham can be useful allies, clearly they are not amenable to your control. On the other hand, with every hour that passes, that remaining grimoire magic is becoming more and more an inextricable part of you—which means it is something you *can* control."

Dunwoody's face had gone blank. "*You hope. Sir.*"

"I am confident in your abilities, Mister Dunwoody. But if you find the notion disturbing, you can take heart from the fact that whatever hexes do remain might well help you to prevent a catastrophe in Splotze."

"*So you're saying I should look on their acquisition as a happy accident?*"

"I am saying, Mister Dunwoody—and not for the first time—that when life hands us lemons it is only prudent to make lemonade."

Very slowly, Gerald Dunwoody nodded. "*Prudent. Right. Any more useful advice, Sir Alec?*"

Not even Frank Dalby had ever tried that tone on him. It was a tone to invite serious censure, if not outright dismissal. But Frank Dalby wasn't a rogue wizard whose formidable powers had been augmented in ways that were, at the end of the day, unspeakable. Because of that, Gerald Dunwoody had to be permitted a little . . . leeway.

He offered his difficult agent a thin smile. "Use your best

judgement. Be careful. Succeed. Thousands of lives are depending on you, Mister Dunwoody."

Dunwoody raised an eyebrow. "*And what would you like me to take care of in my spare time?*"

"Your attitude!" he said sharply, because there were limits. And on that warning note, he disconnected the vibration and sat back in his chair.

Silence shrouded his office. It was late. Even Frank had gone home. Aside from two duty officers, he was alone in the building. Of course, if he went home he'd be alone there, too. But then it seemed more and more often, these days, that he felt alone in the middle of a crowd.

After a while, he slid from his chair, drifted to his office window and stared into the streetlamp-pricked darkness that was Nettleworth asleep. He'd seen too much, and done too much, to harbour any illusions or even much hope that the simple religious teachings of his childhood could ever stand against the evil he confronted every day of his adult life. But even so, he found himself harking back to that kinder, simpler time.

Gerald Dunwoody's a good man, faced with a hard task. If there is a God in this sorry world of ours, He'd do well to keep that young man safe.

With a rattling *chug-chug-chug* the jalopy coasted to a halt in the deep kerbside shadows between lamp posts along the hushed, exclusive suburban Ott street. Breathing out a sigh of relief, Monk turned off the engine then squinted through the open driver's side window. Please, please, let him have found the right place. Dodsworth had given him copious directions, but even so, having never been to the Blonkken embassy in broad daylight, let alone in the practically pitch dark, a mistake was entirely possible. And he couldn't afford any mistakes.

Tickling at the edge of his *potentia*, a tug of familiar thaumaturgics. It felt like the hex he'd given Dodsworth to leave behind so he could get into the embassy undetected. To make sure though, because it was late and he was knackered and couldn't be certain his *potentia* wasn't playing him tricks, he took his little box of special hexes from the jalopy's glove department and held it lightly in his hand. After a moment's concentration he had his answer. Yes, the thaumaturgical signatures matched. He was in the right place.

And now that his eyes were accustomed to the fitful gloom, he could see in the distance the embassy's back garden, tree-fringed and barricaded behind a high brick wall. Beyond that, if he squinted even harder, he could just make out the ambassadorial residence. It was well past midnight, and from the lack of lamplit windows in the ambassadorial residence it seemed fair to assume the occupants were by now conveniently asleep.

Perched on the back of the passenger seat, Reg chattered her beak. "All right then, sunshine. I've been wonderfully patient, but now I think it's time you told me where we are and what we're doing here."

Holding up a finger, Monk continued to squint into the darkness. According to Dodsworth, his expert consultant, the Blonkken embassy wasn't a big building. Two storeys only. For his purposes, its modesty was both good and bad. Faster to get around in, but not so much space to act as a cushion between the offices and the bedrooms. Probably fewer handy hiding places, too, should things go pear-shaped. Still, with any luck—

"Oy!" said Reg, and thumped him with her wing. "Have you gone suddenly deaf, or what?"

He glared at her, rubbing his head. "I wish you wouldn't do that! How am I supposed to hex my way in there if you give me a concussion?"

"Hex your way in where? Monk Markham, *where are we lurking?*"

He couldn't delay the moment of truth any longer. If he could've left her behind altogether he would have, because he knew, he just *knew*, the bird was going to kick up a stink. Except if he'd tried to leave her out of this she'd only have followed him. Like it or not, for as long as Gerald was off janitoring in Splotze, he and Reg were stuck with each other.

"Outside the Blonkken embassy."

"The Blonkken embassy? Why in the name of—" And then Reg's dark eyes widened. "Monk Markham, do you actually think we're going to break into the *Blonkken embassy?*"

"Yes," he said, torn between apprehension and defensiveness. "Well, I am. But don't worry, it'll be fine."

"Don't *worry?*" The bird spluttered. "When it comes to you and your antics, ducky, all I ever do is worry! We can't go staggering about a foreign country's embassy in the middle of the night! What about the guards? If your Blonkken are anything like mine, then they're very big on guards. You can bet your last bottle of brandy they're tramping over the garden beds right now, looking for someone illegal to clap in irons!"

"Reg, I told you, it'll be *fine.*"

"I beg to differ," Reg retorted. "Now just you drive this jalopy back to Chatterly Crescent quick smart, before someone marches out here with a flaming torch, a pointy pike and a lot of bloody awkward questions!"

"Sorry," he said, shaking his head. "But I can't go home until I've had a good poke around in there. I need to see if I can find some incriminating documents that will prove they're the ones up to no good in Splotze."

Reg opened her beak to argue, had second thoughts, then tipped her head to one side. "And what makes you so sure Blonkken's the villain here?"

"I'm not. In fact, I'd be shocked if it turned out Blonkken's behind this wedding mayhem, but I need to keep an open mind."

"*Ha!*" said Reg. "Your mind's already open, sunshine. It's so open I can hear the wind whistling between your ears!"

He glowered. "By all means, feel free to stay behind if you're scared. But I'm afraid *I* have to—"

"*Scared?*" Reg chattered her beak again, furious. "I'm not scared, I'm dumbfounded. If this mad little expedition of yours goes arse over teakettle, and with you in charge of strategics that's more than bloody likely, that mangy Sir Alec will personally string you up by your unmentionables!"

Monk winced. "Yes, well, we'll just have to make sure that doesn't happen, won't we?"

"We? We?" Reg fluffed her feathers in fresh outrage. "Who said anything about *we?* You never asked *my* opinion of your mad plan, did you? You haven't even see fit to tell me what it is!"

"I'm sorry," he said. "I didn't think I had to. I assumed you'd jump on board, seeing as how I'm trying to get Gerald and the girls home again in one piece. But if I was wrong . . ."

Eyes gleaming, Reg rattled her tail so hard she nearly fell off the back of the passenger seat. "Forget it, my boy. That kind of soppy heartstring tugging might've worked on the other bird, but you are looking at a woman who let sentimentality fool her once, and won't ever be fooled again. Got it?"

Swallowing, Monk stared at her. "Sorry," he muttered. "I just—for a moment there, I forgot . . ."

"That I'm not her?" Reg snorted. "Well. I suppose if I squint hard, and twist my head upside down, Mister Clever Clogs, I could see that might be some kind of compliment."

Mister Clever Clogs. Ambushed by unexpected emotion, Monk blinked out of the window. The other Reg had called him that all the time, being sarky. But this was the first time . . .

Reg gave him another great whack on the back of the head. "Just so you know a therapeutic concussion is still on the cards!"

"Bugger it, Reg!" he protested. "I *really* wish you wouldn't do that!"

"Tell me the plan and I'll stop," she said, sniffing. "*All* of it, mind you. Not the edited highlights."

As plans went, he was pretty proud of this one. Especially considering his lack of janitorial experience. But Reg?

"That's your plan?" the bird said, once he'd finished explaining. "Draft a geriatric door-opener to totter about what's technically foreign soil slapping hexes in places you hope won't get noticed, so you can slink in afterwards using your highly dubious counter-hexes and rummage through the privy paperwork of important men who don't give a fat rat's fart if your name ends with Markham? *That's your plan?*"

Squashed as far away from Reg as he could get, which

wasn't anywhere near far enough, Monk cleared his throat. "Ah . . . yes? Yes, that's it. Pretty much. Although I'm not sure *slink* is the right word. And I don't see that it's fair to call Dodsworth *geriatric*, either, when you—"

"*Hell's bells, you mad bugger! You don't need me to concuss you, it's clear as mud you're concussed already!*"

"Look—Reg—"

The bird flapped her wings like a scarecrow in a storm. "Don't you *Look, Reg* me, you daft—you demented—I can't *believe* you'd—without even *discussing* it? What raving loony let you out of the lab?"

"Blimey, Reg," he said, deflated. "All right, so as plans go it might be a little bit tatty round the edges, but I didn't think it was as hopeless as *that*."

More dramatic wing flapping. "*Ha!* Says the man who thought opening a portal into another dimension was a nifty thing to do on a wet afternoon!"

Well, that was just plain mean. "All right!" he said hotly. "If *you're* so bloody clever, Reg, if *you're* such a janitoring mastermind, how would *you* go about uncovering secret information about the people on the Splotze-Borovnik wedding list when you don't have a single solitary reason to go barging in asking pointed questions? Eh? Come on, then. Enlighten me. I am all ears."

Silence.

"I'm sorry?" He leaned sideways. "What was that? I didn't quite catch your answer, seems I'm a bit deaf from all that shouting and wing flapping. Or maybe it's the concussion I didn't realise I had. You'd do *what*, exactly?"

Reg looked down her beak at him. "Ha ha. Very witty. You'll be the toast of your cell block in the Ott prison, I'm sure."

"No, sorry, I still can't seem to find the plan in that delightfully snarky reply."

"Now you look here, Mister Markham!" said Reg, with a truly formidable rattle of tail feathers. "It's all very well you jumping onto your high horse and waving your little fists about like a toddler in a tantrum, but that won't undo the fact that what you're proposing is ridiculously dangerous. I don't care how much of a bloody thaumaturgical genius you are, or how many windows doddering Dodsworth left open for you, or what kind of clever hexes you've got stuffed down your unmentionables, you *cannot* go swanning about a foreign embassy as though you owned the bloody place. Being a Markham might save you out here, but in there—" She pointed her wing towards the embassy. "—you're a nothing and a nobody and when they catch you they'll hang you as a spy."

"*When* they catch me?" Monk shook his head. "Your faith is heartwarming, Reg. Look! I'm going to shed a tear."

"You'll shed more than tears when they've got you standing against a wall with a loaded First Grade staff pointed at your warm heart!" she snapped.

"I thought you said they'd hang me."

"Hang you—shoot you—set you on fire! What difference does it make? The point is, sunshine, you'll be *dead!*"

Monk slumped until his knees knocked the jalopy's polished walnut dashboard. "Blimey, Reg. You really know how to take the fun out of things."

With a softer tail rattle, the dreadful bird hopped down to his knee and fixed him with the sternest of stares. "You silly boy, this was never about fun. That's always been your problem, Mister Markham. You've spent most of your life giggling as you skate over the thin ice. And because you're a Markham, and a genius, and useful to the right sort of people, time and again you get away with blue murder."

Appalled, Monk felt his heart thud. *What is this? First Aylesbury, now the bird. . .* "You make me sound like—like Errol Haythwaite!"

"No, no," she said, impatient. "Errol Haythwaite's a pillock. You're just careless. And thoughtless. You get carried away."

"In other words, I'm a tosser!" he said, still appalled. "I think that's a bit bloody harsh. You don't seem to realise, Reg, that working in Research and Development means I get told things. Dreadful things you'll never read about in the *Ottosland Times*, or are even whispered about beyond our four walls. And then I get told, *Toddle off, Mister Markham, and just make sure that doesn't happen*. So I toddle off and I bend the Laws of Thaumaturgics until you'd hardly recognise them and I come up with a way to make sure *that* doesn't happen. Whatever the *that* is my superiors have stumbled across this week, at any rate. Next week they'll stumble across something else, you can bet your next bowl of mince on it, Reg, and I'll be expected to dream up some other outlandish hex or ridiculous gadget that'll save us, yet again. Because I'm Monk Markham, aren't I, and that's what I do! So if I get a bit carried away giggling while I'm skating on your thin ice, well, I think even you'll agree that giggling's better than screaming!"

Reg blinked at him. "I never said you don't make a valuable contribution to the causes of peace and international freedom, sunshine," she said more kindly. "But if you're looking for a bird who'll hold her tongue when she sees a man merrily tripping down the wrong path, well, don't look at me."

"Look, Reg, you might be right," he said. "This plan of mine might be the wrong plan. But it's the best I can come up with on short notice. Sir Alec just tossed this wedding list thing into my lap and sauntered away. He's like Uncle Ralph and the rest of them, he assumes I can pull a thaumaturgical rabbit out of my hat at a moment's notice, every time. And so I have to, don't I? Bloody Gerald's up to his grimoire-enhanced eyebrows in trouble and he's got my sister and my—my friend with him. I can't leave them twisting in the wind."

Reg looked down her beak again. "No. You can't. But make no mistake—you breaking into foreign embassies using dubious thaumaturgics is a recipe for disaster."

Monk thudded his head against the closed driver's side window. "Then what am I s'posed to do?"

"You let me break into the foreign embassies for you," Reg said promptly. "If your enterprising butler has left a suitably unimportant window open I can fly in and snoop about, and if anyone sees me it'll be *Oh dear, look at the poor little birdy, let's shoo it outside.*"

Oh, lord. "And what if there's a closed door between you

and the room with the information in it? What if what we're looking for is stuck in a drawer? What then?"

"Well, sunshine, what I lack in opposable thumbs I make up for with guile and cunning," said the bird. "And I expect you've got some clever hexwork stuffed down your drawers that'll sort out any inconveniences like locks and closed doors and stuck drawers and what have you."

Monk felt his spirits sink. Really? Just like that? The bird was as bad as Uncle Ralph and Sir Alec and the rest of them, taking his powers of genius for granted.

Although, now that he thought about it . . .

"Could be I do," he said slowly. "A variation on something Bibbie came up with once. Just—be quiet a moment while I work it out."

Amazingly, the bird did as she was asked. What a good thing he always carried a few blank hex matrixes with him wherever he went, on the principle that one never knew when a hex might come in handy. It took him a little under an hour to cobble together what he needed, and then rig up his handkerchief into a nifty sling that Reg could carry into the embassy, laden with the hexes he'd brought with him and the ones he'd just devised.

"So you're clear on all of that?" he asked the bird, once he'd explained which hex did what. "Or d'you want me to run through it again?"

Jumped from his knee down to the jalopy's front passenger seat, Reg stopped poking her beak through the differently coloured hexes piled onto his handkerchief and gave him a look. "D'you mind? *I'm* not a doddling geriatric butler."

"*Reg*—" And then Monk bit his tongue. If they got into another argument now they'd probably still be going at it hammer and tongs when the sun came up. "No, of course you're not. Sorry." He tied up the corners of the handkerchief, then leaned over to the passenger side of the jalopy and thumped down its window. "There you go. Now for pity's sake be careful, because you might be more annoying than a pair of trousers full of ants but I bloody well refuse to lose you again."

Eyes bright, the tricked-up handkerchief with its burden of hexes held firmly in her beak, Reg nodded. "Right," she said indistinctly. "Now bugger off. I'll see you back in Chatterly Crescent."

What? "Reg—"

With a muffled curse, she spat out the handkerchief. "Blimey bloody Charlie, sunshine, must you always *quibble?* There's nothing you can do from out here but find a way to bollocks things up, so go home. Do some dusting. You're always after new experiences, aren't you? Housework'll have all the charm of bloody novelty!"

Defeated, Monk sighed. "Fine. I'll go. Just . . . don't hang about, all right? Because the longer you stay in there, the greater the chance of you getting caught."

"Ha!" she said, and picked up the handkerchief again. "That'll be the day."

She hopped up onto the frame of the jalopy's open window, rattled her tail . . . and launched herself into the quiet night. Heart thudding, Monk watched until he'd lost her among the shadows, then started the engine and chugged away down the street, towards home.

CHAPTER FIFTEEN

" *N othing* suspicious about the Blonkken wedding guests? Or any of the embassy staff? Nothing at all?" Disappointed, Monk slumped in his favourite parlour armchair. "Reg, are you sure?"

Perched on the back of the sofa, the bird looked down her beak at him. "And when have you ever known me not to be sure, sunshine?"

He let the horribly loaded question slide right past them, into oblivion. "Never."

"Then just you put a sock in it and pour me a brandy."

Dawn was fast approaching. Though he'd not yet been to bed, it was still far too early for brandy. But the bird's beak was looking especially pointy and anyway, he had a headache, and nothing was better for headaches than a healthy splosh of fermented peaches. It might not kill the pain, but it swiftly made sure you no longer cared that the top of your head was threatening to explode.

He poured them each a drink and they sipped in sour, contemplative silence.

"You know what this means, don't you?" he said at last, grumpily considering the bottom of his glass. "It means I have to tell Sir Alec I haven't saved the day for him."

"You haven't saved it yet," said Reg, with a genteel, alcoholic belch. "There's still time."

"Not much. And every hour that passes pushes Bibbie and Melissande and Gerald an hour closer to disaster."

Reg rattled her tail. "That's a very glass-half-empty way of looking at the world."

"Actually, my glass is entirely empty," he said. "Did you want some more brandy?"

"No," said the bird. "And neither do you. What you want is a bath and some breakfast. The Sir Alecs of this world are best confronted with a clean face and a full belly."

She was right. Again. Drat her. So he dragged himself upstairs, bathed, shaved, found some fresh clothes, then staggered back downstairs to fortify himself with coffee and porridge. After that, with the sun risen a decent distance above the horizon, he hauled out his crystal ball and gave Sir Alec the bad news.

Sir Alec was unimpressed and said so, at length.

"Well, honestly, sunshine, what did you expect?" said Reg, strutting to and fro across the kitchen table with an irritatingly derisive look in her eye. "You've known him a lot longer than I have and *I'm* not surprised."

Monk dumped three teaspoons of sugar into his fresh cup of coffee and stirred so hard he nearly slopped half of it over the side.

"I didn't say I was surprised."

"Yes, you did," Reg retorted. "Not five seconds ago. You said, and I quote, *That miserable bastard! I don't believe it!*"

Aggrieved all over again, he thumped his fist to the bench beside the sink. "Yes! Precisely! I'm disbelieving, not surprised! Honestly, to hear him talk you'd think I didn't give a toss about Gerald and Bibbie and Melissande!"

"Well . . ." Reg stopped strutting and scratched the side of her head. "To be honest, ducky, I think you're wrong there. Don't misunderstand me, I wouldn't trust that sarky bugger as far as I could spit a hedgehog, but in case you weren't paying attention, your Sir Alec's not looking too flash. Seems to me you caught him in a bad moment, is all. Prob'ly he's got a lot of prickly problems on his plate."

Remembering the pallid cast to Sir Alec's drawn face, and the shadows of strain beneath the tired, chilly grey eyes, Monk tossed his teaspoon into the sink. "So I'm s'posed to feel sorry for him now?" Picking up his coffee, he retreated to the nearest chair. "D'you think he's keeping secrets?"

Reg hooted so hard she nearly fell over. "I don't know, ducky. Do pigeons poop on statues?"

"I *mean* secrets about Splotze," he said, glowering. "I *mean* do you think something's gone wrong with Gerald's mission and he's not telling me because—because—" But a swiftly rising fear wouldn't let him finish. "Dammit, Reg. I never should've let Bibbie set foot out of this house."

"I don't see how you could've stopped her, short of trussing the girl like a turkey and shoving her head first into a closet," said Reg. "Now just you stop carrying on, sunshine. If something has gone arse over teakettle in Splotze, you'd know it. What *you* need to think about is how to fix that clever clogs door-opening hex of yours so that the bloody door *stays* open, right? Because tail feathers like mine don't grow on trees!"

Monk looked at her tail. Thanks to a near-miss on the Blonkken embassy's second floor, it was now minus three of its extravagantly long brown-and-black feathers.

"Yeah. Right. Sorry about that."

"As well you should be," Reg said tartly. "Because I'll tell you this for nothing, my boy. I won't be setting so much as a toe inside another embassy if there's a chance of me flying out of it half-naked!"

He raised his hands in surrender. "I told you, I *promise*, it won't happen again. Now, if you don't mind, I need to brush my teeth then gird my loins to face another day of thaumaturgical adventures in R&D. Can you stay out of trouble until I get home?"

Her offended squawking followed him out of the kitchen, up the stairs and into the bathroom, where he scowled at his reflection while scrubbing his teeth. A tremor of worry shuddered through him as he rinsed his toothbrush.

I hope the wretched bird's right. I hope nothing's gone wrong in Splotze.

"I don't know, Gerald," said Melissande, fiddling with the end of her ribbon-tied, plaited hair. "You paying official sympathy calls? Really that's something I should take care of myself."

Gerald turned away from the window in her guest suite's bedchamber. "Under normal circumstances, perhaps. But none of this business is normal. Besides, there's not a lot of point in you visiting the recently afflicted wedding guests, is there? Not when you've no hope of telling if any of them have been up to thaumaturgical shenanigans. And please, it's Algernon, remember?"

"Fine. Then it's just not done, *Algernon*," Melissande persisted. "Any princess worth her tiara doesn't send a secretary to convey a king's concern. It might easily be taken as an insult, and what good will that do us?"

"How can anyone be insulted if I explain you're still abed, recovering?" he said. "This way you're making a good impression, unwell and still thinking of others, and I'm doing my job. We can't lose."

As Melissande shifted in her chair, unconvinced, Bibbie bounced a bit on the edge of the bed. "He's right, Mel. With everyone recovering from that ghastly State Dinner, and resting up ready for the fireworks this evening, this is an ideal opportunity to run potential suspects to ground. Only . . ." She frowned. "Even though we've sorted through some of them, there are still rather a lot left. Why don't I—"

Gerald turned on her. "Absolutely *not!* You are not helping me with anything *remotely* thaumaturgical. How many times do I have to tell you what Sir Alec said? Do you *want* to see me clapped in irons when we get back home?"

"Faddle," said Bibbie, wrinkling her nose. "*Clapped in irons*. When it comes to exaggeration you're as bad as Melissande."

He loved Monk's sister to distraction, but that didn't mean there weren't times he could easily shake her until her bones rattled.

"Call it what you like, Miss Slack, but my decision is final. You're staying here. I swear, if you so much as poke your nose out of these apartments before I've finished investigating I'll clap *you* in irons and ship you back to Ottosland on the slowest hot air balloon I can find! It'll take you so long to get there that by the time you set foot on Ottish soil they'll be celebrating the turn of the next century!"

Melissande looked at him over her new spectacles. "D'you know, Bibbie, I rather think he means it."

"Yes, well, *I* rather think I mean it too!" he said, harassed. "Please, Bibbie, I am *begging* you. Don't make my job any harder than it is already."

She stared at him, her hexed eyes overbright. "Gracious. And there was me thinking I'd been of use at the Servants' Ball. How silly. What a *gel* I am."

Oh, *damn*. Crossing to the bed, Gerald dropped to one knee and took her hands in his. "I'm sorry. But no matter how brilliant you are, you're not a trained agent and this is no time to be learning on the fly. It's too dangerous. Sir Alec won't risk you, and neither will I."

"Besides," said Melissande, breaking the taut silence. "While I might, at a pinch, send my secretary on this kind of errand, I'd never send my lady's maid. That really would cause a stir."

Bibbie slid her hands free. "Fine. Far be it from me to contradict Your Royal Highness. While our very special Mister Rowbotham's off doing his important, manly duty, perhaps there's a dirty fireplace somewhere I could clean."

"Leave her," said Melissande, as Bibbie retreated to the suite's bathroom. "She'll come round, eventually."

Pushing to his feet, Gerald sighed. "I hope so."

"It's hard for her," Melissande added. "She's easily as talented as Monk, y'know. If life weren't so unfair, if the world wasn't so ridiculously prejudiced and shortsighted, she'd be making her own splashes in Research and Development. She might even be a proper government agent."

The accusing undertone in Melissande's voice had him folding his arms. "It's not my fault Sir Alec and the rest can't see past the fact she's a gel! I'm following orders, Melissande. What else can I do?"

She smiled at him, gently. "You can at least try to see her as an equal, Mister Rowbotham. And stop protecting her. If Ottosland is in danger, then she has as much right as any man to defend it."

Melissande was right. Of course she was right. Except . . .

"If you truly do love her," said Melissande, eyebrows lifted, her gaze challenging, "there's no better way for you to show it."

Bloody woman. She saw too much. He sought distraction in checking his pocket watch.

"It's nearly past luncheon," he said, tucking the timepiece back into his vest. "I should go downstairs. It'll be easier to check on the remaining guests if they're gathered in one place. After that, I'll visit whoever wasn't feeling up to stirring out of his or her chamber." He glanced at the closed bathroom door. "Make sure she stays here, Melissande. Please. There really will be hell to pay if anything happens."

Melissande sighed. "I know. Don't worry, I'll keep her distracted. Now go on—and good luck."

Dear Melissande. She was worth twice her weight in tiaras. Relieved, Gerald withdrew.

Whatever else he might be, Crown Prince Hartwig was a generous host. The grand dining hall, scrubbed and perfumed and redecorated after the state dinner debacle, now boasted sideboard after sideboard of aromatic dishes designed to tempt the most cautious of palates. Freshly cut flowers abounded, and a quintet of fine tenors and baritones serenaded every guest who ventured across the silk-draped threshold.

Sidling his unobtrusive way in, Gerald retreated to an empty corner of the chamber and took a moment to consider the Splotze-Borovnik wedding's potential enemies. There was Ottosland's bumptious Foreign Minister, Lord Babcock. His pallor a trifle waxen, he was exchanging pleasantries with the Zumana of Fandawandi while helping himself to some crumbed lamb cutlets. Over there, already seated, Jandria's Minister of Foreign Affairs and his wife were eating roast squab with gusto. Clearly the tainted crab puffs had made no lasting impression on them. The guests from Graff and Blonkken entered the dining room, amiably chatting. Behind them came Aframbigi's Foreign Minister and his Second Wife. A sideways swipe, that was, leaving the First Wife at home. A petty revenge for a small, unforgotten slight, most likely. Politics. So bloody tedious.

As a handful of impeccably liveried servants carried in more silver platters of food, Gerald half-closed his eyes and focused on his etheretic shield. Its outright lowering was still unwise but perhaps, with his grimoire-enhanced abilities, he could *thin* it a little. Shade it from opaque to translucent, leaving him just enough obfuscation to remain hidden . . . but not blind.

As his *potentia* stirred and he felt its power warm him, like shafts of sunlight through damp cloud. Felt it ripple through his shielding, those shafts of sunlight dispersing mist.

On the other side of the dining room the Jandrian minister's head lifted, sharply, laden fork arrested halfway to his mouth. *Damn.* Holding his breath, Gerald yanked his *potentia* back inside. The Jandrian minister shook his head, then relaxed.

So. It was going to be a case of trial and error until he had the knack of controlling his new powers. Well, at least he was in no immediate danger of being bored.

Heart thudding, he tried again.

A softer stirring. No more than a hint, a whisper, of power. The Jandrian minister noticed nothing. The rest of the room was undisturbed. Imagining himself a searchlight, Gerald swept the dining room with his shrouded *potentia*, seeking something, anything, that didn't feel right. The quintet sang on, joyfully, their music decorating the air.

How odd. I think yes, I can taste the ether. It's sour and thin here, like beer that's aged well past its prime. Gone threadbare. No wonder this region's thaumaturgics are so unreliable.

Nasty. A pain throbbed meanly behind his eyes. He tried to blink it away, marvelling anew at the glory of unblinded sight. When the sharp pulse didn't ease, he did his best to ignore it. Risked eking out a sliver more of his *potentia*. Still the Jandrian minister remained oblivious. Excellent. Even better, he couldn't sense anything immediately untoward in the dining room.

Time to start spreading Princess Melissande's heartfelt good wishes.

After camouflaging himself behind a plate of pickled herring, he descended gormishly upon Lord Babcock, conveniently seated by himself. Despite his pallor, the minister was eagerly tucking into his cutlets and chutney.

"I say, sir," Gerald said, awkwardly bowing. "What a relief to see you up and about after all that recent unpleasantness. Her Royal Highness, Princess Melissande of New Ottosland, particularly asked me to convey her best wishes to you for a speedy recovery. But it seems you're already well on the mend. Her Highness will be *thrilled* to hear it."

Lord Babcock lowered his cutlery and squinted up at him. "Really? That's most thoughtful. My compliments to Her Highness."

Leaning closer, Gerald captured his lordship's gaze. Impressed his will upon the man, feeling again that thrilling surge of power. "I'll pass them along. Tell me, my lord, have you any reason to wish ill upon the wedding?"

"What?" Babcock's squint relaxed into a wide-eyed docility "No. Of course not."

It was the truth. "What about Ferdie Goosen? Does that name ring a bell?"

"Goosen?" Dreamily, Babcock shook his head. "Never heard of him."

And that was true too. Relieved, because the thought of corruption and treachery so close to home was a nightmare, Gerald released his grimoire hold on Babcock and stepped back.

"Thank you so much for your time, Your Lordship. I'll be sure to tell Her Highness that you—"

A wave of etheretic unrest swamped him, strangling the rest of his platitude. Half-discarding, half-dropping his plate of herring on Babcock's table, he slewed around to face the dining room's grand entrance.

And there were the Lanruvians, spreading silence like warm blood dropped into water. Side by side with their Spirit Speaker walked a jovial Marquis of Harenstein, he of the vast paunch and lead-lined stomach. His child-bride wasn't with him. Instead he'd been accompanied by two of his retainers. Both were unfamiliar. They'd not attended the Servants' Ball. Older than the Harenstein minions who'd danced there, they were smiling, coldly polite. The taller one wore a ragged scar on his face.

Instinct had Gerald pouring power back into his shield before that unsettling Spirit Speaker could feel anything amiss. But in the split second before he was hidden completely, a random and terrible premonition stopped the air in his throat.

The fireworks. The fireworks. Something's dreadfully wrong.

As Hartwig's quintet rediscovered its harmonious voice, and conversations stuttered back to life, Gerald fumbled his way to the nearest food-laden sideboard where he could stand with his back to the newcomers and catch his rasping breath. His bones were still shaking with the force of his proofless conviction.

But I'm right. I know I'm right. Only . . . how do I know it?

More grimoire magic? Perhaps. Probably. But did it matter? No. All that mattered was the smothering sense of impending danger. After a moment, he risked a sneaking glance over his shoulder.

The Lanruvians, praise the pigs, hadn't noticed him. Neither had the marquis or his minions. The old fool! Surely he knew Lanruvia's reputation? After so much goodwill garnered by Harenstein's brokering of the wedding, why would he sully his own by cultivating such men?

I've no idea. That's a question for Sir Alec and Monk's uncle. My job now is to see those fireworks safe.

Abandoning, for the moment, his plan to question Hartwig's other luncheon guests, he ghosted his way out of the dining room and headed back upstairs to Melissande's suite.

Bibbie only let him in after he'd spent several minutes grovelling through the front door in a whispered undertone.

"Where's Melissande?" he demanded, following the wretched girl into the bedchamber, where she was packing ahead of their departure that evening on Hartwig's sumptuous royal barge. "I hope she's not off doing something inadvisable."

"She's visiting Crown Princess Brunelda," said Bibbie,

keeping her back firmly turned. "Who's feeling very poorly with her gout. *If* that's any of your business, Mister Rowbotham."

"Actually, it is," he said, frustrated. "There's something I need her to do."

Bibbie sniffed. "I won't bother asking if I can be of assistance."

"As it happens, no, you can't help," he said, retreating to the window, a safe distance. "But only because you're not Melissande."

"Oh." Bibbie dropped a folded silk girlish underthing into the suitcase and turned. Then she frowned. "What's wrong? You look spooked."

"I am spooked," he admitted, and rubbed a hand across his face. "Someone's sabotaged the fireworks."

"*Tonight's* fireworks?" she said, her eyes widening behind Gladys Slack's ridiculous horn-rimmed spectacles. "That's dreadful! What are we going to do?"

Saint Snodgrass save him, did she never listen? "*We're* not going to do anything. I need Melissande to pump Hartwig for pertinent information and then I'm going to *un*sabotage them. And *please* don't argue with me about it, Gladys. We've argued enough for one day."

Bibbie stared at him, her expressive face and eyes full of many shouted objections. Then she nodded. "Agreed. I'll just save up the rest of my arguments for when we get home."

Wonderful. He could hardly wait.

Whoever said the course of true love doesn't run smooth never knew the half of it.

"And instead of simply standing there, laying down your high-and-mighty janitorial law," Bibbie added, "you can give me a hand with the rest of Melissande's boxes. Honestly, the way she packs you'd think the wedding tour was meant to last six months instead of a week or so."

"Fine," he said. "But first I need to contact Sir Alec."

He gave it seven good tries, but with Splotze's etheretics in an uncooperative mood he had to give up. He was in the middle of hauling Melissande's ridiculously large and heavy shoe-case out of the wardrobe when she returned to the suite.

"Honestly!" she said crossly, tossing her fox-fur stole onto the bed. "How many times must I tell you, Algernon? You can't be in here! You're going to ruin my reputation!"

"Bugger your reputation," he said, letting the shoe-case drop. "Someone's fiddled with the fireworks."

Elegant in her best green silk day dress and dainty heels, Melissande frowned. "What d'you mean, fiddled?"

"What d'you think I mean?"

"Oh." Rallying, Melissande lifted her chin. "Are you sure? How d'you know? I thought you were going downstairs to luncheon."

"I did. And when I saw the Lanruvians I came over with a very bad feeling. Melissande, I need to see Hartwig. Now."

"Hartwig?" She was frowning again. "Are you sure? When you've no more proof than a bad feeling?"

"Yes."

"But d'you really want to kick up a stink, throw the wedding plans into disarray, when this might only be indigestion?"

"Don't be silly, Mel," said Bibbie. "If Gerald says trouble's brewing, then there's probably trouble."

Startled, Gerald looked at her. Even angry and hurt, she was defending him. So maybe there was a chance that . . .

But he mustn't, *mustn't*, let himself be sidetracked by hope.

"Trust me, Melissande, the last thing I want to do is cause a public kerfuffle," he said. "The idea is to catch who's behind this, not tip our hand and frighten them off. Please, just take me to see the Crown Prince. If we tell him we want to know about the fireworks for the *Times*, he likely won't fuss about keeping the details under wraps. I need to know how many pontoons there are, where in the Canal they're set up, that kind of thing. The more I know, the better chance I have of figuring out how the fireworks have been tampered with and how I'm going to prevent a disaster."

"*If* they've been tampered with," said Melissande, still dubious. Then she sighed. "Only you're right, of course. You can't afford not to fear the worst."

And speaking of fearing the worst . . .

But before he could open his mouth, Bibbie's hackles were

up. "Oh, no," she said, fists clenched by her slender hips. "We are *not* being left behind in this palace like children."

"Left behind?" Melissande echoed. "Not attend the fireworks, you mean? Sorry Gerald, that's out of the question. Hartwig's barge departs on the tour as soon as the display is over. We have to be on board with the rest of the guests."

"No, you don't," he protested weakly. "You could say you're feeling poorly, then catch up in a carriage first thing tomorrow."

"*No*," said Melissande. "If I try to stay behind, Hartwig will make a fuss and that'll draw everyone's attention. Hardly what I'd call being a secret agent."

Feeling unfairly put upon, Gerald glared at the girls. If only between them they'd bloody well stop being *right*.

"Fine," he snapped. "And for pity's sake, it's *Algernon*. Now, can we please go and interview Hartwig?"

"Actually . . ." Melissande pulled a face. "It might be best if you let me tackle Hartwig on my own. According to poor Brunelda he's in rather a prickly mood after the tainted crab puff calamity. I might have to—" Blushing, she cleared her throat. "—sweet talk him into chatting with me. And if it's all the same to you, I'd rather not have an audience."

As if he had a choice. Without Melissande's help he was hobbled, and she knew it. "All right. But go now. And if Hartwig gets sticky, promise him his picture will appear next to the article. That way you probably won't be able to shut him up."

Melissande bit her lip. "D'you really think the Lanruvians are behind this plot to ruin the wedding?"

"I think they're sneaky, devious bastards with something nefarious shoved up their silk sleeves," he said. "Possibly hexes to turn Hartwig's fireworks into a conflagration. Now, *please*, Melissande, would you go? The clock is ticking."

"Yes, yes," she said, reaching for her fox-fur stole. "But until I get back just you stay in the bathroom. There'll be a maid along any minute and you've no idea how their tongues wag."

Nearly five hours later, almost halfway across the Canal in a stolen boat scarcely bigger than a bathtub, Gerald paused his rowing through the late autumn's swiftly falling dusk to catch his breath and mop the sweat of exertion from his brow.

Saint Snodgrass save me. If it turns out I am imagining things I'll never hear the end of it.

But he wasn't. He *knew* he wasn't. And once he'd saved the day, surely no-one would care how he'd done it, or why he'd been so certain the night's fireworks were in danger. Besides, even if he'd not been so bone-shakingly sure, still he'd have acted. Because if he failed to trust his instincts, let the chance of humiliation stay his hand, and his instincts were proven right? If people were hurt, or worse, if they were killed? Sir Alec really would clap him in irons then throw away the key.

And I'd never forgive myself.

So now here he was, dangerously shrouded in a no-see-'em hex, cultivating blisters as he rowed a purloined, barely Canal-worthy wooden box out to the nearest tethered firework-laden pontoon, while eager crowds of sightseers thronged both sides of the Canal and the wedding party with its glittering comet's tail of guests was boarding Crown Prince Hartwig's royal barge in eager anticipation of the imminent fireworks display.

Watching over his shoulder, Gerald felt a nasty sizzle of nerves. *Damn.* If only the barge wasn't anchored quite so close to those burdened, possibly lethal pontoons.

Because the evening's entertainment was intended as a warm up to the big celebration slated to take place on the night of the wedding, there were only three fireworks pontoons for him to investigate. Thanks to Melissande's clever questioning of the Crown Prince, he knew that each configuration of fireworks was thaumaturgically sequenced and controlled by Radley Blayling, the Ottish wizard who'd designed the display. And since Melissande had managed to wangle herself a last-minute introduction to the man, with himself as her faithful scribe, taking copious notes, he was confident—well, as confident as he could be, anyway—that Blayling was an innocent pawn in the plot.

Which meant the Lanruvians—if it was the Lanruvians—had somehow, whether by bribery, corruption, serendipity, illegal thaumaturgics or a wicked combination thereof, managed to tamper with the fireworks themselves. And if he failed to uncover the mischief in time . . .

Sweating anew, but not from exertion, Gerald started rowing again. Such a bugger he couldn't use a speed-'em-up hex as well. But with the chance of compromised fireworks' thaumaturgics close by, he didn't dare risk it. The speed-'em-up was too volatile to risk.

Off to the right, Hartwig's imposing royal barge glittered and twinkled, bedecked like a queen. Lamps like vividly coloured jewels were strung stem to stern, and across the placid waters of the Canal floated strains of bright music and laughter as the wedding revellers kicked up their heels, sublimely unaware that in the light-flickered shadows danger and death crouched with bared teeth, waiting.

He tried not to imagine the barge exploding in flames. Tried not to hear the screams of the injured and dying. To see Bibbie and Melissande, dying.

It can't happen. It won't happen. I'm not going to let it.

The dreadful sense of danger that had swamped him in the palace dining room, that haunted him now, drove him to forget the sweat stinging his eyes, the blisters stinging his palms and fingers, the fire burning in his shoulders and back. He rowed and rowed, knowing countless lives depended on him. That Bibbie depended on him. That he was the only thing standing between her and cruel murder.

Don't worry, Bibs. I'll protect you.

He nearly fell headfirst out of the stupid little boat, trying to climb onto the first tethered fireworks pontoon. Panting, heart scudding, he knelt precariously on the unsteady platform, unfurled his magnified *potentia* and touched it to the wards set to safeguard the complicated thaumaturgics bound up in the bundles of gunpowder and assorted chemicals. They surrendered to him without protest. Ha. Blayling might be a genius with fireworks, but he was rubbish at protective hexes. And wasn't that a worry? Tampering made simple.

But the fireworks hadn't been altered. Not these ones, at least.

Daunted only by the knowledge that time was fast running out, he clambered back in the little boat and rowed hard for the second pontoon. Took the risk of staying put, this time, and looking for imminent danger from slightly afar. Still nothing. Pouring sweat now, *come on, Dunnywood, row faster*, he headed for the third and final pontoon. Stretched out his senses with a desperate gasp, knowing this had to be it, knowing the danger was here, had to be here—

With a deafening whoosh and an eye-searing flash of light, the floating pontoon of fireworks ignited in a brilliant ball of kaleidoscope colour. He heard the crowd's full-throated roar of delight and wonder. Heard his own shout of angry despair.

And then, for Gerald Dunwoody, the fireworks ended.

CHAPTER SIXTEEN

"Ow! Melissande, d'you *mind?*"

"Not at all, Mister Rowbotham," said Melissande, cheerfully dabbing a disgusting green ointment on his blistered chin. "Now stop being such a baby. You're hardly scorched at all."

"Actually," Gerald retorted, "I'm scorched quite a bit!"

Not to mention embarrassed, stripped down to his still-damp long underwear with his bare torso all exposed. Melissande, bless her, was turning a blind eye, paying him no more attention than if he'd been a horse. She'd even quashed Bibbie, whose utter lack of maidenly modesty had threatened to take full flight.

"And whose fault is that?" said Monk's incorrigible sister, the fiendishly unsympathetic love of his life, perched on the edge of the bed in Melissande's magnificent stateroom aboard Hartwig's royal barge. "I *told* you to be careful, didn't I?"

Melissande scooped more noxious green ointment onto the tip of her finger. "She did. You should've listened. Now do be quiet. After the lies I told Hartwig about you not attending the fireworks because you were indisposed, I can't have the entire barge listening to you bellow like a banshee."

"Why not?" he said, backing away from her. "You could tell them I was in the throes of agony, and you wouldn't be far wrong!"

Melissande smeared the fresh dollop of ointment back into its pot, then held the pot out. "Suit yourself. And while you're at it, treat yourself. But when you're in the throes of a terrible fever, because that frequently happens with burns, I suggest you dive overboard. Maybe a dip in the Canal will save you."

Bumped against a cupboard, trapped, Gerald looked at the smelly ointment, then at Melissande, who was glaring. His scorched bits sang a loud chorus of complaint.

Bugger. "Please finish."

"If you insist," said Melissande, and resumed her questionable doctoring.

Beyond the stateroom's main porthole, Splotze's starlit countryside glided by as Hartwig's enormous and lavishly outfitted barge made its ponderous way down the Canal towards the next day's first official stop at Little Grande Splotze, where they were to partake of a specially prepared luncheon and festive celebration. What a prospect. By the time this assignment was done with he'd almost certainly not fit into a single pair of his trousers.

"Mind you," said Bibbie, idly swinging her legs, "I still can't believe you were wrong about the fireworks."

He glowered at her. "I wasn't wrong."

"Oh?" She feigned surprise. "So that wasn't me and Melissande and those aristocratic whathaveyous and thousands of tourists ooohing and aaahing at all the pretty sparkly lights in the sky?"

"In case you've forgotten, Miss Slack, there are more fireworks planned," he retorted. "I might've been wrong about the timing, granted, but I am *not* wrong about the danger."

"Oh," said Bibbie, and frowned. "You sound awfully definite."

"Miss Slack, I'd bet my life on it."

Bibbie looked at Melissande. "You'll have to warn Hartwig. Get him to cancel the wedding fireworks. He'll listen to you."

Wincing as Melissande dabbed ointment on his blistered midriff, Gerald nodded. "She's right, Melissande. The fireworks must be called off. Talk to him tonight, or at the latest first thing in the morning."

"Well . . . I can try, but I doubt he'll listen," said Melissande. "Hartwig's spent so much money on this wedding, you've no idea. Not to mention its political importance. To convince him there's danger I'd have to give our whole game away. Sir Alec would fall in a foaming heap."

"Not if it saved lives," said Bibbie. "Surely."

Melissande kept on dabbing. "Look, I'm all for saving lives. But we'll be touring for nearly two weeks, so there is still time, isn't there? Algernon? If we can unmask the plotters before we return to Grande Splotze, there'll be no need to tell Hartwig anything. And lo, the happy ending, complete with fireworks and no secret agents revealed."

And better yet, no Sir Alec in a foaming heap. "Yes, I suppose I can—*ow!*"

"Hold still," said Melissande, peering at the charred patch on his ribs. "This is the worst bit. Honestly, how could you have been so silly as to get yourself blown into the Canal? It's a wonder you made it to the barge in one piece, and undetected."

He wanted to hop up and down, the stinging was so fierce. "I'm a wizard, remember? And I came first in swimming class. Hell's bells, Melissande. What's *in* that green muck?"

She shrugged. "I haven't a clue. Holy Man Shugat gave it to Rupert and Rupert gave it to me. I think he said something about cactus juice blessed by the Kallarapi Gods, and possibly some interesting camel by-products, but to be honest I wasn't really listening. All I know is that it cleared up Boris's little problem a treat."

Gerald stared at her, aghast, as Bibbie dissolved into giggles. "*Melissande!*"

"You're welcome," she said, and thrust his wet clothes at him, "Now go away. Get some sleep. Starting with breakfast, we've a lot of work to do."

Morning saw Hartwig's scarlet-painted, three-deck barge gliding majestically down the Canal between lush green meadows dotted with heavy uddered milch cows, who regarded them in bovine astonishment as they passed. At some point during the night they'd left behind the industrial untidiness of the cargo barge docks, and now the landscape was painted in varying themes of bucolic bliss. The sky was blue, the air crisp and florally scented. A glorious autumn day, yet empty of calamity.

But likely that would change.

The barge boasted a huge formal dining room and a dance floor, as well as two saloons, a small salon, a ladies' salon, several games rooms and accommodation in rigorously graded sumptuosity for one hundred and fifty passengers, staff and crew . . . but even so, the wedding guests' minions couldn't be kept entirely out of sight. Which meant that even though they'd been herded down to the far end of the prom-enade deck for their suitably humble fresh air breakfast, they could still see the wedding party enjoying its extravagant silk-canopied, five course repast, waited on by a bevy of servants.

Pretending to listen as the senior lackeys from Graff and Blonkken shovelled down pork sausages and bickered about which country bred the best racehorses, Gerald kept half an eye on the wedding party and brooded.

He'd only slept through part of the previous night. Not, to his surprise, because of his burns. His burns were almost healed, thanks to Holy Man Shugat's dreadful ointment. No, he'd spent most of the hours until dawn cautiously eking out his *potentia*, teasing at the inconsistent etheretics, searching Hartwig's barge for any sign of the wizard who'd set that filthy entrapment hex and used blood magic to hunt Abel Bestwick. To his immense frustration, he'd felt nothing.

But that doesn't mean there's nothing to feel.

He had to be patient. Trust that the villain in their midst would stumble, and reveal himself. Or herself, possibly, if he was wrong about the Lanruvians.

Only I'm not wrong. They're steeped in malice, those three. I didn't mistake what I felt.

As the bickering lackeys paused to take a breath between insults and mouthfuls, Bibbie, seated beside him, leapt fear-lessly into the fray.

"I say," she said, her voice carefully calculated to project a breathy timidity, "does anyone know why the Lanruvians haven't brought any staff with them? I mean, it's rather odd, isn't it, that they don't have any staff?"

The Graffish horse expert, middle-aged and portly, favoured Bibbie with a smug, superior smile. "Miss Slack, isn't it?"

Dimpling, Bibbie conjured a becoming blush. "That's right, Mister Hoffman. Gladys Slack of New Ottosland. How kind of you to remember."

Hoffman preened. "Not at all, Miss Slack. It is hard to forget a personable young lady."

Before Bibbie could further encourage the puffing windbag, Gerald bounced a little in his chair and guffawed. "Yes, isn't it? And you know, by golly, I think our personable Miss Slack is right. They do seem an odd bunch, those Lanruvians. Mind you, there's not much known about them at home." He favoured the table with a gormless smile. "Don't s'pose any of you chaps care to spill the beans?"

"Oh, yes, would you?" said Bibbie, batting her eyelashes outrageously. "Because while of course I wouldn't *dream* of speaking for Mister Rowbotham, I know *I* dread the thought of my ignorance giving everyone a poor impression of Princess Melissande."

Bibbie wasn't the only female lackey seated at the minions' breakfast table, but she was by far the most alluring. It seemed Dowager Queen Erminium had old-fashioned ideas about suitable lady's maids for herself and her daughter. As the men rushed to reassure Miss Slack that on the contrary she was charming, *delightful*, the other two women, older than Bibbie and uniformly hatchet-faced, exchanged disapproving glances then glared at their emptied plates. So far they'd said nothing except "Good morning."

Only one of Harenstein's lackeys had joined them for breakfast. Dermit, the man without the scar. "Miss Slack," he said, his Ottish guttural with gravelly Harenstein inflection, "there is little known about the Lanruvians."

"Surely the Crown Prince knows?" said Bibbie, her dark, incanted eyes round with kittenish surprise. She aimed her limpid gaze at the minion sitting opposite. "Mister Glanzig, can't you shed some light on Splotze's mysterious guests?"

Peeder Glanzig, Prince Ludwig's junior secretary and official wedding dogsbody, was a plain-faced young man afflicted with a sparse beard that did nothing to disguise his woeful lack of chin. He swallowed, flushing under Gladys Slack's melting scrutiny.

"I wish I could, Miss Slack. But as you say the Lanruvians are a puzzle."

Bibbie's bafflement only made her more adorable. "I'm very silly," she sighed. "I thought since they were invited to the wedding you'd know why, and by whom. I mean, they were invited, weren't they? They didn't just turn up hoping to join in?"

"Of course they were invited," Glanzig said hurriedly. "But it's not my place to question who is on the guest list, Miss Slack. And these Lanruvians, well, they keep themselves to themselves."

"That's true, Miss Slack," chimed in Lal Bandabeedi, the Aframbigin ambassador's attendant. "We call them the ghost men. Don't you see them drifting about like shades of the dead?"

Bibbie gave a delicious little shudder. "Oh, my dear sir, you describe them completely. Especially since, well, they don't even seem to be *enjoying* themselves." Then she furrowed her brow in another irresistible display of feminine confusion. "But I'm still all at sea. What is it to Lanruvia who dear Prince Ludwig marries? I *do* wish someone could help me understand."

As servants returned to refresh cups of tea and coffee, clear away the remains of toast and jam, bacon, sausages and scrambled eggs, and deliver some palate-cleansing sliced melon, Bibbie's admirers attempted to impress her with their superior knowledge. Bibbie, bless her, hung on every blustering word, nodding and exclaiming and praising the acumen of her would-be educators.

Taking advantage of the useful diversion, Gerald thinned his etheretic shield. Immediately he felt the nearby Lanruvians' simmering thaumic power, like dragon's breath in his face. But no immediate danger this time, only its sleeping promise. He could also feel the *potentia*-dampening hex he'd cobbled together for Bibbie just that morning, having been struck by the belated thought that she, too, could benefit from a little judicious obfuscation. She'd not been pleased, but she'd taken it. And now he found himself touched that she was wearing it, knowing she trusted him enough to do as he asked, at least this once.

Praise Saint Snodgrass for small miracles.

On and on the men babbled, Bibbie artlessly encouraging them. Keeping a wary eye on the Lanruvians, Gerald dabbled through his fellow lackeys' pallid *potentias* . . . and found nothing. There wasn't a man or woman among them with more thaumaturgical aptitude than a mop. Disconcerted, he let his etheretic shield return to full strength.

Bugger it.

So did this mean the villain, or villains, had been left behind in Grand Splotze? It was possible. Not all the wedding guests' lackeys had come on the tour. If the pre-wedding fireworks were indeed meant to deal the nuptials their fatal blow, then there wasn't any reason for the person responsible to be on the barge. In fact, it made more sense for him or her to stay behind. In which case, should he invent a reason to go back?

No. It's too risky. I could be entirely wrong.

Bloody hell. The uncertainty was going to give him an ulcer.

With the babble dying down Bibbie, still playing her part to the hilt, favoured her eager admirers with another devastating smile.

"Thank you all *so* much, gentlemen," she cooed. "Truly, I'd be lost without your kindness. But there was *one* thing . . ." She looked to the end of the table, where Lord Babcock's priggish private under-secretary sipped tea with his little finger punctiliously crooked. "Mister Mistle? I might've been hearing things, but I'll swear you mentioned something about the Lanruvians and cherries."

Hever Mistle favoured Bibbie with a restrained nod. "I did, Miss Slack."

"Then could you enlighten me? I'd be *ever* so grateful. But, y'know, only if you'd not be speaking out of turn. I wouldn't like you to run afoul of Lord Babcock on *my* account."

"It's unlikely. I am not employed by his lordship to safekeep Lanruvian secrets." Mistle returned his cup to its saucer with a precise little *clink*. "I mentioned cherries, Miss Slack, only because I've heard it whispered that our pale, reclusive and above all insular friends are thinking to look beyond their jealously guarded borders. It seems the Lanruvians grow a variety of cherry to make a liqueur fancier weep with joy."

Gerald hid a frown in his own cup of tea. *Really?* Heard it whispered where, exactly? "I say, sir," he said, as Bibbie's admirers exchanged looks. "D'you mean Lanruvia's thinking of asking Splotze to make its world famous liqueur with *their* cherries?"

Hever Mistle shrugged, his expression bland as milk. "I think Splotze's last two cherry harvests have been . . . unfortunate. And an unreliable harvest leads to unease, wouldn't you agree?" Mistle flicked a sprinkling of salt from his sleeve. "Of course, I don't claim to be an expert. I merely pass along what I've heard."

Yes, and why hadn't the same information been passed along to Sir Alec? If someone had fallen down on the job, heads would surely roll.

"I'd think the cherry-growers of Splotze would have something to say about that," he said to Mistle, who shrugged. "They're awfully proud of their cherries."

He turned to Peeder Glanzig. "Could you even call it Splotze Cherry Liqueur if the cherries were being brought in from Lanruvia?"

Glanzig shifted uncomfortably in his seat. "I don't believe these are proper matters for discussion, Mister Rowbotham," he said, disapproving. Then he laughed, unconvincingly. "I mean to say, all this sombre talk of business, sir. We shall be boring the ladies. Perhaps, Miss Slack, you could entertain us with tales of life in New Ottosland? Such a quaint little kingdom, tucked away in the middle of the vast and mysterious Kallarapi desert. I'm sure we'd all be thrilled to hear more about it."

Chilled with foreboding, Gerald lightly kicked Bibbie's ankle under the table. *Say no! Say you've signed an Order of Discretion!* But Bibbie giggled, ignoring him.

"Oh, Mister Glanzig, I'd be delighted," she gushed. "For you know, I think New Ottosland is an undiscovered jewel!"

But it seemed to Gerald that Bibbie was the undiscovered jewel. Eating his slices of melon, listening to her spin a sparkling cobweb of a story out of what he knew were Melissande's infrequent mentions of her New Ottosland past, he found himself regretting the rigid rules of society that meant Monk's brilliant sister could never be a janitor in her own right.

Because, let's face it, she'd make even Frank Dalby sit up.

Carefully, casually, he let his gaze roam until it rested once more on the Lanruvians. Could the explanation for their presence really be that simple? That innocent? Cherry liqueur?

I suppose it could . . . but since when have I ever been that lucky?

Dowager Queen Erminium of Borovnik was a difficult woman.

"This sauce is too thin!" she announced, poking at her third course of sliced roast beef. "Where is the cook? Can someone send for the cook? I must instruct him in the proper way to prepare a green peppercorn sauce!"

"Please, Mama," Princess Ratafia murmured, seated at her mother's side. "I think the sauce is quite—"

"No, Ratafia, the sauce is not quite anything," her mother contradicted. "Save for too thin."

"My dear Erminium," said Hartwig's long-suffering wife Brunelda, bristling, "this sauce is an old family recipe passed down to me by my late grandmother."

Erminium smiled. "Indeed, my dear Brunelda? Well. Much is now explained."

"Mama," Ratafia whispered, anguished.

"You must allow me to furnish you with a green peppercorn sauce recipe of my own," said Erminium, as though her daughter hadn't spoken. "I fancy you will find it more fashionable."

Brunelda's answering smile was sickly sweet. "To my mind, many things counted fashionable are, in truth, sadly lacking. If there is a fashion for glugsome sauces then I am content to be seen a dowdy and will not lose a wink of sleep."

"Save from indigestion, perhaps," said Erminium, making

a great show of scraping all traces of the offending sauce from her beef. "Or worse. For it is well known among those of us who have made the art of saucery our particular interest, that a thin sauce of any kind must prove an affliction to the bowels."

Ratafia dropped her fork. "*Mama.*"

But Erminium had the bit well and truly between her teeth. "And I think I have even heard it mentioned by some Borovnik doctors that souls of goutish disposition should especially beware, as a thin sauce is well known to agitate the vital humours."

"In*deed?*" Brunelda's vast bosom heaved with barely repressed offence. "Borovnik doctors?"

So sharp was her tone that the rest of the breakfast table was hard-put to go on pretending that here was a honeyed nattering about naught. Ratafia had given up remonstrating, and was gazing at her plate with not quite masked despair. Seated opposite her, Prince Ludwig's stormy eyes suggested he was desperate to defend his mother but knew himself honour-bound not to, on account of his promised wife and the deference due to the woman shortly to become his bride-mama.

Appetite fled, Melissande glanced around the table and saw her own discomfort mirrored in nearly every other face. Only the Lanruvians seemed indifferent, oddly absent even though their presence was oppressively inescapable. Oh—and Hartwig. He was chewing his beef with gusto, thin sauce and all, heedless of the tension. Sometimes he really was a *clod*.

She risked a longer look at the man seated to her left. Why the devil didn't he say something amusing? As Splotze's Secretary of State, Leopold Gertz had made diplomacy his life. There was nothing at all diplomatic about stabbing bits of fried tomato with a fork, not when the mother of the bride and the mother of the groom looked as though they could cheerfully substitute each other for the tomato. Why wasn't he merrily defusing the tension? That was his job, wasn't it? It had certainly been her job, when she was practically a prime minister. Good grief, anyone would think he *wanted* the women to come to blows.

Men! They're all useless!

"Borovnik's doctors," said the Dowager Queen, breaking the glaring stalemate, "are renowned."

"Indeed they are," Brunelda agreed quickly. "I have often heard my own personal physician pass comment."

Her tone left no-one in doubt that the comment in question was anything but complimentary.

Erminium's thin lips pinched to vanishing. "As frequently as he must attend you, my dear Brunelda, I'm sure that's so. I must pass you the stylings of *my* personal physician. Humboldt has cured *countless* cases of gout."

Melissande closed her eyes. If only Brunelda hadn't decided to brave her affliction and join them. Lord, if only Hartwig had appointed a Secretary of State who knew his job. The urge to stamp on Leopold Gertz's foot and wake him up to his obligations was almost overwhelming. Perhaps she should stop resisting it. If nothing else, his screams of pain would provide a welcome distraction.

"You know, speaking of doctors," said the Marquis of Harenstein, with an unexpected chuckle, "I had a doctor once who swore by voles for toothache."

Borovnik's Dowager Queen lifted her quizzing glass on its black velvet ribbon and stared at him through the polished lens. Her eye magnified alarmingly.

"I beg your pardon, Norbert? Did you say *voles?*"

Nodding vigorously, the marquis patted his young wife's hand. "I did, my dear Edwina. No word of a lie. *Voles.* And I tell you, the pain in my tooth was so bad I was desperate enough to try anything. So I did. But the sight of a live vole trussed to my jaw so alarmed my poor little Anadetta, here, that I was forced to dispense with it, *and* the physician, and instead put my faith in the court blacksmith and a trusty pair of pliers!"

Dowager Queen Erminium dropped her quizzing glass. "*Really*, Norbert! You do talk nonsense!"

"No, no, it's true!" the marquis protested, his other hand pressed faithfully to his heart.

"Then I'm sure it was a merciful escape for the vole,"

Erminium snapped. "I can't imagine what crimes a vole might commit, that it should be trussed to your jaw and forced to endure your blatherings!"

Relieved laughter broke out around the table. Even Brunelda was betrayed into a twitch of a smile. Leopold Gertz, stirring himself at last, turned to the Margrave of Blonkken and invited him to expound upon the recent exciting discovery of etheretically sensitive crystal caves beneath his nation's capital.

The breakfast continued, less fraughtly, and two courses later mercifully concluded.

Melissande, thwarted yet again in her quest to capture one of the Lanruvians in conversation, stared after their retreating backs and swallowed an unladylike oath. Then, feeling a light touch to her elbow, she turned.

"Ratafia!"

The soon-to-be Princess of Splotze smiled. "Melissande, I was wondering if you'd care to take a stroll around the barge with me? Only Luddie's gone to smoke a cigar in the saloon with the other men, and Mama says she has the headache and must take to her bed. So I thought I'd partake of the fresh air, in your company. But only if you'd care to. I don't want to impose."

For all that Ratafia was beautiful and polished, her public manners impeccable, still Melissande could hear a note of loneliness in her well-schooled voice. Her inner self rejoiced.

Excellent. She's vulnerable. Twist her arm hard enough and you might get some useful answers.

It was a shameful thing to think, but she couldn't afford to be squeamish. If she didn't do her best to help Gerald get to the truth, lives might well . . . would probably . . . be lost. What price scruples then?

"Impose, Ratafia?" She gave her sister-princess a bracing smile. "Not at all. After that enormous breakfast, I think strolling is a must."

And so, side by side, they strolled and watched Splotze's verdant countryside glide by. The lackeys and their breakfast remains were already cleared away, so they had the spacious promenade deck to themselves.

Tipping her head back a little, Melissande smiled to feel the gentle sunshine on her face. Freckles, shmeckles. How long had it been since she'd strolled beneath a blue sky, with a green-scented breeze caressing her skin? Or listened to the lowing of distant cows, the skirling cries of river gulls, a murmur of voices not tight with tension or grief or impending danger? Too long. She had to do this more often.

"I expect you're wondering," Ratafia said eventually, "why my mother is so quick to raise the dust with Crown Princess Brunelda."

So much for relaxation.

"Actually, no," Melissande replied, "Tell me if I have it aright. Your mother and Prince Ludwig's mother have known each other nearly all their lives, having bumped shoulders at practically every important social occasion since they were let out of the nursery. And thanks to the stupid politics between Borovnik and Splotze, they were never encouraged to be friends, which means they've spent the last fifty-odd years in a vain attempt to lord it over each other every chance they get. And even though your two families are about to be joined in historic matrimony, after so long they can't imagine doing anything *but* squabble."

"Gosh," said Ratafia, awestruck. "However did you know?"

She shrugged. "Because Lional and Sultan Zazoor of Kallarap were in a similar boat. It was all terribly tedious. Lional—"

"I'm sorry," Ratafia said quickly. "Please, don't talk about him if it's painful. If you'd rather, we needn't talk at all."

But she wasn't really listening to Ratafia. Oh, lord. *Lional.* Slowing, she touched her fingertips to Ratafia's rose-pink sleeve. "Ratafia—you do *want* to marry Ludwig, don't you? I mean, I hope nobody's forcing your hand."

"Forcing my hand?" Ratafia stopped, astonished. "Melissande, are you afraid I'm being bullied into this wedding?"

For all the eggshell-walking that diplomacy required as a matter of course, sometimes it was just as important to forge ahead and bugger the mess. She might be in Splotze more-or-less on behalf of the Ottosland government, but if tricky

Sir Alec thought she'd stand quietly by while a sweet young girl was sold into wedlock for a bloody canal then he wasn't half as clever as he liked to think.

"To be honest, Ratafia, I am," she replied. "*Is* that what's happening?"

Ratafia laughed, surprised. "Of *course* not. I told you, I'm terribly fond of Luddie."

Well, that seemed genuine enough . . . but marriage was a two-way street. Struck by yet another horrible thought, Melissande bit her lip.

I wonder if Luddie is terribly fond of her?

It was a ghastly notion, but every possibility had to be considered. What if Hartwig's brother didn't want to marry Ratafia? What if *he* was the one being pressured into the wedding?

What if he's the one behind Abel Bestwick, and the fireworks, and whatever goes wrong next?

CHAPTER SEVENTEEN

Alarmed, Ratafia stretched out her hand. "Are you all right, Melissande? You've gone awfully pale."

"What? Oh. Yes. I'm fine." With her knees suddenly wobbly, she clutched at the promenade deck's polished hand rail. *And that's a lie, it's a great big fib.* Staring over the barge's side, all the way down to the greenish-grey water and the piebald ducks with their yellow beaks and curly tails, industriously paddling, Melissande breathed hard and waited for the horror to subside. "Though I think your mother might be right," she added, over her shoulder. "That peppercorn sauce. Especially on top of everything else!"

"Hartwig does love his food," Ratafia said, with a smothered giggle. "And he loves to share. I shall have to be careful or I'll not fit into my wedding dress."

Ratafia's wedding dress. Her *wedding*. Scant days away now, and no hope of changing her mind. The scandal would be lethal. Frozen, Melissande stared at the ducks. So many of them. This stretch of the Canal was like a little duck city.

How can I ask her if Ludwig's love is real? I can't. She'll pitch me over the side. I'll create an international incident and Sir Alec will go spare.

She uncramped her fingers from the hand rail and made herself turn round. "I wouldn't worry about that, Ratafia. I'm sure you'll look beautiful."

"Well, I hope so," Ratafia sighed. "Because I do want to make Luddie proud. And I want to make Borovnik proud, too. This marriage is so important. It's our chance, perhaps our only chance, for lasting peace."

She really was a sweet girl. Too sweet, perhaps, to survive the shark-infested waters into which she was about to plunge.

Unless of course she's lying. Maybe I'm wrong about Ludwig. Maybe Ratafia is being pressured to marry and the only way out is to sabotage her own wedding.

It wasn't a completely far-fetched notion. Hadn't she done her own feeble best to scupper Lional's mad plan to marry her off? And so what if Ratafia was sweet? That could be an act. Beneath the sweetness, the girl might well be a seething morass of bitter scheming. Look at Permelia Wycliffe, that so-called bastion of Ottish Pastry Guild respectability. As it turned out, the woman had been a bogtrotting nutter.

"Melissande?" said Ratafia, anxious. "Are you sure you're all right? You do look rather odd."

Ignoring the churning nerves, she made herself smile at Borovnik's princess. "Well, to be honest, Ratafia, I am a trifle worried. About you. Because I think I know a little bit of what you're going through just now. Feeling like a leaf swept up in a windstorm, tossed hither and yon, at the mercy of so many powerful forces. It makes you wonder if anyone's stopped to think about you, and what you want."

"Oh." Gaze faltering, Ratafia blushed. "Yes. It is a little— only, not really. I wouldn't like you to think me ungrateful, or unmindful of—"

"It's not about gratitude," Melissande said quickly. "Or owing something to others. Ratafia, your first obligation is to yourself. It must be. How can you make someone else happy if you're miserable?"

Another blush. "Mother says a woman's true happiness is found in the happiness of others," Ratafia said softly. "Especially a husband."

"Oh, really?" Melissande retorted. "Well, your mother might be a dab hand when it comes to peppercorn sauce, but that doesn't make her an expert on everything!"

Ratafia stepped back. "Melissande!"

Bugger, bugger, bugger. "I'm sorry, Ratafia," she said,

grimacing. "It's just—well, the thing is, you remind me of me, from not so long ago. When Lional was determined I should marry Sultan Zazoor. I didn't want to, and he didn't care, and I felt so alone, so *helpless*, that I got drunk and climbed into a fountain full of goldfish. And there might've been singing, but it's all a bit of a blur."

Ratafia's rosebud mouth opened into a perfect little O. "How *awful* for you!" she whispered. "But you're wrong, Melissande. I don't the least bit want to get drunk and serenade goldfish. I *want* to marry Luddie."

"Because you honestly love him? Not because it's the only way to seal a lasting peace over the Canal?"

Ratafia stared across the water at the moist brown clods of earth in the ploughed field beyond the Canal's far bank. Creeping into her lovely eyes, a mingling of iron and acceptance.

"Of course there's the politics. For people like us there's always politics, Melissande. But it isn't *just* politics. I won't let it be just politics. And neither will Luddie."

She sounded so sure of Hartwig's younger brother, Melissande didn't have the heart to question her resolve. If the girl was love-blind, marriage would restore her sight soon enough.

And in the meantime, I'll find out what I can about Prince Ludwig and his resolve.

If it turned out her suspicions were right, and Ludwig proved himself a villain, she'd have Gerald take steps. Which yes, would break Ratafia's heart.

But better a broken heart than a funeral—or a lifetime of being hexed. Just ask Reg.

She and Ratafia started strolling again, companionably silent, the climbing sun warm on their cheeks. They passed one barge-hand polishing the promenade deck's railing, and another oiling some rope. Drifting up from the saloon on the middle deck beneath them, gentlemen's laughter and the teasing tang of cigar smoke. Hearing her Luddie's raucous mirth, Ratafia smiled. The look on her face caught Melissande sharply unprepared. Stirred up thoughts of Monk, who loved thaumaturgics so much it sometimes seemed there wasn't room in his life for anything . . . anyone . . . else.

She winced. *Stop being a gel, woman. You've a job to do, so do it.* Let her be sidetracked into mooning over Bibbie's infuriating, bewildering brother and she'd likely miss an important clue.

"Ratafia, can I ask you something?"

Borovnik's princess trailed her fingertips along a stretch of freshly polished timber hand rail. "Yes, of course."

"You might think me impertinent."

An amused smile. "Friends can't be impertinent."

Friends. It was a nice thought. A pity she was here under false pretences.

Come on, you ditherer. Ask. It's not like you're betraying her. You've only just met, and when this business is over likely you'll never see her again. So what does it matter?

But it did matter. Her scruples, it seemed, weren't so easily abandoned. Going out of her way to befriend Ratafia simply to lull her into sharing confidences? That was cold. Fancy being Gerald, doing this sort of thing for the rest of his life. Hardly surprising he often looked sad.

"Well, I was wondering how it came about, you know, that you and Prince Ludwig—" Annoyed, Melissande felt herself turning pink. "How you—I mean—"

"Fell in love?" said Ratafia, with a swift, mischievous grin, as they swung about the barge's gently rounded stern and started back towards the bow. Their fashionable silk day dresses made little swishing sounds with each measured step. "Actually, it's all Uncle Norbert's fault. He encouraged our acquaintance last year, at Harenstein's First Snow Fair."

And that was unexpected. "*Uncle* Norbert? I didn't realize you're related to the Marquis of Harenstein."

"Oh, I'm not," Ratafia said, pausing to admire the barge's ceremonial brass bell. "It's a courtesy title. To be honest—" Her voice lowered confidingly. "It feels a little odd, acquiring an uncle at my age. But when he asked for the honour I didn't like to say no. He's done so much for me and Luddie, you see."

"So, you and Prince Ludwig hadn't met before the fair?"

Ratafia wrinkled her perfect nose. "Well, yes, we'd *met*. A few times. But I'd hardly said more than hello to him, on account of we're never sure from one hour to the next whether Borovnik and Splotze are at daggers drawn or not. And what with Mama so difficult about Crown Princess Brunelda, and Luddie being a man and me needing to be careful, you know what that's like, there seemed little point in pursuing further conversation. Not until Uncle Norbert stuck his oar in, so to speak."

And thus was the world rearranged. Neatly. On a whim.

"And how will your alliance work, in the long run?" said Melissande. "I mean, Prince Ludwig is Hartwig's heir. The sad truth is that at some point, let's hope it's years from now, he's going to succeed his brother as the Crown Prince of Splotze, which will make you Crown Princess. And one day your mother—" Oh dear. Best not. "Well, she might decide she's tired of being the Dowager Queen. What will happen to Borovnik then?"

"I'll be Queen of Borovnik in my own right," said Ratafia, and flicked her fingernail against the barge's brass bell. It chimed the air, sweetly. "That's one of the marriage conditions. Uncle Norbert was very firm about it."

A skein of grey geese flew low overhead, pinions creaking. Melissande watched them, thoughts awhirl. A moment later an angry shout, as goose-shit splattered a stretch of newly-polished hand rail. She rolled her eyes.

Oh, look. My life in a nutshell.

Glancing at Ratafia, she moved on from the bell. "I hadn't realised the marquis was involved in the legalities of your union with Ludwig."

"No?" Ratafia smiled, and fell into step beside her. "Well, he was, and he's been tremendous. He's helped Mama negotiate the marriage treaty every step of the way. Such a blessing, since more often than not we were dealing with Secretary of State Gertz and Mother can't abide him. She says he's so damp that after an hour in his company, she's caught a cold. But thankfully Uncle Norbert knows just how to handle him."

Melissande felt her stirred instincts stir even harder. Really? Well, well, well. Uncle Norbert had been busy, hadn't he?

The question is, what is he expecting to get in return for all his hard work? And who on this barge would rather he were disappointed?

Another line of investigation that should be pursued. At this rate they'd have to ask Sir Alec for reinforcements. If ever there was a time to be missing Reg . . .

"It sounds rather complicated," she said, cautiously. "How do your people feel about the arrangement? Won't they mind having their queen living in another country?"

Ratafia sighed. "I did rather wonder about that myself. Only Uncle Norbert says that whatever pleases me will please the people of Borovnik. He says a ruler's subjects are like children, they must be kindly guided and firmly led and that under no circumstances can their crotchets be allowed to sway matters of state."

So, Norbert of Harenstein was a glutton *and* a pompous prat. Good to know.

"And Queen Erminium agrees with him?"

"Mama says Uncle Norbert is the answer to her prayers."

Heart sinking, Melissande looked at Ratafia's serenely beautiful face. "And what do you think?"

A pause, then Ratafia's lips firmed. "I think Uncle Norbert is Marquis of Harenstein, and one day I'll be Queen of Borovnik and Crown Princess of Splotze."

In other words, look out, Uncle Norbert. There's a new tiara in town. "Good for you, Ratafia."

"Ludwig and I care a great deal for our peoples."

Yes, but did their peoples care for Ratafia and Ludwig, as a matched set? Pompous prattery aside, the stark truth was that royalty nearly always married without first consulting Mistress Needle the seamstress and the butcher, Master Ham. So what if the plain folk of Splotze weren't all that thrilled with the notion of inheriting the princess next door? What if Borovnik's commonplace sons and daughters didn't care to see Ludwig's face smirking up at them from every coin? What if they resented the Splotzeish imposition of a mostly absent, part-time queen?

"Melissande?" said Ratafia. "You're looking peculiar again."

They'd reached the barge's bow with its cushioned chairs and a scattering of wooden planters riotous with colourful blossoms. The Canal stretched out before them in a long, straight line, the celebrations at Little Grande Splotze coming closer with every copse and cow and cottage they majestically glided by.

Overwhelmed, Melissande stared at Ratafia. The weight of her terrible secret felt suddenly unbearable. This was the poor girl's wedding tour. Soon it would be her wedding. And if she wasn't the one plotting to see it brought crashing to ruin, then didn't she have the right to know that her future was in peril? That Ludwig, or his people, or her people, or the Lanruvians, *someone*, was scheming to make ashes of her dreams?

Of course she does. But I can't tell her. Lord, I hate this. I want to go home.

She smiled. "No, no, I'm fine, Ratafia. I'm just happy for you, that's all."

"Thank you, Melissande," said Ratafia, and impulsively embraced her. "I'm *so* glad you're here."

With an effort, Melissande managed to keep smiling. *See if you still think that when your wedding goes up in smoke.* But no, she couldn't afford to be pessimistic. Things would work out. Gerald was going to save the day . . . with a little help from his friends.

Provided his friends don't lose their marbles in the meantime.

With a sigh, Ratafia gazed at the pretty countryside surrounding them. "I have a confession, Melissande. I appreciate this barge is probably the most wonderful ever built, but I shan't be sorry to leave it behind and continue the wedding tour in the carriages. I'm looking forward to being cheered along Splotze's roads and through its townships."

"I'm not," Melissande said, still distracted. "I always feel like an exotic exhibit on day release from the zoo." And speaking of exotic exhibits . . . "Ratafia, just out of curiosity, why did you invite the Lanruvians to the wedding?"

"The Lanruvians?" Ratafia perched on the edge of the

nearest chair. "Oh, I think Hartwig invited them. As to why, you'd have to ask him."

"I already did. He's not sure what they're doing here."

"Really?" Ratafia shrugged. "Well, I can't say I'm surprised. Every time I turn around there's someone to smile at whom I don't know from a knot in a tree. That's what happens with this kind of wedding. It's never—" And then her face lit up in a dazzling smile, and she pointed at the wrought-iron spiral staircase a little way along the promenade. "Oh, look, there's Luddie, come to make sure I've not fallen overboard. Isn't he *sweet*?" She stood. "Shall I ask him to stroll with us?"

Turning, Melissande considered Ratafia's beloved. Sweet? Not the word she'd have chosen, but he certainly had good timing. Propriety forbade her from pigeonholing Prince Ludwig by herself, but what could be more unexceptionable than a gentle wander and some gossip with Hartwig's brother and his soon-to-be wife?

And while we're wandering ourselves dizzy going round and round this deck, with any luck I'll be able to prise more information out of him than I've managed to prise from his betrothed.

"What a good idea, Ratafia," she said. "By all means, run and ask."

"And the prince couldn't tell you *anything* useful?" Gerald frowned. "That's disappointing."

"I know," Melissande said glumly, reclining on her stateroom's striped and tasselled daybed. "All Ludwig wanted to talk about was the honeymoon. He's taking Ratafia to some private island or other off the Fandawandi coast. I can't believe they're both so *dim*. Apparently there's a scad of palace bureaucrats on both sides of the Canal handling all the 'boring, pettifogging details', like who the devil asked the Lanruvians to the party, but since neither Ratafia nor Ludwig is interested in being bored they've not bothered to keep track. I swear, Gerald, if someone had invited a herd of *elephants* to the wedding, those two wouldn't think to wonder why!"

"You should ask Leopold Gertz," said Bibbie, slouched in

a chair by a gauze-covered porthole. "Uncle Ralph says secretaries of state always know everything about everyone."

Melissande gave her a pointed look. "I did ask him, at the State Dinner. He wouldn't say. I told you that, Bibbie. Why don't you ever listen?"

"*Anyway*," Gerald said quickly, before the girls could start bickering, "perhaps it's an idea to ask him again. You should interview Gertz especially for the *Times*, Melissande. I need to know if he knows about this Lanruvian cherry business, for a start." He glanced at the clock on the cabin's fireplace mantel. "There should be just enough time before luncheon."

Groaning, Melissande draped her forearm over her face. "Luncheon? Today? But I won't be finished digesting breakfast until the middle of next week."

"Never mind about that," he said, and pushed off the stool belonging to the superfluous, velvet-covered piano. "Make yourself presentable, and let's go chat with Secretary Gertz. And after him, if there's time, you can wangle me near Ludwig and I'll see if I feel anything untoward."

"Oh dear," said Bibbie, being waspish. "I think Her Highness is having second thoughts about suspecting Hartwig's brother. It's the billing and cooing. Our pragmatic princess has come over all romantical."

Crossly blushing, making her scattered freckles stand out, Melissande tossed the hand mirror onto the daybed. "I am *not* getting *romantical!* I simply think he's genuinely fond of Ratafia."

"He might well be," Gerald said, hating to burst her optimistic bubble. "Or, as you said, he could just be a very good actor. Or he could love her, but not enough to put her before Splotze."

"But why would he go to all this trouble?" Melissande demanded. "Why not just tell the Marquis of Harenstein to mind his own business and then find himself some other princess to marry?"

"I don't know," he said. "That's what I'm hoping to find out. Now, are you ready?"

"Wait a minute," said Bibbie. "What am I going to do while

you two are off playing journalist? And don't you dare say *stay here*. I won't be cooped up in this cabin like a canary."

"Ha!" Melissande snapped. "More like a moulting parakeet, if you ask me."

It was precisely the kind of thing Reg would say, and had the same bracing effect.

Since speaking up would be as helpful as pouring oil on a fire, Gerald fetched his suitably travel-worn secretarial writing case, made sure he had sufficient paper, fountain pens and ink to hand, jotted down the questions he needed Melissande to ask Leopold Gertz, then borrowed her mirror to slick down his hair, straighten his tie and be certain there were no wobbles in his obfuscation hex.

Only when he was satisfied he still looked like Algernon Rowbotham did he raise his voice. "You two do realise, I suppose, that I'm required to tell Sir Alec *everything* that happens on this mission? Do you really want him reading about moulting parrots and arthritic hens?"

The hurling of hissed, inventive invective ceased, abruptly.

"You might be required to tell him, but I'll bet Monk's jalopy's weight in marshmallows that you don't," said Bibbie, truculent. "I've grown up in government circles, remember? *Nobody* writes down *everything* in their reports."

He smiled, not very nicely. "For you, Miss Slack, I will make an exception. And that goes for you too, Your Highness. I know you're feeling nervy. I know you're waiting for the other shoe to drop. On our heads. I don't care. If you're not helping me, you're in my way. And trust me, girls, you don't want to be in my way."

Bibbie looked at Melissande, and Melissande looked back. Then they both turned identically accusing stares on him.

"Mister Rowbotham," said Melissande, with chilly dignity, "I rather think that was uncalled for."

"*Definitely* uncalled for," said Bibbie. "I'm not impressed."

He gave them a curt nod. "There. You see? I knew if you tried hard enough you'd find something to agree on. Melissande? Let's go. And Gladys, why don't you find someone new to flirt with? I expect you're positively pining for some male attention. Bat your eyelashes hard enough and perhaps your unsuspecting swain will so far forget himself as to spill a few informative beans."

Ignoring Bibbie's offended gasp, he collected his writing case then ostentatiously opened the cabin door for Melissande.

"Algernon?" she said, subdued, as they made their way along a narrow, gaslit corridor. "Just then. What you said. Was that you being frightening by accident . . . or on purpose?"

Ah. "You think I was frightening?"

She caught at his sleeve, tugging him to a halt. The tinted light from the wall-lamp shaded her spectacled eyes and outlined the firm set of her jaw.

"Don't. Please. You know perfectly well you were."

He glanced up and down the corridor, but they remained alone. "I'd apologise for startling you, except I'm not sorry. I meant to."

"Oh." Troubled, she smoothed the sleeve her clutching fingers had wrinkled. "Well. Maybe Gladys and I were being a bit overwrought, but even so . . ." She bit her lip. "It's not like you."

He couldn't meet her concerned stare. "Perhaps it is, though. This isn't Ottosland, Melissande. I'm not your Algernon here. I'm Sir Alec's Algernon. There is a difference."

She snorted. "Believe me, Mister Rowbotham, I've noticed. But I think it's more than that. And I think you know it's more than that."

Of course he knew. The point was how did *she* know? Poor Melissande was as thaumaturgically moppish as the lackeys he'd had breakfast with. It was one thing for Bibbie to notice he was different, but Melissande?

Perhaps it's a good thing we left Reg behind, else I'd have all three of them noticing things, and prodding.

"Algernon . . ." Voice soft now, Melissande stroked his arm. "I can't begin to understand what you've been through, these past weeks. The other Ottosland and—and—everything. But for your sake—for all our sakes—*talk* to someone about it. Monk, or Sir Alec, or an impersonal Department boffin if that would be easier. Reg, even. But *someone*. This awful grimoire magic. It isn't a burden you should carry alone."

Her heartfelt compassion stung him to silence. The corridor wavered and her plain, freckled face blurred and he had to blink hard to see clearly again.

"You shouldn't worry about me, Mel," he said at last, his voice rough. "I'm fine."

She sighed. "Fibber."

Yes. He was. A fibber and possibly much worse. But there was no-one he could talk to about the changes still unfolding within him. Not yet. Not until he'd finished changing. How long that would take, he had no idea.

And by then there might not be any point in talking. By then . . .

He didn't care to finish the thought.

"Come along then, Algernon," said Melissande, with another resigned sigh. "Let's get this journalistic charade on the road, shall we?"

But to his immense frustration, Leopold Getz wasn't free to speak to them.

"I'm sorry, Your Highness," said Peeder Glanzig. "The Secretary's not free to speak with the *New Ottosland Times*. He's in a meeting and can't be disturbed."

"Oh," Melissande said blankly. "How unfortunate. Who with?"

Clearing his throat, Glanzig furtively looked around the barge's Small Salon, which had been set aside for state matters not pertaining to the wedding. They were alone, but it seemed Ludwig's lackey was unwilling to trust even the cushions.

"The Lanruvians," he whispered. "But I didn't tell you that. And I *never* said a single word about *cherries*."

"Ah!" Melissande said brightly. "The Lanruvians! I'm so looking forward to meeting them, Mister Glanzig. When d'you think they'll be free for a chat?"

Peeder Glanzig's finger explored the miserly space between his collar and neck. "I can't say, Your Highness."

Melissande's eyes narrowed. "And does that mean you *can't* say? Or you can't *say?*"

Helpless, Glanzig sought the nearest masculine support. "I don't think the Lanruvians are the kind of gentlemen who give interviews to a newspaper, Your Highness. Not even when it's wearing a tiara. But I shall be sure to convey your interest to Secretary Gertz as soon as he's free."

"Right then," said Melissande, once they were outside on the barge's middle deck walkway. "Ludwig it is. Although really, y'know, I think you should speak to him and Ratafia together. Two birds with one stone. Because as farfetched as it might sound, there's always the chance they're in cahoots."

Yes. There was. The dire truth was that until further notice, everyone on the barge was still a suspect. Though surely some had to be more suspicious than others.

The elusive bloody Lanruvians, for a start.

Above them, from the promenade deck, they heard Bibbie's unmistakable laugh, the girlish trill she used when she was plying her formidable feminine wiles.

"Come on, Algernon," said Melissande. "You can't complain. She's only doing as she was told." A snort. "For once."

He lifted a hand. "I know, I know. Only—"

The sickness came in a thick wave, a roiling churn of nausea riding a dark thaumaturgical cloud. He felt the writing case slip from his numb fingers, heard it crash onto the deck, heard Melissande say something loudly, alarmed. His restored vision was flashing around the edges, drilling an augur of pain through his skull.

Then Bibbie cried out, a dreadful sound of fear and pain.

"Algernon, what is it? What's wrong?"

As deep male voices babbled consternation, and hurried footsteps thudded on the barge's various levels and stretches of deck and on its wrought-iron spiral staircases, Gerald fumbled himself free of Melissande's alarmed grasp.

"Thaumaturgics," he muttered. "The bad kind. Our villain's close. Stay here."

Before she could start arguing, he blundered away. The unreliable, rippled ether surrounded him like sludge, thick and oily and unreadable. More running feet. Slamming doors at the far end of the middle deck, where the important guest cabins were located. Slamming doors and raised voices below him, on the barge's lowest deck. His matchbox-sized minion cabin was down there. So was Bibbie's. Another poisonous ripple through the ether. Stumbling, he fell against a stretch of hand railing. Felt his knees buckle, and had to hold on to stay upright. This was *ridiculous*. He was a rogue wizard. Better. What the devil was *wrong* with him?

Fresh shouting below him, strident with alarm. Bleary eyed, smeary eyed, he struggled towards the nearest staircase. He could feel his grimly enhanced *potentia* writhing in his blood and thought, muzzily, that he knew what was happening. The rotten thaumaturgics were somehow warping Splotze's unreliable ether, and his *potentia* was warping with it. He might as well try to run through cold glue. Bile rose in his throat. He wanted desperately to be sick.

Another familiar feminine cry, not pain this time but outraged surprise. *Bibbie*. She was beneath him now, she'd managed to find her way down to the lowest deck. Was that the source of the filthy thaumaturgics? He thought so, but with his senses so whirligig he was finding it hard to tell. *Wait, Bibbie. I'm coming. Don't do anything—*

Loud protests. Someone bellowed.

"*Good God, no! Look out!*"

A startled scream . . . and then a splash.

"*Gel overboard!*" the someone shouted. "*Gel overboard! Help! Quick! Miss Slack's gone in the drink!*"

CHAPTER EIGHTEEN

"*Good evening, Mister Markham. Or should I say good morning?*"

The cool, acidic voice, coming as it did out of the inky shadows pooled around the rear courtyard of his Chatterly Crescent town house, nearly stopped Monk's heart.

"*What?*" Shying, he tripped over an uneven edge of courtyard paving then had to windmill his arms to keep his balance. "Who the devil—Sir Alec? Is that you?"

A muffled rustle of clothing. A sharp, scraping snick as a match was struck, flaring brief flame. The nose-tickling aroma of burning tobacco. Sir Alec stepped into the back door's lamplight, a thin cigarette neatly balanced between his fingers.

"Where's the bird?"

Wary, Monk held his ground. Shoved his hands in his pockets. *Fabulous, Reg. The one time I could use you sticking your beak in unasked* . . . "Off stretching her wings. Sir Alec, it's the middle of the night. What are you doing here?"

"Waiting for you," said Uncle Ralph's infuriating friend. "Let's go inside, shall we?"

He nearly said, *Do we have to?* but managed to swallow the words just in time. The honed edge to Sir Alec's voice suggested sarcasm wouldn't be wise.

Resigned, he headed for the back door. "Of course, sir. Follow me."

A whispered word and a quadruple finger-tap neutralised his security ward. He led Sir Alec into the kitchen, abandoned him beside the pantry, filled the kettle and put it on the hob. Then he hauled his emergency brandy bottle out of the cupboard, set it without comment on the table, and fuddled about extracting the tin of ground coffee, the milk, the sugar, two mugs and two teaspoons from their various hiding places. Only then did he stop and properly look at his inconvenient, uninvited guest.

Sir Alec looked bloody awful.

"Have you an ashtray?" he asked, oddly polite, and vaguely waved his half-consumed cigarette. "Or should I use the sink?"

"Blimey, not the sink," Monk said quickly. "If Melissande catches you, she'll—" His over-running tongue stumbled to a halt. "Yeah. Fine. Use the sink."

Sir Alec crossed the kitchen in the overly-careful fashion of a man who'd drunk too much . . . or slept too little. A sizzle, and a last pungent whiff of burning tobacco.

"It's a filthy habit, I know," he said, staring into the sink's depths. "I keep telling myself I'm going to stop, only there always seems to be an excellent reason to light up just one more."

In the same way there was always an excellent reason to down just one more glass of brandy. Monk hid a wince. How uncomfortable, knowing that he and Gerald's intimidating superior had even that much in common.

"So," said Sir Alec, turning. "As you have pointed out, Mister Markham, it is the middle of the night. Indeed, it's somewhat past the middle. Which begs the question, where were you? Somewhere I'm bound to regret, no doubt."

Monk felt a sizzle of resentment burn away caution. "If you must know, Sir Alec, I was out doing your dirty work. Actually, *we* were. Me and Reg. We were snooping around the Aframbigi and Graff embassies for clues."

Sir Alec raised an eyebrow. "I take it you've returned empty handed?"

And was that meant to be a criticism? It was hard to tell. "Yes. Sorry. There's no sign either country is up to mischief in Splotze."

"Ah." The small word was almost a sigh. "Then perhaps you might have more luck with this."

From inside his dark blue wool overcoat Sir Alec withdrew a roughly oblong brown paper parcel, lumpily tied with string, and laid it almost delicately on the kitchen table. As soon as he saw it, Monk felt another hot sizzle . . . this time a warning of thaumaturgical danger. Since he'd not felt it before now, it meant Sir Alec's expensive overcoat was protected by a shielding hex.

Crafty.

"This was delivered to my office today," said Sir Alec. "It's—"

"I know what it is," Monk said, fighting the urge to retreat. "A blood hex."

Sir Alec nodded, regretful. "I'm afraid so."

The hex's murky siren call bubbled thickly through his blood. He could feel its residual miasma slickly, sickly, coating his *potentia*. On the hob, the kettle started to boil. Staring at the deceptively innocuous parcel on the table, he ignored its shrill singing.

"And you want me to deconstruct the bloody thing? Is that why you're here?"

Sir Alec nodded again. "It is."

Belly churning, Monk swallowed.

Dammit. Why me?

Up went Sir Alec's supercilious eyebrow. "Because there's no-one else, Mister Markham. I thought we'd long ago established that."

This was his kitchen, in his house, and Sir Alec had barged in without an invitation. "*Look*," he said, close to snarling, and moved to silence the shrieking kettle. The blood hex was scraping his nerves to ribbons. "Stop doing that, all right? I don't like it. And I don't like being taken for granted, either. *Or* being ambushed outside my own bloody home."

"Indeed," said Sir Alec. "And is there anything else you don't like, Mister Markham? While we're on the subject, and before we turn our attention to matters that actually matter."

It would be a grave mistake to throw the kettle. Seething,

Monk made them both coffee, liberally laced it with brandy, then shoved Sir Alec's mug across the table in his general direction.

"Feel free to burn your tongue on it. Sir."

Sir Alec left his mug where it was. "I need that blood hex deconstructed tonight, Mister Markham."

Looking at the seemingly innocuous parcel was hard. His gaze kept trying to skitter away. "Gerald sent it?"

"Yes."

"Whose blood is it? Abel Bestwick's?"

"Yes."

"Have you heard from him?"

"Bestwick?" Sir Alec shook his head. "No."

Glowering, Monk risked a sip from his own steaming mug. "From Gerald."

"No."

Another sip of coffee. The brandy bolstered his faltering courage. "Prob'ly he can't get through. According to R&D's monitors, Splotze's etheretics are a dog's breakfast just now. I've been keeping an eye on 'em."

"As have I," said Sir Alec, and reached for his own coffee. "I trust you're being discreet?"

"No, actually," he said, staring. "Just this afternoon I stood on my desk and made a general announcement."

Sir Alec sighed. "Mister Markham . . ."

"Yeah, well," he muttered. "Since you asked for a list, I'm also not too fond of being insulted."

"Point taken," said Sir Alec, after a moment.

Really? Bloody hell. The man had to be sickening for something. Warier than ever, Monk put down his mug, pulled out a chair and sat. Braced his elbows on the table and forced himself to stare at the paper-wrapped hex.

"I take it you haven't opened this?" he said, flicking a glance at Sir Alec.

"It wasn't necessary."

Now it was his turn to sigh. "I need a minute. Ward the kitchen, would you? Sir?"

There was no actual, university-approved method of

preparing to handle these kind of dangerous thaumaturgics. The closest the textbooks got to sage advice was *don't do it.* But his time in the labyrinth of Research and Development had taught him the hard way that launching into any flavour of compromised thaumaturgical deconstructions without some kind of preparation was a guarantee of blood on the walls. Usually, but not always or exclusively, it belonged to the wizard attempting the deconstruction.

So, as Sir Alec quietly and methodically went about warding the kitchen to prevent the accidental leakage of antithetical subthaumicles, Monk cleared his mind of extraneous thoughts—*Blimey, Gerald, I hope you three are all right*—and encouraged his pulse rate to slow down before his heart wore out.

His hands were sweating. He wiped them dry on his chest.

"In your own time, Mister Markham," said Sir Alec, leaning against the sink with his arms folded and his face blank.

In other words, *Get on with it.*

He took a deep breath. Let it out slowly, willing the fear to breath out too. Glanced up. "I'm ready. But look, if Reg comes back while I'm—"

"Rest easy, Mister Markham," Sir Alec said. "I promise to keep the bird out of your hair."

"Yeah, good, fine," he said, frowning. "Only, y'know, nicely. Don't forget she's had a rough trot and she's still not herself."

"*Mister Markham.*"

Right.

On another deep breath, Monk reached for the parcel. Tried not to notice how his fingers trembled as he unknotted the string and discarded it, along with the crumpled brown paper wrapping. And then stifled a curse as they touched the raggedly square, bloodstained, hexed piece of old blue carpet.

Oh, Gerald. What are you mixed up in now?

Vaguely he was aware of Sir Alec's gasp of startled discomfort. So, the man was human. Vulnerable, even. That was nice to know. Perhaps. And something else to set aside, as he faced the blood magic in all its malevolent perfection.

The warm kitchen seemed to chill as he focused his *potentia* on the daunting task before him. The lamplit air cooled from comforting yellow to unfriendly blue. His heart thumped. His skin crawled. With a growing sense of alarm he began to doubt he was the right wizard for this.

"Yes, you are, Mister Markham," said Sir Alec, from a long way away. "I have every faith in you. Now stop dithering and do your job."

Stop dithering? Stop *dithering*?

You miserable sarky bugger. I hope you choke on those cigarettes.

He closed his eyes. Released his fear. Flattened both palms firmly, deliberately against the hexed piece of carpet, and plunged himself into the dark hell of grimoire magic.

Time melted. Turned liquid. Became molten glass. Trapped in a burning prism, he struggled and shuddered and fought. The hex's filthy thaumaturgical field was an ocean of pitiless acid. Burning, it stripped him to bare, bloody bones, scoured him clean of all conceit and any faith in his powers. He swam its currents with desperation, always two shallow gasps from drowning.

Bugger this, Gerald. I wish you were here.

No. No. He couldn't afford to think about Gerald. Or Bibbie. Or Melissande. Let himself get distracted and he really would drown.

The blood magic incant whipped around him like rope in a tornado. Every attempt to snatch it to stillness failed. He was tired, so bloody tired, but he didn't dare give up. He was a Markham, and Markhams always won.

Except when we lose.

He could feel the panic rising, feel the bitter cold of defeat.

I can't do this. I'm not Gerald. I'm no rogue.

From so far away that it felt like a dream, he heard a soft and familiar voice.

"—age, Mister Markham. Courage. One foot in front of the other. It's not acceptable for you to fall over now."

Irritated, he twitched the words away like a horse wrinkling its skin to discourage a fly.

Bloody Sir Alec Oldman. Sir Manky. Sir Secret Government Stooge. All his fault, this was.

I could be having a bath.

Battered by the relentless thaumaturgical stresses, Monk strained his *potentia* way past what he knew was safe. He could feel the sweat pouring, hear the air rasping in his throat. How long now had he been fighting? He had no idea. The hex was half blood magic, half thaumaturgical barbed wire.

I can't believe Gerald tamed it. What the hell has he become?

A question that had to wait for an answer he wasn't sure he could stomach.

The cruel incant whipped by him yet again, for the hundredth time, the thousandth. Because he had to, because he was a Markham and he couldn't give up, he couldn't *lose*, for the hundredth time, the thousandth, he reached for it with his *potentia*.

And shouted aloud as this time his *potentia* held it fast. He clutched the blood magic hex tight, almost sobbing with relief, eager to rip its strands apart before it escaped him.

What is this thing? Who made it? Have I ever met this brilliant, murdering bastard of a wizard?

Greedy as a little boy tearing the wrapping paper from his birthday gifts, he began to peel away the hex's violently defensive outer layer. And it hurt, bugger, it *hurt*. He was running naked through a briar patch, a ragged dance of blood and pain.

It doesn't matter. It's not important. Winning matters. Nothing else.

And he was winning. Against the odds, he was winning.

There were three distinct thaumic fingerprints tangled up in the hex. That much was clear. He was almost sure one of them was Gerald's. Not positive, though, because it was distorted by the underlying blood magic. The second fingerprint belonged to missing Abel Bestwick. That came from the dried blood. A wizard's *potentia* screamed in his blood. And thanks to Sir Alec, he'd been made familiar with Bestwick's thaumaturgical signature. As for the third thaumic fingerprint, he couldn't quite—it was slippery—what the devil—

And then he realised. *Markham, you dimwit.* It wasn't a thaumic fingerprint at all, it was a powerful deflection incant. Flawless, in fact. Shining and polished, like a mirror reflecting an abyss. Move along now, move along. There's nothing to see here.

Groaning, Monk wrapped his bruised and briar-pricked *potentia* around the incant and wrenched it loose. It dissolved almost at once in the blood magic's thaumaturgical field . . . and at last he was staring into the beating heart of evil.

And could see nothing else. Every element, every syllable, every thread of the incant was warded. Bound and smothered and defended by deflections he'd need a year, at least, to unravel. Churning beneath the pain, the kind of fear he wasn't used to feeling.

Oh, lord. If Sir Alec shoved the wizard who made this in front of me, right now, I wouldn't know. I couldn't recognise him.

So how the hell was that winning?

He felt sick.

"Right then, Sir Alec, that's more than enough," said another distant voice. "He's been playing silly buggers with that filthy hex of yours for nearly three hours. Look at his face! He's the colour of week-old milk." A sharp poke in his arm. A small pain, but rousing. "Come along, Mister Clever Clogs. Time to stop showing off."

Step by feeble step, exhausted, Monk backed out of the thaumaturgical briar patch. Took a moment to catch his breath, then wearily disentangled his *potentia* from the blood magic he had failed to decipher.

When at last he'd gathered enough strength to blink his vision clear, he saw Reg standing on the table in front of him, feathers militantly ruffled, dark eyes alight with a combative gleam. Sir Alec was still leaning—no, actually, he was slouching now, not like him at all—against the kitchen sink and regarding Reg with a definitely jaundiced air. Then his tired gaze shifted, and in his pale grey eyes, a fading hope.

"Well, Mister Markham?"

He scrubbed his fingers through his hair, then dragged his palms down his face, feeling unclean. Badly used. With his elbow, he shoved the bloodstained carpet further away. A damned shame he couldn't burn it.

"Well, sir, it's a blood magic hex and the target was—is—Abel Bestwick."

"And?"

Not at all fooled by Sir Alec's measured tone and seeming indifference, he tried to stifle a wince. The tatty piece of carpet lay on the table like a crime.

"And that's it," he said, fighting the desire to hide behind his hands. "That's all I can tell you. Bestwick's in there, and Gerald. I can identify their *potentias*. But the wizard who created that piece of muck is a ghost." He met Sir Alec's grey gaze defiantly. "I'm sorry."

Silence, as Sir Alec stared. It was impossible to say what he was thinking, or feeling. His tired face was utterly blank.

"Right then!" Reg said briskly, and rattled her tail. "So that was very interesting, and now it's over, and now *you*, Sir Alec, can be on your merry way because our Mister Markham is no longer At Home to visitors."

"Indeed," Sir Alec said, straightening. "I wasn't aware, Reg, that you—"

"No, of course you're not bloody aware," Reg snapped. "Of anything, as far as I can see. People like you never are. People like you, sunshine, are so busy swanning about tossing orders like half-cooked rice at a third-rate wedding that you can't even see that—"

Sir Alec silenced her with a look. "Mister Markham."

Monk shoved his chair back and made himself stand. "Sir."

"You put in a fine effort," Sir Alec said, with every appearance of sincerity. "You shouldn't reproach yourself. Bringing you that hex to break was more a last ditch hope than anything."

What? "Now you bloody tell me!"

A wintry smile. "Indeed."

With a shiver of revulsion, Monk stared at the bloodstained carpet. "You should stick that filthy thing somewhere safe and wait for Gerald to get home. He'll be able to sort it out. Aside from the bastard who created it, I reckon he's the only one who can."

"I'm inclined to agree," said Sir Alec, after a moment. "And if that notion doesn't scare you spitless, Mister Markham, then I am gravely mistaken in you."

Their eyes met in a rare, complete sympathy.

"Now hold on a minute—" Reg began, feathers bristling.

"Don't, Reg," he said. "Please. I'll explain later."

As Reg subsided, muttering darkly under her breath, Sir Alec removed the warding hexes he'd placed around the kitchen. No longer trusting his legs to hold him upright, Monk dropped back into his chair.

"So, sir. What now?"

"What d'you think?" Sir Alec said, shrugging. "We wait and cross our fingers, Mister Markham. Something will happen, eventually. It generally does. That is the nature of the janitoring beast. And in the meantime . . ." His brows pinched in a small frown. "While, for obvious reasons, I cannot officially be aware of your nocturnal perambulations through various buildings of a foreign character . . ."

He swallowed a sigh. He'd spent too long in Uncle Ralph's company not to hear the unspoken request. "You'd be tickled pink if Reg and I kept on perambulating while you very carefully look in the opposite direction?"

A glimmer of weary appreciation. "How many more embassies have you to investigate?"

"There's only Harenstein's to go. The rest are all clear. But there'll be a bit of a delay checking it, I'm sorry. Their regular butler's flat on his back with a nasty case of catarrh, and Dodsworth's not cosy enough with his understudy to risk pushing him for an invitation to afternoon tea."

"*Dodsworth*," said Sir Alec, after a tight-lipped pause. "The Markham family butler, yes?"

"That's right," Monk said, daring him to complain. "He's been helping me—us—out. Don't worry, I haven't told him anything important. Not that he's asked. He knows better than to pry. Alfred Dodsworth is a good man, Sir Alec. You can trust him. My word on that."

Reg rattled her tail. "Oh, don't bother, sunshine. You're wasting your breath. They've got no sense of humour, these bloody Government types."

She was right, Sir Alec was definitely unamused. "Look, sir," he persisted, starting to feel put-upon again, "you did say you didn't care how I went about this. And Dodsworth's been fabulously crafty. No-one suspects a thing. In fact—"

But Sir Alec was shaking his head. "Not another word, Mister Markham. We'll just file this under Ignorance is Bliss and move on, I think."

Sometimes meekness was the better part of not having one's head bitten off. "Yes, sir. Whatever you say, sir."

That earned him another jaundiced look. "How long before the adventurously trustworthy Dodsworth can wangle his useful invitation into the Harenstein embassy?"

"A few days, he said."

Sir Alec's lips pinched again. "No sooner?"

"No, sir. Sorry."

"In that case I'll leave the matter in your hands Mister Markham. But I expect you to apprise me at once, no matter the hour, of any useful developments."

"I will, sir."

"As for this abomination—" With a jerk of his chin, Sir Alec indicated the ragged, bloodstained piece of carpet containing the blood hex. "I've changed my mind. Mister Dunwoody's unique prowess notwithstanding, given the gravity of the situation I'd like to leave it here. So that when you're rested you can make another attempt to identify the wizard responsible for creating that blood magic incant."

Monk made himself look at the hexed bloodstain, not even trying to hide his shudder of disgust. Wrap his *potentia* around that thing again? He'd rather saw off his own head with a blunt butter knife. But how could he say no, with Sir Alec asking him almost politely, for once not making demands, and a tightly leashed tension in him that suggested he was a man straining hard at the end of his tether.

Reg rattled her tail even more emphatically, the gleam in her eyes ominous. "Now look here, sunshine—"

"Reg," he sighed. "It's all right. Someone has to do it and who else can he ask? There's only Gerald. And Gerald's not around."

The bird was practically bouncing with indignation. "I know that, don't I? As if I need you to remind me of that!"

"I'll do my best, Sir Alec," he said, resisting the urge to throw a tea towel over her. "But I'm not making any promises."

Sir Alec nodded. "And I am not asking for them, Mister Markham. Good night."

As the muffled sound of the front door closing reached them, Reg chattered her beak. "That manky bloody man. One of these days, sunshine, I'm telling you. One of these days . . ."

Forcing open eyelids that felt gritty with weariness, Monk considered her. "Why do you always have to give him so much grief, Reg? Is it all government men you mistrust, or is there something about Sir Alec in particular that puts your beak on edge?"

Instead of answering, Reg fluffed her feathers and hunched her head close to her chest. Against every expectation, she seemed almost apologetic.

"Reg?" he persisted.

"Blimey, you're a nosy bugger," she muttered, resentful. "Instead of peppering me with impertinent questions, why don't you wrap that ratty bit of carpet in a nice old-fashioned dampening hex and get it out of my sight before it sends me into a spontaneous moult?"

She might be prevaricating, but she was still right about the carpet. It was unsavoury, and dangerous. He retrieved a biscuit tin from the pantry, tipped its chocolate chip contents onto a plate, dropped in the bloodstained carpet and hexed the lid firmly shut.

"Happy now?" he asked the bird, waving the sealed tin under her beak.

She grunted. "Ecstatic."

"I'm thrilled." He hid the tin at the back of the top shelf in the pantry, then returned to the table. "And now you can bloody well stop dodging me, Reg. What the hell has Sir Alec, *any* Sir Alec, ever done to you?"

Fluffing her feathers, Reg pretended a culinary interest in chocolate chip biscuits.

"*Reg.*"

She gave him a look. "*What?*"

"Talk to me!" he insisted. "I want to know why you're so convinced he's the enemy!"

Mumbling imprecations, Reg hopped from the table to the back of the nearest chair and rattled her tail until its long brown-and-black striped feathers dangled neatly downwards. Then she heaved a great sigh and fluffed herself like a broody hen.

"I never said he was the enemy. And I know Gerald has time for him, so he can't be all bad even if he is a manky government stooge."

Monk felt his empty belly rumble, and reached for a biscuit. "He's *not* bad, Reg," he said, around crumbs. "He's difficult, but that's hardly the same thing. I mean, look at you."

"Cheeky!" Reg snapped. Then she shook her tail, hard. "All right, if you *must* know . . . I can't bear to look at the man. And that's because every time I do, I see *my* Sir Alec, don't I? And I remember how I *begged* my Gerald not to set him on fire then leave him burning alive until the end of time. But my Gerald wouldn't listen to me. I failed. And so—"

Reg's scratchy little voice broke, a dreadful sound of anguish. Biscuits forgotten, Monk picked her up and cradled her against his chest. She felt as fragile as a captive soap bubble.

"Reg, don't do this," he pleaded, fingers gently stroking her drooping wing. "It doesn't help. Come on. Didn't you agree, in this very kitchen, that we weren't going to flog the corpsed horses any more?"

"I might have," Reg muttered.

"Then for pity's sake, *enough!* Because when you look over your shoulder, Reg, you're making me look over mine. And I can't keep tormenting myself with *maybe* and *what if* and *why didn't I.* I can't. I have to move on."

Reg wriggled herself out of his grasp to land flat-footed on the table. Gazing up at him, she tipped her head to one side.

"Deary, deary me," she said gently. "That manky blood magic hex proper took it out of you, didn't it?"

He dragged his sleeve across his face. "I'm fine."

"Eat another biscuit," she suggested. "Rumour has it chocolate's almost as good as brandy."

Another biscuit would make him ill. "No, I'm fine."

"Good. Then you can tell me what's going on with Gerald that's got you and Sir Alec scared spitless."

Damn. He was hoping she'd forgotten. His gaze flicked to the closed pantry. "I don't know that anything's going on, exactly. It's just . . . that blood magic hex is vicious. The worst kind of thaumaturgy."

"I know, sunshine," she said quietly. "I felt it. And yet seemingly our Gerald handled it like it was no more dangerous than a kitten."

Monk felt his mouth dry. "I'm sure there's a reasonable explanation."

"No, you're not, and neither is Sir Alec," Reg retorted. "You're worried, my boy. *I'm* worried. This is Gerald we're talking about. It's his left-over grimoire magic. And if that's not worth worrying over, I don't know what is."

Feeling helpless, he stared at her. "Oh, Reg. What the hell are we doing to do?"

"What d'you think? Get the rest of those manky hexes out of him the minute he's home."

"If I can," he said. "Reg—"

"Don't you start that! You're Monk Markham, raving lunatic and genius." She chattered her beak. "Now why don't you take yourself off to bed for a nice eight hours of shuteye. Your face is enough to frighten a sober woman to drink."

"I can't," he groaned. "We're testing the new and improved oscillating tetrathaumicle containment field this morning and if I leave Walthorpe and Dalrymple to their own devices they'll blow up the lab. Or kill each other the old fashioned way, with their fists, because Dalrymple can't mind his own business and Walthorpe won't put up with being bossed."

"Ha! And you call yourselves grown men."

"Among other things." Creakily, Monk got to his feet. "I'll have a bath. That should help."

But even as the watery heat soaked the ache from his muscles, the ache in his heart and mind, the briar-patch memories in his *potentia*, combined to rob him of relief.

Lord, I hope Gerald's all right. I hope he and the girls are having better luck than me.

CHAPTER NINETEEN

"*Melissande!*" cried Hartwig, practically shoving past her into the stateroom's parlour. "My dear gel, are you all right?"

Rolling her eyes, Melissande tactfully closed her stateroom's door. "Yes, Hartwig, of course. *I* didn't fall into the Canal. That was Miss Slack."

"Indeed it was, the clumsy creature," said Hartwig. He pulled a large red silk handkerchief from his blue velvet coat pocket and dabbed the anxious sweat from his brow. "And I hope you've scolded her severely for giving you such a terrible fright."

"Actually, I've been a bit more concerned with making sure she hasn't contracted pneumonia, but—"

"And as for all those fools who jumped in the Canal after her!" Hartwig flapped his handkerchief to emphasise his distress. "Nine of them. *Nine!* Including my idiot of a brother. What the devil were they thinking?"

"Ah . . . that it would rather put a damper on the wedding celebrations if Miss Slack were to drown?"

"Yes, but she didn't drown, did she?" said Hartwig, sounding almost aggrieved. "Wretched gel swims like a frog from what I saw. Didn't need *one* man diving in after her, let alone *nine.*"

"And how is Prince Ludwig? I hope he's not caught a chill as a reward for his heroics?"

"He's fine," said Hartwig, scowling. "They're all fine. *I'm* the one who's not fine. Because now we're going to be late for the luncheon at Little Grande Splotze! I'll never hear the end of it from that old hag Erminium. She's complained at me for a whole hour without stopping to take a breath! And Brunelda just *sits* there, with *gout*, being no help at all!"

Oh, dear. "I am sorry, Hartwig. You're right. Miss Slack deserves a good scolding." And she'd been getting one, from Gerald, but that was another story entirely. "As for Little Grande Splotze, perhaps it's not such a disaster. We can celebrate over dinner just as easily as lunch, can't we?"

"That's the new plan, yes," Hartwig grumbled. "A message has been sent ahead to arrange it. But that's not the point, my dear. The *point* is that this little kerfuffle gives the Dowager Queen of Borovnik an excuse to find fault with Splotze. Just like the crab puff disaster gave her an excuse. I tell you, Melly, the way that bloody woman's carrying on you'd think she was having second thoughts about her daughter marrying Ludwig!"

Oh, for pity's sake. Not *another* sabotage suspect, surely! Hiding her dismay, Melissande offered Hartwig a sympathetic smile. "Poor Twiggy. It sounds like you've had a terribly trying time. I'm mortified to be the cause of it."

"No, no, no!" cried Hartwig, turning towards her with his arms outstretched. "My dear Melissande, *no!* Believe me when I say that *you* are my sole refuge in the storm!"

Short of running away, there was nothing she could do to avoid his embrace.

"Oh, well, Hartwig, I'm sure that's not entirely true," she said, wriggling to avoid the worst of his wandering hands. "I'm sure dear Brunelda is with you in spirit, even if her sad affliction means she can't throw Erminium overboard as a gesture of support."

Hartwig chuckled. "Minx. You shouldn't say things like that. You'll give me ideas."

He already had ideas, drat him. Pushing his hand off her behind, she stepped back. "Honestly, Twiggy, why don't you tell the Dowager Queen to direct her concerns to your Secretary of State? Let Leopold Gertz deal with her. I mean, you didn't just bring him along for decoration, did you?"

"Oh, *Leopold*," said Hartwig, in deep tones of despair. "That's the worst thing about nepotism, Melly. It means you have to employ family."

"He's family?" she said, discreetly retreating to a safe distance. "I didn't know."

"My third cousin's second husband. There was a gambling debt. And some monkeys. And an ostrich. All very sordid. I'd rather not talk of it, if you don't mind."

"No, no, of course not," she said quickly. "In fact, Twiggy, I don't mean to be rude, but I really should get back to Miss Slack."

"Oh," said Hartwig, disappointed. "Well. If you must, you must."

"But it was lovely of you to come and make sure I was all right," Melissande said, holding the cabin door open for him. "And please thank Prince Ludwig for me. He was very gallant."

Hartwig cleared his throat. "Gallant. Yes. Well, of course y'know, Melly, I'd've dived in to save Miss Slack for you myself, only by the time I got there, well, nine men in the drink already, and I've got this old hunting injury, and—"

"Yes, yes," she soothed. "I know, Hartwig. I know. Please, don't give it another thought. I'll see you for dinner. Lovely. Thank you!"

Heaving a sigh of relief she shut the cabin door behind him. Then, with a certain amount of dread, she returned to her bedchamber where Bibbie, bathed clean of Canal water and changed into dry clothes, sat wrapped in a blanket. Gerald, fuming, stood in a corner.

"—are making me very cross, Algernon!" Bibbie was saying, her cheeks pink with vexation. "Because I could tell you the story a hundred more times and *nothing* would change! I don't remember what happened after I felt that tainted convulsion in the ether, and rushed off the promenade deck to find where it came from. It's all *gone*."

Gerald raised both hands in frustration. "Yes, Gladys, because there's a good chance you've been hexed. So now we have to get the memory back."

"Get it back?" Bibbie tugged her blanket more closely round her shoulders. "What d'you mean?"

"I mean I might know a way of jogging things along."

Silence, as Bibbie stared at him. Then she shook her head. "No."

He took a step towards her. "Bibbie—I mean Gladys—"

"*No,*" she said. "And don't ask me why, Algernon. You know perfectly well why."

"But I don't," said Melissande. "Would someone care to explain?"

Still looking at Bibbie, Gerald smiled, painfully. "She doesn't trust me."

Didn't *trust*—oh. Of course. His grimoire magic. *Damn.*

"Don't be stupid, Algernon," Bibbie said. She couldn't quite meet his eyes. "It's not about trust, it's about being prudent. You shouldn't take it personally."

He shrugged. "It's a bit hard not to, Gladys."

"Actually, Algernon, she's got a point," Melissande said, going to stand with Bibbie. "What if you tried something dubiously thaumaturgical on her and things went pear-shaped? She'd have to go home, which means I'd have to go home, which means *you'd* have to go home, and what would Sir Alec say then?"

She was right, and he knew it. A muscle leapt along his jaw. "Fine," he said, turning. "So what do you suggest?"

He was asking her? Well. He must be feeling dire. "Obviously," she said, "in my capacity as guest reporter for the *New Ottosland Times*, I interview the nine men who threw themselves into the Canal after Bibbie. There was so much hysteria and confusion at the time that there's at least a score of wildly differing bystander accounts. We need to get the facts straight. And if those nine men were close enough to try and rescue Gladys, chances are that at least one of them was close enough to see what really happened just before she went over the hand rail."

"Exactly," Bibbie agreed. "But there's something else to consider. What if one of those nine men is the man with the tainted thaumaturgics?"

"And he dived overboard after you to do what?" said Gerald. "Make sure you couldn't tell anyone what you'd found out? And failed purely by chance? Wonderful." He sat in the bedchamber's other chair. "I *knew* bringing you two along was a mistake."

Melissande felt a stab of fright. "Wait. Are you saying this means our villain knows he's in danger of discovery? Does it mean your *life* is at risk now, Bibbie?"

Bibbie frowned. "*Gladys*. And I suppose it could be, only . . ."

"Only what?" she said, goaded. "What are you talking about? And how can you be so *calm* about this?"

"Why are you cross with me?" Bibbie demanded. "You're the one who always says panic doesn't solve anything!"

"*Both* of you settle down," Gerald snapped. "And then you can tell us, Gladys, what you meant by *only*."

"Well, at the risk of sounding self-serving," said Bibbie, "if our villain does think I've unmasked him, that means I must've done something rather stupid to betray myself. And I don't think I did. I may want to slap you silly now and then Algernon, but I'd *never* do anything to harm you or this mission."

"Right then," Melissande said, very briskly, because there was far too much emotion sloshing about her stateroom's bedchamber. "So we're all agreed it's unlikely Miss Slack is in danger or that the mission's been compromised."

"Yes," said Gerald, slowly. He was still looking at Bibbie, who was looking at him. "But we should be especially vigilant anyway. Just in case."

Yes. Because the mission had to come first, so there could be no prudent running away. Melissande stared at the floor.

Only a madman would choose this life, surely.

She looked up. "Of course, and in the meantime I interview these nine men, you stand by taking notes, and with luck, if our villain is among them, you'll know. All right?"

Gerald nodded. "That sounds reasonable."

Well, praise the pigs for small mercies. "Then, Mister Rowbotham, I suggest we collect your writing case and start our interviews," she said, still brisk. "I'm sure the *New Ottosland*

Times' subscribers will be thrilled to read all about the daring Canal rescue of Her Royal Highness Prince Melissande's beautiful lady's maid Gladys." She pointed a finger at Bibbie. "Only this time, Miss Slack, you're bloody well staying *put.* Show your face outside of this cabin before we get back and I swear by Saint Snodgrass, I'll pitch you back into the Canal myself!"

They weren't far from Little Grande Splotze by the time they'd finished interviewing all of Bibbie's would-be rescuers.

"We might as well have saved our breaths," said Melissande, as Bibbie helped her dress for dinner. "Because after nine hideously boastful accounts of today's adventure, here's what we can say happened for certain. While you were chatting with various minions on the promenade deck, you suddenly took ill and rushed back down to your cabin. Tragically, however, before you could reach it, you were overcome by your mystery ailment and knocked on someone's door asking for help. *Nine* someones came dashing to your assistance, including Prince Ludwig but excluding—and I'm sure this will shock you—the Lanruvians, who it seems are allergic to heroics as well as crabs. But before our nine dashing heroes could clutch you to their stalwart, manly chests you'd had some kind of fit and tumbled into the Canal. Naturally, being men, they tumbled in after you, and were so busy fighting each other off for the chance of being the one to save you from a watery grave that they almost succeeded in drowning each other. So it was left up to me and Ratafia to haul you out of the drink. Which we did. The end."

"Oh," said Bibbie. "Well. *That's* not much help. Whose door was I banging on? Because while I don't remember, I'll bet it's important. I mean, I do know I wasn't really sick. I was pretending. I'll bet the man with the rotten thaumaturgics was behind that door and I was cunningly attempting to get a good look at him!"

Melissande fastened the clasp of her gold-and-sapphire bracelet. "That's what Algernon thinks, too." *Except he didn't say cunningly, he said stupidly. But you don't need to know that.*

"Unfortunately, according to our sterling parade of witnesses, we have four doors to choose from, belonging to Peeder Glanzig, Hever Mistle, Grune Volker and Stani Hoffman."

Bibbie stopped checking a silk stocking for pulled threads and stared. "*Hever Mistle* jumped into the Canal?"

"Yes." She grinned. "Clearly he's more athletic than he looks. Or more besotted."

Putting down the first silk stocking, Bibbie took up the second and made a show of carefully unrolling it. "I can't help noticing Algernon wasn't one of the nine."

Oh, Bibbie. "He wanted to dive in, but I wouldn't let him. He needs to stay as inconspicuous as possible. You know that. Gladys . . ."

"Here you go," said Bibbie, and handed over both stockings and their garters. "Do you want your gown next; or your shoes?"

"Gown," she said, and began putting on her stockings. "Look. About Algernon. You do trust him, don't you? I mean, you're not afraid of him. Are you?"

Instead of answering, Bibbie made a fuss about slipping the dark green velvet evening gown from its hanger.

"*Bibbie.*"

"If Algernon hears you calling me that, Your Highness, he'll go spare."

"Bugger Algernon," Melissande said, and caught hold of Bibbie's hand. "*Are* you afraid of him?"

"No," said Bibbie. "But I am worried for him, Melissande. He's different."

"Well, yes," she said, puzzled, "and I agree, it is worrying. But we knew that before we came."

Bibbie made a little sound of impatience. "No, I mean he's *more* different. Don't ask me to explain, because I can't. I just know . . ." Sighing, she pulled free. "Oh, I don't know what I know. I just know what I feel."

"Worried," said Melissande. *Bugger. I do wish Reg was here.* "Anyway, we asked those four if they recalled you banging on their cabin door for help but they all said no, or they'd not been in their cabin at the time."

"One or more of them could be lying."

"Well, yes, of course, but because everyone's so excitable just now Algernon didn't want to risk using thaumaturgics during the interviews," she said. "He's going to do what he can to get at the truth tonight, under cover of the festivities. I think he's starting to fret, actually, because we leave the barge behind after breakfast tomorrow and he'll never have a captive audience like this again."

Through the closed cabin porthole drifted the sound of the barge's bell, sweetly booming.

"He's right," said Bibbie, tightly. "The clock is running down. We'll have to cross our fingers and toes that my memory comes back."

Melissande bit her lip. "Gladys, are you absolutely sure you don't dare let Algernon—"

"*Yes*," said Bibbie. "Now come along, Your Highness. If we don't get you into that gown we're going to delay everyone for dinner, and Dowager Queen Erminium will complain Crown Prince Hartwig into a fit."

The royal barge reached Little Grande Splotze just on sunset, and the wedding party was greeted in the town square by an enthusiastic throng of town officials and excited townsfolk, complete with streamers, rattles, whistles, a brief but charming display of fireworks, long wooden trestle tables bearing roast meats and baked potatoes and cherry pies and apple strudels and cinnamon cream, and a band that was very nearly playing in tune. Hartwig and Ludwig and their guests were offered fine wine and cherry liqueur to drink. The minions were shown to several barrels of cider.

Gerald resisted the urge to dive headfirst into the nearest one.

Sitting a little apart from the rest of the lackeys, picking at his rustic food and watching Gladys Slack flirt with her many male admirers and charm even the Borovnik handmaidens to smiles, he struggled to keep his mind on the job.

I can't believe Bibbie risked herself like that. After everything I said. The bloody girl could've drowned. She could've been murdered,

*right under my nose. What would I have told Sir Alec? How could
I have faced Monk?*

How could he go on, if something happened to Bibbie?

*I don't know how much longer I can keep on being Algernon.
I'm treading so cautiously that I'm playing right into the enemy's
hands. If I don't learn something definite in the next day then to
hell with being circumspect. I'll start shaking branches to see who
falls out of the thaumaturgical tree.*

And too bloody bad if Sir Alec didn't like it.

After the fireworks and food came the dancing. For a little
while Gerald amused himself watching Melissande adroitly
avoiding the worst of Hartwig's over-enthusiasms. Then,
though it seemed nigh impossible that either of the Borovnik
lady's maids were involved in the wedding plot, he partnered
each woman in a revelly so he could be certain of their innocence. Within a few minutes he learned they were neither
plotters nor dancers.

Smiling bravely, he hobbled on bruised feet back to his
bench, took refuge in a fresh tankard of cider and, under
cover of the laughing and music and general frivolity, risked
lowering his shield completely to hunt for untoward
thaumaturgics.

And felt nothing, again, save the tortured writhings of
Splotze's distorted etheretics.

Bloody bloody buggering hell.

So that was that. He had no choice. No more walking on
egg-shells. Time to start throwing a few thaumaturgical
punches, starting with those damned Lanruvians, who'd
already left the party and returned to the barge.

*Because nobody is that elusive and innocent. Nobody is so secre-
tive about bloody cherries. Somehow, I swear, I'll see them stripped
of their disguise.*

But he had to be careful not to fixate on the Lanruvians.
Because despite the fact he *knew* they were rotten, it turned
out they'd not been anywhere near Bibbie when she fell—or
was pushed—into the Canal. He had to remember there
were other suspects. Dear lord, a *lot* of other suspects. In fact
he was starting to wonder if he'd ever sort through them in

time. He was even starting to wonder if Sir Alec hadn't made a mistake.

I know he wants to keep our presence here secret, but if I can't unmask the villain before we get back to Grande Splotze, that might not be possible. I mean, we can't let people die just so Hartwig never finds out we put a spy in his palace.

Could they?

A shadow fell across him, and he looked up. Bibbie, showing no outward sign of harm from her plunge into the Canal. Bright eyed and rose-petal cheeked, she gave him a dimpled smile.

"Aren't you going to ask me to dance, Mister Rowbotham?"

He put down his tankard. "I wasn't sure if you'd want to, Miss Slack."

Her dimples vanished. "Don't be silly."

She'd as good as said she didn't trust him. Was afraid of him. How was he meant to feel about that?

"Algernon . . ." Bibbie held out her hand. "*Dance* with me."

He needed her to trust him. He needed her not afraid. His life would be dust and ashes if she feared him. He took her slender hand in his, and they danced.

The next day got off to an unfortunate start.

"I swear," Melissande muttered through gritted teeth, "that before this wedding tour is over, Algernon, you're going to be arresting *me* for murder and international sabotage."

If they'd been safely alone, Gerald would have given her a kiss on the cheek for comfort. But since they were seated with Bibbie in an open horse-drawn touring carriage, third from the front in a long line of elaborately old-fashioned equipages that were supposed to have left the royal barge behind on the Canal nearly two hours ago, he could only offer her a brief, understanding smile.

"I'm sure we'll be on our way soon, Your Highness," he said, politely diplomatic.

"And y'know, things could always be worse," Bibbie added, her brilliant eyes wickedly amused. "I mean, Dowager Queen Erminium could be *your* mother."

Seated opposite the girls, facing backwards, Gerald narrowed his eyes. Clearly, in Bibbie's world, polite diplomacy was committed by other people. What a good thing their coachman was standing at the fractious horses' heads . . . and that everyone else was too busy with their own complaining to overhear her remark.

Drifting on the late morning breeze, the sound of Queen Erminium's querulous dissatisfaction as she questioned every twist and turn of the day's proposed itinerary. Hartwig and Ludwig, decanted from their respective carriages, fruitlessly tried to satisfy her endless demands.

"For pity's *sake*," said Melissande. "It's bad enough we had to wait for poor Brunelda to be carted back onto the barge with another attack of gout. Bloody Erminium's had *months* to approve this tour. I wonder how much Borovnik had to pay Ludwig to propose to Ratafia, knowing it was a marry-the-princess-and-get-a-dowager-queen-for-free deal!"

Gerald winced. Apparently Bibbie's rampant allergy to the diplomatic niceties was contagious.

All along the line of carriages stretching behind theirs, the horses stamped their feet and tossed their heads, tails swishing. Every so often he saw somebody lean over the side of his or her carriage, eyes shaded by one hand, and stare towards the front of the line where there was absolutely no movement.

"Oh dear," said Melissande, as the Dowager Queen's strident voice shifted up another octave. "I wonder if I shouldn't—"

Gerald half-raised a warning finger. "Actually, Your Highness, it looks as though the Marquis of Harenstein is coming to the rescue."

"Well, thank goodness someone is, because—"

Hearing the marquis's heels thudding on the Canal towpath's tangled grass, Melissande hushed. A moment later Norbert of Harenstein reached them, his impressive bulk swathed in primrose-yellow velvet and silk.

"Marigold," he grunted, nodding at Melissande as he slowed almost to a halt. "Don't despair. I'll soon have this unfortunate fiddle-faddle smoothed over."

Melissande favoured the marquis with an uncharacteristic

simper. "Really, Norbert? Oh, it would be marvellous if you could. Harenstein to the rescue again!"

The marquis pressed a pudgy hand to his heart. "Fret not, Your Highness. Our wedding tour is as good as underway."

"Marigold?" said Bibbie, once the marquis was safely out of earshot. "Don't tell me I've been mispronouncing your name all this time."

"He's just got a little trouble with his memory," said Melissande, sighing. "The poor man."

"So he's a poor man now? *And* you're calling him Norbert? Melissande, is there some news you'd care to share?"

Melissande frowned. "Don't be vulgar. I've changed my opinion about him, that's all."

"Since when?"

"Since he very kindly rescued me from Hartwig last night," said Melissande. "Twice. And if you hadn't been so busy flirting with all and sundry you'd know that, Miss Slack."

Unrepentant, Bibbie grinned. "Slack by name but *not* by nature. Besides, Your Highness, I was only following orders. And very successfully, I might add. Give me another day or two and I'll have completed my conquest of every male in the wedding party."

"So nine men—including a prince—diving into the Canal on your behalf wasn't enough?"

"Your Highness, nine men was but the beginning!"

Gerald blinked. *Saint Snodgrass defend us. I've created a monster.* "Your help is appreciated, Gladys, but for all our sakes, please don't get carried away. Your Highness, I don't suppose Norbert said anything useful while he was rescuing you?"

"Unfortunately not," said Melissande. "Every time I asked him about his involvement in the wedding he launched into another story about his childhood. I did try to divert him, but once he gets going, well, stopping him is a bit like stopping Hartwig's barge."

"Never mind," he said. "Maybe you'll have better luck next time."

"Maybe we both will," said Bibbie, wrinkling her nose.

"Because I'm afraid Norbert's minions weren't any more helpful than their master. Horribly rude, the pair of them. I tried to thank Grune Volker for diving into the Canal on my behalf and he had the nerve to lecture me about unlady-like romping! And his friend, Dermit? All he can do is grunt."

"Really?" Melissande fought not to smile. "So not *every* male in the wedding party can be counted your conquest."

Bibbie squinted at her, unimpressed. "I feel bound to point out, Your Highness, that gloating is a most unattractive—"

"*Excellent!* Then I think we can be on our way at last!"

Crown Prince Hartwig's shout reached almost to the last carriage. Wilting wedding tour guests immediately perked up. The horses perked up too, responding to the stir.

Giving up her promising squabble with Melissande, Bibbie slumped in her seat. "Saint Snodgrass be praised. Although why your Norbert waited so long to take charge is beyond me."

"Good manners?" Melissande suggested. "You must have heard of them. And he's not my Norbert."

On his way back to his own carriage, Harenstein's marquis slowed and favoured Melissande with a broad wink. "All settled now, Madrigal."

"Yes, and I'm ever so grateful, Norbert," she said. "However did you manage it?"

Flattered, he stopped. "Dear Ermingard," he murmured. "She's getting quite emotional at the prospect of handing her only daughter over to Splotze. Though it's to be expected, I suppose. A mother's love."

"Heartbreaking, I'm sure. But can we leave now?"

"Yes, yes," said Norbert of Harenstein. "Although sadly, since we've lost so much time, we'll have to forgo the pleasures of this region's best scenery, and instead play catch up travelling by way of Putzi Gorge."

"Oh?" said Melissande. "You mean we shan't be visiting Tirinz? Princess Ratafia will be so disappointed."

"Can't be helped, I'm afraid," said the marquis. "What with gels falling willynilly off perfectly safe barges and so forth."

Melissande cleared her throat. "Yes. Well. These things happen, Norbert. Ah—did you say *Putzi Gorge?* That sounds rather alarming."

"Alarming?" The marquis laughed indulgently. "Not at all, Marybelle. If I've traversed the gorge once I've traversed it a hundred times. It's a bit dramatic, of course, but safe as Central Ott's High Street, I promise."

"Well, Norbert, if you say so."

"And the good news is," the marquis added, oblivious to the fact that now he was the one holding up the proceedings, with the Dowager Queen and Crown Prince Hartwig and Prince Ludwig returned to their respective carriages, "that even though we're being denied Tirinz, and must settle for second-best scenery, we'll still be spending the night at Lake Yablitz. And that means crossing its famous Hanging Bridge. So cheer up, Matilda! All is not lost."

"Hmm," said Bibbie, once Norbert of Harenstein was safely out of earshot. "Putzi Gorge. Is it me, or does that sound like a suspiciously convenient place for an accident?"

"What?" said Melissande, her eyes widening. "You think our mystery villain might try something in the gorge?"

"I think I didn't lose us that much time yesterday, falling into the Canal," Bibbie said darkly. "And we made most of it up last night. But now, thanks to Erminium . . ."

"You think *Erminium* would—"

"Erminium, or someone taking advantage of her ghastly tantrums."

"What d'you think, Algernon?" said Melissande. "Are you worried something awful could happen in Putzi Gorge?"

Gerald felt his muscles tighten. What he wouldn't give to say no. But they'd know if he lied, and they'd never forgive him. "Anything's possible, Melissande. But don't worry. I'll be watching."

"No, *we'll* be watching," said Bibbie, and patted Melissande's knee. "It's all right, Your Highness. Algernon and I won't let anything happen."

Ah, yes. That was his Bibbie. Fearless and beautiful. An unstoppable force of nature.

And then there was no time for more discussion, because their coachman climbed back onto his seat. What a mercy the carriage design had him perched right out the front, a good distance from his passengers. So long as they kept their voices low they'd be able to speak freely. Whips cracked, hooves stamped, and the cavalcade of carriages finally took to the road.

CHAPTER TWENTY

If there was anything worse than waiting and waiting for something terrible to happen on the road to Lake Yablitz, not knowing when or where or how disaster would strike, Melisssande didn't want to experience it. Stomach twisted into knots, she sat with Bibbie and Gerald in Hartwig's beautifully sprung touring carriage and tried to enjoy the sunshine and fresh air, but it was a dismal struggle. Her nervous tension made it almost impossible to enjoy Splotze's second-best scenery, which was full of flower-dotted meadows and cherry orchards and milch cows and brown goats with tinkly silver bells around their necks. There also seemed to be rather a lot of rabbits, which insisted on making suicidal leaps in front of the oncoming carriages.

Whenever she felt their own wheels bump, she closed her eyes, crossed her fingers and made sure not to look behind them.

Gerald had sunk himself into some kind of inconspicuous thaumaturgical trance, doing his utmost to stay two steps ahead of trouble. As the carriage bowled along Hartwig's immaculately maintained road, the horses' hooves swift trotting clip-clop reliable as a metronome, she gazed into his disconcerting Algernon Rowbotham face and marvelled.

I don't know how he does it. Not just the thaumaturgics. I don't know how he can bear to have so many lives depending on him. On what he does. On who he is. It really is mad, this life.

She'd had a taste of it herself, in New Ottosland, and the

weight of responsibility had nearly broken her spirit. But Gerald seemed to be managing.

I hope Bibbie's wrong, about him changing again. He's had enough changes to be going on with. He needs to stand still for a while, settle back inside his skin. And anyway, what does that mean, changing again? I wish she'd tell me. I know she knows more than she's saying. How could she not? She's Emmerabiblia Markham. But I wonder if she realises that she's treating me like a gel?

Beside her, Bibbie stirred. "At least we're making good time," she remarked, stifling a little yawn with her gloved hand. "Provided nobody loses a carriage wheel, and none of the horses breaks a leg, we should still be able to enjoy this evening's reception at Lake Yablitz."

Melissande looked at her. "I don't suppose it ever occurs to you to think *happy* thoughts?"

"Your Highness . . ." Bibbie shrugged. "Those *are* my happy thoughts."

Her stomach knotted tighter. "Oh."

Somewhere ahead of them was the Putzi Gorge. She tried not to think of sudden stops and long, screaming plunges. If the wedding's masked villain really was one of them, travelling in front or behind as part of their merry cavalcade, surely he—or she—wouldn't be so reckless as to endanger his or her own life?

Unless, of course, this is a cause worth dying for.

No, no. Happy thoughts, Melissande. *Happy* thoughts.

Lolling now against her side of the carriage, apparently heedless of creasing her green-striped muslin dress, Bibbie stifled another yawn then waved vaguely at the passing countryside. "Oh, look. Another bunny. I'm not sure I can stand the excitement."

Melissande nudged her sharply. Their coachman was yet to utter a word, but that didn't mean he wasn't listening like a bat.

"Thank you, Miss Slack. That will be quite enough from you. I'm sure Splotze's rabbits are the most picturesque in the world."

"They'd be picturesque in a red wine gravy," said Bibbie. "I'll grant you that much."

"I think," said Gerald, surprising them both, "that what Miss Slack means is that she's feeling peckish."

"Mister Rowbotham!" Bibbie stopped lolling. "Everything all right, is it? You're enjoying the fresh air? And the scenery? Marvellous bunnies they have here, don't you think?"

There were shadows of strain beneath Gerald's Algernon Rowbotham eyes. "Everything's fine, Miss Slack," he said, with a small, reassuring nod. "The bunnies are delightful and the fresh air is very bracing."

"It is, isn't it?" said Bibbie, sounding relieved. "But actually, you're mistaken. I'm not peckish. I'm famished. When d'you suppose the Crown Prince will call a halt for lunch?"

As soon as it had become sadly obvious that the wedding party wouldn't have time to enjoy the picnic that was planned for the daisied banks of the Heffershtet River *and* reach Lake Yablitz before sunset, Brunelda—in magnificent defiance of her gout, and doubtless to score a pointed victory over Erminium—had arranged for luncheon baskets to be made up for each carriage and stowed under the coachman's seat. Bibbie pressed a hand to her stomach.

"Can't we ask the coachman to pull over a moment, so we can liberate a sandwich or two?" she said, plaintive. "I swear, my ribs are playing knucklebones with each other."

"Absolutely not," said Melissande. "That would be a gross breach of good manners."

"Whereas me dropping dead of starvation would be the height of polite conduct, I suppose?"

She smirked. "I wouldn't go that far. But at least we'd have some peace and quiet."

Bibbie flounced into silence. Meeting Gerald's wearily amused gaze, Melissande rolled her eyes. Not for the world was she going to admit that she, too, was famished.

But as it turned out, Bibbie wasn't the only one in imminent danger of perishing from hunger. Several miles further along the road, Hartwig called a halt to their travels. Unfortunately, by this time, the pretty countryside had been left behind. Now they were in the midst of some half-hearted woodland, surrounded by spindly trees, many of them dead or dying, with some straggling bushes, tumbled rocks and a few stubborn blades of green here and there for added variety.

"Blimey," Bibbie muttered, as their carriage eased to a creaking stop. "It's about time. I'm ready to devour rabbit without the red wine gravy. I think I'd even consider it raw." She contorted herself into a ladylike stretch. "Oooh, I'm all knots and tangles. Can we walk about for a bit, d'you think? I can't possibly stay cooped up in this carriage until Lake Yablitz. And anyway, there is the small matter of . . ." She frowned. "Personal comfort."

Yes, indeed. They'd been bouncing their bladders for several hours, hadn't they? But that wasn't something that got mentioned in polite company.

"Look," Bibbie added, pointing. "All the men are deserting us for the nearest convenient tree or clump of foliage. I'm telling you, I can't possibly squirm all the way to the lake." With a glance at the coachman, she added, with an eye roll, "If you please, Your Highness."

It was true. The wedding party's various gentlemen were indeed answering nature's urgent call. Even the aloof Lanruvians weren't immune. Melissande turned to Gerald. Curse the bloody coachman, stolidly sitting in his seat.

"I suppose it's safe to go wandering off, is it, Mister Rowbotham?"

Gerald's Algernon eyes lost focus as he plunged once more into his *potentia*. Waiting for his verdict, Melissande became abruptly aware of her own personal comfort issues, and saw that a few of the ladies in the wedding party had begun discreetly withdrawing to find some privacy, wearing expressions that said *Certainly I Am Not Doing What Everyone Knows I Am Doing. In Fact I Am A Figment of Your Imagination.*

Blinking, Gerald came back to himself. "You should be safe," he said, his voice low. "I can't sense any lurking thaumaturgics."

"Praise the pigs," said Bibbie. "Come along, Your Highness. I'll safeguard your modesty if you'll safeguard mine."

Gerald leapt up to open the carriage door and hand them down to solid ground. Melissande shook out her green muslin dress then marched off, leaving Bibbie to trail minion-like in her wake.

Afterwards, having silenced noisy nature, she left Monk's sister to amuse herself and took advantage of Hartwig's preoccupation with a complaining Erminium to snatch a private word with Ludwig, hard to miss in peacock-blue velvet and perched on a slab of rock by the side of the road, contemplating the drab scenery.

As she approached, she found herself considering him through her recently acquired filter of secrets and lies.

Could he be our villain after all? Oh, how I hate suspecting people I'd much rather like.

Yet another reason for never becoming a janitor.

"Hello, Melissande," Ludwig greeted her, so morose that he neglected the common courtesy of standing in her presence. "Everything all right? Your carriage snug and comfy and so forth?"

She nodded. "Everything's lovely, Ludwig, thank you. I'm thoroughly enjoying myself."

The look he gave her suggested he wasn't convinced. "Very sporting of you to say so, I'm sure."

She considered his carriage, where Ratafia was being kept company by damp Leopold Gertz. It seemed as though he was trying to distract Borovnik's princess from her mother's latest tirade.

And if he is, Melissande decided, *it's the first useful thing I've seen him do since we met.*

"No, Ludwig, I mean it," she said, turning back. "But I will confess I'm sorry we've missed taking the scenic road to Lake Yablitz. Family, eh? We can't choose them. We can only survive them. Though I suppose . . ." Another glance at Ratafia. "That's not always so, is it? I mean, you did choose Ratafia."

Ludwig snorted, a sound of hollow amusement. "No, I didn't. Hartwig and Norbert and that bloody hag Erminium, they formed the Committee to Find Ludwig a Wife and presented Ratafia to me on a gilded platter."

For a moment, she couldn't speak. *So I was right the first time? The marriage is forced? But—all that billing and cooing! The island honeymoon! Good lord, how could I have been so bamboozled?* "And you agreed to take her?" she said at last, faintly. *Does Ratafia know? Oh, lord. Wait until Gerald finds out.* "Ludwig . . ."

He shrugged. "Of course I agreed. How could I refuse? I'm Hartwig's heir and I'm duty bound to do what he couldn't, guarantee the family's line of succession. And, well, since I hadn't found a bride on my own I can't really blame the old boy for losing patience and forcing my hand. Not getting any younger, y'know. I won't see thirty-five again."

"But, Ludwig, I thought—I was convinced—that you *love* Ratafia."

"Love her?" Ludwig stared. And then, to her surprise, he broke into a sweetly shy smile that almost managed to make him handsome. "Dammit, Melissande, I adore her. Thought I made that clear, back on the barge."

So she *wasn't* wrong. Good. For a moment there she'd really thought she was losing her touch. Why wasn't there another rock? She needed to sit down. "Oh. Yes. I mean, you did, yes, only—"

"Never expected to, y'know," Ludwig confided. "Wasn't even sure I wanted to. Love makes everything so bloody complicated. If you want a quiet life you steer clear of love, that's my advice."

Yes, well, she didn't seem to be having any trouble on that score. "Yet you haven't followed it yourself."

Ludwig's smile was sheepish this time. "Our family motto. *Do as I say, not as I do.*" He linked his fingers around one raised knee. "And I really do love my girl." The sheepish smile crumpled into a frown. "It's her bloody mother I can't stand."

And what was she supposed to say to that? "Well . . . perhaps you won't need to see much of Erminium, after you're married. You know. Being newlyweds, wanting your privacy. Matters of state. If you play your cards right you could keep her at bay for months on end."

"That would be my cunning plan," Ludwig said, with a

swift, conspiratorial grin. "But don't tell Ratafia. For some reason she's quite attached to the old bat."

"I won't breathe a word, I promise. Ludwig—"

"Yes?" he said, after a politely patient moment. "Something the matter, Melissande?"

"No, no," she said hastily. *Come on, woman, spit it out. Too bad if you make Gerald cross. Are you here to help him, or aren't you?* "I was just wondering . . . everything's all right, isn't it? With the wedding preparations. Nothing's been giving you cause for concern?"

Ludwig pulled a face. "What, aside from the crab puff catastrophe and your lady's maid falling into the Canal and Brunelda having to abandon the wedding tour on account of her gout and the Lanruvians set to upset Splotze's cherry cart and Erminium, you mean? No. Why would I be feeling concerned?"

She felt her heart leap. "Y'know, it's funny, I do believe I heard mention of cherries. And the Lanruvians. But it sounded so peculiar I thought it must've been a mistake."

"No mistake," said Ludwig, morose again. "You got me thinking the other day, Melissande, about those bloody Lanruvians and what they're doing at my wedding. So I tackled Hartwig."

It was a struggle to keep her eager excitement from showing. "And what did he say?"

"That it was all Leopold's idea. Making up our cherry harvest shortfall by bringing in the Lanruvians. Using my wedding to cover up any questions about their presence. Hartwig's livid, but by the time he found out it was too late to uninvite them. So we've got to put a brave face on things until the wedding treaty's signed. There are all kinds of concessions and loopholes and what-have-yous to do with the Canal in the cherry arrangement, y'see. Punitary fines. Reversions of rights. Transfers of titles. If the Lanruvians start rocking the barge now, well, the whole bloody Splotze-Borovnik partnership could capsize. Disaster."

"I'm sorry, Ludwig," she said at last, after trying to think it through. "I don't quite see it. If it's that important, how could Secretary Gertz do something so silly?"

"He panicked," Ludwig sighed. "Everyone knows we float through the world on our cherry liqueur. He was afraid two bad harvests might turn into twenty."

"Which would put something of a dent in Splotze's reputation and revenue."

"And change the balance of power between us and Borovnik." Ludwig heaved another sigh. "Which explains the urgent desire to prop up our cherry supply. Bloody Leopold. Always doing the wrong thing for the right reason."

Melissande inspected a loose thread in her sleeve. Lord, what a tangle, with the Lanruvians slap bang in the middle of it. The question was, did this make them the villains? Or were they simply the happy beneficiaries of someone else's villainy?

And if that's the case, then whose?

"Ah . . . Melissande?"

Looking up, she saw that Ludwig's demeanour had shifted from woeful to anxious. "Yes?"

"Need to ask you not to repeat any of this," he said. "Shouldn't have told you, really. But it's on my mind and, well, you're a good listener."

And now she was going to lie to him with a reassuring smile on her lips. *I hate this. I really do.* "Oh, Ludwig, of course. I'll not breathe a word."

"Much appreciated," said Ludwig, expansive with relief. He clambered down from his rock, took up her hand and kissed it. "Hartwig always said you were a right one, and he wasn't wrong."

"And of course when he said *that*," Melissande concluded, "I wanted the earth to open up and swallow me."

"I'm sorry," said Gerald. "I know this is uncomfortable for you."

"But it's life or death," she said. "Yes, yes. I understand."

Understanding, however, didn't necessarily mean acceptance, or approval. One of the things he loved most about Melissande was her unflinching dedication to honesty.

Whereas janitors are dedicated to uncovering the truth . . . and sometimes the only way to get at the truth is by lying until you're blue in the face.

Something that would never sit well with Rupert's sister.

As the coachmen watered their horses from special barrels attached to the carriages, and inspected them for harness galls and stones in their hooves, the wedding guests had spread out along the side of the road to eat their picnic lunches and chat. Taking advantage of the lull, he and Melissande had removed to a discreet but socially acceptable distance, pretending to consult on her next article for the *New Ottosland Times.*

"You don't have to go on, y'know, Mel," he said gently. "Being involved. If you'd rather step back. I'll not think any less of you. How could I? You've been marvellous. You've done far more than Sir Alec expected you would. Or could. Truth be told, if you did step back now I've no doubt he'd be relieved."

Melissande managed a wobbly little smile. "Him and Rupes. But Ger—sorry, Algernon, how can I? The job's not finished. You need me to be your camouflage, so you can keep on janitoring without raising suspicions."

"The *Times*, you mean?" He shook his head. "No. We can get around that. I've been thinking. All you need do is fall victim to a vague indisposition. You tell Hartwig you're terribly sorry, but you don't think you can go on. He makes an embarrassing fuss over you then reluctantly agrees and orders the carriage to take you and Bibbie back to Grande Splotze, leaving me behind as your proxy for the *Times.* Under those circumstances, no-one will object to me asking them all kinds of questions."

"Oh," said Melissande. "Yes. That does sound like it would work."

It certainly did. In fact, the more he thought about it, the harder he could kick himself for not having come up with the plan much sooner. Like before he'd ever let Bibbie set foot on Hartwig's barge. If he'd done that, he might've saved himself an awful lot of aggravation.

Only, of course, if I had left her behind in Grande Splotze, probably as soon as my back was turned she'd have picked up the hunt for Bestwick where I left off.

Hell's bells. Abel Bestwick. So much had happened, the missing janitor had slipped his mind. Or maybe it was more that he didn't *want* to think of him. Too much guilt there. For all his superior *potentia*, he'd failed to find the poor bastard. Save him.

But if Bibbie went back to the palace, she'd make a point of visiting that kitchen maid. He knew it. And if the girl started weeping for her lost Ferdie again, and begged Bibbie for help . . .

Of course she'd laugh at the danger and go hunting for Bestwick. Bibbie's a Markham. That's what they do.

He looked over at her, at the moment doing her best to charm a smile out of Norbert of Harenstein's man, Dermit. Norbert's man was still resisting.

Blimey. He must be carved out of stone.

"Actually?" said Melissande, who was giving Bibbie the same frowning, considering look. "I think it'll be safer all round if Bibbie and I stay. Saint Snodgrass alone knows what she'd get up to that far out of your sight." A little sigh. "Don't worry about me, Algernon. I'm just being overly nice in my scruples."

"Are you sure?" he said, and wished he could hug her.

Her chin tilted, in that particular way that made her quint-essentially, uniquely Melissande. "Quite sure. Now, what are we going to do about the Lanruvians?"

"*We* aren't going to do anything," he said firmly. "Whether they're behind the plot or simply taking advantage of it, they're still bloody dangerous. You stay away from those buggers, Mel. They're my problem, and I'll deal with them."

Behind her spectacles, her eyes narrowed. "And there you go being frightening again."

"In which case, my work is done," he retorted. "For the moment. So why don't you go and rescue Dermit? He might be a dour stick, but as far as I can tell he's done nothing to deserve Bibbie's undivided attention."

"Yes, Mister Rowbotham," Melissande murmured. "Whatever you say, Mister Rowbotham."

But the rescue wasn't needed, because a moment later Hartwig was chivvying his motley assortment of guests back to their carriages. One by one they clambered into their seats, the coachmen roused the horses, and the cavalcade rolled on.

Gerald, seeing Bibbie's eyelids droop, couldn't resist. "Oh dear. Is all that flirting wearing you out, Miss Slack?"

She glowered at him, sleepily. "Drop dead, Mister Rowbotham."

And on that cordial note, their journey to Lake Yablitz continued.

For the next two hours, nearly, while Bibbie and Melissande dozed, Gerald hid behind his own closed eyelids and used as much of his *potentia* as he dared to search the surrounding ether for signs of danger. But beyond the discomfort of Splotze's cantankerous etheretics, and the Lanruvians' hot, bright *potentias*, he found nothing and no-one to give him pause.

Which was both a relief, and profoundly disturbing. It didn't make sense. If the Lanruvians couldn't hide their power from him, really, could anyone else? Somewhere, somehow, he must've taken a wrong turn. Something Melissande had said, earlier. Something about scruples . . .

From the start I've been assuming there's a wizard at work here. But what if there's not? What if there's simply an ordinary, every day villain armed with a rotten wizard's filthy thaumaturgics? Grimoire magics created for mischief, and sold without scruple to the man with the most coin.

Damn. It made sense—and he should've considered the possibility from the beginning. Instead, he'd let the Lanruvians' presence blind him. *Idiot.* He had to get hold of Sir Alec. See if his superior had been able to trace the provenance of that blood magic hex. If they could work out who'd created it they'd be several steps closer to finding out who'd bought it, and once they knew who'd bought it . . .

Bibbie cleared her throat, inquiringly. "Are you all right, Mister Rowthbotham? You look like someone's jabbed you with a very large pin."

It could still be the Lanruvians, of course, attempting to

hide their tracks by using another wizard's incants and hexes. He felt sure there was more to their presence in Splotze than cherries.

But as various people keep on telling me, feelings aren't facts. I might be wrong.

"Algernon!" Bibbie said sharply. "What's the matter?"

"Nothing," he said, blinking himself free of furious thought. "Where are we?"

"In Splotze," Bibbie said sweetly, a glint in her eyes.

Melissande poked Bibbie in the ribs with her elbow, then pointed. "I'm no expert on landscapes, but I think we're coming up on Putzi Gorge. I mean, look around us. The countryside's looking awfully gorge-like, if you ask me."

They were travelling through more spindly woodland, flanked left and right by large patches of dry ground scattered with leaf litter and rocks. Leaning over the side of the carriage and twisting round, through the thin scattering of trees Gerald saw the road ahead start to wind and dip.

"You're right," he said, and felt his heart thump. *Is it now? Is this it? Was I wrong about the fireworks after all? Does our villain intend the Splotze-Borovnik dream to die here?* "That's a gorge."

"I wonder how deep it goes . . . and how long it'll take us to reach the other side," said Melissande.

She sounded like someone who was nervous and trying hard to be brave. He pulled back inside the carriage.

"I'm sorry. I don't know. Your Highness, d'you mind if Miss Slack and I swap places? I'm afraid travelling backwards down a gorge will play havoc with my insides."

"And what about my insides?" said Bibbie, prepared to be indignant. And then, bless her, she realised that he needed to be able to see what lay ahead. "Never mind. By all means, Mister Rowbotham, let's swap."

So they changed seats, and he settled himself next to Melissande. Risked taking her hand in his, and giving it a quick squeeze.

Bibbie bent forward, her gaze intent. "I don't feel anything beyond Splotze's loopy etheretics. Do you?"

Lowering his voice to match hers, a near whisper, he shook his head. "No." At least not yet. "Gladys—"

"I've been thinking too," she said. "Perhaps even if our mystery villain does try something, it won't work. The etheretics here are *ridiculous*. I don't see how—"

False hope was dangerous. "You felt what I felt on the barge, Gladys. The power of those thaumaturgics. Our villain must've been planning this for months. D'you really think he's going to let some ridiculous etheretics get in his way?"

She wanted to argue, but she was Emmerabiblia Markham. She didn't fear to stare a hard truth in the face. "No."

Melissande's fingers laced in her lap. "Are you saying you can't stop him?"

"Of course not," he said. "I'm saying he's good. But don't worry. I'm better."

And for the love of Saint Snodgrass, don't let *that* be a lie.

Ludwig and Ratafia's carriage led the wedding tour party down into the forested gorge. They lost the sunlight quickly, the cloudless blue sky soon criss-crossed by a latticework of branches. The air grew cool and damp. Water trickled over the mossy rocks that edged the inner side of the fern-fringed and downwards-winding road, and shadows pooled beneath the gnarled and overhanging trees.

Only the horses' hooves, the carriage wheels, the trickling water and the belling of hidden birds broke the deep silence.

Gerald felt his *potentia* stir, its grimoire magic roused by the ether's twists and folds and pockets of darkness. *Cantankerous* was a kind word, compared with what he sensed here. But was there villainy, too? He couldn't sense it. Could Bibbie? Like him she was seeking trouble, and even with his dimming hex in place her *potentia* glowed before his mind's eye, bright amid the gorge's gloom.

"Careful, Gladys," he murmured. "You don't want the wrong people knowing what you are."

Dreamily she nodded, and a moment later her brightness faded a little.

The road unwound steadily, lowering them further and

further from the sky. Here and there the trickling water turned into tiny falls, droplets splashing and spinning, making the lush green fernery dance.

"Well," said Melissande, hands still folded tightly in her lap. "So far, so good."

In front of them, one of the horses drawing Hartwig's carriage spooked at a bird clattering out of a tree, in turn spooking its three companions. All four horses leapt forward in fright, crowding into the back of Ludwig and Ratafia's carriage. Its team of four shied sideways, dangerously close to the road's edge. Ratafia and Ludwig cried out. Small rocks tumbled, waking echoes all the way to the bottom of the gorge.

Melissande squeaked as their own carriage lurched, its horses quick to believe there was danger. "Algernon!"

Bloody horses. Bloody *hell*. Any moment now, any moment, the rest of the wedding tour's carriage teams would start to panic . . . and there wasn't any way for him to calm them with thaumaturgics.

"Hold tight, Your Highness," he said. "Gladys?"

Bibbie's face was pale, her hexed brown eyes narrowed in concentration as their carriage bounced alarmingly. "Nothing," she muttered. "No incants. What about you?"

Did he dare drop his shield entirely? Could the writhing etheretics hide him, or would his true nature be revealed? And there was Bibbie, so close to him, lord, close enough to touch. What would she feel? Nothing? Or would she feel everything and turn away from him in fear?

Coward.

In a short, sharp burst he reached out with his full *potentia*, swift and searing like a lightning strike. Splotze's ether convulsed. He heard Bibbie's shocked gasp, feeling him untrammelled, then felt her take the same risk. Inspiration struck. He reached out again, letting her *potentia* blur his own. Bibbie gasped again, startled, and then she followed his lead. Used her *potentia* to hide his completely, leaving him free.

Desperate, he searched the ether. Clutched at the side of the carriage as it lurched again. The coachman was cursing in ripely inventive Splotzin, and he could hear other voices raised in alarm. Was this sudden upset the villainy he'd dreaded? And if it was, could they find the culprit and stop him in time?

Come out, come out, wherever you are.

But like Bibbie, he found nothing. The only grimoire magic in Putzi Gorge was his own. He opened his eyes.

"Nothing."

Bibbie was staring, her eyes crowded with difficult questions.

He shook his head. "Not now, Gladys."

"Not now what?" said Melissande, alarmed. She was clutching the side of the carriage, too. "Mister Rowbotham—"

"Everything's fine, Your Highness," he said, squeezing her hand again. "No need to worry. Look, Prince Ludwig's coachman has his horses under control."

And so did their own coachman, praise Saint Snodgrass, and the burly man in charge of Hartwig's carriage team. Above the calmed thudding of hoofbeats they heard relieved laughter from Ludwig and Ratafia, booming praise to his coachman from Crown Prince Hartwig . . . and a rising tide of complaint from Borovnik's Dowager Queen.

Melissande sighed. "Oh dear. She just can't help herself, can she?" Then she leaned a little closer. "You're quite sure we're safe, Algernon?"

"As sure as I can be," he replied softly. "As hard as I looked, there were no rotten thaumaturgics. I really do think we're fine."

"But from now on," Bibbie added, scowling, "*nobody* is allowed to say *so far, so good*. Right?"

CHAPTER TWENTY-ONE

Not quite an hour later, the wedding party emerged unscathed from the shadowed cool of Putzi Gorge into warm afternoon sunlight.

As Gerald and Bibbie changed seats again, she raised her eyebrows at him. Whatever qualms she was feeling, given what she knew of him after their little thaumaturgical adventure, she was keeping them well hidden.

"First the fireworks and now this," she said lightly. "I wonder, Mister Rowbotham, if you've ever heard the story of the janitor who cried wolf?"

"And *I* wonder, Miss Slack," said Melissande, "if the old saying *better safe than sorry* rings any bells for you?"

He gave them both a warning look. "Perhaps we should enjoy the scenery. Quietly."

"Good idea!" said Bibbie. "And the first one to spot a rabbit wins a seat beside Dowager Queen Erminium at dinner."

Really? Sitting back, Gerald folded his arms.

I wonder if it wouldn't have been smarter of me to fall in love with Melissande, instead.

The carriages bowled on without further incident. Several more miles closer to Lake Yablitz, as they passed through countryside featuring trees and hedgerows but thankfully no rabbits, Crown Prince Hartwig called another halt so the horses could be watered again, and his guests could stretch their legs and so forth.

With nature remaining silent this time, Gerald and the girls contented themselves with alighting from their carriage and unkinking their various kinked bits.

"No, Gladys," said Melissande, as Bibbie looked longingly along the verge at Norbert of Harenstein's men, who stood apart in deep conversation. "I think, in this case, the time has come to accept defeat. Hard as it must be to admit, Bern Dermit and Grune Volker are apparently immune to your charms."

Bibbie heaved a sigh. "Well, I suppose there must be a first time for everything. Although now I really am sorry Volker didn't catch pneumonia when he went over the barge's railing with me into the Canal."

"When he what?" Gerald stared. "Went over *with* you? But he dived in after you. Didn't he?"

Bibbie was frowning at the two men, clearly rankled by her failed conquest. "With me, after me, does it really matter which?"

"I don't know," he said, and resisted the urge to shake her. "Maybe. Do you actually *remember* him going in with you or is it just a figure of speech?"

"Oh," said Bibbie, abruptly seeing his point. "You mean did Dermit lie? Well—I'm not sure. It's all still a blank, what happened. Only for some reason, just then, I thought . . . I felt . . ."

"You felt what?" he persisted. "Come on, Gladys. *Think*." She swatted at him. "I *am* thinking. Don't bully me."

"You're not suggesting Volker was trying to harm Gladys, are you?" said Melissande, disbelieving. "On purpose? But Algernon, why would he? He's from Harenstein."

Biting his lip, Gerald stared at Grune Volker. Yes, he was. And at first glance nothing could be more ridiculous than the notion that Harenstein was behind the plot against the wedding.

But nothing is impossible. And someone here is guilty.

With another gusty sigh, Bibbie pressed fingertips to her temples and turned away. "No. I'm sorry. Whatever I thought I felt, or remembered, it's gone."

He smothered disappointment. "Never mind. Melissande's probably right. The notion of Harenstein as the villain is rather far-fetched."

But as soon as he could punch through Splotze's ether to Sir Alec, he was going to ask his superior to take a very close look at bluff, bumptious Norbert and his men.

And then Princess Ratafia joined them, resplendent in turquoise silk and glowing like the happiest bride-to-be in the world. Playing the part of well-trained secretary, Gerald retreated a few paces, taking Bibbie with him. She didn't pull away from him. He had to think that was good.

"Putzi Gorge was exciting, Melissande, wasn't it!" Ratafia exclaimed. "Especially when the horses decided to be silly. Were you frightened? I was. But then Luddie put his arms around me and I knew we'd be safe."

"The gorge certainly had its moments, yes," Melissande agreed. "But does it make up for missing the cheering townsfolk in Tirinz?"

The princess giggled. "Oh, I'm not bothered about missing Tirinz. I don't care where I am, so long as I'm with Ludwig. Anyway, Hartwig says we need to get on. So I'll see you again at Lake Yablitz!"

"Don't suppose anyone's got a lemon handy, have they?" said Bibbie, as Ratafia of Borovnik danced away. "Only that much sugar makes me feel ill."

"Since when?" said Melissande, snorting. "I'm not the one who ate four office sticky buns in one sitting."

I miss Reg, Gerald thought, as he ushered the bickering girls back into the carriage. *Where's Reg when I need her? If I poke them in their unmentionables I'll end up behind bars.*

More miles through second-best scenery, still no rabbits. Hedgerowed fields gave way to open moorland. More miles and the countryside grew hilly, the road undulating, in places quite steep.

Remembering his Department briefing notes, and the photographs included with them, Gerald looked at the girls. "I think we're quite close, now."

"Good," said Bibbie. "Because my posterior's positively snoring."

"That's not very delicate, Gladys," said Melissande.

Bibbie grimaced. "You think of something, *any*thing, delicate about a numb bum, Your Highness, and *I'll* sit next to Erminium at dinner."

Ignoring that, Melissande clasped her hands in her lap. "And everything's still all right, is it, Mister Rowbotham?"

"I think so," he said, after a moment. "My bum's not numb, anyway."

That made her smile, which was what he'd wanted. Poor Melissande. She wasn't having much fun on this mission. In her own way she was as brave and bold as Bibbie, but she really wasn't cut out for the janitoring life.

They lapsed back into silence. Another few miles rolled by. He risked lowering his shield, yet again, to test the surrounding etheretics. Nothing different. No alarm bells. Only the same busy, tizzied twistings.

Four years in this place? I don't know how Bestwick didn't go mad. It must've been like sleeping under sandpaper sheets, all this rubbing against his potentia.

Then again, Bestwick did succumb to the charms of kitchenmaid Mitzie, knowing full well what Sir Alec would say. So perhaps he had gone mad.

The carriages followed the road round a wide, sweeping bend. Bibbie sat up and pointed. "Oy. Out there. Am I seeing things, or does that look like a bridge?"

As Melissande shaded her eyes and squinted, Gerald shifted round on his seat. Leaning sideways again, so he could see past the coachman and horses and the two carriages in front of them, he squinted too until the hazy suggestion of bridginess resolved into solidity: Splotze's famous Hanging Bridge of Yablitz. His parents had sent him a post-card, and covered the back with exclamation marks.

Constructed of ornately carved wood, the bridge stood high and deceptively fragile above a narrow silver ribbon of river, which doubled back on itself in a long lazy loop to pour into distant Lake Yablitz. The horizon-sliding sun gilded the wide, still water and burnished the roofs of picturesque Lake Yablitz township.

As the road began to drop away before them, leading down

to the bridge, the carriage horses slowed from a trot to a walk. The road's left-hand side was open, while up ahead its right-hand side was crowded by a high and wide rock-strewn slope of hill. Spindly saplings struggled for life between the stones.

"Algernon . . ."

Gerald pulled himself back into the carriage, nerves scraped by the warning note in Bibbie's voice. "Gladys?"

"What's wrong?" said Melissande. "Is something wrong?"

Brows pinched in a frown, Bibbie was staring at the top of the hill, where rocks were carelessly scattered like a giant's abandoned game of knucklebones.

"I don't know," she murmured. "Algernon?"

His rear end might not be numb, but his *potentia* was feeling muffled. The grimoire parts of it, especially, resented Splotze's tortured ether. He followed Bibbie's troubled gaze to the hilltop, and risked a thaumaturgial look. Felt his own face collapse in a frown.

"I don't know, either. There might be something. It's hard to say." The frown twisted into a sarcastic grimace. "I don't like to cry wolf."

Bibbie shook her head. "I take that back, Mister Rowbotham. You cry wolf as many times as you like."

He was almost sure he couldn't feel any rank thaumaturgics. But she was Monk's sister. He'd be mad not to take her unease seriously.

Damn. And now I really wish Reg was here.

What he wouldn't give to have her flying up there for a good stickybeak around. She'd become his second set of eyes, and he'd hardly noticed. Just taken her for granted.

I won't do that again.

"Look," said Melissande, "I don't like to nag, but are we in trouble or aren't we? Because if we are, I think someone has to tell Hartwig what's going on."

"Really?" said Bibbie. "You want to confess you've been lying to him since you got here? I don't see how that'll help."

"No, it'll be awful," Melissande said, her expression dogged. "But that's beside the point. I won't sit here saying nothing if Ratafia and—"

"Stop it," Gerald said. "Nobody's saying anything, not unless I—"

Shooting bolts of pain obliterated coherent thought. As he slid boneless off his seat and onto the carriage floor, he heard Bibbie cry out, echoing his distress.

"Algernon! Gladys!" cried Melissande. "Coachman, coachman, stop! Something's terribly wrong!"

Splotze's ether had turned whiplike, lashing him in fury. The stench of grimoire thaumaturgics smothered his *potentia*, clogged his senses. He could barely breathe. He heard Bibbie's harsh sobbing breaths, felt her fingers groping for his hand. He caught hold of her, a lifeline.

Another whipcrack of tainted magic, much closer this time. Coming from one of the other carriages? He thought so, but which one? The writhing ether was a blanket, blotting out sight.

Then Melissande gasped. "Oh, no! *Look!*"

Fighting pain and confusion, Gerald opened his eyes. Saw Bibbie, and tried to smile. And then he heard a deep, ominous grinding, rock against rock. The ether twisted tighter, convulsing. Horses whinnied in fear. Raised voices, coachmen shouting. Their carriage slewed to a halt, hard behind Hartwig's carriage, nearly sliding off the road.

Melissande was on her feet, gaping in alarm. Gerald hauled himself to his knees, hauling Bibbie with him. Dazed by grimoire magic he looked at the bridge—just in time to see the first of three huge rocks plunge down the side of the steep hill and strike it. Timber shattered. Splinters flew. Water plumed as the hexed rocks smashed into the river below.

"Ratafia!" cried Melissande. "And Ludwig!"

Their carriage was a mere stone's throw from the ruined bridge. Its horses reared and whinnied, terrified. The coachman was doing his best to control them, but he was losing the fight.

Shouts from Hartwig's carriage. Then more shouts from behind, as the other guests panicked. Another stony, grinding rumble. Gerald choked on fresh pain, feeling Bibbie's fingers close vise-like on his hand. He turned to see two more enormous boulders ponderously skipping down the hill, dragging with them a horde of smaller rocks, raising a dirt cloud, knocking stubby trees aside like skittles. The rocks struck the road, blocking it, scant feet from the rear of the last carriage containing Lord Babcock of Ottosland and his secretary, Hever Mistle. Its horses rose onto their hind legs, their terror leaping to the team pulling the Lanruvians' carriage, directly in front.

There was nowhere to run. The wedding tour party was trapped.

Yet another deafening rumble and a shower of small stones. More rocks were sliding towards the road, towards the bridge. All the horses were fear-blinded now, rearing dangerously high and waving their forelegs, threatening to hurt themselves and each other. It was Putzi Gorge all over again, only a hundred times worse. The air was full of dust and shredded leaves and terror.

"Gerald, *do* something!" said Melissande, close to tears. "Those rocks are going to hit Ratafia's carriage!"

He smeared his vision clear. Dammit, she was right. More rocks were sliding fast, half the hillside sliding with them. Where were Ratafia and Ludwig? *Damn*, they were still in the carriage, too frightened to leap out. Or maybe they were hurt. Either way . . .

He turned to Bibbie. "Hide me, Bibs. Now. Like you did in the gorge."

A flash of her smile, still hers though she was Gladys. Burning within her, the wild, reckless courage that would not be denied. She flung her *potentia* around him . . . and he threw away his shield. Familiar light and strange darkness, bound within him as one. His grimoire *potentia*, twisted like the ether, shuddering to break free. If he let it loose, would he be safe? And could he find himself again? No choice. He had to risk it. If he got lost, Bibbie would find him.

Trusting her, he let go.

And nearly fell over with shock, because the *Lanruvians*, his prime suspects, were using their powers to avert disaster. Or trying to. Only they were failing. The men from Lanruvia weren't the right kind of wizards.

But I am. Bloody hell.

Bibbie's *potentia* was on fire, swirling around him like living flame. He was hiding in her inferno. He was running out of time. He let blind instinct guide him. Let the blocking and binding incants pour out of him in an almost silent stream and focused his will on preventing bloody death.

Come on, Dunnywood! Time to earn your damned keep!

The swiftly sliding rocks had been hexed to tumble and kill. A small part of his mind was screaming *How? Who?* But investigation had to wait. Drenched in sweat, his muscles shaking, he over-rode the filthy, murderous incants and bent the rocks to his will. Slowed them . . . and slowed them . . . and told them to crack. He could hear Bibbie gasping as she kept him from sight, could hear Melissande's whispered encouragement. *Come on, come on, come on.* And then Melissande shouted, gladly, and he shouted too, as the rocks shattered into shards that struck the road and the carriages and the unfortunate horses, drawing blood, gouging splinters . . . but not taking life.

With a strangled groan he collapsed in a heap on the floor of their carriage. Half a heartbeat later, Bibbie collapsed beside him. Her shroud of flames fell with her, leaving him exposed. But that didn't matter, because he was his changed self again, his grimoire *potentia* under control. He wasn't lost. He was safe. Not caring who could see him, he reached for Bibbie's hand. Pulled her close and kissed her.

The world and its terrible troubles went away.

A hundred years later he opened his eyes and let her go. He could feel his silly Rowbotham face stretched wide in a smile. Gladys Slack was smiling too, but behind her face was Bibbie. His Bibbie. His heart.

Somewhere close by there was a lot of shouting and chaos. Horses whinnying. Dust settling. There was weeping, he could hear it. He looked up. It wasn't Melissande. He'd have been very surprised if it was.

Still. She did look shaken, down to her bones. He clambered upright and put a hand on her shoulder.

"You're all right, Mel? We're all right. It's over now, I think."

She was staring at the wedding party's first two carriages, their horses finally tamed, and at Hartwig and Erminium and Leopold Gertz and Ludwig and Ratafia, standing on the rock-strewn road clutching at each other in desperate relief.

"Well, they seem fine, Saint Snodgrass be praised," she said, with only the faintest tremor in her voice. Then she turned, revealing her eyes stark with what might have been. Nearly was. "Well done, you two. Oh, *bloody* well done."

Their coachman was seeing to the horses, and from the hubbub of the other guests, a babbling of so many different tongues the party sounded like a debate at the United Magical Nations, it seemed that not a soul was paying them any attention.

"It was wizardry, wasn't it?" she added, her voice safely lowered. "This time, it was wizardry."

Bibbie sat up. "Yes."

"Oh." Melissande's lips trembled, then firmed. "Well, then. At least now we know for sure." Her chin lifted. "And do we know who's behind it?"

Gerald shook his head, feeling his elation collapse. "Sorry."

"The hexes on those rocks felt the same as the thaumaturgics on the barge," Bibbie said, sounding grim. "I think."

And the same as the deadly incants at Abel Bestwick's lodging, the blood magic hex too, but he didn't want to say that. Not until he'd had a chance to talk to Sir Alec. Call him old-fashioned, accuse him of treating them like gels, he didn't care. Bibbie and Melissande had been frightened enough for one day.

Instead of answering, he helped Bibbie to her feet.

"Well, even if they're not the same," said Melissande, "we can be sure of one more thing." She nodded at Hartwig and Ludwig and the rest, still embracing and exclaiming and consoling each other. Norbert of Harenstein had joined them, and Ratafia was clutched to his breast in an extravagance of tearful relief. "Whoever's behind this, they can't be here. We were all of us nearly killed. So the culprit must be elsewhere. Agreed?"

"Agreed," said Bibbie. "Algernon?"

Gerald hesitated. He wanted to say yes, if only to calm their fears, but there were too many blank spaces. The Lanruvians. He still found it hard to fathom that *they'd* tried to help avert the bloodshed. And there remained that question mark raised over Norberts' minions . . .

The thought turned him towards Harenstein's carriage. Volker and Dermit stood in the road beside it, their faces pale with shock.

"Algernon?" Bibbie prompted again.

He looked at her. "It does seem unlikely."

"Unlikely?" Melissande snorted. "That'll do. So if you'll excuse me? I'm putting a stop to this."

What? "Wait—Melissande—"

"No, Gerald," she said sharply. "It's over. Yes, I know, you saved us all. This time. But what about next time? Now both of you, stay here."

And before he could restrain her, she'd leapt down from their carriage and was marching towards the shattered bridge, and Hartwig.

"Melissande, my dear!" cried Hartwig, his voice shaking. His face was chalky pale, his eyes wet. "My dear, are you unharmed?"

He was a grabby old goat but she hugged him anyway. "Yes, Twiggy, I'm fine. You?"

"Yes, yes," he said, blustering. Defying her to notice that he'd just been scared out of his wits. "Of course. I'm the Crown Prince of Splotze, m'dear. Takes more than a few stray pebbles to unseat me!"

Neatly extricating herself from his fervent clasp, to her surprise she found herself being clutched by Norbert of Harenstein.

"It was a close thing, Millicent," he declared fervently. "A damned close thing!"

Good lord, the marquis was *shaking*. She patted his back. "But we're all safe, Norbert, and that's what counts." After a second strategical extrication, she looked to Borovnik's Dowager Queen. "Your Majesty?"

A splinter of carriage-wood or boulder had struck Erminium's right cheek. A swollen bruise was forming, and there was blood on her parchment skin and dust all over her tawny silk dress. But her head was high and her spine was straight and there was as much anger as fear in her eyes.

"Disgraceful," she declared. "*Disgraceful*. Hartwig, this is no way to treat your guests! Have you never heard of hillside maintenance?"

Happy to be ignored, leaving Hartwig to defend his honour, Melissande joined Ratafia and Ludwig, who looked as though they wanted nothing more than to remain in each other's consoling arms forever.

"You must've been so frightened, both of you," she said, and took one of Ratafia's cold little hands in hers. "But you're not hurt, praise Saint Snodgrass. And just think of the story you'll have to tell your children!"

Though she was tear-stained, Ratafia smiled. "Yes, I suppose you're right."

"Of course she is," said Ludwig, and kissed Ratafia's dusty cheek. "I shall put them to bed each night with tales of their sweet mother's courage."

"Oh, *Luddie* . . ."

Tactfully turning aside from the fresh billing and cooing, which surely they'd earned, Melissande saw that all the wedding tour guests had clambered out of their carriages and were picking their way along the road to join them. Even the Lanruvians were approaching, their disconcerting detachment unshaken. Spying Gerald and Bibbie, inching closer, she started to shake her head, warning them off, but an indignant cry from Erminium distracted her.

"*No*, Hartwig, I *demand* that you make arrangements for us to go back to Grande Splotze *tonight!*"

"Oh, Mama, that's not necessary," Ratafia protested. "This was an unfortunate mishap, that's all. Please, don't make us go back!"

"There, you see?" said Hartwig. "Such a brave gel, she'll make Splotze a wonderful Crown Princess! Now Erminium, I know we've had a fright but we can't let this little mishap spoil the rest of the wedding tour. All those people, waiting to see Ludwig and Ratafia. Besides, we don't want to give anyone an excuse to say Borovnik's easily rattled, do we?"

Erminium's fear for her daughter had drained the colour from her cheeks. Now it flooded back. "Do not insult me, Hartwig! The courage of Borovnik has never been in doubt!" Elbowing Ludwig aside, she took her daughter by the shoulders. "Ratafia, are you quite sure?"

"I am, Mama," said Ratafia. "Hartwig's right. I owe it to the people of Splotze to keep going. And I warn you, I'll swim the river if I have to and walk the rest of the way on bare feet. The tour *must* continue."

Melissande ground her teeth. Bugger. Just when she'd thought she'd get what she wanted without having to lift a finger.

Curse you, Ratafia. Of all the times to be brave and stalwart and princessly.

"Well, I'm sorry, but I won't!" she announced. "I think it's madness to go on. I think we should all return to Grande Splotze at once."

"What's that?" said Hartwig, staring. "But Melissande, you said you were fine!"

She pressed an artfully shaking hand to her face. "I lied, Twiggy. I'm sorry. I shouldn't be such a ninny but I'm afraid I can't help it. I'm afraid I'm *afraid!* Oh, Hartwig. Dear Hartwig. I beg you . . . I *implore* you . . . take us home to Grande Splotze!"

And on a deep breath, she burst into noisy tears and flung herself into Hartwig's surprised but welcoming arms.

"There, there, Melly," he said, patting her shoulder. "It's all right, m'dear. Don't cry. Of course we'll go back to the palace, if that's what you want."

Oh, lord, she thought, feeling a pang of guilt at the genuine distress in Hartwig's voice. *When Sir Alec finds out I've stuck my oar in, he'll go spare.*

Another day, another six hours spent fighting idiots in the Department of Thaumaturgy's unswept halls of power.

And to think his day was still only half over.

Resisting the urge to bang his head on his desk, Sir Alec initialled the last page of Mawford's final report on the latest nastiness in West Uphantica. Perhaps now someone other than Ralph would believe him when he said trouble was brewing again.

As he replaced his pen in its holder, someone tapped on the closed office door. "Come," he said, flipping the file's folder shut.

Frank took one look at his face and rolled his eyes. "West Uphantica?"

A sigh. "What else?"

"And Gaylord's being a pillock."

"He is."

"You put up with too much shite from that tosser."

"I do."

"I've got a plan to take care of Ravelard bloody Gaylord," Frank said, shoving the door closed with his foot. "Want to hear it?"

He kept his lips from twitching, but only just. "No."

"Fine." Frank crossed to the desk and held out the steaming mug he'd brought with him. "Then listen to this. And while you're listening, pour some bloody tea down your throat."

"I can fetch my own tea."

"By the looks of you, Ace, you wouldn't make it to the stairs. *Drink*."

So he took Frank's mug and swallowed, welcoming the warmth and even the sugar. "You were saying?"

"Aylesbury Markham was right," said Frank, dropping into the visitor's chair. "The Lanruvians have been getting cosy with the Maneezi."

The unwelcome news woke his lightly sleeping megrim. "It's confirmed?"

"Pribble got a message to us through Bisphor in Tarikstan. Had to use word of mouth with a courier."

How disturbing. "He couldn't risk regular channels?"

"There's been an uptick in etheretic monitoring," Frank said, moodily fingering the half-hearted crease in his trousers. "The Maneezi are bloody nervous, he says."

"They must be, if they're risking eavesdropping on our embassy."

"And he's seen Lanruvians coming out of their big Research facility," Frank added. "Which is another bloody worry we don't need right now."

Perplexed, Sir Alec sat back in his chair. "It makes no sense. The Maneezi aren't stupid. Why would they risk everything by getting into bed with the Lanruvians?"

Frank shrugged. "Could be they're more scared of those pale skinny bastards than they are of sanctions." His face twisted with derision. "And not without cause. When the political winds blow left to right, the powers that be are toothless and three-quarters blind to boot."

"Or those pale skinny bastards have something the Maneezi want, so they're willing to chance giving them a thaumicle extractor in return." More sharp pain stabbed through his head at the thought of the Lanruvians with access to that kind of equipment. "All right, Mister Dalby. Here's what we'll do. First—"

"It's taken care of," said Frank, with a swift half-smile. "Field agents on alert, Customs on standby, wizards known for particle thaumaturgics flagged, ditto all PT equipment."

The pain in his head eased. "Good, Frank. Keep me apprised."

"Will do. Mind you, Ace, the Maneezi are bound to notice this little flurry of activity. Which means the Lanruvians'll notice."

"In which case they might reconsider their ill-considered plans."

"We can only bloody hope." Frank rubbed the side of his nose. "Heard anything more from Dunwoody?"

Sir Alec put down the half-emptied mug of tea. "No. Communications with Splotze continue problematical. Sir Ralph's boffins are calling it 'the etheretic storm of the century'."

Frank grunted. "Not having second thoughts about sending him in, are you? Like, maybe it was too soon after that other mucky business?"

"No."

Frank crossed an ankle over his knee, comfortable as a cat on the uncomfortable visitor's chair. "If you are, you should bring him home."

"I'm not," he said tightly. "I have every confidence that Mister Dunwoody can resolve this Splotze-Borovnik business efficiently and discreetly."

"If you say so, Ace." With another grunt, Frank stood. "Any road. Nice chatting with you. Don't bother getting up, I'll show m'self out."

But before Frank's fingers touched the door's handle, it flew open. In the doorway, Ralph's nephew, looking rather the worse for wear.

Sir Alec nodded. "Thank you, Mister Dalby. I'll take it from here. Come in, Mister Markham."

As Frank closed the door behind him, Monk pulled a familiar, bloodstained square of blue carpet from under his coat and tossed it on the desk.

"I'm sorry," he said. "I couldn't do it. And I wrecked the damn thing trying."

Sir Alec folded his hands neatly on top of the West Uphantica file and considered the thaumaturgically inert carpet in silence. Then he sighed.

"These things happen. Sit down, Mister Markham. Before you fall down."

Grey-faced and hollow-eyed, Monk folded onto the chair Frank had just abandoned. "I really am sorry, sir. It was an accident. I got carried away."

"As I said," he replied, in the tone that until now only Frank Dalby had heard—and, even then, very seldom. "What we do is not an exact science."

Monk dragged shaking fingers through his hair. "*Blood magic*," he said, with deep loathing. "I used every decoding hex I could think of. I even invented a new one." He pulled a face. "I think that might be what killed it. I was going to try putting it back together again, only Reg threatened to poke out my eyeballs so I stopped. Because, y'know, for once I think she really meant it."

Good for the bird. "Go home, Mister Markham. Get some sleep. You've earned it."

Ralph's nephew stood. Swaying a little on his feet, he stared at the wrapped square of carpet soaked in blood, and ruined blood magic. "Heard from Gerald?"

"No."

"Me neither. So let's hope no news is good news." Another frown. A jerk of his head at the desk. "Anyway. I'm sorry."

Alone again, Sir Alec dropped the useless piece of carpet into his office rubbish bin. Thought of Abel Bestwick . . . and in a single explosive sweep of his arm sent the West Uphantica file flying.

"*Damn!*"

CHAPTER TWENTY-TWO

When Monk reached his jalopy, parked on the street outside the Nettleworth building, he found Reg perched on the bonnet like an oversized hood ornament.

"Well?" the bird said. "How did he take it?"

"Better than I thought he would. What are you doing here, Reg?"

She flapped onto his shoulder. "Making sure that government stooge didn't turn your guts into his garters. Blimey, sunshine. You look like a walking corpse. Anyone ever tell you natural light is not your friend?"

Buzzing with exhaustion, Monk unwarded the car door, opened it, and slid behind the wheel. "Look, Reg," he said, as the bird hopped onto the back of the passenger seat. "I don't need a nursemaid. I'm going straight home and then I'm crawling into bed."

Reg rattled her tail. "Well, you're going straight home. But your bed'll have to stay empty a while longer, sunshine."

He stared at her. "*What?*"

"Dodsworth's waiting for you at Chatterly Crescent, all gee'd up about something and raring to go."

Dodsworth? "Gee'd up about what? Did he say?"

"Oh, yes," Reg said, looking down her beak at him. "Once I'd let him in through the locked and warded front door, your butler and me had ourselves a lovely chinwag over tea and toast. And he wasn't the least bit discombobulated to find out I say a bloody sight more than Polly wants a bloody cracker and make sure it's got no sesame seeds. I'm only holding back the particulars because I don't want to spoil the surprise."

Right. With a sigh, Monk fired up the jalopy and pulled away from the kerb. "Sorry. I'm a bit tired."

"Yes. Well," the bird muttered. Then she slapped him with her wing. "Oy. Don't suppose you thought to ask that manky Sir Alec of yours if he's heard from our Gerald?"

"I did, and he hasn't."

"Bugger," said Reg. "What's our boy up to? Didn't his mother teach him it's polite to call home?"

Monk winced. A steady drumbeat of pain was booming in his skull. He pulled down his driver's side window for some fresh air, then nosed the jalopy into the heavy flow of traffic along Kastelan Street.

"I expect he's a bit busy, Reg. Please. Don't go on."

She considered him closely, head tipped to one side. "On second thoughts, maybe I should've poked Dodsworth in his unmentionables until he went away. If you go wandering about the place looking like that, Mister Markham, you'll frighten the horses into hysterics."

Dodsworth wouldn't have come to see him if it wasn't important. "Bugger the horses, Reg. They can take care of themselves."

His family's butler was perched on the front steps of the Chatterly Crescent town house. Seeing the jalopy turn in to the driveway, he got up, creakily, and tottered to meet it.

"Master Monk! I'm sorry to disturb you, but I thought you'd want to know at once," he said, bending down to peer into the car. "I've just had word from—" Dodsworth frowned. "Master Monk, there is a bird on the seat beside you."

"Ah—yes, I do believe there is," he said, carefully not looking at Reg. "I found it lying stunned on the side of the road, poor thing. Couldn't leave it there, could I? Anyway, you were saying?"

"I feel bound to point out, sir, that it is no longer stunned and is in possession of a very long, sharp beak."

"Is it? I can't say I noticed. *Anyway*—"

Keeping one eye on Reg, Dodsworth managed to collect himself. "Yes, sir. I've had word from my friend, the Harenstein embassy's butler. He's back at work, but now that useless guffin who filled in for him has succumbed to dropsy and there's an important supper at the embassy this evening. He wanted to know if I couldn't see fit to lend him a hand."

Despite his headache, and his bone-shattering weariness, Monk felt himself start to grin. "Really?"

"Yes, really, sir," said Dodsworth, with an answering smile. "And seeing as how I know you're interested in getting in there, and Master Aylesbury's away on business and your dear parents are off visiting Lord and Lady Patchoo, I thought I could, without compromising my position, answer my friend's cry for help and take you with me as my assis—"

Monk reached through the open driver's side window and seized Dodsworth's lined, retainerly face between his hands. "Alfred, I swear, if there wasn't a jalopy between us I'd kiss you."

"Indeed, sir?" said Dodsworth, slightly muffled. "How very enthusiastic of you, to be sure."

He let go. "When do we leave?"

"As soon as possible, Master Monk," said Dodsworth. "Apparently there's a great deal to do."

"Then come inside and wait while I sort out a few things, would you? And if you felt like it, you could maybe make me some toast? I haven't had anything to eat since—" His mind blanked. "Anyway. Toast would be nice."

Stepping back, Dodsworth frowned. "Now, now, Master Monk. I think we can do a little better than *toast*."

Monk unfolded himself out of the jalopy. "Actually, I was hoping you were going to say that."

"Ah—the bird, Master Monk?" said Dodsworth, as they headed for the town house's front door.

He didn't look back. "Never mind about the bird, Dodsworth. I'm sure the bird, like hysterical horses, can take care of herself."

*　　*　　*

After a quick bath, a slightly longer hunt for clean, suitably assistant butler clothes, a large handful of headache pills and some of Dodsworth's exemplary coffee and scrambled eggs, it was time to go. Pretending he'd forgotten to lock the back door, Monk left Dodsworth in the jalopy worrying about hidden birdshit and caught up with Reg, who was lurking in the rear courtyard.

"Follow us to the embassy," he said quickly. "And once you're there make sure to stay out of sight. Find a handy tree or something. I'll signal you from a window if there's anything you can do to help."

Balanced on the edge of a flower pot, Reg gave him a look. "I don't know, sunshine. I'm not sure you're up to this."

"I'm fine," he said, impatient. "I've had a bath, I've had breakfast."

"So now you look like a clean, well fed walking corpse," said the bird. "The horses will still go into hysterics."

"I'm *fine*. Blimey, how does Gerald put up with you?" Bending, he dropped a kiss on the top of her head. "Fly safe and whatever you do, don't lose the jalopy."

He and Dodsworth were admitted to the Harenstein embassy without incident. Kreski, Dodsworth's butler friend, fell upon them with a cry of relief and immediately put them to work in the kitchen. Three hours later, still slicing vegetables, Monk made a note to himself to tell his parents that Dodsworth deserved a raise.

Another hour of slaving, this time over a hot stove stirring an endless array of sauces, and the embassy supper's guests began to arrive. That meant he had a snatch of time to himself.

Catching Dodsworth in passing, he pulled the butler aside. "Look, I need to do something. Hopefully it won't take too long. But if Kreski comes looking for me—"

"Don't worry, sir," said Dodsworth. "I'll keep him occupied. Master Monk—"

Monk turned back. "Yes?"

Lines of worry were creasing the butler's lugubrious face. "What we're doing. It is important, isn't it?"

"Oh, Dodsworth, my old friend," he breathed, and clasped the man's bony shoulder. "You have no idea."

Dodsworth cleared his throat. "Very good, sir. Off you go, then, and I'll see you in due course."

After countless hours of battling to unlock the blood magic incant's secrets, and failing, Monk found that the simple task of wrapping himself in a no-see-'em was a lot harder than it should've been.

Bugger. I didn't realise I was this stonkered.

Maybe he should've paid more attention to Reg's pointed walking corpse remarks.

Gritting his teeth against a hot surge of pain, he roused his battered *potentia* and hid himself inside the hex. As always, the no-see-'em turned his surroundings to watercolours, rendered them thin and slightly sloppy as he drifted up the embassy's servant stairs, crossed the green baize door threshold into the privileged world of titled ambassadors and their guests, then trod lightly up more stairs to the official offices above the ground floor. Music floated up after him, full of trumpets and hints of war.

His no-see-'em hex was the best ever devised. It slid him past the embassy's wardings like water through a sieve.

Two chattering maids passed him, oblivious, going downstairs. As he explored his first corridor, a uniformed junior secretary came out of a room and closed the door behind him. Monk waited until he heard the man's booted feet on the stairs then poked his head inside the room. A stationery cupboard. Probably no secrets in there.

It took him nearly half an hour, but at last he found the office he was looking for. Ornately furnished in the flamboyantly overdone Harenstein style, crowded with books, the paperwork on the desk confirmed that it belonged to Ambassador Dermit who was, according to Sir Alec, uncle to the Bern Dermit currently serving on the Marquis of Harenstein's personal staff.

Breathing softly, willfully ignoring his body's urgent need for sleep, Monk stood at the desk and coaxed his reluctant *potentia* to do his bidding. A heaviness. Hexed resistance. And then the warded drawers on the desk surrendered to his illicit coercion and he was able to open them and start rummaging.

He found what he was after in the second-bottom drawer. A sealed envelope, warded three different ways. His fingers tingled against the thaumaturgics. Powerful, yes, but no match for him, not even when he was tired enough to fall asleep in a gutter. He broke all three wards and pulled a folded sheet of paper from the breached envelope.

It was coded in a cypher he'd never seen before . . . but at first glance, it made him blink. Blimey. Somebody really didn't want this letter being read by strangers. It'd take more time than he had now to break it. In fact he had the nasty suspicion it'd likely take a whole day. And even when it was deciphered, there was no guarantee that it had anything to do with the Splotze-Borovnik wedding. But this letter was the closest thing he'd come up with yet to a clue. So he was going to take a leap of faith. What other choice did he have?

"Bloody hell, Reg!" he whispered, hanging out of the office window. The sun had set a while ago, and light from the embassy garden's decorative lanterns brushed her feathers as she thumped onto his outstretched arm. "Where were you? I've been signalling for five minutes at least and having multiple heart attacks because I've switched off my no-see-'em!"

"Keep your underwear on, sunshine," the bird retorted. "Have you counted how many windows this embassy's got? I've been hopping from tree to tree since I got here. It's a wonder I can fly straight, I'm so dizzy."

He waved his other hand at her. "Yes, yes, all right, never mind. Take this."

She eyed the envelope he was clutching. "And what's that? It bloody stinks of thaumaturgics."

"I don't have time to explain! Please, just take it and fly back to Chatterly Crescent before somebody sees you and Kreski comes looking for me!"

"Kreski? Who's Kres-mmph!"

"And try not to drool on it," he added, as the bird glared

at him over the envelope, which he'd shoved into her open beak. "You might set off the thaumaturgics."

Dark eyes promising a proper poking of his unmentionables, Reg rattled her tail, flapped her wings, and launched herself into the night.

For one precious moment he let himself sag over the office windowsill. *Please, please, let that note be what gets Gerald and the girls home in one piece.* And then he pulled back inside, reignited the no-see-'em, breathed hard until his protesting *potentia* settled, and made his way back downstairs to tackle the embassy supper's dirty dishes.

"Well," Bibbie remarked, once again comfortably sprawled on the royal bed in the palace's sumptuous guest suite. "You've done a bang-up job, Mel, I must say. After that stunt you pulled at what's left of the Hanging Bridge, now the only person speaking to you is Hartwig."

Melissande, seated in the bedchamber's largest plush velvet chair, folded her arms. *Y'know, I'm getting rather tired of this.* "That's not true. You're speaking to me. And so is Algernon."

Cross-legged on the carpeted floor, Gerald grunted, not looking up from his crystal ball. "Only because I have to."

She kicked her heel against the carpet. "Honestly, Algernon. I think you're being rather mean."

"*Mean?*" Gerald laughed, unamused. "Wait till you hear what Sir Alec has to say. Trust me, Your Highness, *that's* when you'll hear *mean*."

"Only if you can get that wretched crystal ball to work," she said. "Can you?"

"No," he said curtly. "The etheretics are still out of whack. Which means the portals won't be working either. We're stuck here, curse it, with no way of reaching Sir Alec."

"Maybe you should let Gladys have a turn," she said, feeling nasty. "A fresh eye. A woman's touch. That sort of thing."

"There's no point, Melissande," said Bibbie. "If Algernon can't get that crystal ball working, nobody can."

Disbelieving, Melissande stared at her. *Bibbie giving up on a thaumaturgical challenge? Bibbie surrendering the high* ground to a wizard? And then she saw the look that passed between Monk's sister and Gerald. It was full of secrets. Of the mysterious thaumaturgical communion they'd shared at the bridge. She remembered there were things about him that Bibbie still hadn't told her. Remembered their shocking, heart-stopping kiss. Passion and need and triumph, inextricably intertwined.

So much for her not being sure he loved her. So much for him worrying that for her, he was the wrong man.

Gerald had confided that fear, late one night a few days after coming home from the mess in that other, dreadful Ottosland. But apparently things changed. *Monk*. She felt a little ache in the region of her heart. Perhaps if she ignored it, the bothersome pain would go away.

"*Anyway*," said Bibbie. "We're back in Grande Splotze, after a lovely cross-country motorcar dash, and the second fireworks display is set for tonight." She frowned. "Algernon—"

Gerald picked up his crystal ball and stood. "I told you already, Gladys. *I don't know* if there's danger tonight. I was convinced the first fireworks were a trap and it turned out I was wrong. Perhaps my funny feeling was actually about the bridge. Who can say? Not me. I don't have much experience with thaumaturgically-induced premonitions."

It felt most peculiar, being in disgrace with Gerald. Melissande found herself faltering. Reluctant to speak up. But then she felt her chin lift.

I'm not going to let him shut me out. I did what I thought was right, what I thought would save lives. I answer to my conscience, not to him . . . or Sir Alec.

"Perhaps it was, and perhaps it wasn't," she said. "But I don't think we should take any chances, do you? I think you should trust your instincts, Algernon."

"Mel's right," said Bibbie. "Because in this case, yours are the only instincts we *can* trust." She groaned. "Lord, thaumaturgically-induced premonitions give me a headache!"

"And what gives *me* a headache," said Gerald, crossing the bedchamber to glare out of the window, "is that after everything that's happened we *still* can't give a name to our villain."

"Perhaps we will, after tonight," said Bibbie. "Or perhaps it won't matter. If you've been right all along, and Ratafia and Ludwig really are in danger from the pre-wedding fireworks, then there's still time to save them. With the wedding set for midnight, we've hours to go yet. So really, it's simple."

Gerald stared at her. "Simple?"

"Yes!" Bibbie said brightly. "You get us through the fireworks in one piece, Grande Splotze's bells ring out with joy, Hartwig heaves a sigh of relief, Erminium complains about something else entirely trivial, the cooing lovebirds get married then sign the Splotze-Borovnik treaty, and that's that. There's no urgent reason to kill anyone, then."

Gerald frowned. "Yes. Right. Simple as pie. Only you're forgetting there's the chance that if they're killed soon enough after the wedding, say on the honeymoon, the Canal treaty might still be at risk."

"True," Bibbie said, sliding out of her chair. "What matters, though, is that we'll have bought time for Sir Alec to work with Uncle Ralph and bodgy up a story about accidentally stumbling across a plot against the wedding. Time to keep on investigating too, if we still haven't worked out who's behind it. That way nobody need ever know there were janitors involved, or that the three of us were here under false pretences. It'll be an international diplomacy affair . . . and we can go back home leaving no-one the wiser."

The smallest smile tugged at the corner of Gerald's mouth. "Beautifully reasoned, Bibbie. There's just one tiny fly in your ointment."

"No, there's not, Gerald," said Bibbie, determined. "Because we *are* going to make sure nobody dies tonight."

Secretary of State Leopold Gertz jumped so hard, hearing his name called, that he nearly fell off the royal dais.

"I'm so sorry," Melissande said quickly. "I didn't mean to startle you."

The damp little man waved a hand, pretending indifference. The beads of sweat rolling down his face told another story. He'd been placing scallop-edged, gold-chased name cards at each setting on the official wedding table. She had to wonder if he realised his fingers were slowly crumpling the ones he had left.

"Princess Melissande," he said, close to squeaking. "I didn't hear you come in. Was there something you wanted?"

She looked around the palace's state dining room, which had been decorated all over again for the post-nuptial feast. A few servants were adding some finishing touches: silver streamers, potted flowers, ribbon rosettes in crimson and royal blue, each one centred with a simpering portrait of the happy couple.

"It all looks lovely, Secretary Gertz," she said, hoping to charm him. "You should be very proud."

"Yes, yes, thank you," he said. "It's a blessed occasion." His eyebrows pinched. "Rather rushed now, of course, with the wedding tour being cancelled."

"Which is my fault. I know," she said. "That's why I've come to see you, Secretary Gertz. I'm at a bit of a loose end, and I thought you might like an extra pair of hands. My way of making things up to you."

Secretary Gertz stared as though she'd grown another head. "But—you're a Royal Highness, Your Highness."

"True. For my sins. But that doesn't precisely make me incompetent."

"But—but—" Gertz looked around the dining room, his expression hunted. "Your secretary. Your lady's maid. Surely it's more appropriate that *they* should—"

"Well, yes, but they're not here," she said, unable to take her eyes from the expensive place cards he was slowly destroying. "I gave them leave to visit the township."

Gertz, realising at last the mess he was making, dropped the ruined cards on the official table as though they'd burst into flame.

"You sent your servants away? You're *unaccompanied*?"

She shrugged. "Only for an hour or so. I had to do it, Secretary Gertz. After that awful business at the Hanging Bridge, Slack could do nothing but burst into tears. She was getting on my nerves. I thought an outing with Rowbotham might cheer her up."

"I see," said Gertz, clearly not seeing at all. "Well, Your Highness. I'm sure if your brother His Majesty King Rupert has no objection to his royal sister being left unchaperoned, then *I* have nothing to say on the matter."

Fresh sweat was trickling down Gertz's thin, sallow cheeks. A nervous tic flickered beside his left eye. He was looking positively ill with wedding strain. Though he irritated her, to her surprise Melissande felt a welling of sympathy.

"Are *you* all right, Mister Secretary?" she asked. "After what happened, I mean? You were even closer to danger than I was, and I know it gave me a nasty turn."

Gertz tugged at the high, braid-covered collar of his official uniform tunic. "Yes. I am. Thank you for your asking, Your Highness. It was a most unpleasant experience, but it's behind us now and that's all that matters."

He didn't look like a man who'd left a brush with death behind him, but there was no point contradicting him.

"So, Secretary Gertz, *is* there a way I can help?"

Looking hunted again, Gertz surrendered to the inevitable, produced a white silk handkerchief from his pocket and mopped his face. "I suppose—if you insist—you might pass a message to Mister Ibblie, Your Highness. He should be in his office on the fourth floor. If you'd remind him that Goby *must* follow the musical program as it has been arranged then I would be—"

"I'm sorry, but who—?"

"Goby," said Gertz, sounding almost impatient. "Dowager Queen Erminium's music master. He's conducting tonight's ensemble at the reception prior to the wedding ceremony." Another flourish with the handkerchief. "*Twice* now in rehearsal he has substituted his own compositions for those of Crown Prince Hartwig's court composer." An offended sniff. "It seems that the honour of conducting the ensemble is insufficient to Goby's needs. I have spoken with him most directly, but he seems determined to go his own way. If he should try the same knavish trick tonight then I tell you plainly I shan't be responsible for the consequences!"

Oh dear. Politics *and* Erminium. A lethal combination. No wonder the poor man was on the brink of a breakdown.

"Yes, Secretary Gertz, I quite understand," Melissande said gravely. "It would be a debacle."

"These bloody Borovniks," Gertz said under his breath, surprisingly savage. "It's a pity we never drowned them in the Canal when we had the chance."

A mutually shocked silence, as they stared at each other.

"Oh my," Gertz said faintly. "Oh dear. Your Highness, forgive me, I—"

She held up her hand. "No. No. It's quite all right, Leopold. I didn't hear a thing. I'll just—I'll go and see Secretary Ibblie now. Good day."

Leaving Hartwig's damp, distraught Secretary of State to his card placing, she took herself off to see Ibblie. And as she toiled up the stairs, thought: *Poor little Leopold. I think the pressure has finally got to him. A good thing for his sake it's all nearly over.*

Mister Ibblie, having risen to greet her, took the news of Erminium's music master with commendable equanimity.

"Yes, Your Highness, I was aware there'd been . . ." A diplomatic smile. "Some friction. Should the chance arise, you might reassure Secretary Gertz that steps have been taken to contain Master Goby's—" A pause. "Unbridled enthusiasm."

Impressed, Melissande nodded. "He'll be very pleased to hear it, Mister Ibblie. I'm afraid Secretary Gertz is a little overwhelmed just now." Then she winced. "Oh. Perhaps I shouldn't have said that. Only, to be brutally frank with you, sir, I'm not entirely convinced he's as sanguine about the accident at Lake Yablitz as he'd like everyone to think. And since Hartwig—the Crown Prince, I mean—relies on him so heavily—and, indeed, since they're *family*—"

Ibblie offered her a small bow from the other side of his desk, which was thickly papered with notes and memos and scribblings. It brought back not-so-fond memories of her time as practically a prime minister.

"The gracious delicacy of your feelings, Princess Melissande, does you great credit," Ibblie replied. "If I may be so bold as to say? And might I also say that I, for one, am most grateful that you saw to the safe return of our wedding party." He shuddered. "So much rests on the success of this marriage. Any threat to it *must* be seen as a threat to both nations."

"Mister Ibblie," she said, completely charmed, "I could not agree more. And if I might say something else, intending no offence? If ever the day should come when you feel the need for new surroundings—notwithstanding your natural allegiance to your homeland, of course—I wish you would come to me. My brother, King Rupert, is always in need of good men upon whose expertise and counsel he can rely."

And who aren't staring the age of ninety-four in the face.

Another bow. "Your Highness, I am deeply touched," said Ibblie. "And I shall remember your flattering offer."

"Do, Mister Ibblie," she said. "Now, unless there's something I can help you with, I'll return to the Secretary and set his mind at ease over the Dowager Queen's music master."

"Thank you, Your Highness, that's very kind," said Ibblie. "But I'm tolerably confident I have everything under control. Although—"

"Yes?" she said, helpfully.

Ibblie was staring at a hand-scrawled note, his expression fastidiously displeased. "It has just been brought to my attention, Your Highness, that the Lanruvians have departed Splotze. Without, I might add, formally informing the Crown Prince."

"Departed?" She stared. "You mean they're not attending the fireworks? Or the reception? None of it?"

Ibblie let the note drop. "Apparently not."

"But . . . what about their cherries? I thought they wanted to sell you their cherries?"

If he was surprised that she knew of that, he was too self-disciplined to let it show. "I'm afraid I couldn't say, Your Highness. The ways of Lanruvia are a mystery to me."

And me, Melissande thought, staggered. *So does this mean they were* never *part of the plot against the wedding?*

She had no idea. She couldn't begin to imagine what Gerald was going to say.

"Mister Ibblie, I'm astonished. Does Hartwig know?"

"He does not," said Mister Ibblie. "But if you could inform

Secretary Gertz, then the Secretary could inform the Crown Prince. That is the proper way such news is delivered."

In other words, *You and Hartwig might be chummy, but I'd rather you kept your nose out of this.*

And she was more than happy to oblige.

Leaving Ibblie to his ruthlessly efficient organisation, she went back downstairs to Leopold Gertz and gave him the good news about the music master, followed by the bad news about the Lanruvians. Then she escaped the state dining room—Gertz's agitation was contagious—and, unsettlingly adrift, wandered aimlessly around the armour display in the palace's Grand Entrance Hall.

What use am I now? None. Gerald and Bibbie don't need my help to investigate the fireworks. Mister Ibblie doesn't need me. Leopold Gertz doesn't want me. And neither does Ratafia any more. Even Ludwig's cross, since I upset his little snowbud. Hartwig would be pleased to see me, but I don't think I could cope with his wandering hands.

The enormous clock in the hall chimed a quarter to three. Lord, it was hours yet before she needed to dress for the fireworks. Assuming, of course, that they went ahead. Assuming Gerald and Bibbie didn't blow them up early, by accident, or discover some terrible thaumaturgical tampering they couldn't undo and had to call a halt to the whole event.

I could read a book, I suppose. Or knit.

And then she had an idea. Mitzie! She should do the right thing and visit Bibbie's sad little kitchen maid. See how the girl was faring, make sure she didn't need anything.

Now with something useful to do, Melissande abandoned the horse armour and spiked dog collars—though really, in hindsight, they'd have come in rather useful around Hartwig—and made her way below stairs to the palace's vast kitchens.

CHAPTER TWENTY-THREE

Down in Hartwig's underground kitchens, Melissande found a level of busyness to make an anthill look lazy. Kitchen maids and pot boys and under-cooks and spit turners and an assortment of culinary dogsbodies scurried under the lash of the highly strung—but apparently sober—head Cook's sharp tongue. The lamplit air was rich with the mouth-watering aromas of roasting meats, frying meats, baking pies, stewing fruit, boiling sugar syrup and cakes cooling on racks. Knives scythed against sharpeners, pots and pans rattled, oven doors slammed. Someone dropped a plate. Shouts mingled with the smashing. Someone else cut themselves, and curses curdled the thick air.

Unnoticed at the foot of the staircase linking kitchen complex to palace, Melissande took in the mayhem with appalled admiration. Hartwig's kitchens made Rupert's look like child's play. Even Lional, whose appetite for fine food and entertaining had been far from modest, never achieved a choreographed pandemonium like this.

A pot boy staggered by her, burdened with dirty saucepans. She stopped him with a smile and a raised hand.

"Essa?" he said, fox-red curls lank with steam and grease, eyes wide with surprise at the sight of a well-dressed lady.

Essa. That was Splotzin. Of course the child didn't speak Ottish. And she hadn't even a smattering of his tongue. What was *essa?* Yes?

"Mitzie?" she said hopefully, and pointed to the outer

kitchen where a couple of maids were frantically working. Then she pointed to herself. "Mitzie."

The boy was young but not ignorant. He grinned. "Mitzie, essa." A jerk of his chin suggested that she stand where she was, then he staggered away.

Eager to avoid a confrontation with the near-hysterical cook, Melissande shuffled into a conveniently shadowed corner and waited.

"Psst. Miss! Miss? Were you wanting me?"

She turned, and saw a kitchen maid's astonished face peering round a nearby whitewashed archway. "Are you Mitzie?"

Nodding, the incredulous maid stepped into view. She was a plumply pretty lass, her plain blue dress swathed in a juice-stained white apron, with a limp white cap on her curls and her cheeks pink from the hot ovens.

With another cautious look in the loud cook's direction, Melissande darted to the archway. "Mitzie, I'm Princess Melissande of New Ottosland. I was wondering if you had a moment to talk, but—" Another look at the kitchens. A few of the bustling staff had noticed her, but were too busy to stop and point and stare. If that changed . . . "Perhaps this isn't a good time."

Mitzie's mouth dropped open. "You're Gladys's princess?"

Oh, thank Saint Snodgrass. "I am. Gladys told me all about you, Mitzie. I just wanted to see if you were—Mitzie? Mitzie! What's the matter?"

The kitchen maid's cheeks had blushed a deeper pink, and she seemed on the point of tears. "Oh, *Miss!* Are you come to help me with Ferdie?"

Help her with—*Oh, lord*. Heart racing, Melissande took the girl's arm. *Abel Bestwick's alive?* "Mitzie? Are you saying you know where Ferdie is?"

With an anguished glance at the head cook, who had his back to them for the moment, Mitzie pressed a finger to her lips, then daringly took hold of Melissande's sleeve.

"Will you come, Miss?" she whispered, almost tugging. "Please?"

Melissande nodded. "Of course."

She hurried after the maid, who whisked through the kitchen labyrinth like a field mouse going to ground. They scuttled past rows of benches, bake ovens, spit ovens, an enormous pantry, the buttery, the cold larder and the wet larder and the hanging room ripe with game.

"Up here, Miss. To the servants' wing. Mind your step," said Mitzie, and after ducking between two halves of a heavy leather curtain they toiled up a narrow, winding staircase, higher and higher, up to the miserly maids' rooms beneath the palace's lofty roof.

"Ferdie's in here, Miss," said Mitzie, stopping at a door painted a dingy dark green. It was the last room in the narrow corridor leading off the staircase landing. A small, grimy window leaked grudging light onto the uneven timber floor. "I leave a lamp lit. Oh, Miss, I know it's wrong of me, but I been hiding him. I had to. He's my Ferdie. And oh, Miss, he idn't a bad man, he's only in trouble."

Melissande, still panting after the staircase, pressed her palm to the girl's flushed cheek, then took the small brass key that was fumbled into her grasp. "Bless you, Mitzie. You were right to tell me. And as for hiding him, well, you'll likely never know what a good thing you've done."

"Miss, I can't stay," the maid said, her eyes anxious. "They'll be shouting for me in the kitchens."

And the last thing either of them needed was a Mitzie hunt, raising a ruckus and making inconvenient discoveries. "You go. I'll talk to Ferdie. And Mitzie?"

"Yes, Miss?"

"Don't you worry," Melissande said, patting the girl's arm. "We'll sort this out. You'll not get in trouble, I give you my word."

Mitzie's dimples were as pretty as Bibbie's. "Thank you, Miss. I'll find you later, if that's all right."

"Yes, yes. Now go!"

The dingy green door swung open with a soft creak. Melissande slipped into the room beyond and pushed the door until she heard its latch quietly click. Then, clutching the key, she turned and looked around. A small room, holding only a single bed, a chest of drawers, an elderly wardrobe and one rickety wooden chair. It was pushed next to the bed, a dim oil lamp burning on it.

Close to tip-toe, she crossed to the bed and touched her fingers to the bare shoulder of the man asleep beneath its blanket. "Ferdie. Can you hear me?"

With a muffled oath the man startled awake, twisting away from her. His breath caught, a sound of sharp pain. The lamplight fell over his face, revealing cheeks stubbled and sunken, eyes bright with lingering fever. A plain face. Unremarkable. A Sir Alec kind of face, that wasn't noticed in a crowd.

"Who the devil are you?" he demanded hoarsely. "And how the hell did you find me?"

"Mitzie." Ignoring his curse, she sat on the edge of the bed. "As for me, I'm Melissande Cadwallader. And you are Abel Bestwick. Sir Alec's man in Splotze."

Sir Alec's man in Splotze choked. "*What?*"

Oh dear. Was he going to be difficult? "Look, Mister Bestwick, we don't have much time. I know who you are, I know why you're here, and I know about the message you got through to Sir Alec. He's sent in another janitor. Gerald Dunwoody. D'you know him?"

With a pained effort, Bestwick shoved and wriggled until he was sitting up against his pillow. The blanket fell to his waist, revealing faded bruises and a bloodstained bandage wrapped around his skinny ribs.

"No," he said, his eyes hard with suspicion. "And I've never heard of you."

"Well, actually, you might've," she said. "I'm also known as Princess Melissande of New Ottosland."

"I've heard of New Ottosland," Bestwick said grudgingly.

"Oh, for pity's sake," she muttered. "Will you at least admit you know Sir Alec? Medium height, brown hair, grey eyes, a disturbing habit of chilly sarcasm? Does that ring a bell?"

A cautious nod.

"And Monk Markham? Don't you dare tell me you've never heard of him!"

Another cautious nod. "Who hasn't?"

"Well, it's a start," she said, cross with relief. "Mister Bestwick—Abel—I do appreciate this is confusing. And that you're under strict instructions not to reveal your true identity. But I think we're a bit past that now, don't you?"

Mutely, he stared at her.

"Abel, please, you must believe me!" she said, trying not to sound desperate. "I'm not secretly working for the Jandrians or the Lanruvians or whoever the enemy is this week. I'm on your side! Gerald and I and Monk Markham's sister are trying to finish what you started and stop whoever's out to ruin the Splotze-Borovnik wedding. We've already foiled one attempt that we're sure of. There might've been more, but—"

Abel Bestwick was shaking his head. "I must be dreaming. Delirious. This can't be real. Sir Alec would never send *women* into the field."

Oh, yes. He was going to be difficult. "We're not in the field, Abel," she said, cajoling. "Bibbie and I aren't janitors. At the most you could call us *honorary* agents."

"Honorary agents," Abel Bestwick murmured. "Right. I wonder if this means I'm dying?"

She could slap some sense into him, but then he might really die and she was in enough trouble already. "Look, Abel, we don't have time for this. You'll simply have to trust that we do have experience and we really have come to help. Please, *please*, won't you believe me?"

"I must be mad," Bestwick said. "All right. You're an honorary agent. Now what?"

Oh, Saint Snodgrass be praised. "Well, for one thing, can you tell me who's behind the plot? We thought it was the Lanruvians, but—"

"It's Harenstein," said Abel Bestwick.

"Oh, no," she said, stupidly. "That can't be right. Harenstein? *Norbert*, you mean? But—Erminium says Norbert's been an answer to her prayers. He brought Ratafia and Ludwig together in the first place. And he was nearly killed at the bridge. No, no, Abel, you're wrong. It *can't* be Norbert."

"I don't know if the marquis is involved," said Bestwick.

"But two of his men are. I overheard them plotting in the stables. I *saw* them."

Mitzie's tiny room was warm, but Melissande felt herself starting to shiver. "Dermit and Volker? Is that who you mean?"

Bestwick's face darkened. "Yes. Them. One of the bastards stabbed me. Him with the scar."

"Is your wound bad?" she said, because that was the proper thing to ask. But she could hardly see Abel Bestwick's blood-stained bandage for the tears crowding her eyes.

Poor Erminium. Poor Ratafia. And Ludwig. And Twiggy. Poor everyone, when the truth comes out.

"Hey. Miss Cadwallader, or whoever you are," said Bestwick. "D'you mind? Cry later."

Blinking hard, she glared at him. "You're bloody rude!"

"I'm bloody perforated," he retorted. "I nearly died. If it hadn't been for Mitzie . . ." His plain, angry face softened. "Look. Where's—what's his name, again? Dunwoody?"

"Yes. Gerald."

"If he's a janitor, why isn't he here?"

"He doesn't know *I'm* here," she said, and slid off the edge of Bestwick's mattress. "Nobody knows, Abel. Everyone thinks you *are* dead. As for Gerald, he's convinced tonight's fireworks have been sabotaged. If so, he and Bibbie are going to unsabotage them."

Somehow.

"Why not call them off?" said Bestwick, frowning. "Better yet, postpone the wedding?"

She gave him a look. "I'll give you three guesses, Mister Bestwick."

Abel Bestwick sagged. "Right. Politics. I wasn't thinking."

Her eyes were dry again. Now she was far too angry to cry. *All the lies. All the heartache. Someone's going to pay.* "I have to go, Abel. I have to find Gerald, and tell him what you've told me."

"Tell Sir Alec while you're at it."

"I wish I could," she said. "Only the etheretics aren't co-operating. No crystal ball, no portal. And even the fastest airship is too slow. We're on our own, I'm afraid."

Bestwick grimaced. "Don't worry. You get used to it."

He sounded bitter, and she supposed she couldn't blame him. An undercover janitor's life looked anything but glamorous.

"You've had a bad time of it," she said. "I'm sorry."

He grunted. "Thanks. Now you should go, while I—"

"Don't be ridiculous, Abel!" she said in her best no-nonsense voice, pressing him back to the narrow bed. "You're staying here."

"But—"

"But nothing," she snapped. "You're in no condition for janitoring, and you know it. Now, I'm warning you, don't you dare step foot outside this room! There's no need to worry. I'll take care of everything. And if the worst happens, and you're discovered, tell whoever's found you that you're under my protection. Her Royal Highness, Princess Melissande of New Ottosland, remember? Tell them Crown Prince Hartwig and I are particular friends." When Bestwick's eyes widened she added crossly, "Not *that* kind of particular, thank you. But I've known Twiggy for donkey's years. Mention both of us and you should be all right. *If* you're discovered. But let's hope you're not."

"Yes, let's," said Abel Bestwick, giving in, and rolled his tired, pain-filled eyes.

She left Sir Alec's other janitor locked in Mitzie's room. Made her way back down the long spiral staircase, through the heavy leather curtain and into the kitchens, caught Mitzie's eye and dropped the little brass key on the floor, in passing. Then she returned to the Entrance Hall, where she took a moment to catch her breath amid the shining suits of armour.

Saint Snodgrass preserve her. What should she do now? Tell Hartwig? Lord, no. He likely wouldn't believe her. Or worse, he would, and he'd confront Norbert, and all hell would break loose. No. Her only choice was to find Gerald. She nearly laughed out loud.

Find Gerald? Down at the Canal? When the Canal's overflowing with tourists? How am I s'posed to do that? Stand on a rubbish bin and wave my arms until he sees me?

Well, yes. If she had to. If that was what it took. What a mercy she'd not changed out of her second-best day dress and comfortable shoes.

Heart racing, once again despicably close to tears, she took a deep breath, then another, and then headed down to the Canal.

Not hand in hand, but nearly, Gerald walked with Bibbie along the noisily festive streets of Grande Splotze, at long last close to reaching the Canal. Splotze's capital was more crowded than ever, the air fairly humming with excited anticipation for the fireworks, and the wedding, and the dawn of a new day for Splotze and Borovnik.

"Blimey," said Bibbie, her voice almost lost in the babble and din. "If we walk any slower we'll be going backwards. I've never seen so many different nationalities in the same place at the same time."

"It's a sight, isn't it?" he agreed. "Careful. Mind your step."

Bibbie neatly avoided tripping into the smelly gutter. Bumped shoulders with a man from Graff, prettily apologised, then laughed.

"Lord, Algernon. What a crush!"

Yes. So many people. Too many. Imagining the panic and chaos if the fireworks went wrong, if he failed to prevent disaster, he shuddered. And then he jumped, as Bibbie took his arm.

"Stop that, Mister Rowbotham. Everything's going to be fine."

He looked down at her, and felt his heart leap. Breaking every promise he'd made to Monk, to himself, he'd kissed her. Abandoned cautious pragmatism . . . and opened the floodgates to love.

And I'm not sorry. In fact, as soon as I can I'm going to kiss her again.

"Algernon?" Bibbie gave his arm a little shake. "What's wrong?"

"Nothing," he said, and smiled, despite the danger. "Hold

tight, Miss Slack. I'm done with dawdling. We're going to pick up the pace."

Using his *potentia* to nudge laggardly pedestrians out of their way, he hurried them across the last main thoroughfare and down several winding side streets until they reached the Canal promenade.

"Oh!" said Bibbie, delighted by the clowns and the jugglers and the cheeky dancing monkeys. "What a pity we don't have time to play."

He bent his head to her. "Maybe tomorrow. Let's get past today first."

"All right," said Bibbie. "But before we do anything else, can we stop for a drink and something to eat?"

"Are your ribs playing knucklebones again?"

"They're considering it," she said. "Please, Algernon? We've got time."

They had a little time, yes. And truth be told, he was hungry too. So they chose a food stall with the shortest queue, and bought cups of fresh cherry juice and fat spiced sausages, their skins split and dribbling juices. Then they cheated their way to a patch of grass on the Canal green and sat in the gradually waning afternoon sunshine to enjoy their hasty meal. To be safe, even though the tourists around them were caught up in the excitement of their own lives, Gerald blurred himself and Bibbie so they couldn't be overhead.

"Clever," said Bibbie, noticing. "And tricky. Learn that one in the Department, did you?"

No. He'd made it up just then. *I want something, I get it. As simple as that.* Except it wasn't meant to be so simple. That was how the other Gerald had thought. That was grimoire magic's slippery slope. And was he even now starting that insidious slide?

Bibbie was waiting for him to answer. "Must've done," he said, and pointed. "Look. Doesn't that monkey there remind you of Errol Haythwaite?"

Giggling, she poked him. "Now, now, Mister Rowbotham. Poor little monkey. It's not nice to make fun."

"It isn't? Then please accept my apologies, Miss Slack."

She grinned. He grinned. They drank their cherry juice and ate their sausages and pretended they were two regular people without a care in the world.

Meal finished, licking grease from her fingers, Bibbie looked at him sidelong. "Algernon, you're not *really* furious with Melissande, are you?"

Bloody Melissande. "I was. Maybe I still am. A bit. She crossed the line, Gladys. She agreed I was in charge here, and then—" He ate some more sausage. "She agreed I was in charge."

"Yes, I know, but she's Melissande," said Bibbie. "You can't really be surprised."

No. Not really. "Sir Alec's going to go spare."

Bibbie shrugged. "Maybe. I think it depends on how everything turns out."

Trust Bibbie to make him confront the unpalatable truth. This impromptu picnic was nothing but a mirage. He wasn't Algernon Rowbotham on an outing with his young lady. He was a janitor with a job to do.

And Bibbie shouldn't be here.

"But I am here, Gerald," she said sharply. "And I'm not going away."

How did she *do* that? How did she always *know?*

A fleeting, dimpled smile. "Monk's not the only one who can read you like hieroglyphics."

"Bibbie—"

She covered his hand with hers. Her touch was warm. Exciting. Comforting. Perilous. If he closed his eyes he'd see her true face, not the made-up brown eyes and dark hair of demure Gladys Slack.

"There's something I need to tell you, Gerald," she said quietly. No smiles now, no teasing. "I know what's happened. To you. The grimoire magic and your *potentia*. I'm not entirely sure when, but I'm guessing it was in Abel Bestwick's lodging."

His mouth was dry, his heart sickly pounding. "You can't know that."

"Of course I can," she said. "I'm Emmerabiblia Markham. And just so you know? I'm not afraid of you."

He had to look away. "Perhaps you should be."

"Gerald . . ." She sighed, her fingers tightening around his. "Listen to me. *You aren't him*. He was a monster . . . and you're the man I love."

It couldn't be right, to feel this happy. Not when the fate of two countries and countless lives hung in the balance, depending on him. Not when he could hear that other Gerald's grimoire magic whispering in his blood.

Bibbie leaned in and kissed him, the merest butterfly brushing of her lips against his. "We need to get down to the Canal front. It's time to inspect those fireworks pontoons."

Yes. It was. But, as it turned out, that was going to be a great deal more easily said than done.

"Blimey," said Bibbie, as they stood before the crowded Canal wall and stared across the water at the twenty pontoons tethered ready for the night's event. "I wish you'd been right the first time, Algernon. I don't think we're going to get this done with a pilfered rowboat."

"Even if there was a rowboat to pilfer," he agreed. "And there's not."

The Canal had been entirely emptied of water craft. There wasn't even a royal barge, because these were the wedding fireworks and after the last gloriously burning ember winked out, the wedding party would be returning to the palace for the reception, crab puffs to be conspicuously absent, then the marriage ceremony, then the treaty signing, and last of all the fifteen-course State Dinner.

Bibbie was frowning. "Gosh. I can feel the wardings from here. Can't you?"

He certainly could. It seemed Hartwig was taking no chances with these fireworks, relying on someone sterner than Radley Blayling to keep them safe from Splotze's erratic and exasperating etheretic field. But were they also stern enough to keep them safe from something worse?

"I can't feel anything else, though," Bibbie murmured. "Nothing rotten. No tampering."

And neither could he. It was almost as though that sickening sense of danger he'd felt in the palace had been no more substantial than a dream.

"Mind you," she added, "I didn't feel the hexes at the Hanging Bridge until it was too late." She shivered. "Whoever's behind this is awfully good, Algernon."

He nodded. "I know. But we're better."

We have to be. Because if we're not . . .

Two sections of the Canal front had been cordoned off from the general public, with floating platforms put in place for a uniquely intimate view of the fireworks. One section was for the wedding party and its important guests, and the other was set aside for the lucky minions and lackeys who'd been deemed worthy of a front row seat.

Gerald patted his coat pocket. "Here's an idea. We've got our passes, and without a rowboat I think that floating platform is the nearest we're going to get to those bloody pontoons. If I'm right and something happens, sitting right down the front gives us our best chance of foiling the plot."

But the palace guard they showed their passes to wouldn't let them through the cordon. Far too early. Come back at sunset. Crown Prince's orders. Go away.

Gerald was tempted to compel him, but Bibbie hustled him off before he could succumb.

"It was a good idea in theory," she said. "But I think we'd cause a stir, sitting there all by ourselves for the next two-and-a-bit hours. It's best if we blend in. Isn't it?"

He was getting impatient. Letting fear over-ride good judgement. If Frank Dalby was here, there'd be some withering scorn.

"You're right," he said. "But we'll keep wandering around the promenade. If there's a change in the ether, if any grimoire thaumaturgics start stirring, here is the most likely place we'll feel them."

This was a mistake, Melissande thought, fetching up against a Canal promenade lamp post to catch her breath. *What was I thinking? I'm never going to find Gerald and Bibbie in this wretched crowd.*

Tourists and dancing dogs and jugglers and food stalls and ridiculous people on stilts. What sane adult staggered about the place on stilts? She must've been out of her mind. She should've stayed in the palace and waited for Gerald and Bibbie to come back. Or dragged Abel Bestwick out of Mitzie's room and taken him to see Hartwig and *bugger* the politics. What was a little spying between not-currently-enemies when lives were at stake?

Harenstein? This is all Harenstein's fault? How did I not see it? How did Gerald not see it? He's the janitor here. It's supposed to be his job!

It was getting late. According to Mister Ibblie's polite list of instructions, anyone fortunate enough to be included with the wedding party should be dressed and ready to depart the palace at dusk. That meant she should go back now, because of the crowds and having to bathe and dress up for the night. And if Bibbie wasn't waiting for her in their guest suite she'd have to dress herself, which would be interesting. She might need to kidnap a passing maid.

Saint Snodgrass preserve me. I never asked for this. When I get home, Sir Alec and I are going to have words.

"Look," said Bibbie, pointing, as the gathered crowd on the promenade began chanting and cheering. "There's the wedding party. Doesn't Ratafia look sweet? Oh, and there's Melissande. In purple. Hmm." She frowned. "Which means she dressed herself. What a pity. Maybe that's why she looks like she's swallowed a hedgehog. But she did know not to expect us back, didn't she?"

Gerald nodded. "I thought so."

"Then maybe Ratafia's still not speaking to her. Or maybe Erminium is."

"Maybe," he said, but he wasn't really paying attention. They were standing on the Canal green edge closest to the cordoned-off royal enclosures. The promenade was lamplit now, dusk velvety and star-studded. Moths flirted with the glowing gaslights. Everywhere he looked he saw Grande

Splotze's townsfolk and visitors, laughing and cheering and clapping and innocent.

"Oh, at last," said Bibbie. "They're letting the minions into their pen. Come on, Algernon, quickly. Before we're left stuck up the back. Although perhaps it won't matter, since everything's so quiet."

Yes. The ether was quiet, more or less. Still twisted. Uniquely Splotzeish. But not tainted or tortured, ready to erupt in killing and maiming grimoire magic.

So why do I feel so jittery?

"Algernon?" Bibbie tugged at his sleeve. "Let's go."

There was a band playing on the Canal green. Too big for the gazebo, it had swallowed up half the grass and was serenading the crowd with cheerful music, lots of horns and trumpets, merry tunes to tap the toes. He wanted to clap his hands and melt those trumpets. He wanted to snap every violin string with a thought.

"*Algernon.*"

He took a step back. Looked at Bibbie. "No, Gladys. I can't."

"Why not?"

How could he explain his sudden sense of dread? There weren't any words that made sense. But then he didn't make sense, did he? That was what being *rogue* meant.

Bibbie's expression changed. "I don't feel anything. What do you feel?"

"Afraid," he said. "I can't go down there, Bibbie. And I can't stay out here, with the crowd. Too many people. I can't see. I can't think. I need *space*, I need—"

The Grande Splotze observation tower.

"Up *there?*" said Bibbie, following his gaze. "Gerald, are you sure?"

He took her hand and pulled her with him, reckless with his *potentia* as he bullied tourist after tourist out of their way.

The observation tower was closed to the public, its gate secured with chain and lock. A wave of his hand blurred him and Bibbie from detection. A single word swung the gate wide.

"Ah . . . Gerald . . ." said Bibbie, stepping over the discarded security chain. "Perhaps you'd better—"

He snapped his fingers twice, and the gate clanged closed and warded behind them.

"Right," said Bibbie, half-laughing. "Very efficient."

"I'm sorry, there are quite a lot of stairs," he said, looking up. "Four hundred and twenty-three, if you're counting. I know—" he added, as she groaned. "It's a bugger, but there you are."

The cheerful band music helped them keep time as they climbed. The jostling crowd below made a sound like the ocean, no words up here, only a susurration of voices. They reached the top of the tower, panting, and gasped for air beneath the darkening sky and the distant stars.

Bibbie moved to the viewing platform's warded edge and looked down at the Canal, crowded with fireworks pontoons. Then she looked back over her shoulder, her eyes bright with courage.

"Right, then, Mister Dunwoody. What now?"

CHAPTER TWENTY-FOUR

The fireworks were about to start any moment. Seated with Hartwig on the crowded wedding party viewing platform, since poor gouty Brunelda was *still* confined to her couch, Melissande craned her neck to see in between the guests from Ottosland and Fandawandi and Graff and Blonkken, across to the next platform where various and sundry minions and lackeys were laughing and chatting and drinking cider.

Algernon Rowbotham and Gladys Slack, who'd not returned to the palace, weren't among them.

Oh, lord. Oh, Saint Snodgrass. I hope they're all right.

She also hoped the fireworks weren't tampered with, because thanks to their special viewing platform she was sitting awfully bloody close.

Erminium, ruler-straight in the chair on Hartwig's other side, was making clear her opinion of spoiled rotten servants who didn't know how to enjoy themselves quietly.

Norbert of Harenstein, standing nearby with his young, beautiful wife, sighed and wagged a finger at the Dowager Queen. "Come, come, Erminium. It's not so bad."

Swallowing, Melissande stared at him as he coaxed Ratafia's perpetually dissatisfied mother into taking another glass of cherry liqueur. How could Norbert be involved in the plot? He was here, with his empty-headed marquise. If the fireworks had been tampered with he'd be somewhere else, surely.

Like Volker and Dermit. They're not here either. But then, they really are villains.

Of course, if Gerald was wrong again, and the fireworks were safe, then perhaps Norbert *was* a villain, too.

I hate this. I've had enough. I want to go home.

"Melissande?" said Ratafia, who'd decided to forgive her. She stood resplendent in topaz-gold silk, with Ludwig's arm about her slender waist, blooming like a bride. "Is everything all right?"

"Yes, of course," she said, smiling, feeling sick enough to weep. "I'm just excited."

"So am I!" said Ratafia, her beautiful face aglow. "I love fireworks, and I love Luddie. This will be a perfect night!"

Melissande nodded, not trusting herself to speak.

A perfect night, or perfectly dreadful. If only I knew which.

"*Blimey*, I hate waiting," said Bibbie. "How lucky are you, Gerald, that I'm not scared of heights?"

Pacing the observation tower's viewing platform, skin crawling, palms sweating, Gerald stared down at the fireworks pontoons.

"Very. Can you feel anything yet?"

She sighed. "No. Still not yet."

No. He dragged his hand down his face, felt the tremble in his fingers. Dread was alive in him now, howling through his bones.

Damn and blast. What I wouldn't give to be wrong.

With a whistling rush the first fireworks ignited, tracing lines of green and gold against the deepening night sky. The crowd roared, drowning the screaming whizz of the thaumaturgically enhanced gunpowder. All the smiling upturned faces, splashed with colour, reflected wonder and joy. Next came a blossoming of flowers, gold and crimson and purple and white, promise of a distant spring.

Bibbie turned, laughing. "Look at them, Gerald. They're fabulous!"

He wanted to smile back at her, to share in her wonder. But the howling dread wouldn't let him, wouldn't stop shaking his bones. Roiling beneath the beauty was a filthy promise of death.

Between heartbeats, Bibbie's pleasure died. Her face twisted with pain.

"Gerald—"

"I know, Bibbie! I know!"

He fought to stay on his feet, but these thaumaturgics were worse than the blood hex, worse than what they'd faced at the Hanging Bridge. They beat him to his knees.

"*Gerald!*"

"Stay back, Bibbie!" he groaned, shuddering. "Please. Stay back."

With an effort he got rid of Algernon, needing to be himself. Wanting her to see *him*, not that counterfeit face. Just in case . . . in case . . .

"Bloody hell, Bibs." He was nearly sobbing. "It's close, so damned close—"

And then she was kneeling with him, her fingers warm and strong around his wrists. A twisting ripple and she was herself again, Gladys Slack cast aside. The brilliant blue eyes he'd missed so much were wide with fear.

"Gerald, I don't know how to—it's grimoire magic, I'm not strong enough, I can't—"

"I can," he said, gasping. "But not alone."

"Do you want me to hide you? I can do that much, at least, I can—"

"No!" He didn't want her anywhere near what was coming. "It might make things tricky, this time. Two *potentias*."

"Then what do you need, Gerald?" Her breath caught. "Anything. It's yours."

"Tell me again, Bibs. I need to hear it."

She framed his face with her warm hands. Pressed her forehead to his. "I love you, Gerald Dunwoody, and I am not afraid."

"Damn," he muttered, torn between delight and dismay. "Sir Alec will go right round the bend. And your uncle!"

A small shrug. "Probably. But I say we jump off that bridge tomorrow."

"Tomorrow," he said, and kissed her, too briefly, making the word a promise.

Four hundred and twenty-three steps below them, the crowd roared and cheered as fireworks streaked the night sky all the glowing colours of dawn. Melissande was down there. Rightly or wrongly, she mattered more than the rest. If he failed here, her death would belong to him forever. The ensuing Splotze-Borovnik conflict would be his too, countless deaths, rivers of spilled blood, a continent plunged into chaos.

So don't fail.

Something malevolent shuddered through the ether. A putrid flower, unfurling, its petals stinking of decay. Another roar from the crowd, this time pocked with alarm. There were wizards among the thousands watching, and witches. They knew.

With an effort Gerald stood, and Bibbie stood with him. Walked beside him to the edge of the platform so he could see the tethered pontoons and the fireworks and the people he had to save.

"I don't know who or what I am any more, Bibbie," he whispered. "I don't know what I'm doing. I'm making this up as I go."

She laced her fingers with his, cool and slim. An anchor. A lifeline. "It's all right, Gerald. I won't let you get lost."

And that was her promise. Believing it, he made his leap of faith into the dark.

The tainted thaumaturgics in the fireworks were rank and riddled with decay, dreamed to life by a twisted soul. He felt his changed *potentia* quail at the touch of them, changed not so much, it seemed, as he feared. He rode the roil of dark magics through the ether like a kestrel in a storm, feeling the whip and wash toss him, feeling his soul fight to stay free. Here there was no distance, he was a mere hairsbreadth from the terrible incants. Reach out his hand and he could touch them. Reach out his mind and see them crushed.

Provided they didn't crush him first.

Don't let go, Bibbie. Don't leave me here alone.

He fought to remember all he knew of thaumaturgics. The lessons Reg had taught him. The things he'd learned on his own. What he'd discovered by accident in the attics at

Chatterley Crescent, arguing mad experiments with Monk. And of course the grimoire magics that he'd given himself.

Every incant created contains the seed of its own destruction. For every syllable there is a silence. For every take there must be give.

He was standing on a viewing platform, high above Grande Splotze. Stretch up with his fingers and he'd touch the sky, catch a falling star, make the moon his toy. He could feel the ground below him and the emptiness of air. Behind his closed eyelids he saw traceries of fire.

And fire is ravenous. Fire feeds until it's dead.

All the wicked, wicked magic. Before its gluttonous feast was over half the world or more would be consumed. Abandoning himself to instinct, to his remade and terrible *potentia*, he planted his own seed within the heart of every tainted incant. Showed it silence. Gave it death.

The incants screamed with their dying, died cruel, died hard. He struggled not to die with them but they were tearing him apart. Tearing quickly. Or was it slowly? He'd lost all sense of time.

The last incant perished. In its dying wake, a different, kinder silence. And then he heard, from far away, someone call his name, weeping.

"Gerald . . . Gerald . . . it's over. Come back. Please, please, come back."

Was he leaving? He didn't want to. He had a reason to stay. Blood tasted like salt and iron. It was warm, and stank of life. He could feel somebody's fingers, tightly interlaced with his. Someone's tears fell on his cold face, warm as blood on snow.

Bibbie.

Gerald opened his eyes. He was sprawled on his back, the tower's platform hard against his flesh and bones. But his head had a fine pillow, beautiful, wonderful Bibbie Markham's lap, and she was stroking his hair with her cool, slim fingers, brokenly saying his name again and again. As he smiled up at her, not leaving, not dying, the crowd far below them roared its approval . . . and in the starry night sky above them untainted fireworks danced with joy.

*   *   *

A princess should carry smelling salts upon her person at all times.

It was one of the oddest admonitions she'd ever encountered, growing up, but as she bent over a stricken Lord Babcock, Melissande found herself grateful to the governess who'd left Dashforth's *Precepts for Young Royalty* in the nursery's library.

Lord Babcock, pale and clammy, slumped in a chair at the back of the viewing platform, breathing in shallow groans. He wasn't alone in his discomfort. Aframbigi's Foreign Minister, and Jandria's, were also suffering pangs of some kind. Just not badly enough to require smelling salts—or so they claimed.

She wafted the foul salts under Lord Babcock's nose one more time, to be on the safe side. As he snorted and spluttered, a fresh roar of appreciation from the crowd and much clapping from her fellow wedding guests and their minions on the other platform tipped her face skywards, but it was too late. The astonishing burst of fireworks was no more than a swiftly fading memory of blue and green.

The fireworks.

She felt her stomach jitter. There'd been a moment, just a moment, when she could have *sworn* she saw something creepily wrong in the brilliant, fiery lights bursting overhead. But then the moment passed, the fireworks continued beautifully brilliant, nothing creepy about them at all, and she'd thought, *I really must learn to curb my imagination.*

That was when someone said, "Oh dear, Lord Babcock's not feeling too well."

And naturally she'd gone to help, because that's what one did. It was the reason one carried smelling salts at all times.

Satisfied that Babcock was coming around with no harm done, Melissande put the stopper back in the bottle of salts and returned it to her reticule. A pity she couldn't put her suspicions away just as neatly.

I'll swear this isn't another case of finger food gone wrong. Something dreadful was about to happen with the fireworks, I know it. Something thaumaturgically catastrophic. But then . . . it didn't.

Because of Gerald and Bibbie, she'd stake her life on that.

And she'd bet it was the near-thaumaturgic disaster that had skittled Lord Babcock and the other two. Chances were that all three men, given who they were and where they came from, had finely tuned etheretic sensitivities.

On the other hand, Norbert of Harenstein hadn't noticed a thing. She wasn't sure what to make of that.

Another glorious burst of light and colour. More cheering. More clapping. The fireworks were reaching their breathtaking crescendo, boom boom boom, bloom and burst, a battering of beauty. Shaky with relief, Melissande smiled.

Well done, Radley Blayling. Unless of course you're part of the plot, in which case, shame on you.

With another spluttering snort, Lord Babcock collected himself out of his slump. Bending again, she patted his arm. "Feeling better, Your Lordship? Oh, I am pleased."

"What happened?" Babcock muttered, hand pressed to his head. "What the devil's going on?"

Well, my lord, if it turns out I'm right that's for me to know and Sir Ralph Markham to tell. Eventually. If he feels so inclined. Which he probably won't.

"I'm not sure, Lord Babcock," she said kindly, because the poor man did look seedy. "A little too much cherry liqueur, perhaps."

His gaze sharpened, turning inwards. "Yes. Yes. Most likely. Thank you, Your Highness."

Government ministers, no matter how exalted, did not dismiss royalty. Except when they did. Ah, the Ottish. Unoffended, because really, what would be the point, Melissande made her way through the well-bred cheering back to Hartwig's side.

"Old Babcock all ship-shape, then?" he asked, his arm going around her, his hand resting, inevitably, on her hip.

"He's fine," she said, giving up. He was Hartwig, he was harmless, and he had a lot on his plate. "Twiggy, the fireworks were wonderful."

"Yes, well," he said gruffly, and smoothed his moustache. "Only got one brother, haven't I? Got to do the right thing by him. Even if he is an idiot who dives into canals."

Carriages were waiting to take the wedding party back to

the palace. Riding with Hartwig, the horses trotting through a storm of cheering and tossed confetti, Melissande searched every face in the crowd as it passed. But no Algernon. No Gladys. She wanted to weep.

It didn't kill them, did it? Saving us? Please, please, don't say I brought them here to die.

"Look at that," said Hartwig, pitching his voice above the happy throng. "We've got clouds coming in. Think it might rain a bit, later tonight. S'posed to be a good omen, a touch of rain at a wedding. Brings luck, the old wives say."

She glanced at the sky. He was right, the stars were clouding over. "Let's hope so, Twiggy."

Because right now I need all the luck I can get.

Toiling her way up to her suite, she debated with herself about whether or not she should tell Hartwig she'd misplaced her secretary *and* her lady's maid and ask him to send out a search party for them. She knew he'd say yes in a heartbeat . . . but if she did ask, might she unwittingly be putting Gerald and Bibbie in danger? Assuming, of course, they weren't—weren't—

No. I refuse to entertain the possibility.

She was still trying to decide on the best thing to do when she walked into the guest apartment's bedchamber.

"Good, there you are," said Bibbie, neat and tidy in a primly demure dark blue satin dress. "I've got your green silk evening gown pressed and ready, because you can't stay in that hideous purple thing. Honestly, all it's good for is dusters."

Melissande blinked. For a moment it was a toss up, whether she hugged Bibbie or slapped her. In the end she simply sat on the bed, beyond caring if she crumpled her maligned mauve dress.

"You wretched bloody nuisance," she said, her voice unsteady. "Don't you realise I thought you were *dead?*"

Bibbie's brittle brightness faded. "Oh. Look, Melissande, there's—"

"No, Bibbie. There is no *looking*. No *there's no need to make a fuss*. Not after what happened with the fireworks. Something did happen, didn't it? I mean, I'm not losing my mind?"

Her Gladys Slack face sombre, Bibbie perched on the edge of the nearest chair. "No. Something happened. Or rather nothing happened. Thanks to Gerald."

It was a different kind of relief, to know she'd not been wrong. "And where is Gerald? Is he all right?"

"Honestly?" said Bibbie, after an unnervingly long silence. "I'm not sure. I think so. He didn't die or go mad, which is good. Only . . ."

"Only *what*, Bibbie?" she demanded. "Please. Just say it. You're frightening me."

Bibbie looked up, her eyes haunted with wonder. "Well, the thing is, Mel? I think he should have. The grimoire incants in those fireworks?" She shivered. "I've never felt—I never *imagined* . . ." She pressed her hands to her face, briefly. "They were brilliant, y'know. Wickedly, dreadfully brilliant. Monk could've made them. He wouldn't, but he could. I don't know who else is good enough. And I don't know any wizard besides Gerald who could've destroyed them, and survived."

Melissande stared. "Not even Monk?"

"No, not even Monk. Because Monk isn't—he hasn't—"

And now Bibbie was *really* frightening her. "What? Monk hasn't what?"

But Bibbie shook her head. "I can't, Melissande. I'm sorry. It's not for me to say. You'll have to ask Gerald."

She slid off the bed. "Fine. Where is he?"

"In his room, getting gussied up."

"Go and fetch him, would you? I needed to talk to him anyway. You two aren't the only ones who've had an interesting night. *Now*, Bibbie. Or I'll be late for the party."

But when Bibbie returned, she was alone and frowning. "He's gone down to the reception. He left a note."

"The *wedding* reception?" Melissande said, disbelieving. "But you minions aren't invited, he knows that. You've got drinks in the Servants' Hall. What is he thinking? Upstairs isn't going to let Algernon Rowbotham crash the pre-wedding party."

"Trust me, Melissande," said Bibbie, her expression grim. "He won't give them a choice. He's so angry about the fireworks. I've never seen him so angry. He swore he was going to unmask the plotters tonight or tear the wedding apart, trying."

She could've screamed with frustration. "I've already unmasked them! It's Dermit and Volker. Quick, Bibbie. Help me get changed. We need to find Gerald, just in case those Steinish bastards have figured out who keeps putting a spoke in their dirty wheel."

But Bibbie was so still she might've been nailed to the carpet. "*Dermit and Volker?* Are you sure? How do you know?"

Heedless of seams and buttons, Melissande started undressing herself. "Abel Bestwick told me."

"*Abel Bestwick?* When did you—"

"A few hours ago." Melissande flailed out of the purple dress and flung it on the bed. "And no, I wasn't holding a séance. He's not dead, Bibbie. He's been hiding in Mitzie the kitchen maid's room in the palace."

"Good lord," Bibbie said faintly.

"I told you I'd had an interesting time," she retorted. "Anyway, once I'd convinced him I wasn't a madwoman, or an enemy agent, he told me everything he knew."

"And he says it's Harenstein? But—but what about the Lanruvians?"

"The Lanruvians have gone home," she said, fumbling with the buttons on her boots. "I have no idea why. All I know is that Abel Bestwick swears blind that Dermit and Volker are our villains, and seeing as how one of them stabbed him I rather thought contradicting him would be impolite."

"Good lord," said Bibbie. "Dermit and Volker. Well, at least that explains why they wouldn't succumb to my charms."

Oh, for pity's *sake*. "Yes, Emmerabiblia," Melissande said slowly. "Because that's what *really* matters. I'm so glad we've cleared that up. *Now fetch me my bloody evening gown before I forget I'm a bloody princess and do you a bloody mischief they'll write up in the* Times*!*"

Bravely undeterred by the memory of crab puffs, and lured by the promise of limitless cherry liqueur, the well-placed and well-dressed of Hartwig's acquaintance had arrived promptly to celebrate Splotze and Borovnik's highly anticipated nuptials.

Eating, drinking, gossiping, the wedding guests swirled in a colourful cloud of national dress and perfume and sprightly music. Watching from a discreet nook halfway along one wall, almost but not quite hidden behind a crimson velvet curtain, Gerald paid special attention to the dancers who'd gone on the wedding tour . . . and admitted to a grudging respect. Life in the rough and tumble worlds of politics and international diplomacy certainly hardened the nerves. Not a one of them showed any sign of nerves over the near-tragedy at the Hanging Bridge. And if one of them was disappointed, well, he couldn't tell that, either. Which was a damned shame.

The guests from Blonkken arrived, and were immediately plied with refreshments. But still no Lanruvians. Probably planning to make yet another fashionably late entrance. Puzzling bastards, they were. Try as he might, he couldn't figure them out. He'd not felt them at the fireworks . . . but what did that mean? Perhaps nothing. Perhaps everything. It was too soon to know.

The fireworks.

A dull, persistent ache was throbbing behind his eyes. And he felt oddly disconnected, as insubstantial as the music being played by Hartwig's favourite ensemble. Echoes of the observation platform, belling through his blood.

I don't know who or what I am any more, Bibbie. I don't know what I'm doing. I'm making this up as I go.

It was true then. It was true now. What he'd become . . . what he was becoming . . .

What I did tonight was impossible. Damn that other Gerald. Only a madman would meld a rogue potentia *with grimoire magics.*

What a blessing he'd had Bibbie. Without her to hold on to, to come back to, he'd never have survived. The observation platform, the Hanging Bridge. She'd saved him both times.

And when Sir Alec finds out . . .

But that was another bridge that could wait till tomorrow. Lord Babcock and the Jandrians entered the reception chamber together, playing nicely for once. Behind them a clutch of local dignitaries and their wives. He'd seen them before, at the doomed State Dinner. Still no soon-to-be happy couple though, or their families. No Melissande, either. But Secretary of State Leopold Gertz was here, doing his damp best to jolly things along as discreet palace servants brought in more finger food on silver platters. Though he was bone weary, and hurting, Gerald felt himself smile.

Tuck in quick, everyone, before the Marquis of Harenstein arrives.

Cautiously he unshielded his *potentia*. Touched it lightly here and there, but felt nothing untoward. And perhaps he wouldn't. Perhaps whoever had failed first at the Hanging Bridge and then with the fireworks had belatedly come to his senses.

But I won't hold my breath. This villain, whoever he is, has come too far to turn back now.

By now the reception chamber was so crowded and gabbleish that Hartwig's ensemble was having to play twice as loudly to be heard. And blimey, what were they playing? It was awful. But as he winced at the tuneless collection of sharps and flats, something distracted him.

Shifting his gaze towards the chamber's far end, he glimpsed a man dressed in severely fashionable black and white sidling his way through a large knot of guests who stood beside an enormous urn filled with Borovnik wildflowers.

Losing sight of him, Gerald cursed. Too many men dressed in black and white, too many parading silver platters and eager hands reaching for the food. Stirred instinct prickled an urgent warning. There'd been something . . . furtive . . . in the way the man moved.

Dammit. If only I'd seen his face.

And then a commotion erupted before the loudly playing ensemble, raised voices and a ragged expiration of music.

"—too bad, Goby, this is entirely too bad! You were told *not* to play that caterwauling rubbish! Are you an imbecile or a typical Borovnik, too arrogant to live?"

The commotion rippled outwards as guests retreated, snickering and muttering and even laughing out loud. Gerald saw

Leopold Gertz, like a damp bantam cockerel, fists clenched and chest thrust forward, confronting a man who clutched a conductor's baton and seemed dangerously inclined to use it.

Excellent. Perfect timing. *Thank you, Secretary Gertz*.

Under cover of the swiftly escalating dispute, Gerald wove his unobtrusive way through the goggling guests to the far end of the chamber. Pressing his back to the nearest empty bit of wall, he closed his eyes and let loose his *potentia*.

And this time he felt them, the slumbering grimoire thaumaturgics. After the fireworks they couldn't hide from him any more. The man, the mysterious villain he was hunting, had attached four sickeningly powerful hexes to the back of that flower-filled urn.

A touch, a thought, and he'd killed them. No-one was dying here tonight. Grimly smiling, he looked across the crowded room . . . straight into the shocked eyes of Bern Dermit. Who like himself was a lackey, and shouldn't have been allowed into the reception.

But I have my potentia. *What's his excuse?*

From one breath to the next, Dermit's shock twisted to incredulous fury. To understanding. To hate.

I'll be damned, thought Gerald, blinking. *It's you*.

Melissande and Bibbie had nearly reached the bottom of the palace's sweeping staircase when they crossed paths with the wedding party and got swept up in Hartwig's expansive enthusiasm.

"Of course, Melissande, of *course* you must make a grand entrance with us," he protested. "Why, you're as good as family. *Isn't* she, Brunelda?"

Poor gouty Brunelda, reduced to hobbling with a stick, seemed about to remonstrate . . . until she caught sight of Erminium's face.

"Absolutely she's like family, Hartwig," she said, sweetly smiling. "The daughter we never had, my dear."

With Hartwig choking on that one, and Erminium at long last speechless with rage, Melissande risked an eloquent glance at Bibbie.

Stay close. I'll find Gerald.

Bibbie nodded, bless her, and demurely retreated to bring up the rear.

Ratafia smiled, radiant, soppily entwined with her besotted Ludwig. "I'm glad you're here too, Melissande. And that's a *very* nice dress. Green suits you."

"Thank you," said Melissande. And when she heard Bibbie giggle, thought, *Oh, shut up.*

They arrived at the reception chamber to find Leopold Gertz and another man hurling spittled insults like hammers, much to the astonished amusement of Hartwig's many guests. Melissande looked at the other man's waving baton.

Good lord. Master Goby, I presume.

But then Leopold Gertz realised the wedding party had arrived, and the altercation collapsed in a mutual exchange of fulminating glares. Goby turned back to his musicians, and a moment later the chamber was blasted by a brass fanfare.

As Gertz retreated in embarrassed confusion, Melissande looked for Gerald. And there he was, standing beside a huge flowerpot, his expression oddly blank. She bounced a little bit and waved to attract his attention. No response. And then he saw her.

"Won't be a moment," she said to an oblivious Ratafia, and braved the crush of guests to join him. They collided almost halfway.

"It's Harenstein!" they declared in simultaneous undertones.

"How did you know?" Gerald demanded, catching hold of her arm and tugging her towards the wall.

"Abel Bestwick told me. Have you seen him too?"

"*Bestwick?*" Gerald gaped, then shook his head. "No. I just caught Bern Dermit setting grimoire hexes. It's all right, I killed them, but the bastard's given me the slip. He could be anywhere in the palace setting some more. Where's Bibbie? I need her to help me find him. And I want you to warn Hartwig, politics be damned."

Her head was spinning. "Bibbie's outside. Gerald, are you *sure* about telling Hartwig? Sir Alec—"

"Damn him, too," he said, furiously intent. "If we don't stop Dermit, Sir Alec will be the least of our worries."

Very true.

But they'd not made it five paces before Leopold Gertz appeared in front of them, holding two glasses of richly red cherry liqueur.

"Your Highness!" he said, his face pallid and sweating. "Don't go. Master Goby has played his last trick, I promise. Here." He held out a glass to her. "We'll drink to it, shall we? Here you are, sir." He gave the other glass to Gerald, then snatched a flute of sparkling wine for himself from a passing servant. "To Splotze and her music! May she reign forever sovereign!"

It would take more time to protest and excuse themselves than make the toast. With a flicker of his eyelid—*Come on, let's drink and run*—Gerald raised his glass.

"Indeed. To Splotze!"

Loathing cherry liqueur, Melissande pressed the lip of her glass deceptively against her teeth. Pretending to sip, she watched Splotze's Secretary of State watch Gerald drain his glass dry. Lord, Gertz really did look dreadful. And his *eyes* . . . Hungrily avid. Almost *manic*.

Then, just for a moment, his alarming gaze shifted past Gerald towards something, or someone, standing behind them. Terror. Triumph. Shame. She saw them all in Gertz's sweating face, and spun round.

Bern Dermit. Standing with him, Grune Volker. And in their faces she saw nothing but gloating hate.

Dropping her own glass she grabbed Gertz by the arm. "Leopold! *What have you done?*"

Gertz pulled free and backed away. "What I had to do. For Splotze. You wouldn't understand."

With a grunt, Gerald pressed a fist to his belly. Then he looked at her, astonished pain dawning.

"Melissande?"

Catching hold of him as he folded, she turned on Leopold Gertz. "You've *poisoned* him?"

Not waiting for Gertz to answer, because she already knew, she started dragging Gerald towards the reception chamber's door . . . and saw Dermit and Volker, those two Steinish bastards, bullying their way through Hartwig's heedless guests with murder in their eyes.

"*Bibbie!*"

And Bibbie was beside her, taking Gerald's other arm, helping to drag him towards the chamber doors. Now people were turning, curious, too bloody stupid to get out of the way. Dermit's hand was in his pocket. Everything about him screamed: *You're dead*.

"Bibbie, he's got hexes," she said, nearly sobbing. "We need a diversion!"

Bibbie clenched a fist and whispered. All around the chamber, curtains burst into flame.

"Done," she said, vicious. "Now let's get out of here."

CHAPTER TWENTY-FIVE

"*O* *y, you pair of hoydens! Put a sock in it, right now! And*
then tell me what you've gone and done to my Gerald!"

An ambush of tears, hot and smarting. Melissande blinked
them away. Help had come at last.

"Reg? How did you—"

Flapped onto the Canal wall, Reg was staring at Gerald.
"That Markham boy made himself useful for once." She jerked
her beak. "Is it poison?"

"Yes," said Bibbie. "Where's Monk? For pity's sake don't
tell me you came alone!"

"I'll remember that, madam," the bird said with a pointed
sniff. "What kind of poison, d'you know?"

"No," said Melissande. "But he drank it, if that helps." Her
voice was wobbling. Very unroyal. "Oh, Reg, it started working
so *fast* and we—"

"And you thought the best way to help my Gerald was take
him on a midnight tour of Grande Splotze?"

Bibbie turned on her. "If you've portable portalled all the
way from Chatterly Crescent to do nothing but carp, then I
suggest you portal yourself back again right now, you—you—
bloody *imposter!*"

On the cobbles at their feet, Gerald rolled his head
and moaned. The small sound was shockingly loud in the
silence.

A sniff. A soft rattling of long tail feathers. "So," said Reg.
"Are you two running to somewhere in particular, or—"

"Abel Bestwick's lodging," said Melissande, subdued. "It's at—"

"45b Voblinz Lane. I know." Reg gave her tail another good shake. "But why take him there? Why not send for a doctor? You were in the palace weren't you? Don't tell me Hartwig doesn't keep a doctor in his pocket, just in case he collapses with an attack of ingrown toenail."

She glanced at Bibbie, but Monk's sister had dropped to one knee beside stuporous Gerald and was chafing his wrist between her hands.

"There wasn't time, Reg. The bastards who did this were about to finish the job. We *had* to run. And we thought Abel might keep some kind of all-round poison remedy. You know, since he's a janitor." A bubble of despair rose in her throat. "Only those poisoning pillocks must be following us and I think we're lost and—"

Reassuringly brisk, Reg rattled her tail again. "Not to worry. Along with a locator hex for finding Gerald, that Markham boy gave me excellent directions to Mister Bestwick's humble abode, just in case. So let's get cracking, shall we? Miss Markham—it'd be a good idea if you tarted up your obfuscation hex before we go."

Another appalled silence. Melissande stared at Bibbie, and Bibbie stared back.

"Oh, my giddy aunt," Reg said, disgusted. "Call yourself a witch, madam? Call yourself a Markham? I know what I'd call you, I'd call you—"

"The woman Gerald loves, actually," Melissande snapped. "So leave her be, Reg, and lead the way to Voblinz Lane. *Now*."

"No, wait," said Bibbie. "She's right. Let me just—"

Oh, lord. At this rate they were going to argue themselves right into Dermit and Volker's murderous clutches. "There's no *time*, Bibbie! Those bastards could stumble over us at any moment! Now come on. I'll take his top half and you take his legs, just like before. Don't worry. We've made it this far. We'll make it the rest of the way."

"Blimey," said Reg, when they had Gerald once more slung

between them. "There's a circus act in there somewhere." With a flapping of wings, she was airborne. "Well, ladies, what are you waiting for? Follow me!"

She led them through the hushed, shadowed streets to Voblinz Lane without making a single wrong turn. *Thank you, Monk.* The narrow street was darkly narrow and noisome, scattered with rain-sodden refuse. Only one of its gaslights was working. And that was the first and last bit of good news to be found.

"I don't *believe* it," Bibbie said, both hands pressed to the warped and paint-peeling front door of 45b. "Gerald's *warded* the wretched hovel. Running after blood magic and he still remembers to lock the door!"

Melissande swallowed another bubble of despair. *Oh, lord. I can't take much more of this.* "You're sure it's Gerald's hexwork?"

"Yes," Bibbie said, with an impatient glance. "I can feel some older hexes too, probably Bestwick's, but they're all kaput. Trust me, this is Gerald's doing. I'd know one of his hexes anywhere."

Wonderful. As if they didn't have enough headaches to be going on with. "Well . . . can you break it?"

"She has to," said Reg, sitting on the cracked pavement beside Gerald. Her beak caressed his cheek, once. "Because our boy is fighting the fight of his life and we're not going to be any help to him out here."

"Bibs . . ." Afraid, uncertain, Melissande rested a hand on Bibbie's shoulder, feeling her tense and trembling. "You and Monk and Gerald, you've spent months and months mucking about with thaumaturgics in the attic. Monk says you're easily as good as him these days. I know there's a difference between witch and wizard *potentias*, but—"

"No, there's not," Bibbie said tightly. "That's nonsense put out by manky old men like Great-uncle Throgmorton, who want to keep *gels* in their place."

"So your *potentia* and Gerald's, they're compatible? I mean, you worked together at the Hanging Bridge, didn't you? The way Monk and Gerald work together at home? And—you know, when they were stuck in the other Ottosland."

"Sort of," Bibbie said, after a moment. "But teaming up *potentias* isn't the same as breaking each other's thaumaturgics. It's true, I've managed to crack a few of Gerald's hexes." Her flattened palms became fists, and banged her frustration on the door. "But that was before he—"

Suddenly, it seemed Bibbie had to stare at the peeling paint.

"Before the grimoire magic?" Crossing her arms, Melissande rubbed her hands up and down to chase away the chill. "I know you said he's changed, but even so . . . he got rid of it, didn't he? He's not—not permanently tainted, or anything? Is he?"

Bibbie uncurled her fisted fingers one by one. "No. Of course he isn't."

And that was a lie. Goaded beyond self-control, Melissande gave temper free rein. "*Stop* it, Emmerabiblia! I'm sick and bloody tired of you treating me like a *gel!* You of all people! I don't know how you can!"

"What's this?" Reg demanded, abandoning her vigil on the pavement to hop onto a nearby step. "Has something else happened to Gerald?"

"It's not for me to say," Bibbie answered, mulishly stubborn. "You'll have to ask him."

"Well, ducky, I would, only he's a bit *poisoned* just now!"

"I'm sorry. I can't—I *won't*—tell you," Bibbie said, dogged to the end. "So you might as well stop asking."

"All right, Emmerabiblia," Melissande said wearily. "Keep your secrets, I don't care. Just get us inside, will you, before we're discovered?"

Bibbie's reply was to rest her forehead against the warded door. She stood there for what felt like hours, the fingers of her left hand gently drumming the wood, her Gladys Slack prettiness twisted ugly with painful effort. Beads of sweat stippled her skin, and her cheeks paled to sickliness. Her breathing deepened. Harshened. Became pants. Became gasps.

And then, on a cry of anguish, she fell back.

"It's no good," she said hoarsely. "His *potentia*'s too different now. I can't get past his—there's a thaumaturgical kink in there somewhere and I'm not strong enough to—"

"Codswallop. You are strong enough," Reg snapped. "You're Emmerabiblia Markham."

"Yes, but *he's* Gerald Dunwoody! And you don't know what that means, Reg. Not any more."

Reg's eyes gleamed in the miserly gaslight. "Oh, don't I? Well, madam, speaking as an imposter, I'd say I—"

"I didn't mean that," said Bibbie, the heel of her hand pressed to her temple. "Gerald's not *that*."

Head tipped to one side, Reg narrowed her eyes. "Then what is he, Miss Markham?"

Turning away, Bibbie picked up her reticule from the front door step. Retrieved from it a small crystal ball and tried to open a connection.

"Oy!" said Reg. "That belongs to Gerald. Thieving now, are we, madam?"

"He brought three with him," Bibbie said distantly. "And it's not like he's using any of them at the moment."

Somewhere along the shabby lane, a cat yowled. Startled, Melissande stared into the shadows.

Oh lord, this is taking too long. Why did we run? I should've screamed for Hartwig, not Bibbie.

"Can you get it to work?"

Bibbie cast a swift look around, as though she were examining the invisible air. "It feels like the ether's starting to settle. I just hope it's enough."

"If it is, contact Sir Alec. He should—"

"No, I need Monk. I need to ask him about—well, never mind. It's thaumaturgical. You wouldn't understand."

No. Right. Of course she wouldn't. Trying not to be offended, Melissande left Bibbie to her etheretics and retreated to crouch beside Gerald. A moment later Reg joined her in a flapping of wings.

"His colour's bad," the bird said. "And he's in a muck sweat. But he's still breathing, so there's hope. Even if his lungs are whistling like a kettle." A thoughtful sniff. "I thought you said the poison acted fast?"

"It did," she said. Oh, Gerald. He looked so helpless, so vulnerable lying on the cobbles. *This is all my fault. If I'd never asked him for help in New Ottosland* . . . "Moments after he drank his cherry liqueur, he doubled over in pain and collapsed."

"Hmm," said Reg. "Open his shirt, ducky." With Gerald's slowly rising and falling chest exposed, she leaned down for a closer look. "Bugger. See those little purplish blisters? I've seen 'em before. There's a good chance our boy's swallowed tincture of *dirit*."

"*Dirit?* I've never—"

"It's a weed," Reg said darkly. "And a scourge. If you're a witch or a wizard and you smoke the stuff, nine times out of ten you'll croak yourself. Slowly. Might take a few months. But if you drink it . . ."

The grim finality in Reg's voice iced her blood. "Is there a cure?"

Reg's feathers flattened. "Not that I've ever found."

"Oh," she said, and fastened Gerald's shirt and smart evening jacket with fingers gone cold and numb.

"The mystery *is*—" Reg chattered her beak. "—why isn't he dead already? Because if we are talking tincture of *dirit*, and I'm pretty sure that's it, he should've turned up his toes long before you girls reached the Canal."

Shivering, Melissande smoothed Gerald's blond, Algernon hair. She was finally starting to get used to it. "Don't tell me you're *complaining*, Reg."

"Don't be bloody silly," the bird retorted. "But—"

"Oh, you poxy, *poxy*—" Bibbie snarled, shaking the crystal ball. "Make the connection!"

Distracted from belly-churning thoughts of death, she frowned at Monk's sister. "Why won't the call connect, Reg? If you portalled in—"

"In's not the same as out when it comes to Splotze's dodgy etheretics," said Reg. "In my case it was a one way trip. It's just a bloody shame I couldn't get here an hour or two earlier. Then I could've stopped those buggers from feeding Gerald tinctured *dirit*." An angry chatter of beak. "That manky Sir Alec! This *never* would've happened if he'd let me come with you. First rule around these parts: never accept a drink from a man of the Steinish persuasion! I'm speaking from personal experience, you understand. When I—"

"It wasn't Dermit and Volker who gave him the liqueur," Melissande said, following Bibbie's example and chafing Gerald's lax wrist. Beneath her cold fingers his pulse alternately stuttered and raced. "It was Leopold Gertz, Hartwig's Secretary of State." And though she'd stood there and *watched* that damp little man poison Gerald, still she was finding it almost impossible to believe. "But *why* he'd do it, why *he'd* be working with—" And then she realised what the bird had said. "Wait a minute. How do *you* know Harenstein is up to its armpits in this mess?"

"Ah," said Reg, raising her voice over the top of Bibbie's extravagant cursing. "Well, me and that Markham boy and the Markham family's doddering butler, we've been doing a little sleuthing of our own. Popping in and out of a few foreign embassies, looking for clues. Only you didn't hear me say that."

A rush of relief. "Monk found something."

"He did," said Reg, sounding pleased and proud. "Encrypted instructions from the Marquis of Harenstein to Roland Dermit, his Ambassador to Ott. Be so kind as to contact that terribly helpful blackmarket wizard you know, and present him with this wish list of highly illegal and dangerous thaumaturgical hexes. Money no object, time of the essence. Or words to that effect." A thoughtful sniff. "Y'know, if ever he gets tired of inventing portable portals, that young man of yours has quite the future in codebreaking."

Dermit. There was the connection. Feeling ill, Melissande carefully tucked Gerald's arm back to his side. Some of those blackmarket hexes must've been for protection. Against the rock slide, against the fireworks. Against who knew what else?

So Norbert is to blame. And none of us saw his true face behind the jovial mask.

"Now, now, ducky, don't go hating yourself for getting hoodwinked," said Reg. "Some buggers are very, very good at being bad."

Yes, they were, weren't they? Buggers like Lional, and Permelia Wycliffe and her ghastly brother. Quite a list of villains she was accumulating.

Remembering Permelia and her use of illegal thaumaturgics, she looked at Reg. "The wizard who sold Norbert all those hexes . . . is there any chance that—"

"That he's the same blackmarket wizard what's put the cat among the pigeons at home?" said Reg. "The thought did cross your young man's busy mind. I expect he's telling that manky Sir Alec about it right now. Always assuming said government stooge hasn't bitten his head off for sending me here without mentioning it beforehand."

"What?" said Bibbie, giving up on the crystal ball. "Monk's gone and thumbed his nose at the Department *again?* Oh, *honestly!*"

Reg shrugged. "First rule of dealing with Departments: forgiveness after the fact is come by faster than permission before. *Especially* if you make the Department look good."

"Maybe," said Bibbie, scowling. "But if I end up back on a stationary pushbike in the bloody attic because of Monk, *I'll* be buying hexes from that damned blackmarket wizard!" With an exasperated sigh, she returned the useless crystal ball to her reticule then crouched beside Gerald and took hold of his hand. Her Gladys Slack face was suddenly tender. Pressing her other hand to his cheek, she bent down. "Gerald. It's Bibbie. Can you hear me?"

Gerald's closed eyelids fluttered. His breathing hitched. His eyebrows pinched in a frown.

Bibbie bent lower and brushed her lips against his. "Please, Gerald? I need you."

Gerald moaned, the faintest breath of sound.

"Gerald, you have to help me get past Abel Bestwick's front door. I need the key to that hex. *Please*, Gerald. Don't give up. You beat the fireworks. You can beat this too."

He moaned again, as a shudder ran through him. Seized with painful hope, Melissande squeezed his knee. "Listen to Bibbie, Gerald. Come on. What's the point of being a rogue wizard if you're just going to lie there taking a nap?"

A muscle leapt along his jaw.

"Keeping trying," Reg urged. "I don't know how, but you're getting through."

Now Bibbie framed Gerald's face between her hands. "I can't break your hexes, Gerald," she whispered. "Not any more. And I can't reach Monk. *Please*. You have to fight, you have to help me, because if you don't—"

They all heard it. The clatter, bang and scrape as a piece of discarded tin was kicked across the cracked and broken cobbles of dirty Voblinz Lane. And then they saw, shadow-like and back-lit, the indistinct figures of two men standing motionless at the lane's southern end.

Fear, cold and curdling. *Dermit and Volker. It was to be.* Melissande lifted her chin. "Well, they've certainly taken their time. They must have strolled here. I'll bet they've not even broken a sweat. If I were Norbert, I'd be docking their pay."

"Right," said Reg, and fluffed up her feathers. "You two hoydens sit tight with Gerald, while I go and—"

"No, Reg," said Bibbie. "You're not going anywhere."

Reg chattered her beak. "I beg your pardon, ducky? I don't recall making you the captain of me!"

Bibbie leapt to her feet and looked down at the bird. "If that is Dermit and Volker, Reg, then they strolled here because they didn't need to run. They knew where to find us. Last time they brought a blood magic hex. There's no saying what they've got in their pockets this time."

"All the more reason for me to flap on down there and take a look!" said Reg. "Because *you* can't go and wag your finger at them for being naughty!"

Bibbie smiled. "Actually, I think I can."

"No, you bloody well can't! Those buggers are dangerous!"

"True," she admitted. "But as you pointed out, Reg? *I'm* Emmerabiblia Markham. In fact . . ." She snapped her fingers. The illusion of Gladys Slack wavered, then vanished. In the gloomy light, her hair gleamed a bright gold. "There. That's better."

Melissande bit her lip. "I don't know, Bibbie. Is that a good idea? Sir Alec did stress how important it is for you to—"

Bibbie's glance was scornful. "D'you really think that matters now? Anyway . . ." Another smile, this time with edges. "I want those bastards to see the real me. I want them to know exactly who they crossed tonight."

It was no good. She couldn't argue on her knees. Standing, she reached out an imploring hand. "Please don't, Bibbie. If anything happens to you, what do I tell Gerald? What do I tell *Monk?*"

Bibbie pointed to the end of the alley, and the shadow figures standing there who still hadn't moved. "What d'you want to do, Mel? Wait for them to make the first move? Or would you rather cross your fingers that Splotze's ridiculous etheretics will miraculously clear in the next three minutes, and a team of Sir Alec's janitors will come galloping to our rescue?"

Dammit. The girl was impossible. Melissande turned to Reg. "Well? Are you just going to *sit* there?"

"No," said Reg. "I'm going to give Gerald my moral support."

"*Oh!*" She could slap the damn bird. "Bibbie—"

"Don't bother, Melissande. I've made up my mind." Looking like an ice maiden, Bibbie stared down at Gerald. "If this goes pear-shaped for me, and he pulls through, tell him . . . tell him . . ." Eyes glittering, her chin tilted defiantly. "Tell him to tell Monk that if he doesn't put an end to this bloody blackmarket wizard, once and for all, then I shall come back and haunt him for the rest of his life!"

"Well, well," said Reg, as Bibbie walked away. "And here's me thinking your Miss Markham and the other one have bugger all in common." A snort. "She set the palace on fire, I s'pose?"

Melissande clutched her hands together, so they couldn't tremble. "I don't think she meant to."

"No," said Reg, very pensive. "Her sort never do."

There was just enough light at the southern end of Voblinz Lane for her to see Dermit and Volker's arrogant assurance fade to confusion as she approached.

"Good evening, gentlemen. Are you lost?"

Norbert's henchmen exchanged unsettled glances, then Dermit folded his arms. Such a manly man. *Urrggh*. To think that she'd *simpered* at him. And as for Volker, he was looking at her in the way some men did. *Here's a pretty piece of crumpet.* His gaze kept dragging chest-wards as though she had a magnet in her dress.

"Who are you?" Dermit demanded, so arrogant.

Bibbie smiled. "A friend of Gladys Slack's. You might as well know, she's told me everything. Well . . . almost everything. I am rather curious about Leopold Gertz. How much did you have to pay him, to poison the wizard?"

He blinked. "What do you know of Gertz? And poisoning?"

"I *told* you." Bibbie held up crossed fingers. "Gladys and me? We're like *that*."

"We paid him nothing," said Volker. Now he was undressing her with his eyes. "Gertz is a crackpot Splotze patriot. He did it for Crown Prince and Country."

Ah, Bibbie thought. *So they have come to kill. Nobody answers awkward questions unless they think what they say will never be repeated.*

Funnily enough, it felt rather liberating, staring into the faces of the two men she and Gerald had managed to thwart at every turn. Who mistakenly thought they were going to kill her. And Gerald. And Melissande. Yes. Definitely liberating . . . and exhilarating.

But then Mother does say I have no proper sense of decorum.

"The wizard," said Dermit. "Is he dead yet?"

"Not even a little bit," she said cheerfully. "But you did give it your best try and, after all, that's what matters, isn't it? Anyway, gentlemen, here's what I really can't fathom. Were you or were you not working fist-in-glove with the Lanruvians? Because everyone *I* know says they're right proper villains, but then they tried to stop the landslide at the bridge. So which is it, Dermit? Are they friend or foe?"

Volker's scarred face tightened. "I do not like this, Dermit. The girl knows too much."

"She does." Expression menacing, right hand hovering near his pocket, Dermit took a step forward. "*Who are you?*"

Bibbie sighed. "Oh, all right then, if you *must* know."

Snap, snap, went her fingers. Gladys Slack appeared, then vanished.

As the men gaped at her, momentarily stunned to frozen silence, she tried to read what was in Dermit's pocket. But she wasn't Gerald. Their hexes could hide from her. *Damn.* Still, it was safe to say their commissioned thaumaturgics would be hazardous to her health.

And Gerald's, and Melissande's, and Reg's too. Probably. I can't let this drag on much longer.

Dermit recovered first. "You are a foreign agent? But you cannot be. Women are not agents!"

"That's true," she said, shrugging. "At the moment. But times change. Ah—Lanruvia?"

"Who do you work for?" said Volker, his eyes narrowed.

"Myself, actually."

Dermit sneered. "A lie."

"No, it isn't," she said, feigning indignation, keeping an eye on his hand, so close to his pocket. Of the two men, he was by far the more dangerous. "*Lanruvia.*"

"Enough of this," said Dermit. "It does not matter who you are, girl, or who has sent you." He jerked his chin towards the other end of the lane. "We are here for the wizard."

She let her teeth show, just a little. "He isn't for sale."

"Stupid girl!" Volker shouted. "You know what we can do!"

"I've a fair idea, yes," said Bibbie, watching Dermit's fingers slide into his pocket. "But here's the thing, gentlemen. That Gladys Slack trick I showed you? I know a better one. Look!"

Her hands came up. Fisted. Then she spat the words no-one, not even Monk, knew that she knew.

Bern Dermit and Grune Volker dropped dead at her feet.

Oh, she thought, staring down at them. *That was . . . easier than I expected.*

There were feelings, somewhere. She didn't have time to feel them now. After emptying her would-be slayers' pockets, she returned to Gerald and the girls. Met Melissande's shocked stare with a small, complicated smile.

"It turns out Great-uncle Throgmorton owned a lot of *very* naughty books." And then she shrugged. "Besides. I'm a Markham. And a Thackeray. *And* they hurt Gerald. Now, would you mind handing me my reticule? Make sure you take the crystal ball out first."

As Melissande, still stunned silent, did as she was asked, Reg chattered her beak. "Not that I'm sorry those buggers are dead, you understand," she said. "But I feel bound to point out that they might have been useful."

Bibbie shook her head. "No. They'd never have spoken willingly and besides, Dermit was about to use one of these filthy things. Thank you, Mel." Grimacing, she tipped the hexes she'd collected into her reticule. "And we wouldn't have survived."

"So you saved our lives," said Melissande. "And I'm sure we're grateful. But *Bibbie* . . ."

The look on Melissande's face told her what she was supposed to be feeling. Faint. Shocked. Remorseful. Guilty. But she was pretty sure she didn't feel any of those things.

Mostly, it seemed, she felt pleased.

"Here," she said to Reg, and held out the two other items she'd taken from Bern Dermit. "I'm thinking one of these vials is tincture of *dirit*—and the other one is what a smart man carries with him when he's carrying tincture of *dirit*. You'd better tell me which is which. I wouldn't like to make a mistake."

Gerald had been battling the poison for so long that it took nearly twenty minutes for the antidote to take effect. When at last he stirred, and opened his eyes, Reg leapt onto his chest and burst into sobs.

Sitting on the cold pavement beside him, Bibbie smiled and touched his hand. Algernon Rowbotham disappeared. Rolling his head, Gerald looked at her. Smile fading, she looked back. They had so much to talk about. There was so much to say. But for now, *right* now, it was enough that they sit beside each other in silence on the cold damp cobbled pavement, while the bloody bird wept and scolded and Melissande, whose eyes weren't dry, fretted aloud about how they'd get home.

"Don't worry, Mel," she said, and looked at the crystal ball cradled in her hand. "The ether really is starting to clear. Give it a few more minutes and I'll be able to get a call through to Monk. Then he'll call Sir Alec, and everything will be fine."

Epilogue

"**B**loody hell, Alec. Bloody, *bloody* hell! Do you have *any* notion of what you've done?"

Sir Alec finished signing his name, neatly placed his pen on the desk, set aside his monthly expense report and then looked up.

"By all means, Ralph, come in. Take a seat. But be so kind as to shut the door after you first."

Shutting his office door was of paramount importance. It might be late—these kinds of conversations were always conducted in the dead of night—but Nettleworth was never entirely deserted.

Ralph slammed the door and started pacing. "I told you, Alec. Didn't I tell you? Didn't I say this damned mission would end in tears?"

Sitting back in his chair, Sir Alec swallowed a sigh. "Surely it's to be expected. Weddings are, I'm told, emotional affairs."

Ralph's glare was hot enough to combust a forest. "I'm not talking about the bloody wedding! I could care less about the Splotze-Borovnik wedding! *Damnit*, Alec! What the devil are we to do with this—this—*creature* you've created? That bloody *dirit* should've killed him stone dead in heartbeats. And thanks to those grimoire incants and his rogue *potentia*, it didn't! What have you to say about *that*? About any of it? The things he did—he's unprecedented, Alec! And it's all your fault!"

Creature. Resisting the urge to swear, Sir Alec kept his

expression impassive. "Calm down, Ralph, before you burst a blood vessel."

"*Trust* me, Alec, this *is* bloody calm!"

Ah. "Would you care for a drink?"

"No, Alec, what I'd care for is an explanation!" Ralph retorted. "What I'd care for is knowing how you intend to stuff this bloody genie back in its bottle!"

It would be far easier to answer Ralph's ire if he weren't, in his own way, feeling equally alarmed. "Ralph, you are borrowing trouble. There's no need. Mister Jennings tells me—"

Ralph waved a furiously dismissive hand in passing. "To the devil with Jennings, Alec! He's as clueless as the rest of us. Admit it. You don't know what Gerald Dunwoody's turned into and you've no more idea of how to control him than I have!"

"What I know, Ralph," he said, very carefully, because his own temper was starting to stir, "is that Gerald Dunwoody saved the day for us. Again."

"With a lot of help from my niece!" said Ralph, still glaring. "And that's another thing, Alec. Emmerabiblia! D'you know she's started dropping hints the size of carthorses about *gels* in the *Department?*"

Because he was more than a little irritated with Ralph, he smiled. "Indeed? Well, she certainly proved her mettle in Splotze."

Ralph leapt to the desk and banged both his fists on it, hard. "Don't you dare, Alec. I'm warning you. *Don't you bloody dare*. I won't have Bibbie dragged into our world. Not again. This Splotze business will never be repeated, do I make myself clear?"

He stared at Ralph's fists until they were removed, then looked up at his sometime friend, sometime foe, and shrugged. *Emmerabiblia Markham.* What a surprise that young lady had turned out be. The various mission reports had proven to be . . . interesting . . . reading.

"Quite clear, Ralph. Only I expect, at the end of the day, it won't be up to me. Or, dare I say it, you."

"Perhaps not," said Ralph, close to snarling. "But it won't be up to her, either."

He wasn't sure about that, but neither was there any point

in arguing. Young Bibbie was Ralph's niece. Let her be Ralph's problem, at least for the time being. He gestured at the chair on the other side of the desk.

"I understand. Now, please, Ralph, do sit down. There's no reason that we can't discuss this like sensible men."

Ralph stepped back. The mingled despair and contempt in his eyes were a sharp reproof. "There's nothing to discuss. Clearly you're not interested in entertaining any suggestion that Gerald Dunwoody might now be more than even you can handle."

He dropped his gaze to the desk. *Dammit.* He'd never seen Ralph so angry, at least not at him. The situation was untenable. Ralph Markham was an indispensible ally. If he let pride destroy their complicated relationship . . .

"I'm sorry," he said, resting his clasped hands before him. "If I gave you the impression that I feel your concerns are trivial, Ralph, I apologise."

Which neatly took the wind out of Ralph's bellicose sails. He sat. "You did."

"Then I was clumsy."

"You were."

"I am sorry."

"Yes. So you've said." Ralph drummed his fingers on the arm of the chair. "But let's not get maudlin. What matters now is how we're going to deal with your precious Mister Dunwoody." A shiver. "Who makes my skin crawl, Alec. I'll not pussyfoot around it. These changes in his *potentia?* They make my skin crawl."

Jennings had said the same thing, in a slightly more technical manner. And as for his own skin . . .

Dunwoody's more unsettling than ever. I can't deny that. But unsettling isn't evil. Gerald Dunwoody isn't evil.

"Something's got to be done, Alec," Ralph said, more kindly. "I know you're fond of the lad, but—"

Fond. A ridiculous word. "I agree," he said briskly. "Mister Dunwoody's situation cannot be left unaddressed. For any of our sakes. But I'm not prepared to let fear propel me into a decision I might later regret."

Ralph was bristling. "Fear? Who said anything about fear?"

You did, my friend, and we both know it. "A poor choice of words," he said smoothly. "My point is that we can't unring a bell, Ralph. What we need is a little breathing space, so we can think the matter through calmly, and decide what to do next."

Ralph snorted. "And I suppose you've got that all organised, have you?"

"Well . . ." He permitted himself a small smile. "As it happens, I do have an idea."

"And am I going to like it?"

"I hope so. King Rupert of New Ottosland has expressed a desire to introduce a little modern thaumaturgy into his moribund kingdom. Nothing too extreme. A limited public portal network, a few labour-saving devices here and there. He wondered if I might be able to assist him. I thought perhaps Mister Dunwoody could prove helpful."

"New Ottosland," Ralph said slowly, considering. "That's a nice long way away. And then there's the Kallarapi desert. All that sand, and New Ottosland like a little island in the middle . . ."

"Precisely."

"Out of sight, out of mind, that sort of thing."

"Indeed."

Now Ralph was smiling. "And in the meantime, Alec, while Dunwoody's busy emptying scorpions out of his underwear, you and I—and possibly that ghastly nephew of mine—can come up with a way to get him under control. Permanently."

Not at all. But he wasn't about to spoil things with another argument. Not yet, anyway. "So, you agree?"

Ralph sighed. "Do I have a choice?"

"Always," he said, lying without compunction. "But I really do feel this is the answer, at least for the time being. Now, Ralph, are you quite sure I can't pour you a drink?"

Nine days after his return to Ottosland, Gerald found the events in Splotze were starting to take on a slightly unrealistic air. Even with the report writing, and the hours of poking, prodding, intrusive tests with Mister Jennings, and the scattering of conversations that had taken place here in Chatterly Crescent, a certain dreamlike feeling persisted.

Of course, that bizarre sense of *I wonder if I didn't imagine it all* wasn't helped by the sight of Sir Alec at the town house's kitchen table, sharing an informal meal. He'd turned up at the front door, uninvited, just as Melissande was making mushroom gravy, despite unsolicited culinary advice from Reg, and Monk and Bibbie were laying the table. So of course he'd been asked to stay.

To their scarcely hidden alarm, Sir Alec agreed.

Now it was nearly half-past eight. Over the course of an hour and a half they'd eaten their way through an appetiser—onion soup, *not* crab puffs—then roast beef with all the trimmings, and finally an apple and blackberry pie with generous dollops of cream. Conversation had been desultory and mostly about the foibles of famous thaumaturgists, long dead. Nothing awkward or Department-related at all.

"So," said Sir Alec, elbows negligently resting on the kitchen table. "The Splotze-Borovnik affair."

Gerald exchanged glances with Monk. *I knew it was too good to last.* Then he looked back at Sir Alec. "Yes, sir? What about it?"

"In the end, it was a rather grubby crime, really," Sir Alec said, sounding mildly offended. "A distasteful dog's breakfast of passion, misplaced patriotism, and greed."

That was one way of looking at it, certainly. A very *simplified* way. But given the enormous list of secrets, both classified and unclassifiable, that the six of them now kept, he had to wonder how long simple could last.

And what was the tally this time? Bibbie's two dead bodies and his own grimoire-enhanced *potentia* and the restoration of his sight and Reg and Monk's enterprising but completely illegal forays into espionage. And Dodsworth, of course. There were probably more, but he was tired and full of food. Those were enough to be going on with.

Perched on the back of her chair, Reg rattled her tail. "What *I* want to know, Mister Government Stooge, is did we ever uncover the truth about those bloody Lanruvians?"

Sir Alec nodded. "As a matter of fact, Reg, we did. Ambassador Dermit has proven himself to be a fascinating conversationalist."

"And?" said Reg, when it seemed no-one else felt brave enough to prod. "What did our Steinish chatterbox have to say?"

Sighing, Sir Alec steepled his fingers. Though he was dressed in his customary nondescript grey suit, he had unbent far enough to loosen his tie. It made him look positively debauched.

"Let's see if I can keep this straight," he murmured. "Since between them, our players have turned this into something of a melodrama. Norbert of Harenstein encouraged the match between Ratafia and Ludwig in order to lull Hartwig and Erminium into a false sense of security regarding his friendship *and* the disposition of the Canal. His intent, however, was to bind Erminium to him, encouraging her to rely on his judgement above her own, so that he might in due course undermine the newly formed alliance between Splotze and Borovnik, and the marriage between Prince Ludwig and Princess Ratafia, thus ensuring that the Canal came under Steinish control, with Borovnik the paper partner."

"Yes, yes," said Reg. "The political quickstep. It's all horribly familiar, I've seen it a hundred times before. But what about the bloody *Lanruvians?*"

"Yes," said Melissande. "And Leopold Gertz?"

Sir Alec's lips twitched, very faintly. "Former Secretary of State Gertz's motives were, alas, driven by the personal. In some ways he, too, is a victim. Norbert of Harenstein learned of his history and ruthlessly manipulated it for his own ends."

"What history?" said Bibbie, drawing patterns on the table-cloth with the tines of her fork. "I never thought Gertz was enough of a person to have a history. He was always just . . . that damp little man."

Sir Alec's gaze was cool and steady. "We are all of us persons, Miss Markham, however plain and damp and lacking in brilliance we might be."

As Bibbie's cheeks tinted pink at the reproof, Gerald reached for her other hand under the table and squeezed. His precious, precocious Emmerabiblia. They'd have to talk, and soon. What with one thing and another there'd been little time before now. And, if he was honest, a need for some distance. She'd felt it too. They'd both been hiding.

But that can't go on. There are things we need to say. Things we can't hide from, even though they're hard to look at.

Under the table, Bibbie's fingers closed around his.

Melissande rearranged her spoon on her empty plate. "What *was* Leopold's history, Sir Alec?"

Sir Alec's expression softened ever so slightly towards regret. "When he was a child, his father was killed in one of the Splotze-Borovnik Canal skirmishes, and apparently the loss disordered his wits. Seeded in him a hatred of Borovnik that bordered on madness. It seems he genuinely believed that in ruining the wedding and the treaty he was saving both Prince Ludwig and his beloved Splotze from a fateful mistake."

Monk was frowning. "Fine, I can see where and why Gertz did his bit. But that rockslide at the Hanging Bridge—from what Gerald's said, it could easily have killed Ludwig and Ratafia. How could Norbert's plan have worked if they were dead?"

"Obviously it couldn't," Sir Alec said, his eyes faintly approving. "That was a miscalculation on the part of Dermit and Volker. Fortunately for Norbert of Harenstein, Mister Dunwoody was at hand."

Gerald cleared his throat. "And Miss Markham."

"Indeed." Now Sir Alec's expression was repressive. "But the less said about that, the better."

Right. Giving Bibbie a quick nudge under the table, he risked a sideways glance at Monk, whose shoulder twitched in the smallest of shrugs. They'd not done much private talking either, since his return from Splotze . . . and now there was more to say then ever. The grimoire magic. Bibbie. Where they all went from here.

But that can wait, too. Right now I need everything to wait.

"All right, all right," said Reg, with an emphatic tail rattle. "So we've established Norbert's a villain and poor little Leopold was simply misunderstood. Not that it excuses him poisoning my Gerald, but since the boy didn't die I'll let that pass. For now. But that *still* doesn't explain—"

"The bloody Lanruvians," said Sir Alec. "Indeed. An intriguing puzzle piece, they've proven to be. According to Ambassador Dermit, Norbert had reached a mutually beneficial agreement with our pale friends. In return for giving their cargo barges unrestricted and uninspected access to the Canal, once it was in Steinish hands, the Lanruvians would give him the wherewithal to take control of the region's unreliable etheretics."

"What?" said Bibbie, astonished. "But—is that even possible?"

"Maybe," said Monk, after a look at Sir Alec. "That restricted equipment Aylebsury said they were trying to get their hands on? There's a good chance it would've helped them make good on their side of the bargain."

"Or at the very least advanced their cause far past the point where I, and Sir Ralph, and any number of other concerned parties would be comfortable," said Sir Alec. He gave Bibbie a small nod. "So now it seems we are in debt to *both* of your brothers, Miss Markham."

"So . . . what?" said Melissande, frowning. "After the near-disaster at the bridge they decided Harenstein couldn't be trusted to succeed?"

Sir Alec sat back. "Certainly that's one explanation. But I don't begin to understand the machinations of the Lanruvian mind."

"Speaking of the bridge," said Reg, "has that manky bugger Dermit turned up yet? Or his knife-happy offsider?"

Gerald held his breath. Dermit and Volker's bodies had been thaumaturgically disposed of, their deaths comprehensively lied about. As far as Sir Alec and Sir Ralph and everyone else was concerned, Norbert of Harenstein's co-conspirators had seen the writing on the wall and fled. He'd not wanted to lie about it, not to Sir Alec, but what could they do? Risk Bibbie being arrested for murder?

Bloody hell, Reg. What are you playing at?

But Sir Alec was shaking his head. "No, they remain unaccounted for."

"Well, I hope you find them," said Bibbie, playing dangerous games. "*And* throw them into a dungeon. I mean, they did try to drown me in the Canal."

"Indeed," said Sir Alec, at his most bland. "We're doing what we can."

Did he harbour even a sliver of suspicion? Nothing in his expression suggested it. But then, he was an expert at keeping secrets . . .

"And what about the cherries?" Bibbie added. "Was that Leopold's daft idea?"

"Yes," said Sir Alec. "Norbert encouraged him since it helped undermine Splotze, which was his primary goal. I understand the marquis promised Gertz a great deal of influence in the cherry liqueur business as a reward for his help."

"*Norbert*," said Melissande, in tones of deep loathing. "Honestly, I could kick myslef. I should've known he was rotten. I mean, how difficult is it to remember someone's name?"

"Don't be too hard on yourself, Miss Cadwallader," said Sir Alec, surpringly kind. "Nobody suspected Harenstein. After all, not every villain struts the stage twirling his moustache and loudly proclaiming his evil plans. Which is a pity, since it would certainly make my job a lot easier."

"What's going to happen to him?"

"Nothing public," said Sir Alec. "There are talks going on, behind firmly closed doors. Everything is being handled with the utmost discretion."

Monk shook his head. "The whole thing's been handled that way. It's been very impressive, really. Well. You know." He looked at Bibbie. "Except for the part where the palace burned down."

Bibbie thumped the table. "It did *not* burn down! Will you stop saying it burned down? There's still a palace there, right?"

"Yes," Monk murmured. "A charred, sooty, smelly, *burned* palace."

"*Anyway*," said Melissande, with a daggered look at Monk and Bibbie, "my point is, Sir Alec, will Norbert be punished for what he did?"

Sir Alec hesitated, then nodded. "Yes, Miss Cadwallader. He will."

"*Good*," she said, fiercely smiling. "Then please be so kind as to give me his postal address when he's settled in his new and hopefully very dungeon-like accommodation. I shall write to him once a week. Dear Norris. Dear Nigel. Dear Neville. Dear *Nugent*."

Gerald, watching Sir Alec, thought it was the closest he'd ever seen his self-contained superior to outright laughter.

"So it's over?" said Bibbie. "We won, they lost, three cheers, pip pip, hoorah?"

"As far as anything like this can ever be said to end, Miss Markham? Yes," said Sir Alec, very cool. "Ludwig and Ratafia are now man and wife, the new Canal treaty has been signed and ratified, and as a result we can look forward to a new era of peace and prosperity in the region."

Melissande snorted. "Provided Erminium stays out of the way. But I, for one, won't be holding my breath." She favoured Sir Alec with a narrow-eyed stare. "Now, since it seems we're tying up all the loose ends, what about Abel Bestwick? I mean, without him Norbert would've got everything he wanted."

Ah, yes. Bestwick. Talk about complications . . .

"That's a Department matter, Miss Cadwallader," Sir Alec, his expression bland again. "Don't let it concern you."

Melissande pointed a finger at him. "But it does concern me. I want your word he'll not be punished for wick-dipping with Mitzie. She helped save the day too, y'know. *And* they're in love."

A pained look ghosted across Sir Alec's face. "Indeed."

"Well, then?"

"Well, then, Miss Cadwallader . . ." Sir Alec shrugged. "You have my word."

Gerald nearly swallowed his tongue.

"And what about—" Monk hesitated. "Well. You know." He waved his hand. "Everything else."

Sir Alec raised an eyebrow. "I'm not sure I know what you mean, Mister Markham."

"*You know*," Monk said, scowling. "The embassies and so forth. You were s'posed to sort that out with Uncle Ralph."

The eyebrow climbed higher. "Was I?"

Sitting beside him, Bibbie patted his hand. "Ignore him, Monk. He's teasing. I had tea and crumpets with Uncle Ralph this morning and everything's fine."

Monk slewed round to stare at her. "You did? Why didn't you invite me?"

Bibbie's smile was poisonously sweet. "You told Dodsworth the palace burned down."

"Bloody hell," Monk muttered. "I give up."

Under cover of more lively sibling nattering, Gerald looked at Sir Alec. "And what about me?" he said quietly. "Does Mister Jennings have an opinion?"

"Perhaps, Mister Dunwoody, this is neither the time nor place to—"

"You might as well tell me, sir. We both know I'm going to tell them after you're gone."

Sir Alec frowned. "Indeed. Well, Mister Dunwoody, in a nutshell? Mister Jennings is reluctant to draw a definitive conclusion as to what has happened to you."

"Ha," said Reg. "I'm not. You should sack that tosser Jennings and give me his bloody job. What happened, Mister Clever Clogs, is exactly what you *hoped* would happen. The grimoire magic you left behind in Gerald, on *purpose*, and don't you think for a moment any of us was fooled by *that* little ploy, has grafted itself well and truly into my boy's rogue *potentia*. Whatever he was before his little jaunt into my world, well, he's twice that now, at least . . . and it might be only the beginning. *That's* the explanation, sunshine. So. Are you happy now?"

Silence, as they all looked at Sir Alec. Silence, as Sir Alec looked back at them.

"Obviously," he said at last, "there will be no discussion whatsoever with anyone outside this room regarding the events that transpired in Splotze. In fact, it would be best if you never discussed them again, either." His lips pinched. "Of course, I say that purely as a matter of form, since I know perfectly well you'll talk of nothing else for the foreseeable future. But as far as my Department is concerned, the Splotze-Borovnik file is closed. And I think I can safely say the same opinion is held by Sir Ralph. Mister Markham, you'll return to your duties in Research and Development, while the rest of you will get back to Witches Inc. And should I have need of your services again, Mister Dunwoody, be sure I shall find you there. And now I'll bid you good night." He stood. "It was a delightful meal. Thank you."

They sat in silence after he left. Then Reg broke the hush with a vigorous rattle of her tail.

"*Right*," she said briskly. "So that's that. At least for now. And you know what they say. All's well that ends well. So, who wants more pie?"

Acknowledgements

Bernadette Foley, who has the patience of a saint

The wonderful team at Orbit, all over the world

Abigail Nathan

Glenda Larke, Mary GT Webber and Elaine Shipp

Ethan Eltenberg, my lovely agent, and his team

The readers who love Gerald and co.

extras

orbit

meet the author

K. E. MILLS is the pseudonym for Karen Miller. She was born in Vancouver, Canada, and moved to Australia with her family when she was two. She started writing stories while still in primary school, where she fell in love with speculative fiction after reading *The Lion, the Witch, and the Wardrobe*. Over the years she has held down a wide variety of jobs, including horse stud groom in Buckingham, England. She is working on several new novels. Find out more about the author at www.karenmiller.net.

introducing

If you enjoyed
WIZARD UNDERCOVER,
look out for

THE LEGEND OF ELI MONPRESS

by Rachel Aaron

*Eli Monpress is talented. He's charming. And
he's a thief.*

*But not just any thief. He's the greatest thief of the
age—and he's also a wizard. And with the help of his
partners—a swordsman with the most powerful magic
sword in the world but no magical ability of his own, and
a demonseed who can step through shadows and punch
through walls—he's going to put his plan into effect.*

*The first step is to increase the size of the bounty on his
head, so he'll need to steal some big things. But he'll
start small for now. He'll just steal something that
no one will miss—at least for a while.*

Like a king.

*This omnibus edition contains the first three novels in
The Legend of Eli Monpress series:* The Spirit Thief,
The Spirit Rebellion *and* The Spirit Eater.

In the prison under the castle Allaze, in the dark, moldy
cells where the greatest criminals in Mellinor spent the
remainder of their lives counting rocks to stave off madness, Eli Monpress was trying to wake up a door.

It was a heavy oak door with an iron frame, created
centuries ago by an overzealous carpenter to have, perhaps, more corners than it should. The edges were carefully fit to lie flush against the stained, stone walls, and
the heavy boards were nailed together so tightly that not
even the flickering torch light could wedge between them.
In all, the effect was so overdone, the construction so
inhumanly strong, that the whole black affair had tran-
scended simple confinement and become a monument to
the absolute hopelessness of the prisoner's situation. Eli
decided to focus on the wood; the iron would have taken
forever.

He ran his hands over it, long fingers gently tapping
in a way living trees find desperately annoying, but dead
wood finds soothing, like a scratch behind the ears. At
last, the boards gave a little shudder and said, in a dusty,
splintery voice, "What do you want?"

"My dear friend," Eli said, never letting up on his tapping, "the real question here is, what do *you* want?"

"Pardon?" the door rattled, thoroughly confused. It
wasn't used to having questions asked of it.

"Well, doesn't it strike you as unfair?" Eli said. "From
your grain, anyone can see you were once a great tree.
Yet, here you are, locked up through no fault of your own,

shut off from the sun by cruel stones with no concern at all for your comfort or continued health."

The door rattled again, knocking the dust from its hinges. Something about the man's voice was off. It was too clear for a normal human's, and the certainty in his words stirred up strange memories that made the door decidedly uncomfortable.

"Wait," it grumbled suspiciously. "You're not a wizard, are you?"

"Me?" Eli clutched his chest. "I, one of those confidence tricksters, manipulators of spirits? Why, the very thought offends me! I am but a wanderer, moving from place to place, listening to the spirits' sorrows and doing what little I can to make them more comfortable." He resumed the pleasant tapping, and the door relaxed against his fingers.

"Well"—it leaned forward a fraction, lowering its creak conspiratorially—"if that's the case, then I don't mind telling you the nails do poke a bit." It rattled, and the nails stood out for a second before returning to their position flush against the wood. The door sighed. "I don't mind the dark so much, or the damp. It's just that people are always slamming me, and that just drives the sharp ends deeper. It hurts something awful, but no one seems to care."

"Let me have a look," Eli said, his voice soft with concern. He made a great show of poring over the door and running his fingers along the joints. The door waited impatiently, creaking every time Eli's hands brushed over a spot where the nails rubbed. Finally, when he had finished his inspection, Eli leaned back and tucked his fist under his chin, obviously deep in thought. When he didn't say anything for a few minutes, the door began to grow impatient, which is a very uncomfortable feeling for a door.

"Well?" it croaked.

"I've found the answer," Eli said, crouching down on the doorstep. "Those nails, which give you so much trouble, are there to pin you to the iron frame. However"—Eli held up one finger in a sage gesture—"they don't stay in on their own accord. They're not glued in; there's no hook. In fact, they seem to be held in place only by the pressure of the wood around them. So"—he arched an eyebrow—"the reason they stay in at all, the only reason, is because you're holding on to them."

"Of course!" the door rumbled. "How else would I stay upright?"

"Who said you had to stay upright?" Eli said, throwing out his arms in a grand gesture. "You're your own spirit, aren't you? If those nails hurt you, why, there's no law that you have to put up with it. If you stay in this situation, you're making yourself a victim."

"But..." The door shuddered uncertainly.

"The first step is admitting you have a problem." Eli gave the wood a reassuring pat. "And that's enough for now. However"—his voice dropped to a whisper—"if you're ever going to live your life, *really* live it, then you need to let go of the roles others have forced on you. You need to let go of those nails."

"But, I don't know..." The door shifted back and forth.

"Indecision is the bane of all hardwoods." Eli shook his head. "Come on, it doesn't have to be forever. Just give it a try."

The door clanged softly against its frame, gathering

its resolve as Eli made encouraging gestures. Then, with a loud bang, the nails popped like corks, and the boards clattered to the ground with a long, relieved sigh.

Eli stepped over the planks and through the now-empty iron doorframe. The narrow hall outside was dark and empty. Eli looked one way, then the other, and shook his head.

"First rule of dungeons," he said with a wry grin, "don't pin all your hopes on a gullible door."

With that, he stepped over the sprawled boards, now mumbling happily in peaceful, nail-free slumber, and jogged off down the hall toward the rendezvous point.

In the sun-drenched rose garden of the castle Allaze, King Henrith of Mellinor was spending money he hadn't received yet.

"Twenty thousand gold standards!" He shook his tea-cup at his Master of the Exchequer. "What does that come out to in mellinos?"

The exchequer, who had answered this question five times already, responded immediately. "Thirty-one thousand five hundred at the current rate, my lord, or approximately half Mellinor's yearly tax income."

"Not bad for a windfall, eh?" The king punched him in the shoulder good-naturedly. "And the Council of Thrones is actually going to pay all that for one thief? What did the bastard do?"

The Master of the Exchequer smiled tightly and rubbed his shoulder. "Eli Monpress"—he picked up the wanted poster that was lying on the table, where the roughly sketched face of a handsome man with dark, shaggy hair grinned boyishly up at them—"bounty, paid dead or alive, twenty thousand Council Gold Standard Weights. Wanted on a hundred and fifty-seven counts of grand larceny against a noble person, three counts of fraud, one charge of counterfeiting, and treason against the Rector Spiritualis." He squinted at the small print along the bottom of the page. "There's a separate bounty of five thousand gold standards from the Spiritualists for that last count, which has to be claimed independently."

"Figures." The king slurped his tea. "The Council can't even ink a wanted poster without the wizards butting their noses in. But"—he grinned broadly—"money's money, eh? Someone get the Master Builder up here. It looks like we'll have that new arena after all."

The order, however, was never given, for at that moment, the Master Jailer came running through the garden gate, his plumed helmet gripped between his white-knuckled hands.

"Your Majesty." He bowed.

"Ah, Master Jailer." The king nodded. "How is our money bag liking his cell?"

The jailer's face, already pale from a job that required him to spend his daylight hours deep underground, turned ghostly. "Well, you see, sir, the prisoner, that is to say"— he looked around for help, but the other officials were already backing away—"he's not in his cell."

"What?" The king leaped out of his seat, face scarlet. "If he's not in his cell, then where is he?"

"We're working on that right now, Majesty!" the jailor said in a rush. "I have the whole guard out looking for him. He won't get out of the palace!"

"See that he doesn't," the king growled. "Because if he's not back in his cell within the hour..."

He didn't need to finish the threat. The jailer saluted and ran out of the garden as fast as his boots would carry him. The officials stayed frozen where they were, each waiting for the others to move first as the king began to stalk around the garden, sipping his tea with murderous intent.

"Your Majesty," squeaked a minor official, who was safely hidden behind the crowd. "This Eli seems a dangerous character. Shouldn't you move to safer quarters?"

"Yes!" The Master of Security grabbed the idea and ran with it. "If that thief could get out of his cell, he can certainly get into the castle!" He seized the king's arm. "We must get you to a safer location, Your Majesty!"

This was followed by a chorus of cries from the other officials.

"Of course!"

"His majesty's safety is of utmost importance!"

"We must preserve the monarchy at all costs!"

Any objections the king may have had were overridden as a surge of officials swept down and half carried, half dragged him into the castle.

"Put me down, you idiots!" the king bellowed, but the officials were good and scared now. Each saw only the precipitous fall that awaited him personally if there were a regime change, and fear gave them courage as they pushed their protesting monarch into the castle, down the arching hallways, and into the throne room.

"Don't worry, Your Majesty," the Master of Security said, organizing two teams to shut the great, golden doors. "That thief won't get in."

The king, who had given up fighting somewhere during the last hundred feet, just harrumphed and stomped up the dais stairs to his throne to wait it out. Meanwhile, the officials dashed back and forth across the marble—locking the parlor doors, overturning the elegant end tables, peeking behind the busts of former kings—checking for every possible, or impossible, security vulnerability. Henrith did his best to ignore the nonsense. Being royalty meant enduring people's endless fussing over your safety, but when the councilors started talking about boarding over the stained-glass windows, the king decided that enough was enough. He stood from his throne and took a breath in preparation for a good bellow when a tug on his robes stopped him short. The king looked down incredulously to see who would dare, and found two royal guards in full armor standing at attention beside the royal dais.

"Sir!" The shorter guard saluted. "The Master of Security has assigned us to move you to a safer location."

"I thought this *was* a safer location." The king sighed.

"Sir!" The soldier saluted again. "With all due respect, the throne room is the first place the enemy would look, and with this ruckus, he could easily get through."

"You're right about that," the king said, glowering at the seething mass of panicked officials. "Let's get out of here."

He stomped down the steps from the high marble dais and let the guards lead him to the back wall of the throne room. The shorter soldier went straight to an older tapestry hanging forgotten in one corner and pushed it aside, revealing, much to the king's amazement, a small door set flush with the stonework.

"I never knew this was here," the king said, genuinely astonished.

"Doors like these are standard in most castles this

age," the guard said, running his gloved hand over the stones to the right of the door. "You just have to know where to look." His fingers closed in the crack between two stones. Something clicked deep in the wall, and the door swung open with a soft scrape.

"This way, sir," the soldier said, ducking through.

The secret passage was only a few feet long. This was good, because it was only a few inches wide, and the king was getting very claustrophobic sliding along sideways between the dusty stone walls, especially when the second soldier closed the door behind them, plunging the passage into darkness. A few steps later, they emerged into the back of another large tapestry. The soldier pushed the heavy cloth aside, and the king was amazed to find himself in his own drawing room.

"Why did no one tell me about this?" he said, exasperated, watching as the second soldier draped the tapestry back into place. "It will be fantastically useful the next time I want to get out of an audience."

"Over here, sir," the shorter guard said, waving toward the wide balcony that overlooked the castle garden. The king didn't see how a balcony was much safer than a throne room, but the guard seemed to know what he was doing, so the king followed quietly. Perhaps there was another secret passage. The king frowned, regretting all those times he'd chosen to go hunting rather than let the Master Builder take him on that tour of the castle the man was always so keen on. Well, the king thought, if the Master Builder had put more emphasis on secret passages rather than appreciation of the flying buttresses, perhaps he would have been more inclined to come along.

The balcony jutted out from the drawing room in a

large semicircle of pale golden marble. His mother had had it built so she could watch the birds up close, and the handrails brushed right up against the leafy branches of the linden trees. The king was about to comment on how peaceful it was compared to the nonsense in the throne room, but the shorter of the two soldiers spoke first.

"I'm really sorry about this."

The king looked at him quizzically. "Sorry about wha—" His question was answered by a blinding pain at the back of his head. The trees and the balcony swirled together, and then he was on the ground with no notion of how he'd gotten there.

"Did you have to hit him that hard?" The soldier's voice floated above him.

"Yes," answered a voice he hadn't heard before, which his poor, aching brain assigned to the tall solider who hadn't spoken while they were escorting him. "That is, if you want him to stay quiet."

The shorter soldier took off his helmet, revealing a young man with a head of dark, shaggy hair. "If you say so," he said, tucking the helmet under his arm.

The shorter soldier trotted to the edge of the balcony, where the trees were thickest. Spots danced across the king's vision, but he was sure he saw what happened next. One of the trees moved to meet the solider. The king blinked, but the tree was still moving. It leaned over as far as it could, stretching out a thick branch to make a nice little step up off the railing. So great was his astonishment, the king barely felt the bigger soldier heft him over his shoulder like an oat sack. Then they were up on the tree branch, and the tree was bending over to set them gently on the ground.

"Thank you," said the shorter soldier as they stepped onto the grass.

And the king, though his ears were ringing horribly, could have sworn he heard the leaves whisper, "Anytime, Eli."

That thought was too much for him, and he dove into unconsciousness.